Conscience

A Novel

Alice Mattison

PEGASUS BOOKS
NEW YORK LONDON

CONSCIENCE

Pegasus Books Ltd
148 West 37th Street, 13th Floor
New York, NY 10018

First Pegasus Books hardcover edition August 2018

Interior design by Sabrina Plomitallo-González, Pegasus Books

ISBN: 978-1-68177-789-4

10 9 8 7 6 5 4 3 2 1

Printed in the United States of America
Distributed by W. W. Norton & Company, Inc.

For Nina, Henry, and Jesse

one

Olive Grossman

Life—make no mistake—is not a story. Naturally, I could think of parts of my life as stories if I reordered and changed them, putting more stress here, less there. But I'd be distorting them. Paying close attention to my own history, I've learned, leads to trouble, confusion, and anxiety. I will never write a memoir.

Without having planned to, though, I often catch myself determining exactly when something that happened to people I know—or even to me—began, the moment after which it would have required cop cars and handcuffs to keep particular people from catching sight of one another and getting ideas, when a word came out of a mouth that eventually led to all the good stuff and all the misery. A story I did not seek but have found myself silently recounting—in the shower, on a walk—began, I think, on a Wednesday morning in late February, a few years ago. My husband, Joshua Griffin—called Griff—strode into our bedroom, dressed for work—I was naked—and asked to borrow *Bright Morning of Pain*, Valerie Benevento's famous novel about love and politics in the Vietnam era.

I was reaching toward my underwear drawer. "I thought you left," I said, straightening up. He had said goodbye as I proceeded toward the shower. Griff is the principal of a small, innovative high school that serves troubled kids. That morning the principal wore a tie over his white shirt and a brown cardigan with cables, knitted not by me but by our daughter Annie.

"You never wanted to read it before," I said, about the book he'd asked for, "and that's probably a good thing."

He was smiling a little, I suppose at the joke of catching me naked or at my being characteristically ready to argue, even in the nude. Or just at the sight of his woman. I am tall with big hips, a belly, and fairly big breasts, and Griff has always made it clear that he likes my body: I suppose that was partly why I fell in love with him all those years ago. He is sinewy but narrower than I am and only slightly taller, a dark-skinned black man with well-defined features.

"Why?" I said, because he was just standing there waiting. "There's no reason, at this point."

The book had come out decades earlier, and Griff emphatically didn't read it, but he certainly knew about it, then and later. We had separated for a time, and this book had been one of our problems. Val Benevento and I were high school friends, and the book mattered to me—it was painful but important. For Griff, who knew what it was about, it would also have been painful to read, so he avoided it. By the time we'd come back together, the book was no longer on my mind or, I suppose, his.

Until now. I'd been asked—and instantly agreed—to write a long essay about *Bright Morning of Pain* for a magazine, in conjunction with forth-coming new paperback and e-book editions with a readers' guide. The night before, when I'd told him about the assignment, Griff had little to say—but he'd thought it over.

I hooked my bra. I put on my panties and a shirt while he watched.

"I was up at three," he said. Griff didn't generally wake in the night unless something was wrong at school, at which point he paced, checking the lead stories in the *Times* on his phone, turning the TV on and off, picking up books and leaving them in unlikely places. "I should have read it long ago."

"You won't like it," I said.

"All these years, I've never read it! I *ought* to read it." His voice became higher. Griff's persuasive voice—his friendly-principal-who-nonetheless-stands-for-no-nonsense voice—went up and down, up and down. "Come on, Ollie. I'll give it back on Friday."

I was leaving for two days, going to a conference in Boston. I earn my living as an editor at a small press near New Haven—where we live—that specializes in books about handicrafts, but years ago, I wrote a biography of Edith Wharton. Since then, my work—not always paid—has included the writing of essays and two obscurely published books, also about writers. The conference was on Edith Wharton; I was going to moderate a panel.

"This way," he said, "when you write the essay, I'll know what you're talking about."

"You'll tell me why I'm wrong? It's not due for months, and it won't be out for a year."

Bright Morning of Pain would bring up questions we didn't need to revisit, certainly not as I started thinking and writing about the book. Also, Griff would hate it. He'd claim he had wasted his time, and then tell me I was wasting *my* time and why, and once his ideas penetrated my thoughts, I'd be unable to think at all.

"I won't care in a year," he said. "I care now."

"I don't believe you." I put on my pants.

"I know," he said. "It's inconsistent."

My train was imminent.

Apparently, Griff had forgotten his desperate need for a novel while we ate breakfast but had recalled it on his way out. Then, being himself, he couldn't wait. He's a fast reader, but two days for a whole book, given everything else he was doing, seemed unlikely.

However, I wouldn't be thinking about the book or my essay while I was away, and probably not for weeks after that. Now that he'd gotten the desire into his head, maybe it would be preferable to hear Griff's inevitably idiosyncratic opinion—and explosive personal reaction— soon, and try to forget it by the time I started writing. He'd nag until I gave it to him.

Also, borrowing the book—asking to borrow it—was, for Griff, an act of love. I associated impetuosity with the good times in our mar- riage. When life was bad—or even just adequate; most often life was just adequate—his gestures in my direction were self-conscious, and he rarely inquired about my concerns. During the time we'd lived apart, we each had a couple of embarrassing affairs, but mostly during those years we both replaced spouse with work. Our daughters were young, and we alternated weeks with them. The weeks I had neither husband nor children to distract me, I lived in a writing blur. I'd come home from my job and write all evening, drinking wine and snacking on crackers and cheese, finally stopping late to eat oatmeal or soup. Griff was a high school history teacher then, and he could always find more papers to grade, projects to invent, extracurricular activities to supervise. After he moved back home, it was simplest for either of us, when the other was difficult, to separate in the same house by working.

Forgetting to mention the book before my shower was more char- acteristic of Griff than waking at night to think of it or bursting into the bedroom to request it, but those unpredictable moments, his wide-awake face turned in my direction, were something to hold on to. However hard I worked when Griff and I were at odds, I did better work, smarter work, when we were getting along, when his wit and good mind made the rooms I passed through quiver with energy and with the surprise that comes when someone else's unexpected thoughts intersect with your own.

Griff would read the book, he'd be upset—even angry—but maybe it was finally time. Maybe, once Griff read it and we lived through that, life in this house would be friendlier for it. Griff usually reads books about history, religion, education, and race; rarely fiction. He is a passionate thinker who needs books but not works of the imagination. Griff is the son and grandson of clergymen: the successive pastors of one of the oldest and most dignified black churches in New Haven, men who looked and sounded like what they were. He has his father's and grandfather's shrewdness, civic presence, and unabashed interest in life's large questions, without their faith.

For years his family was nicer to me than to him because at least I had a religion. Two of his female cousins are ministers, and most of his relatives are churchgoers. I'm Jewish, if only intermittently and selectively observant, but after we married, they sent me greeting cards on Jewish holidays and later encouraged me to take the girls to services. Our daughter Martha insisted on a Bat Mitzvah; Annie, three years later, decided against it, at the exhausted end of a long afternoon full of hugs and tears during which her grandmother—Griff's mother, not mine—tried to talk her into it.

I was flattered by Griff's sudden interest in Val Benevento's book, even his sudden need for me after we said goodbye. Maybe because of the time when we didn't live together, nakedness before my man still felt slightly thrilling. Sometimes our resumed marriage, even decades after we'd returned to it, was a return to the uncertainty of courtship, if not quite to the period when we staggered from a political protest to whichever of our apartments was closer and slept in a single bed.

What I'm saying is that Griff's need for the book was sexy. It was also something else, though Griff wasn't talking about Val Benevento's book that morning as anything more than a book that mattered to me. Griff too had a connection with this book. Some men would have seized it the day it was published, read it, dismissed or condemned it, or become briefly famous discussing their connection to it. Another sort of man would be more comfortable pretending it didn't matter and could be left unread, and Griff was one of those. This was different—and despite my nervousness, I was curious. Barefoot, I crossed the hall into my study and took my copy of *Bright Morning of Pain* from the shelf: the hardcover first edition, with its familiar green-and-gold matte dust jacket (green tree, gold lettering, against a blue sky). The paper had soft, frayed edges and a row of tiny parallel tears at top and bottom that looked familiar. I had marked it up—both years earlier when I first wrote about it and later, when I wrote about it again. The older marks were in ink, the newer ones in pencil.

"Thank you, Ollie," Griff said. My name is Olive. Well, Olivia, but I've called myself Olive since high school. His voice was husky, almost sentimental. We kissed, he departed, and I finished dressing and drove to the train station.

■

I always write about women novelists. I like finding a story in the life, and I feel superior, knowing something about a woman that she may not have known about herself. I also feel guilty for invading her privacy and relieved that she can't reciprocate: she can't examine *my* life. And so it makes me uncomfortable to write down this story, in which I am a character—the story that began the day Griff walked into our bedroom demanding my old friend's book.

Unless it didn't. Unless it began the day Valerie Benevento sat down with a ream of paper and an Olivetti in the late seventies. But the truth is, that wasn't the beginning either. The story begins in the Brooklyn high school I went to in the mid-sixties. And when I think of high school, I think first not of Val but of Helen Weinstein, a short, thin girl with untidy light brown hair. You may recognize her name, but if you do, you're not thinking of the girl I mean—and I don't mean two women shared that name.

■

I met Helen when she sat next to me in biology class sophomore year. We dissected a frog. "What if we had to choose one of our relatives to dissect?" Helen said as we worked, looking not at me but at the frog, snipping out its heart, which was still beating, and picking it apart from the rest of the stunned little animal splayed on a board.

"I couldn't choose," I said, though inwardly I—horrified—was already choosing.

"You'd rather dissect your grandmother, selected by someone else, than choose to dissect her?"

"Oh, not my grandmother."

"But she's old, right? Isn't it better to choose someone who's had a life already?"

"Stop it!" I said. I was enthralled.

Soon, Helen and I were spending afternoons together, taking extended walks from our school into a cold wind (could there always have been a cold wind?) in a direction that led neither to her house nor mine. When I spoke of a feeling I had, one that annoyed or baffled my parents, Helen would say, "Exactly." We parted late on those afternoons, tightening our scarves around our necks and walking home separately on darkening streets. Can the wind have blown at both faces not only on our long walks together but on the subsequent walks to our houses? The sixties was a tempestuous era. Wind blew all the time from all directions.

Helen loved analyzing our friends and relatives, but after devising extreme punishments for those who had treated us unjustly, she insisted that we think again. Had she misinterpreted her mother? Was it unfair of me to feel slighted by a classmate's remark? In Helen I had a confessor, an exacting mentor ten months younger than I.

I don't know how she came to think this way. Neither of us had much religious training. Her parents and brother were easygoing, unschooled. They were large, loose, and vague while she was small and exact. Her hair was kinky, and she had strong, active hands with prominent knuckles. She was short, but her hands might have belonged to someone tall and rangy.

Helen's parents spoke in simple sentences, but her pronouncements were complex, delivered with emphasis. Her father had a shabby grocery store, and the family lived upstairs. I went to Helen's house only once after school, and she chose a snack from the store: a can containing a loaf of date nut bread and a package of cream cheese. She brought them up to her room, and we spread cream cheese on round slices. I had never eaten such a thing and took many slices, but Helen nibbled. In the next room, her brother was playing the Beatles's album *Help!*, but Helen shrugged when I mentioned it.

Valerie Benevento was a blond, vigorous girl with big breasts, a confident laugh, and bouncing, well-washed hair. Somebody told me she rolled it at night around frozen orange juice containers. I met her in Latin class, where we were rivals for top marks.

"What's your name again? Olive?" Val said as we left the classroom one afternoon.

I started to say I was Olivia but then said yes. I had decided at that instant to be Olive: firm, green—the olives we had at home were green, with pimentos—bitter.

"See ya," she said, and was gone.

Talking to Val, when we did talk, was like being with someone from a different culture whose unfamiliar assumptions are so self-evident to the holder that it's impossible to make clear that one doesn't share them. Val was a Catholic from an Italian family, but it wasn't religion or ethnicity that made us different.

At times I felt vaguely dissatisfied with myself for spending time with her, as if doing so were frivolous. The day she first spoke to me, I didn't tell Helen, but I suggested that Helen might like to call me Olive, and she said, "Don't be silly." I agree, it was silly, and my parents—when I began to insist that my name was Olive—scoffed. But except on my driver's license and passport, I've been Olive from then on. Never to Helen.

■

Near the start of our junior year, signs announcing an after-school literary club appeared on bulletin boards. I proposed that we attend the meeting. Helen and I both wrote poetry. We read aloud from books of poems we bought in Greenwich Village. We had shown our poems to no one but each other, and if asked, we would have denied we wrote them.

"Those girls don't like me," Helen said.

"What girls?"

"Valerie Benevento and those irritatingly perfect seniors she spends time with." She named two girls I had never heard of. "They all write," she said. "Plays, novels. They think poems are what kids write on Mother's Day."

"How do you know?" Val was surely not a writer. Writers did not have beautifully waved hair or sweaters that showed off their breasts. They were sloppy like me, but thinner. Or they looked like Helen, whose stiff, oversize clothes in dull colors were made by her mother and were too big and too young for her.

"I see them around," Helen said. "They don't deign to know me."

Still, we went to the meeting. Helen was right—Val attended with two other girls who looked like cheerleaders. "Hi, Olive," Val said when we came in, and Helen made a sharp sound.

I had thought of writing as a highly significant secret that nobody would admit to it except in circumstances of intimacy and trust. Meetings of a literary club would consist of shy discussions of Emily Dickinson—and maybe, thrillingly, eventually, our own poems. But one of Val's senior friends called the group to order as if it were an actual organization, and somebody proposed that we start a magazine to publish our own and other students' writing—as if the school were full of writing. These big, bonny girls talked about writing as if it were a friendly sport involving balls and shouting. When the meeting ended, we had officers. Val was treasurer. She said she'd ask the principal for money to print the magazine, and she'd work out assignments for selling ads.

"You're friends with her?" Helen said when we'd made our way out into the wind. It was almost dark.

"You mean Valerie?"

"Of course Valerie. What do you want to know her for?"

"I don't know her."

"But she called you Olive." I told her what had happened, months earlier.

Helen said, "You could have just said she got your name wrong. You made much of her little mistake, Olivia; you know you did—you made much."

Then we both laughed, and for a few weeks I'd tease her, saying, "Wait—am I making much?" Now I said, "But how do you even know her?"

"I've known her for years," she said. She paused, then said in a low voice, "Her sister was my babysitter." She tugged at her jacket, as if the thought of having needed a babysitter—of not being independent—made clothing tight. We were standing on a street corner, the wind blowing as usual, and I was freezing. I said I had to go, then leaned in and kissed her cheek, and she flicked a cold fingertip over my face—an odd gesture; it hurt a little.

■

We published an issue of *Sidewalks* that spring. Helen attended no more meetings, but she submitted a poem for that first issue, and we printed it, though none of us understood it. It began:

> *A small face, ghostly, crying,*
> *floats, lonely, over*
> *Coats, purses, hair.*
> *Now it is gone.*
> *It reminds me of what I*
> *Have not yet done.*

Helen told me that one day as we walked, she'd seen a child's face reflected in a store window, superimposed on adults inside the store. She didn't seem to mind that we hadn't guessed what she was describing. She wouldn't say what it was she hadn't done yet.

Val was the editor of *Sidewalks* our senior year, and three more issues appeared before we graduated. I still have them all. The group—mostly girls—became friends. I pretended to be as easygoing as they were, not requiring as much of myself when I was with them. We smoked. We saw *The Sound of Music*. At a party, someone passed around a marijuana cigarette.

Helen said my friends were shallow, and sometimes, in bed at night, I made up my mind to drop out of the *Sidewalks* staff. But I had discovered the delight of literary association. I was an active member of the editorial board, though I never had the nerve to walk into stores and try to sell ads. We considered submissions—there were plenty—late in the afternoons in an empty classroom, arguing. We were proud of ourselves for rejecting work we disliked and made enemies with glee. My poems were usually accepted. Val wrote stories about college girls having abortions or slitting their wrists, and we invariably took them. It was not easy to edit them in her presence, but we sometimes talked her into changing a few words. After a long argument between Val and me—the others were too intimidated to speak—I once persuaded her to replace "the scarlet fluid" with "blood."

I told Helen I still found it hard to imagine Val writing—alone, not speaking, her head bent over a desk. Helen disliked Val's stories when she read them in the magazine, but I admired them, though they seem simpleminded now. "They're loud," I admitted at the time. I thought Val was brave to write stories that included strong feelings and violence, even though we might laugh—and we did laugh. She didn't think first of protecting herself.

■

The Friday after Griff borrowed *Bright Morning of Pain*, my train from Boston reached New Haven early in the evening and I drove home. The conference, with its rushed schedule, crowded elevator rides, and hastily swallowed coffee, had created anticipation that was never quite satisfied, as seems to happen at these events. I moderated my panel, competently but without flair.

I came home tired, irked with myself for not having led a life that would somehow have directed me to a different, better conference. The dog, Barnaby, came thumping to meet me, his tail oscillating. I haven't mentioned Barnaby, an enthusiastic black shelter dog, mostly pit bull, with a body so solid it might have been designed to bore holes in things. When Griff was asking for the book right after I stepped out of the shower, Barnaby would have watched from the hall between the bathroom and the bedroom, thumping his tail on the floor. Perhaps I heard the thumping. I think I did.

I let the dog out and then fed him, poured a glass of sauvignon blanc, and called Griff's phone. He was unlikely to be at school at that hour, and board meetings—Griff belonged to two nonprofit boards— didn't happen on Fridays.

I knew from his tone—"Olive. . . ," he said, instead of "Hi" or "Ollie"—that something was wrong. I had a moment of anxiety about our daughters, Martha in New York and Annie in Philadelphia. It was noisy around him. "Are you still at school?" I said.

"Stop and Shop."

"I thought we'd go out."

"I'll cook."

"Let's go out," I said.

"It won't take long. I just paid."

"What's wrong?" I said. Even for someone talking on his cell phone at the supermarket, Griff sounded terse.

There was another pause. "Well, I'm outside." I felt him settle, as if the darkness and fresh air made directness easier. "I—I screwed up," Griff said.

He sounded so bad now that I thought of crime, injury, sickness. Had he been stopped in a suburb for driving while black, even distinguished-looking Griff? Being a white member of a black family meant that I frequently discovered I had no idea what life was like. But this wasn't, as it would turn out, one of those occasions. "What is it? For heaven's sake!"

"Ollie." I heard him swallow. "I am so sorry. I lost your book."

"My book?" I wasn't thinking about Valerie Benevento but about the book I'd been reading on the train, the book I was writing—about yet another obscure novelist—the books my panel had discussed.

Then I understood. "You lost it?" I had a physical reaction—a lurch in my throat—as if he'd lost a baby or the only copy in existence. And a familiar ache began in my chest—disappointment in Griff, disappointment in Griff's awareness of me and what had to do with me. Even then, even under my dismay, I felt something else, something like relief—but primarily I was hurt and angry.

"How did you contrive to lose it? You didn't want to read it so badly that you had to make it physically impossible?" Which made no sense. I hadn't wanted him to read it.

"I had it," he said, "and then I didn't."

"It vanished like smoke?"

"No," he said needlessly. "I lost it. I feel bad enough, Ollie—you don't have to talk me into feeling bad."

"I'll find it." I was already looking around.

"It's not at home," Griff said. "I brought it to school, and it disappeared there."

"Why did you bring it to *school*?" I was pacing. "Why didn't you just go to school without it, once I gave it to you?"

"No, no. I didn't bring it on Wednesday—I brought it on *Thursday*. Yesterday."

"But why?"

"But when I looked for it later, I didn't have it, and it's not in the car. I made everyone crazy, searching. I've been shouting at innocent people."

I was expected to chuckle sympathetically, but I didn't. "If it's lost in that school—oh, honestly. . . ." I continued studying the room I was in. "Probably you only think you brought it. Probably it's here."

"No," he said quietly. "Well, I'll see you in a few minutes."

I hung up and gathered books and newspapers—we still take print newspapers. I was hungry and angry, becoming angrier as I became hungrier. If only he had consented to eat out, we could have taken our two cars, met at a restaurant, and been eating already. As things were, instead of cooking he'd explain interminably how he'd lost the book. This kind of trouble—something minor (nobody died) that didn't feel minor—made us fight too hard. We dropped the exasperated but ultimately married tone of ordinary disagreements in favor of something uglier, a sound we'd learned in the months before we separated, all those years before.

Eventually, we'd eat out, barely speaking, ordering dishes we wouldn't enjoy. Or we'd find the book, and the fight—though I'd still be hungry and angry—would turn into lovemaking, which happened occasionally when we were finishing a fight. I'd be half willing, half resentful, preferring to argue. And *then* what about food? Griff had now forfeited the right to read *Bright Morning of Pain*, whether he wanted to or not. I stopped searching and ate some crackers.

The book was probably under the seat of his car, and if not, it was here in the house after all, somewhere he wouldn't look, like the top of the refrigerator, where one might put something temporarily so as to have two hands free to take out a heavy container of ice water, something Griff often did. He never drank alcohol, after a short period of dissipation before I knew him.

As I resumed searching, eating crackers, I found myself mentally emailing the editor who had assigned the essay about *Bright Morning*. Sorry, can't write it, husband lost book. That was nonsense. True, a new copy would be less useful than the lost one with my marginal notes. But apparently I was less eager than I thought to write the essay.

In a minor way, I was connected in the public mind with Val's book. On the rare occasions when I spoke in public about my own work, I was often asked about Val's, which made me uncomfortable, and not just because I thought it should finally be my turn. Some things about the book had always bothered me, and Val knew that, starting the day I blurted out that I hated the title, while she was still writing it.

But I thought I'd dealt with all that. My official stance was affectionate but rueful; I spoke of the book as not quite up to the classics—but after all, what is? And I spoke of famous Val, shaking my head and smiling, in a tone I might have used for a flawed but loved relative. I had believed I knew how to write this essay without discomfort, using just the few disclaimers I invariably employed. I thought I was in rough agreement with the editors about the essay's direction, and I wanted the nice sum they intended to pay me. It would be fun to write it, intellectually satisfying.

But no. Apparently that wasn't what I felt at all.

Griff's mind is not like mine. I hadn't wanted him to read the book, because he'd make me unsure about it in unexpected ways. Now, instead of reading it, he had lost it. That should have been a relief and told me what to do—order a used copy online and not let him see it—but it troubled me, as if I *had* wanted him to read it, as if I had wanted him to ask questions I couldn't answer. He'd turned my writing assignment from something simple—if simple only in the way things are when you haven't yet begun to look into them—into something complicated. I would be angry whether I found the book or not.

I heard him come in. We live in an old one-family house that had once been divided into two apartments. When we'd first moved in, we'd rented the first floor. We'd long since bought it, and eventually we spread out over the whole house, but to a degree, that night when I searched for Val's book while eating crackers, it still felt like two apartments. When our kids were teenagers, they took advantage of this characteristic: they sneaked out, or sneaked boyfriends in. We sometimes talked about restoring the house to the way it was when it was built, but I liked the possibility of being elsewhere, alone.

From upstairs, I distantly heard Griff bring in his groceries—what had he bought? Didn't we *have* groceries?—as one might hear the downstairs neighbor.

I went down the stairs, preceded by Barnaby. Griff stooped to touch the dog. How satisfying it would be, from a competitive viewpoint, to spot the book behind him, on top of the microwave or next to a plant on a shelf in front of the window, hard to notice amid our clutter, which included much that we should have discarded long since. Griff can make a case for everything, as he can make a case for any of his apparently indefensible students.

He didn't look sorry enough as he put down his bags of groceries. Griff's method of getting what he wants is to claim that reasonable people will naturally forgive even misdeeds that fall just outside what they actually consider acceptable. Soon he would be defensive about losing *Bright Morning of Pain*, proving that losing books was the same as *not* losing books. "You lost it on purpose," I said. "You hid it."

He turned, stricken, a wrapped package that seemed to be fish in one hand. "No!"

I'd hurt him. I hadn't quite meant what I'd said. I'd meant he hadn't taken the book seriously enough; he hadn't made sure not to lose it. But now he put down the fish and gripped my shoulders silently. This suggested—of all things—drama of which I was not yet aware. Had he found the book?

He backed up and looked at me with his expressive, slightly asymmetrical face, as if he had forgotten I was angry, as if we were engaged in a conversation too important for anger to interrupt it. "I read it," he said.

"You read it? You said you lost it."

"Before I lost it. I have to talk about it. But don't tell me how it ends."

"When did you read it?"

"I didn't finish it."

"Then it's where you were sitting when you stopped reading."

"No—that's why I took it to school. I wanted to Xerox my favorite pages."

Suddenly—now—I was dealing with what I had decided I didn't want to deal with ever: Joshua Griffin, complete with opinions about *Bright Morning of Pain*. Yet I still had to find it.

"Only thing I don't like—" he said.

"What?"

"It's not always accurate about historical events. For example—"

"Oh, let's just find it," I said.

"I read almost all of it Wednesday night. It's—It's— I stayed up most of the night, but then I got too sleepy to finish it."

"I'm hungry," I said.

"It's irresistible," Griff said, sounding sentimental.

"I'm going to look for it here," I said firmly, ignoring this new development—which for some reason made me angrier yet. "If that doesn't work, we'll look in your school tomorrow." Griff could get in on a Saturday. "In between we can look under the seat of your car. In fact, that's where it is. Go out and find it. And while you're out there, drive to the Indian restaurant and bring back dinner. I want the thing with chickpeas." It would be a pleasure to have him out of the place, however briefly.

"I'm cooking," he said.

I wanted him absent. "That will take too long."

"No, I bought fish. Much faster than takeout."

He moved briskly into the kitchen and began emptying grocery bags, and I gave way. I could search his car more thoroughly than he would, and I went out to do that. I remembered the crevice at the back of the back seat, the space under the front seats, to no avail. In the house, I resumed searching upstairs, in our bedroom and Annie's old bedroom, where Griff sometimes worked at night. I lifted papers I found and put them down again.

The time when we were separated had left me with a slight self-consciousness about touching his things, such as I don't think wives usually feel. His objects remained intense for me, as they were when I fell in love with him and part of him still seemed out of reach. I half expected to find not the book but something else revelatory—but I didn't. He wasn't having an affair and leaving the credit card receipt for flowers in a random pile. What I found was a cookbook—not damning, though odd. Griff did not consult cookbooks. He cooked what his mother had cooked after teaching kindergarten all day: not the great African American meals of his mother's mother, who was from the South, but meat or fish, frozen vegetables, and Rice-A-Roni or mashed potatoes. I lingered awhile in the quiet rooms upstairs, but I was hungry.

When I came down, Griff said, "Not there, right?"

"No."

He put down the spatula and walked toward me, lowering his face onto my hair. "I can't believe I lost *that* book," he said. "I know there are other copies. They're printing more now in honor of whatever anniversary it is. But I want to finish it. I'm fifty pages from the end."

The loss of the book had become his personal tragedy. "Would you cook that fish, please?" I said. I returned to the living room, where I found my glass of wine half full and drank, looking around again at our bookcases and reading lamps and worn-out furniture, trying to find the dear old hardcover copy of my high school friend's book. As I searched, I called, "Why were you reading cookbooks upstairs?" He said something I didn't hear.

■

In our senior year, Helen volunteered at a day care center in a poor, mostly black neighborhood. She was often too busy for walks in the afternoons, but one cold afternoon after school—it must have been November of 1965—she was free, and we had just set out together when she uncharacteristically said she was starving. We walked in a new direction, to a commercial street where there was a Nedick's. Between us, we had enough money for one hot dog, and Helen said we'd share, but she stepped back when we entered the store. I took her money and stood at the counter while she waited behind me. After I bought the hot dog, I moved to another counter to put mustard on it. I turned, in the store's steamy warmth, tearing the hot dog and its bun in half, but I didn't see her. She stood outside, her back in its dark wool coat and her swirl of hair pressed against the plate glass window. When I offered her half of the frankfurter, she pushed my hand aside.

She was crying. "I don't want it."

"What's wrong?"

She shook her head again. "Let's go. You eat it."

I took a bite of my half.

"I haven't eaten all day," she said as we began to walk.

"Are you sick?"

Helen never talked this way, in inarticulate bursts, so I thought she must be. We paused at a corner, then crossed. I felt awkward and angry—as if she'd set this up just to demonstrate that I was greedy and fat while she was above corporeal needs. But the hot dog tasted good, and it warmed me. I continued eating, as delicately as I could.

"It's something I saw on the news," she said finally. "I can't eat. I can't stop thinking about it."

"What?"

"Norman R. Morrison. Do you know who that is?"

"No," I said, and then remembered.

But Helen was already talking. "He immolated himself." She spoke slowly, stopping between words. "He burned himself up in front of the Pentagon."

I was saying, "I know, I know," trying to quiet her. It had been a protest against the war in Vietnam.

"He poured kerosene on himself and lit himself on fire."

We walked. People looked at her curiously, and at me with my torn hot dog. Finally, I finished my half and threw hers into a trash can. I was afraid observers would look at fat me eating and thin Helen crying and think I had refused to give her any.

I didn't want to think about the man who had burned himself up, but Helen had found out all she could. Norman R. Morrison was a Quaker living in Baltimore with a wife and three young children. The youngest, a baby, was with him in Washington, and he put her down on the sidewalk at a little distance before he lit the fire. A question we considered, when Helen could talk again, was whether that proved he had lost his mind. I said that if Mr. Morrison were sane—if he had been immolating himself as a clearheaded protest against the Vietnam War rather than because he had suddenly become deranged (I wanted him to have been deranged, so I wouldn't have to think that his action might make sense)—he would not have put the baby in danger. Helen disagreed. Helen thought the baby was part of the point. In Vietnam, the baby might have been killed.

"Do you know how many civilians have been killed by American soldiers?" she said. "The day before he died, there were forty-eight. Maybe that's why he did it."

Helen thought Mr. Morrison was saying that we in the United States lived such protected lives that a baby left on a city street would come to no harm—and indeed, someone rescued his baby—while our country wantonly killed babies elsewhere.

We had not talked before about the war in Vietnam, and my parents had done so only peripherally, but I knew I was opposed. A teacher had pointed out that the invented word "escalation" was a way of avoiding saying in plain terms what President Johnson was bringing about, after advocating peace before he was elected: more bombing, more fighting, more dead Vietnamese and dead Americans. I glanced at news programs my parents were watching. There were the sharp cracks of explosions, footage of people running, sometimes with naked children dangling from their arms, legs trailing. Helen knew more than I, but until the day we talked about the man who immolated himself, the war—and current events in general—were not among our topics. For me, private life—the inner life, the emotional life—was so compelling that I had little strength left for the questions of the day, and I loved Helen because she too cared about the inner life. But for

Helen, the man who immolated himself was recognizable because he couldn't subsume the questions of the day to the questions raised by his own life, even "Who's watching the baby?"

The next time an antiwar activist, Roger Allen LaPorte, immolated himself—a week after Norman Morrison's death—Helen was able to talk about it, and we discussed it at my house, eating apples and raisins in my room. I'd learned that Helen was likeliest to eat wholesome snacks.

LaPorte was a young ex-seminarian who set himself on fire in front of the UN and lived long enough to say that he'd done it because he didn't believe in war.

"But how could *anybody* do it?" I said.

"I know," Helen said, to my relief. It scared me that she was so willing to think about the act itself.

"I don't know enough about this war," she said. "I've been wasting time. I went shopping for clothes. My mother says she can't make my clothes now that I'm going to college." She plucked at the sleeve of her drab sweater. I felt guilty because I liked buying clothes.

"I don't think I want to be—" She paused. "A *woo-man*."

"I do," I said. I wished I could go to Barnard, where Helen was applying. Her parents had more money than mine. I applied only to Brooklyn College, because it was free. Val, to my surprise, was also going to Brooklyn. She seemed like the kind of girl whose parents would have sent her away with puffy dresses in a big trunk.

"She'll be your new best friend," Helen said when I mentioned Val. "You'll listen to the Beatles."

"Don't be silly." But it was true that Val might be a compensation. She made me feel that more was possible than I had known.

For Helen, life could lead to the unexpected, but only after you'd squeezed yourself through a narrow tube of self-scrutiny and considered everything up to and including burning yourself to death. Val's idea of the possible was only slightly freer than mine, but in a significant way, as if she saw a few inches around corners.

Just recently, a parent had complained about a sex scene in a story of Val's that we'd published in *Sidewalks*. I didn't like the story. Upon hearing that someone had phoned the principal, I expected the magazine to be shut down, and, to my shame, I'd have accepted that. But Val wrote a letter to the editor of the school paper about the importance of free speech. Then she asked the principal, her old acquaintance by then, if she could put together a discussion at a school assembly on the subject of freedom of the press. She would invite a constitutional lawyer, the editor of *The Nation*, and our congressman. The principal—a kind, foolish man—was dazzled.

The school paper ran an article on the coming discussion, including an interview with Val. The assembly never took place. Val told us the luminaries had all said no. I wondered if she'd invited them. It didn't matter. Her purpose had been served, and among the faculty and the more intellectual students, censoring anything had become not just unthinkable but *notoriously* unthinkable, the first example anyone would have thought of if asked for an instance of the unthinkable. Social studies teachers held units on the Bill of Rights. English teachers discussed the censorship of *Ulysses*.

"It was like a commercial on television," I said to Helen. We were still eating apples and raisins, now arguing about whether Val was someone we respected.

"Exactly," she said, running her fingers through her tight curls. "It was cheap."

"I just mean it got everyone's attention!" I said. "Like a jingle you can't stop singing. Honestly, Helen."

"But that's what I mean," Helen said. "It was in a good cause, but it was a gimmick." She was accusing me of being taken in by a worthless trick.

I was hurt—I did admire what Val had done—but Helen had returned to the subject of Roger Allen LaPorte. "What can it be like to be that sure?" she said. She still nibbled at her apple. I'd thrown my core in the wastebasket a half hour earlier. "I want him to be my boyfriend," she said, "now that he's dead."

Joshua Griffin

God, you watch me as if you were real. I put butter in the frying pan— my mother used margarine—salting and peppering the slices of cod, pouring flour in a bowl and turning the fish over in the bowl. I've known this bowl for a long time. Ollie kept it, at the end that was not the end, when I lived upstairs and she downstairs, because she was the one who wanted to be apart—and then when I lived in a different house, because she wanted that, too. The bowl was still here when I came back, to this house where she can pretend she lives somewhere else. She rarely uses this heavy tan bowl with a blue stripe, but I like it.

I tell you this because I have always mumbled and you have always been the recipient of my mumbles, though for decades I haven't believed that you are real in the sense that my daughters, my parents, the woman I love, or I am real. My students. Can a man who has believed in a deity cease to believe? Is it possible? Can he do more than make a claim not to believe? I am still demanding that you cure my doubt.

I need to take my wife to bed.

It's true that I read most of Val's book, true that I loved it, not true that I was too sleepy to read the end. I know that at the end, the character of Harry appears. I'll read those pages, but not yet. Surely I can be forgiven for wanting to postpone that. I didn't mean to lose the book. I have no idea where it is.

I always ask the same questions: Is it possible to cease to believe? Is it only a claim? And I ask them while doing something that doesn't require attention—chopping at a block of frozen green beans with the sharp knife, chipping at it until it fits into a saucepan. I add salt as we speak. I am real enough to add salt, and I can't say the same about you. I imagine myself saying, *Ollie, let me tell you about my student who's in trouble. I lost the book because I was thinking of him.*

We talk for a long time. Then I stand up and she stands up and I put my hand on the small of her back.

All day at school I didn't miss it, but when I saw it was gone, what I wanted again was the pleasure of forgetting my life, reading not to learn but to be someone else. All that evening, the evening I read, I thought about nobody but those made-up people, not my marriage that isn't exactly a marriage, my school that can't save its pupils, my family that will never believe that I have been worthy of my inheritance.

No, that's not true. I thought also of the past, the difficult past, gunshots and blood. But apparently even that was preferable.

I want a drink. And won't have one. Will eat this plain food without even a beer, though I want a beer. We don't keep beer because I would drink it, even after all these years. What will make her sit and watch me cook and talk to me? Make me know that, God, and I'll believe.

two

Jean Argos

I'm avoiding patches of old snow, hurrying through the parking lot from my Toyota to the midsize, semi-lovable agency I am in charge of, not knowing what I'm about to find. We just hired a new assistant director. This morning, as I rushed out to a meeting downtown for which I was already late, I heard her shout at my community service worker. Shouting is not how we do things. Useful community service workers are hard to come by, and the kid we have now is useful but easily upset.

The meeting was fine but long, and I'm eating lunch at last, ham and cheese on rye. I made the sandwich at home, with Dijon mustard and red-leaf lettuce, and all I ask is to eat the second half sitting. It's in my other hand. So I'd like ten minutes in my office before I have to confront Paulette Strong, the new hire.

Barker Street Social Services is in an old factory building. This is New Haven, so the factory once made guns or parts of guns. The parking lot looks like a factory parking lot from the days when nobody put trees and bushes around a factory. Three clients, young guys, come out of the front door as I climb the steps. If the building was still a factory, they'd be workers, but they don't look tired enough to be getting off work, and yet, in a different way, they look too tired. No place to go. I'd like to put them to work, though making guns would not be my first choice. I know two of them, not by name. The third, whom I don't know, is tall, walking a little behind the others, stretching his hands wide like the daddy, urging them along. As they pass me, he says in a deep voice, "May I have a bite?"

"No way!" I say. The other two laugh, so everybody knows everybody's kidding. We already knew. People with nowhere to go have time for subtleties.

"Miss Jean," I hear one of the shorter men say—not talking to me but about me. I'm responsible for the lunch they just ate, he means. "Miss" makes that clear.

The tall man turns and calls, "I'm Dunbar."

"Pleased to meet you!" I yell without turning. I hold both halves of the sandwich in the same hand to open our heavy old metal door. I brace it with my shoulder. Our building is the last one left on a one-block street. I like our high windows, with lots of panes, but I don't like how wind moves across the open space or how the sun cooks it.

Barker is a drop-in center, a place that isn't the public library where people with nowhere to go can get out of the rain. An outreach team of three finds homeless people hanging out and talks to those who are most afraid of the shelters, most wary of people with social work degrees. We get them to take something—food, a doctor's appointment, a referral. We're open during the day, when the shelters are closed. We serve a light breakfast and lunch. An APRN comes in twice a week. We have two washing machines and a dryer, much used and often broken. Yale students who must change from year to year but who look alike—always a blond girl, an Indian girl, a black boy with glasses—show up and help people write résumés, which rarely lead to jobs, but it has happened. Groups hold discussions in which they sound more in charge of their lives than they are. Some people come in for a half hour, get warm, and leave without sitting down.

The front door of Barker is between our two main rooms. To

my right as I enter is a room with donated computers, sofas, chairs, books, magazines, a TV that doesn't get cable but on which we sometimes show movies. To the left is a larger, drafty room with tables at one end. Lunch is ending as I pass. The last eaters—five guys—are at the other end of the big room. As I move toward the stairs, I hear a few words of their conversation: joking, bragging. Nothing troubling. We have echoing halls and iron handrails on metal stairs, so every walk is a big deal, with clanging and thumping. When I'm in my office, I hear people coming up and people coming down. There's a mental health clinic on the third floor, but they're moving out at the end of the winter. I'm drooling over the space. I have big, high rooms, but not enough of them.

But before I can get into my office and close the door, Darlene, my office manager—who knows the sound of my footsteps—pops out of her office and plunks her tough little self between me and my door.

"She left something out," she says, and hands me a form. She has a wide, pale face and a short brown ponytail with a plain, tight rubber band. Paulette had paperwork to fill out. Darlene doesn't like her and is in a hurry, so I postpone the second half of the sandwich, leave it on my desk, and go back down to find Paulette, carrying the form.

The dining room serves thirty. We want people to go to the big soup kitchens, where they get a hot lunch, so we hand out nothing but cold sandwiches, apples, granola bars, and coffee. No cookies except on Christmas. The big dining room windows give us peace. Barker is a nicer place to be than you'd think, because of those windows. Now the clients ending their meal are standing up, throwing away trash. Beyond the dining room is the kitchen, which is small and old, and at the time I'm talking about, there's an ancient, unreliable gas stove, since replaced. The walls are covered with small six-sided chipped white tiles.

As I cross the dining room, I hear arguing from the kitchen. Not shouting, not like this morning, but arguing. Through the open door, I catch sight of a stranger, a large man in a sweatshirt. Light-skinned, maybe white.

It's Paulette's third day. I don't trust her because I let myself be talked into hiring her by my board. The decision was mine, but the board takes an interest. I couldn't say why I didn't like Paulette. Her credentials were good. The only board member who agreed with me was the president—the outgoing president, whom I don't like—so since he was against her, I decided in her favor. Paulette is a tall, light-skinned black woman with skinny arms. I don't trust her skinny arms. They're too long. What will she do with them that she should back away from?

Now she's having an argument with the community service worker, whose name is Grant, and the stranger. Nobody except staff is allowed in the kitchen, but there he is. The kitchen window is cloudy glass, with wire woven through it slantwise. The light is softer, and it falls on Grant's face. He looks scared. Community service workers have something to be scared of—if we complain about them, they could go to jail. Paulette is facing him, her back to me. He's filling a bucket with hot water to mop the dining room. It's half full, at his feet, but he's facing Paulette, not the sink. The other man is off to the side.

I say, "The utility sink for the pail, remember?"

Grant stays where he is. The stranger stands next to him. Heavy arms and shoulders, wild dark hair.

"It's under control, Jean," Paulette says. She glances over her shoulder. "I told him to do it here."

"No, we're not supposed to," I say. "These are for cooking and dishes. Health department."

"Jean," Paulette says. She faces me. "This is something you can delegate. I promise."

"But wait a second," I say. "Is there a problem here?"

"It's okay," Grant says. "It's okay, it's okay." He's scared to fill the bucket at the sink and scared not to. Not liking Paulette makes me extra careful. Maybe she has a reason, I'm thinking. Maybe a boa constrictor in the utility sink is going to strangle our community service worker.

"Paulette, let's go talk about this," I say. "I've got this form, too— you left something out. And this morning, I thought I heard—" But I will never get a chance to mention this morning.

"Just leave it," Paulette says. "I really can handle it, Jean." Then to Grant, "Okay, use the other sink."

"It's okay, it's okay," he says again. He dumps his bucket out in the kitchen sink ("Sweetie, you didn't need to do *that!*" I say) and carries it into the laundry room, and I hear the faucet run. The other man follows him. I put myself where I can see them both. They fill the bucket.

"Who's that?" I say in a low voice, shrugging one shoulder toward the man.

"I get it," Paulette says. "It's hard to delegate. I've had the same problem."

I feel like hitting her. "Who is that man?" I say in a low voice. "Nobody's allowed in the kitchen except staff. And what was the argument?"

"He offered to help when he finished his lunch," she says. "His name is Arturo. Volunteering is something we ought to encourage."

"I suppose," I say, working hard at staying calm, "but it's not a great idea with somebody we don't know. And not in the kitchen." It takes a while for new hires to learn our way of being both lax and strict. We have to be loose, friendly, and kind, or nobody will come near us—and we have to admit that some clients are dangerous, and be careful. I glance toward the utility sink. Arturo and Grant have gone out to the dining room.

"You can trust my judgment," Paulette says. "And the reason I shouted? Well, you saw for yourself. He was filling the bucket at the wrong sink."

"But you told him to," I say. "You didn't know it was wrong until I told you."

"No, he was filling it in *there*. I didn't want the volunteer in there where I couldn't keep an eye on him."

"That doesn't sound like a reason for an argument."

"You're saying I'm lying?" Paulette says.

I will certainly not mention this morning. "Of course not," I say. "Could you fill that out now, please? Darlene needs it."

"I don't have a pen," she says. "I'll bring it soon, I promise."

I don't have a pen either. I turn, ending the conversation. Almost over my shoulder, I say, "Just try to stay professional."

The dining room, as I pass through, is almost empty, with the calm look it takes on some afternoons, when traffic slows and the sun makes patterns on the floor. Arturo is mopping, and Grant is watching him. The rest of the group I saw are on their way to the door, stopping to talk. There's an AA meeting in the computer room pretty soon.

I walk slowly. I'll never know why Paulette shouted, either this morning or now, and it probably won't matter. But my good mood is gone. I feel like going into my office, closing the door, lying down on the battered and stained orange couch I have in there, and going to sleep. I've done that only once, after a board meeting when the president—the one who's leaving—argued against giving my associate director, Jason King, more hours. Jason is also one of the outreach workers and supervises the other two.

That was a year ago. I was afraid Jason would leave, but he didn't. He took a part-time job at Walmart. I knew he thought I hadn't argued enough. I argued hard but not skillfully. I've been director for five years, and I've hardly ever clashed with the board. The members are people I talked into taking on the job for nothing, people who work in similar agencies, but I didn't know the outgoing president before he joined the board. He's difficult. He'd say I'm difficult.

Upstairs, Jason is outside his office, talking to one of the other outreach workers, blocking the narrow corridor to my office. He's leaning on the wall. His right foot, in a heavy brown leather boot, is braced against the opposite wall. The sole of his shoe is pressed against the green paint, which already has a few faint outlines of the sole of Jason's right shoe. Sometimes I tease him that I'm going to make him repaint that wall. His leg in tan pants makes a barrier. The outreach worker, Mel, is leaning on the opposite wall, next to Jason's shoe. Her feet, in running shoes, are planted in the middle of the corridor, so between me and my office, as I reach the landing, are both her feet and one of Jason's legs. Jason's a good-natured bald man in his forties. He raises a finger to ask if I have a minute. He won't mind watching me eat the second half of my sandwich. He and Mel seem to have been discussing something for a while.

"He's not ready," she says. "No, that's wrong. He is ready. He's just not doing it."

Someone is supposed to come to the center, or allow us to place him in a detox program, or phone for a job interview, or bring in the record of his citizenship, his application for a pardon, his GED certificate. . . .

"I need you," Jason says to me, somehow lowering his leg without sliding onto the floor. He never slides onto the floor. "Sorry, Mel."

"No, we're done," Mel says. "Hi, Jean." She bumps down the stairs.

Jason and I go into my office, and I sit on my orange couch. "Sorry," I say, and pick up the second half of the sandwich.

There's a book on the couch—an unfamiliar book. I've been vaguely aware of it for a few days. Whatever the book is about, it's not about Paulette Strong, so it's appealing. My door is often open when I'm out, and I figure someone is lending it to me. Once a week, a poet teaches a writing workshop downstairs. Poems about homelessness and other topics are tacked on bulletin boards. The poet pushes me to read her favorite books. I don't remember her mentioning this one—*Bright Morning of Pain*, a creased dust jacket with a picture of a tree and gold lettering—but I figure it's hers. I liked one book she lent me, didn't like another one. She'll be annoyed if I disagree a second time.

"We've got a problem," I say to Jason.

"It'll be fine," Jason says.

"What'll be fine? Don't cheer me up until you've heard."

"No, we're okay. Paulette, right? That's what I wanted to talk about. She's going to be fine. You worry too much."

Jason has a wife—a nurse—and four children. He's a social worker by training. He defers to me as his boss, but I know he thinks he could look after me and correct my mistakes, maybe because I'm just me and he's a crowd, if you count his wife, children, and pets. His dogs sometimes come to work with him. I have no pets and no people. Early in life, I was married and divorced.

I haven't told Jason I'm afraid I made the wrong choice when I hired Paulette, but I'm not surprised that he knows. Either of the other candidates—a white woman or a black man—would have been fine. I suspect that Paulette was popular with the board because they thought a black woman would fit nicely with a white woman (me) and a black man (Jason), instead of adding another example of what we already have. Paulette adds something, no question, but it has nothing to do with race or sex.

"She's good," he says. "Yesterday, she was great."

"At what?"

"Intervened in a fight."

"Where?"

"Sidewalk."

"Physical fight?"

"I saw it from the window and ran out. That man with the bike?" I know who he means—he's trouble.

"And who?" I say.

"Dude I never saw before. The bike guy is going with fists—I'm thinking, *Knife, knife, get there before he goes for the knife.*"

"He's not allowed in here with a knife."

"I knew he had one. The way he moved—he knew he could do something else when he got into trouble."

"So?" I pull my feet out of my shoes. I put down my sandwich.

Jason's in my chair, which has wheels, and he's scooting slightly forward and back as he speaks. "So Paulette comes along—back from lunch. And she doesn't say anything."

"She didn't yell?"

"She didn't yell; she just put her hand on Bike Man's right arm and started walking him backward. Then she sort of hugs him—she gets herself around him, and by that time, three guys pull the other man away, and that's that. She kept him talking until he calmed down and the other guy was gone. She's good, Jean."

I finish my sandwich.

I decide not to tell him what happened. I'm bothered about the stranger she let into the kitchen—and how she acted when I told her about the rule—even more than the shouting, but maybe she's one of those people who gets her back up but then does what she should. I ask him what the man in the fight looked like.

"I don't know. Big."

"White?" I said. "Long hair?"

"Maybe Latino. I don't remember the hair." There's no way to know if the man is today's volunteer. I say thanks and stand up, to make him get up. When he leaves, I close the door.

I don't take a nap. But I pick up the book the poet left for me. An old hardcover novel. I don't look at the back cover or read the flap; I just open it at the beginning and start reading.

Leaves drooped in clusters close to the screen, tossed lightly by wind. Some were bright, touched by sun. Then the light changed, gray clouds spread, and the leaves flipped to gray. Maybe it would rain. My boyfriend's arm was stretched across my stomach, and I smelled his sweat.

The words or the rhythms make me drowsy. My legs are drawn up under me, and I lean sideways on the sofa. It's old but has high sides.

The woman thinking it might rain is in bed with her boyfriend in Brooklyn, looking out the window at the backyard. They have come from a demonstration against the war in Vietnam. (I check the copyright date: 1980.) She lightly draws her hand in circles over his back, but he shifts away. The book seems a little dumb, but that's okay. I've never read a dumb book with politics in it before. I would keep reading, but Darlene sticks her head in. This time it's the payroll. I sit down at my desk to look over what she's done, and as I scoot my chair closer to hers, I see a scrap of paper on the floor with unfamiliar handwriting on it.

Someone left me a note that blew onto the floor. I pick it up.

Thurs. am

Jeanne—

Where are you?

JG

"Whoever wrote this spelled my name wrong," I say.

"JG is Joshua Griffin," Darlene says.

"Was I supposed to meet him yesterday?"

"No idea."

I'm used to Darlene.

Today is Friday. I talked to Joshua Griffin early in the week, but we didn't talk about a meeting. Then I realize that the note has been there since *last* Thursday, and when I check my calendar, I see that, sure enough, I wrote "Griffin?" on that Thursday morning. I don't know where I was when he came by. When we talked, he sounded annoyed, maybe surprised that I hadn't phoned him instead of the other way around—now I know why. And I remember that after the last board meeting, he said, "I may drop in on Thursday on my way to school." I took that to mean, "I may or I may not and I'll let you know," but I guess that's not how Joshua Griffin thinks.

Barker is tense, these weeks, partly because we hired Paulette and partly because nobody likes the board president. He announced he was quitting, but we're afraid that he'll change his mind. Two other board members want to be president. I'm for the woman—a psychologist named Ingrid, a friend. The other is this very Joshua Griffin. He serves on several boards and has been on ours for only a few months. He does something in the school system. He's a presence: Griffins have been leaders for decades in the middle-class black community of New Haven, especially the churches. Joshua Griffin is reserved. I'm thinking that with him in charge, I'll be dealing not with a man but a scion. He's not Reverend Griffin, but so many of his relatives have been Reverend that people sometimes call him that.

Ingrid serves on no board but ours. She may not be tough enough to be the president of our cheerful but cantankerous group, but I figure she'll grow into the job. She and I agree about most things. I don't know what Joshua Griffin thinks about anything. When Darlene leaves, I send him an apologetic email.

At the board meeting next week, we'll elect the new president—unless the old one doesn't quit. Or even if he doesn't, I now understand. Joshua Griffin will make him quit. For a second, I want Joshua Griffin to be president of the board, because things will happen. Board meetings now are more talk than action. Maybe the board members are *too* sympathetic to me—except for the president, who has objections but no ideas. Joshua Griffin would have ideas. He would be forceful, and that would be exciting. But it's dangerous to give forceful people too much freedom. My brief support of Joshua Griffin ends; I want Ingrid again.

What might have occurred to someone else—that the mysterious book is Joshua Griffin's and that he put it down on the couch when he wrote the note and forgot to pick it up again—does not occur to me. By this time, I almost remember a moment when the poet mentioned it.

■

A few days later, I find Paulette Strong surrounded by boxes, reorganizing a stuffed supply closet. Darlene has been promising to do it. But Paulette does a better job—she ruthlessly throws things out. I congratulate her and say she should ask me about anything doubtful, and she says, her back to me, "I'm not stupid. I'm not throwing out what we need."

I hurry into my office before I can say something I'd regret. But I like "we."

Though I've been director for five years, I'm still getting used to the job. I'm often surprised to count up and realize how long I've had it and how much time I've spent doing the two jobs in other agencies that led up to it. Surprised that I'm doing this at all and surprised that I'm spending my life at it. I grew up in New Haven and majored in economics at UConn. Then for five years, I worked for a chain of women's clothing stores based in Atlanta, traveling a few days each month. I was slightly powerful and pretty good. My decisions worked out. I had money. I thought about clothes and felt stylish—faking it, but even so. I got married. But after some disappointments (and my divorce), as well as successes that didn't feel as great as I expected, I got disgusted with myself and the job. I quit, moved back to New Haven for the summer, and stayed with a widowed aunt in a house that was too big for her. My parents had moved to Florida. I took a summer job that a friend of my aunt's heard of while I thought about graduate school in anthropology.

I had a little money saved up, and I wanted to learn something hard. I had an idea about coming to understand people different from myself and the people who worked for my old company. The summer job was at a food bank, and I was glad when it continued into fall, because I hadn't found out much about graduate school. Then a woman I met urged me to apply to the agency where she worked, because I understood computers and money. Soon, I was managing the budget and raising money for a shelter. The pay was low, but I still lived with my aunt.

I assumed I would leave the job soon. But I made friends with people who expected to keep doing this kind of work. Even then, before the recession in 2008, we only sometimes got funding for the projects we thought up. My friends and I topped one another's stories about the tricks our agencies came up with just to keep providing whatever services we offered.

A group of us, men and women, got into the habit of drinks on Friday evenings. That's how I met Ingrid. We'd talk about our own sorry prospects and the even sorrier ones of our clients. At first I was silent, because, after all, I was leaving. It was a secret—my life was going to be better than theirs. When my friends and I separated for the weekend, I'd intend to spend it investigating my future studying anthropology far from New Haven, then doing research on some remote continent—but I didn't investigate too hard.

One spring evening, maybe three years after I moved back to New Haven, as we hung around outside the bar, then started down the block, shouting goodbyes as each of us came to his or her car, I noticed that I was feeling regret, even a little envy at what my friends would keep that I planned to give up. There was much to like. The agency where I worked was haphazardly organized, and jobs were fluid, with people taking on something they wanted to do that hadn't been in their job description. I still spent most of my time on money issues, but I talked with clients as much as with other administrators. My curiosity about people different from me (who often were more like me than I expected) might be satisfied by staying where I was.

The casual mixing of races fascinated me, too. Though I'd grown up in this racially mixed town, I rarely had black friends. Now I did. The people I exchanged jokes and plans with on Friday evenings were sometimes white, sometimes black. The client body was more than half black. I'd finally lost my old self-consciousness in the presence of black people, had finally realized that I should notice people for other reasons—they were competent or inept, shy or bold, funny or dull, friendly or unpleasant.

I wouldn't miss the belief that I was helping people, because the feeling was rare. Far more frequent was knowing that despite all I'd tried, what I had done had not helped, maybe made things worse. The benefit to humanity was not an argument for staying in this life.

But there was something else, which made me postpone leaving for what turned out to be year after year, until it became clear what my life had decided for me. What we did was finally so simple, in all these agencies: we offered people who needed it rest, food, apartments, sometimes jobs, or just clear explanations of why they couldn't have what they wanted.

The people we work with have little, sometimes not even sanity. I would be appalled if I noticed myself using their misery to cheer myself: to think that I shouldn't complain because I was better off. If I did that often, I'd quit. I mind my own problems—lack of a man, for example. My clients complain, whether their problems are their own fault or society's or somewhere in between, and so do I.

Here's what finally made it impossible to go away. What we do is so simple and yet so hard. The clients need so much yet are often uncooperative. The American people give us less and less money to help them with. Some people in the field are cynical, lazy, or corrupt. Given all that, what exactly should we do? How, above all, do we keep the agency open?

I stayed for the pleasure of figuring out how to keep doing it. And because now and then I found someone to think about it with. But something remains of my old plan to get out of here. Now and then, I suddenly notice where I am, as if I had actually forgotten I wasn't somewhere else—and now, I suddenly notice that I'm the director. Responsible. In charge. And past fifty.

In charge of my aunt's house, too—she left it to me. I catch myself thinking of "her damned closet" or "that impossible basement," when I could now clear out or change anything I wanted to.

As for love, I have the Eight-Year Disease. I meet men, we fall in love, we live together. After eight years, though—okay, six to ten years—we stop being happy. I had three such relationships before I was fifty. The third was in New Haven. After my aunt died, my boyfriend moved in with me for a while, but I was too glad when something took him out of town for a few days, and I broke up with him. It takes a long time to fall in love again after a breakup of a six-to-ten-year love. It's not like finding yourself alone after being with someone for a year or two, and that's hard enough. I was a part of families. I didn't have a child, but once I was almost a stepmother. Each time, the stretch between loves has been longer. Now—the week Paulette starts working, Dunbar says hello, and I find Joshua Griffin's note—I'm fifty-two. I've been alone for six years.

three

Olive Grossman

Throughout our senior year, Helen made sure I knew what was happening in the war. The number of our troops—mostly reluctant draftees—went way up. Resistance increased, and Helen was often busy in the afternoons. She didn't invite me along, as if, like writing, protest was private.

But one February day in 1966 she asked if I wanted to go to a demonstration outside the Waldorf Astoria. President Johnson would be speaking inside. Of course, I said yes. The next day, Val and I were the last to leave a meeting of the *Sidewalks* staff, and as I erased some notes on the blackboard, I sensed that she was stuffing papers into her large leather satchel extra slowly. She wanted to talk with me alone. I felt a brief thrill.

"Johnson's speaking at the Waldorf," she said. "Next week."

I didn't answer, wondering if Val was proposing that we go to hear the president. She didn't seem like a protestor any more than she seemed like a writer. Had the school paper assigned her to report on the speech? But she said, "There's a protest." She had a flyer. She described what it said at some length. "Want to go?"

"I'm going with Helen Weinstein," I said.

"You knew about it? Why didn't you say so?"

"Want to come with us?" I said, hastening past the embarrassing moment. Helen, I tried to persuade myself, would be glad to hear that Val was antiwar.

"Sure. It starts at six," she said. She announced that we'd go straight into the city after school, so as to eat first. I—even I—would not have thought of food, and it would have been a matter of principle for Helen to remain hungry.

Explaining all this the next day, I talked fast. "You can have a glass of water while we stuff our faces," I said—surely a mistake. We didn't acknowledge that Helen didn't eat.

She was silent. "It's not a party," she said then. "Does Val think it's for fun?"

"That's not fair."

"Go with her."

That made me angry, but I understood. Protest was sacred. If Val was involved, it would be an ersatz protest, a glamorous protest that serious people should ignore. I agreed with Helen—but compromise seemed easier than trying to explain to Val how Helen and I felt.

"Anyway," she continued, "my parents need me in the store after school. I'll see you at the Waldorf."

I knew they didn't need her in the store, but I gave in, remembering that if Helen and I went together, I would get no supper.

Helen was exhausting but correct. The rally was not trivial. Vietnamese people were being killed, and their villages were being destroyed—the trees knocked down, the land left bare. The boys in my class who didn't have the grades for college were grim with the approach of graduation, knowing that without student deferments, as they turned eighteen they'd be drafted and quite possibly killed.

Still, it was a relief to go with Val. Bundled in scarves and hats, we took the subway into Manhattan, and she led me to a luncheonette where we ate hamburgers and drank Cokes. I forgot to leave a tip, and Val sent me back. By the time we reached the Waldorf, others surrounded us—small groups with printed posters or homemade signs. I didn't see Helen.

I thought we might spot President Johnson getting out of a limousine and going inside, but someone said he had been brought in the back way. It was hard to believe he was there.

When it was almost over and Val and I were moving stiffly toward the subway, I saw Helen standing by herself, staring at the door of the elegant hotel. I took Val by the arm and dragged her to Helen, then linked my other arm through hers. Helen resisted, but I didn't let go, and we took the subway home together. Val found a seat, but Helen and I stood, and then Helen dropped her face into my shoulder and cried. I was holding the pole with one hand, steadying my big bag with the other, but I tried to make my arm enclose her, and my fingers stroked her curls.

"We accomplished nothing," Helen said the next day. Four thousand people had attended the rally, she said, but Johnson had never seen us. She'd read in the paper that he'd seen only one man—carrying a sign that read "Bomb Hanoi." The newspaper had printed the president's speech, in which he explained why objections were incorrect: the war would merely prevent North Vietnam from taking over South Vietnam. Our country would nobly help the South Vietnamese remain democratic.

I thought Helen was wrong—that gradually people would come to agree with us—but she was right. The war worsened for many years, though protests forced Johnson not to run again in 1968. Nixon won, and the war continued.

■

Two weeks after Griff had contrived to lose my copy of *Bright Morning of Pain*, I had done nothing to replace it, and despite his protestations, neither had he. Either of us might have procured a cheap old copy that would arrive packed by hand in a used, cut-down carton. I was writing about some novels written in England after the First World War, but I ordinarily acquired whatever I needed for other projects promptly and established off-center piles on the big table in our living room. I continued enjoying the delusion that if my copy of *Bright Morning* was gone, I couldn't write about it.

Griff was busy, certainly. He was invariably overcommitted at school and served on two boards, both going through changes requiring extra meetings. He was often asked to speak at public events. But I thought his tardiness might have to do with how far he'd read when he lost the book: he had been near the end. He had stayed up late, then gone to bed when the suspense was greatest. I didn't remember the structure of Val's book precisely, but I knew what happened at the end. Griff was afraid to finish *Bright Morning of Pain*.

During those weeks, he was often gone for dinner or even breakfast. He'd get up early, buy coffee on his way to school, and have time to work in his office before anyone else arrived. When Griff was absent, I ordinarily reveled in solitude—or solitude with dog. Not this time. I wanted him to worry about me, I noticed one morning, while I ate breakfast by myself. I wanted solicitous inquiries about whether the loss of Val's book was ruining my work life, whether the deadline for the essay was imminent. I wanted him to be curious about what I was working on—the novels about which I was writing an essay, the book I was editing for my job. I wanted the approval conferred by curiosity.

And then, as I had these thoughts, I heard his key in the lock, his step in the hall. Our kitchen had a small square table shoved into a corner, and two chairs. When we ate meals together, we sat at right angles to each other, on the sides of the table that weren't against walls, with an imaginary diagonal line separating our personal plates or mugs from the box of cereal, the coffeepot, or the platter of food. Alone, I spread out, the dog at my feet. When he came in, I was sitting with my feet on his chair. My food, as well as the *New York Times*, covered the entire table.

He said, "Hi," and began rummaging in the cupboard. I took my feet off his chair. Griff likes instant oatmeal. He put water into a bowl without measuring, shook in the oatmeal, put it into the microwave, and punched buttons. I would never touch that stuff. "I told you I'm running for president of the Barker board, right?" he said.

He hadn't told me. "You don't need that!" I stood, as if to act, then sat down again.

"If I don't, the present guy will stay. A good man, but terrible. This smiley Ingrid wants to do it, but I don't trust her, and anyway, he'd win. He won't bother to run if I want it. So, I have to." The microwave chimed. "Nobody else will stand up to Jean Argos."

"She's so bad?" I tried to remember if I'd ever met Jean Argos. I'd heard him say the name often enough.

He laughed. "Oh, she's scary. Drives down the hill at you with her high beams on and her horn blasting." He put milk, brown sugar, and raisins on his oatmeal. "That's not fair. But no executive director should push any board around."

"You push everyone around. Is she fiercer than you?"

"Much," he said.

"Have I met her? What does she look like?"

"Like anyone. Dyed blonde, fifties."

"Like *anyone*?"

"A classic director of an agency." He tucked a dish towel into the neck of his shirt, arranging it like a big apron, then ate his oatmeal standing up, though I had taken my feet off his chair. Instead of making him look silly, the dish towel bib made him even more dignified.

"A lesbian?" I said. Several women I knew with jobs like that were lesbians.

"I never asked her."

He left quickly—as if he'd come only because our house was the most geographically convenient source of microwaved oatmeal—and I was disappointed in myself. I had wasted our first conversation in days by talking about what didn't matter. I didn't care about Jean Argos. Griff and I both knew too well how to be offhand, but that tone was an inaccurate measure of what we were. We had fallen into sharp chatter, like people who only just happened to share a kitchen, as if we had no right to strong opinions around each other. It was appalling.

I didn't want Griff to extend himself still further into the doing of good, which already used up too much of him. Educated, civic-minded black people in New Haven are much in demand—on boards and commissions, as spokespersons, candidates, campaign managers, and board presidents—and he'd told me he had to be careful not to feel flattered when someone phoned to say he was the best person for some job. What had become of that rueful, insightful grasp of his place in our city?

Griff did matter, and I was glad he knew that. But when he decided that
he was the only one who could do something, I'd learned to be suspicious. I was angry that he hadn't talked to me about this. He hadn't even
remembered whether he had or not. It was the opposite of wanting to
borrow my book—and more like losing it. I surprised myself by thinking
that I should have burst into tears. I don't cry much. Thinking about
it, I actually did cry—didn't burst into tears, but enough to have to wipe
my eyes. Not only had Griff lost it, but after initial dismay, he seemed
to have forgotten he'd lost it.

I stood to wash my mug, feeling even worse—though enjoying the
slight satisfaction that comes from understanding what's wrong. The
mug was handmade, dark blue, with ridged circles around the outside, a present from an author whose book on ceramics I'd edited.

Then I left for work. I was working on a book about weaving. While
I work on a book, I become an expert, and shortly after I finish, I again
know nothing. I'd been hired originally at this house that specializes
in books about crafts because in addition to being literate, I could
truthfully say that I knew how to knit and sew, though I remarked even
back then that I hadn't done either for years.

"You never forget," the woman who hired me said, but the last time
I picked up my daughter Annie's knitting project, I had forgotten.

The spring when Griff lost *Bright Morning of Pain*, I could say a good
deal about warping a loom, and because weaving was even more complicated intellectually than some of the crafts about which I edited
books—I was astonished at how many ways there are to weave—I found
this book particularly challenging and engrossing. Because I thought
about weaving techniques all day, I was free to think freshly of literature

at night or on weekends, and now that I had cut back my hours at the job, I could have spent a couple of days a week on my own work. I should have been able to do it well. But I wasn't able.

Joshua Griffin

Wouldn't it have been reasonable to purchase a larger table years ago? We're not rich, but that rich we are. The kitchen is small, but there is room for a larger table. Or it would be possible to eat at the table in the living room, if it weren't covered with books and papers 98 percent of the time. She has a room upstairs to work in, but she works at the big table in the living room—and I understand that. I like that. But we could have bought another table—either for the kitchen or the living room. I might have said, *I will no longer perch on a corner of the table.* Or we could break down the wall to Martha's old room, have a good big kitchen and get a good big table. A likely idea.

Sometimes I look to see if she's taking the clothes she puts on out of a suitcase. I hang my clothes on decent wooden hangers in a decent closet, because I know where I live and I own my house, but her clothes are in piles on the floor, as if she's getting ready to travel. The basics, the basics—is it a quirk of mine, a quirk of mine as a black man to say *here* is the proper way to live, let us live in the proper ways, cleaning ourselves and our possessions, making room, smoothing what is rough until we get no splinters, or else we dishonor ourselves?

Making a kitchen in which we can drink coffee while facing each other, with room for bowls and spoons.

I parked the car at the coffee shop, walked in, opened my mouth to ask for a medium coffee and a cranberry muffin, then turned, saying, "I am sorry," to the baffled barista, who recognized me from yesterday and the day before that, and was reaching for the cranberry muffin. I left the coffee shop, returned to the car, drove to the house, and went inside. Her legs stretched across the chair. Her legs stretched across the chair. As if she was glad to have the extra room.

How can a man who is helpless before the quandaries of his own life exert influence on children in trouble? The boy yesterday. *My father, my father, my father*, he said—how he is helpless before whoever this father is. I pictured my own father, but surely his—younger than I, an unjust man who is a victim of injustice, a man with prison in his past— is nothing like mine. I urged and advised, provided reasons, provided rationales, provided solutions. He left relieved. I should have said, *Let us mourn together the death of what you want to have with your father, what I wanted to have with my father—who is dead—and what I want to have with my wife.*

If I'm not careful, I'll be president of the board of Barker Street. My pride disgusts me.

Olive Grossman

Helen Weinstein took Latin for the first time as a freshman at Barnard. I had studied it in high school, but Helen, atypically, was afraid. Few students learned Latin even then, but she believed she should, and couldn't. I assumed Helen regarded me as sweetly inferior in intellect and skills, but when I saw her in those first months of freshman year, it was supposedly to help her with Latin. We both lived with our parents and commuted to college as we had to high school—but one of us was at Barnard, the women's college at Columbia University, way up on Manhattan's West Side, and the other was at Brooklyn, a public college inconveniently located, even for many Brooklynites, an hour and a half or more by subway from Barnard.

"Explain," Helen would say, thrusting her page of exercises under my nose, and I would discourse on how the farmer, *agricola*, became *agricolae* when a horse belonged to him, while the horse, *equus*, became *equum* when the point was that the farmer owned it. I wondered what was on her mind for which Latin was the excuse to see me. My college work was not onerous, but despite pretty buildings, Brooklyn College was an insufficient destination: going to class felt like running an errand, not joining a community of scholars. I didn't know what to do with myself between classes. Living with my family, I had no social life.

Helen made friends at school, even though she didn't live in the dorms. At home, I gathered, she was a boarder who came and went, shutting herself in her room to study. Her parents, darting up from the store and rushing back, apparently considered Helen and her slightly younger brother a project they'd finished, except for tuition payments.

But my brother and sister were in elementary school, so our household still existed primarily for the care of children—inoculations, teachers' conferences, outgrown shoes. I was an assistant adult. I did homework at the kitchen table or in a big chair in the living room, as I always had, interrupting myself to participate in whatever was going on. I was jealous of Helen's brooding self-discipline, her distinguished private college, and her adult, solitary days, yet despite myself, I encouraged my family to treat me as someone whose life was still primarily with them. Helen was coming to know Manhattan, the exotic borough, while I was stuck in Brooklyn, the boring one. I preferred not to hear about what she did.

Inserting my key into the lock in our apartment door, I'd often recognize her voice and discover her watching my mother cook dinner, talking. Helen would insist that I take a quick walk with her, or she'd tell me her news in a corner of the living room. She'd have brought her Latin text, but we'd soon put it aside. Now I can't forget those unexplained visits. I should have behaved differently—and maybe everything would have been different. I should have had the sense to feel confident about my own life, confident enough that maybe she'd have continued to think that what I thought and did might be something she too could think and do.

Helen had joined an antiwar group and expressed surprise that I hadn't. I said, "I'm still figuring out where the library is," and she made an impatient noise with her mouth.

She told me less about the political group than about a program she'd signed up for, tutoring poor kids after school. She'd locate their apartments and sit down with the children amid crying brothers and sisters and harried parents, trying to teach them reading or arithmetic. I asked, "Are there bugs?" and she scolded me. Like me, Helen spent much of her time on public transportation or with children, but she seemed adult, productive, and unselfish, while the same actions—deprived of meaning because they took place in my own neighborhood and my own house—made me pathetic. So I didn't argue enough.

I'd hear not just about the children but about their parents. Adeline understood her kids in a way Helen's parents never could, she told me. Adeline wasn't afraid to laugh, and once she cried openly. Adeline was the mother of a girl called Tania. There was also a little brother who was not Helen's charge, but she was teaching him letters and numbers.

One late fall afternoon, we were perched next to each other on the broad curved arm of the sofa in my parents' living room. Our arms in their sweaters touched as we gestured, talking while looking out the window at rain. My mother came through the room and said, "Something's wrong with my chairs?" but we ignored her. We had begun talking where we were, studying the rain to see if we wanted to walk, and there we remained.

"I could have shot her," Helen was saying. I hadn't been paying attention.

"Who?"

"Adeline. I *said* 'Adeline.'"

"I'm sorry. I was looking at the rain."

"She yelled at Godfrey for coloring a horse green. She said he should know better."

"I guess he never saw a horse," I said.

"That's not my point. He knows they're not green!" Her voice turned sarcastic. "Even black kids know horses aren't green, Olivia!"

"That's the three-year-old? The little brother?"

"Four. He's four."

"Four," I said evenly, trying to avoid an argument. "I don't remember what kids know at four."

"My point," she said, "is not what he knows. She's squelching his imagination—everything has to be accurate. 'The teacher will holler if you make the horse green!' He'll get rich quicker if he makes it brown? For God's sake."

I was silent.

"What?" she said.

I hesitated to make her own argument back to her. "You said Adeline understands her kids. Maybe it makes sense—if they're poor, getting high marks and a good job will be important."

"Don't condescend! Adeline is perfectly capable of thinking any thought you can think."

That silenced me, and I heard nothing similar for weeks. I didn't know Adeline, but I was uncomfortable hearing so much praise, then anger.

Helen almost never ate with us, despite all this turning up at suppertime. My mother couldn't easily add an unexpected guest. Some cooks can cheerfully take five baked potatoes, mash the interiors with butter and cheese, and calmly serve six people, doing something crunchy with the liberated potato skins. Never my mother. Helen's appearances embarrassed or annoyed her.

Twice a week I had a class from four to six, and my mother refused to serve dinner until I got home, though I'd have preferred otherwise. One evening, when I finally arrived, Helen was there. She'd never come this late before. She was reading in the living room, and she followed me into the room I shared with my sister, whose voice I heard coming from my brother's room.

"What's going on?" I said, irritated. I wanted her to tell me quickly what was wrong—obviously something was wrong—and leave.

"Adeline threw me out," she said.

"How come?" I was taking off my coat, putting down my books.

"It's my own fault. I was supposed to tutor Tania, but I kept arguing with her mother. Now what will happen to her?"

"What did you argue about?"

"Lots of things. TV. Adeline wants a color TV more than anything. It's depressing."

"She'll take you back."

"I don't think so. It's terrible for Tania." She stood in the middle of the room, her hands at her sides. "I did wrong, Olivia."

My mother appeared in the doorway, shrugging meaningfully. I smelled food cooking. I was hungry. Helen—who missed nothing—seemed to miss my mother's discomfort, as, apparently, she had missed Adeline's.

"If only you'd told me," my mother would say, later that evening. "I'd have baked another potato!"

Now Helen, her small face full of misery, turned wordlessly to my mother. I think she was just noting the interruption, not pleading for food, but my mother said brightly, "Helen, stay for supper! I thought there wasn't enough, but we can be a little creative here!"

I didn't want to hear about creativity. For once, Helen stayed and ate, and my mother refused a potato. Helen's scrupulous mind was as exacting as ever, but something had shifted. I was used to feeling inadequate when considering Helen's noble feelings, and at first, I didn't quite know what to conclude about the black welfare mother who wanted a color TV. If it had been Helen's rich relative who wanted a color TV, I'd have cheerfully looked down upon her along with Helen. Color TVs, I would agree, were materialistic, showy, pointless: people would be better off buying Latin textbooks. Helen and I had been snobs together on many occasions—and then reconsidered, when her sense of fairness returned.

But never before had Helen questioned the values and tastes of the poor women she'd come to know. The term "black" was just replacing "Negro": black history, black power, black is beautiful . . . and I ruminated with interest about the black woman rejecting a black-and-white television. I wrote a poem that I showed Helen, in which "black and white" had different meanings in different lines. But I was troubled. I was determined to argue, not just listen.

"I think she knows best," I said, on another evening when Helen had stayed late. She was still criticizing Adeline about the TV, but she had uncharacteristically stopped blaming herself for spoiling Tania's chance to be tutored.

"Don't be silly," she said quickly. "This is just capitalism teaching her to want what she can't buy. She's a victim. More TVs, more money, more soldiers, more killing. She'll spend the rest of her life wanting what won't make her happy."

"Maybe she gets tired at work. She likes watching television at night."

At that point, my mother in her apron appeared once more. Helen cut her off before she could speak. "That's okay, Mrs. Grossman, I'm leaving. I have a paper to write."

"I wish—" my mother began.

"No, I can't, thank you." Helen thought she was being invited, not sent away. She wrapped a fuzzy blue scarf around her head and let herself out. Helen always liked scarves, even when it wasn't especially cold. She looked like someone in a poem.

"Sweet," my mother said, when she was gone. "You should have told me . . ."

"It's fine, Mom," I said.

Helen was making me uncomfortable, but I disapproved of myself when I discovered that I was looking forward to time with my parents and sister and brother. My sister was a funny, chatty girl of twelve who took modern dance; my brother was shy and sweet, only nine and in awe of his sisters. My classes had not yet seized my attention—that would come later. I joined an antiwar group at Brooklyn College, but though I agreed with what I heard, I didn't say much.

Val Benevento was already on the staff of the newspaper, and soon I heard that she was dating one of the editors. I began seeing her byline. When we'd meet on campus, she'd propose having lunch together at a restaurant nearby, and I was flattered that she wanted to. As always, Val was fun. She knew where to go and what to order, and told me I looked good in brown and green. We were both English majors, and Val had found out which professors to avoid. When I told her stories from my life, she claimed I was funny. Val had a part-time job at Lord & Taylor and had more money than I. I couldn't afford lunches out, but I never said no when she suggested one.

As I became more sure of myself, I began to miss Helen instead of resenting her greater fortune. Now I think that maybe her fortune wasn't so great after all, that her life was more than she could handle. As high school girls who were aware of the war and opposed it, we had been about as praiseworthy—at least in my mind—as possible. Helen's new acquaintances asked themselves not merely to oppose the war but to end it. She seemed to think that *she* was supposed to end it.

If we had been men, we might have been sent to kill and be killed, and as women we might have been sleeping with men getting ready for war, but because we were students, our personal worries were postponed. The men's student deferments kept them from being drafted. The system changed in 1969—when my classmates and I were twenty or twenty-one—with the lottery that made every nineteen-year-old American male a potential soldier, not just those who weren't in school. In high school, boys I knew who were going to college had been relieved to have student deferments and didn't think much about the men who didn't have them. But the students Helen and I met now were self-conscious about it. Bourgeois privilege was a big subject with Helen, who sometimes behaved like a visitor from college observing people in the slums and sometimes like a visitor from the slums (she retained several tutees but stopped mentioning conversations with their mothers) observing those in college. She began to speak disdainfully of boys with deferments.

One winter afternoon (piles of coats were stacked at the back of a room with a piano, and embarrassed students pawed through them at the end), I attended an audition for a chorus. I had remembered that I liked to sing. I have a reliable alto voice and had sung in the high school glee club until time with Helen and the literary club became priorities. The students looking for their coats were embarrassed, or angry, because they hadn't been picked. I was picked, though only two altos were accepted that day. I was so startled to hear my name read that I wondered for a moment if there might be another Olive Grossman. It was my first distinction in college. I phoned Val that night to tell her, and she promised to come to our first performance. I suspected she wouldn't, and she didn't. By then, we were seeing less of each other, if only because of where our schedules took us, when we happened to meet.

The chorus sang Orff's *Carmina Burana* that spring. I found its percussive energy irresistible. And most of it was in Latin. I felt distinctive in the world for knowing the *Carmina Burana* and distinctive in the chorus for knowing a little Latin. Singing, I had power—nothing tentative about this music. I bellowed some of the songs at home and taught bits to my brother and sister. Much of the piece is about the wheel of fortune; my own wheel had turned a degree or two.

When I stepped out of the building at five, each week it was a little less dark; that felt like a personal achievement. A girl in the chorus was in one of my classes, so I had a reason to speak to her. She knew a tenor named Patrick—a friend of her boyfriend—and soon the three of us would emerge together, sampling the weather and putting on hats and gloves. At last, I had friends. We'd find a place to drink coffee. I had finally persuaded my mother not to delay dinner for me, and sometimes my friends and I ate hamburgers. I'd never tasted coffee before—the first time, I said, "Black for me," because they drank it black; it took years to discover that I don't like my coffee black.

Sometimes we got into trouble for singing bits of *Carmina Burana* in a booth at the luncheonette, banging on the table with the heels of our hands. Helen and I had never walked down a street singing; when I asked, it turned out she couldn't sing on pitch. My new friends and I sang on our way to our bus or subway stops.

Sometimes Patrick and I were alone. He was a dark-haired, sturdy boy, a little older than I, and lived not with his parents but with cousins, a young couple with a baby. He smoked cigarettes, and I liked his smell. Patrick offered to teach me the guitar. I began smoking regularly instead of only when a friend gave me a cigarette, but I never learned guitar—I was too self-conscious to let him watch me make mistakes. Still, I discovered the pleasure of visiting him at his cousins' apartment, where he slept on a couch in the living room. We sang folk songs together. I knew every Weavers song by heart, and so did he. He could sing the Kingston Trio song about Charlie on the MTA, and soon we sang that. And he could sing Bob Dylan songs, which I found difficult. Learning to produce raspy, angry, rhythmically complex sound and still be making music was irresistible.

Once, his cousins were away, and Patrick began groping and kissing me, first my neck, then my body. His hands were enormous and hot, and every place he touched felt erotically charged. Then he said sensibly, "I didn't think we'd get to this point for months, but we may not have another chance, and I can't afford a hotel." I was shocked for half a minute, both at what he was proposing and at his lack of sentiment—and then I decided that the girl I wanted to be would not be shocked. We took off our clothes in his cousins' bedroom and got into their bed. He had condoms. We were clumsy, frantic—but excited and happy. When we were done, I insisted that we had to change the sheet (which had a little blood on it), and I suppose the cousins guessed what happened, because the clean sheet we found was a different color. Delighted with myself but self-conscious, I dressed fast and left.

Soon Patrick and I were not just sleeping together but singing protest songs at antiwar rallies. We'd walk up to the microphone, and people would yell. I knew they weren't yelling because we were *good*— but maybe we were good. The yelling resumed after we sang. People grabbed us as we left, glad to spot us in the crowd. We called ourselves "Pat and Ollie," and people began using those names, though we always said "Patrick" and "Olive" to each other.

I did all right in my classes, and at the start of my sophomore year, I found a couple of professors who knew more than I'd ever know. All I wanted was to listen to them—no, I also wanted them to think I was remarkable; there were hints that they did.

■

One Saturday afternoon in February of 1968, I was playing Scrabble with my mother when the phone rang. Patrick had become less attentive except when we sang, and I worried that he had found a girl with her own apartment. I hoped it was Patrick calling, but it was Helen, who hardly ever phoned. She invited me to visit her the next day.

"I haven't told you," she said. "I moved out."

She had a job sorting books in the Columbia library and had moved into a cheap apartment where two other women lived. "They're letting me stay in the living room. They need the money."

"Like my friend Patrick," I said, and would have liked to say I had a boyfriend, but I didn't feel sure enough. I envied her once more and wondered if her parents paid some of the rent. I thought, as I often did, that I should have been more like Helen—I should have found a way to move out.

"It's cheaper than the dorms," she said. "And the train takes so long."

She said she had a boyfriend, and I tried to suppress competitive thoughts. "I met him at a rally," she said. "He'll probably stop by tomorrow."

I wondered why she wanted me to come, and to come now. This was the first time I couldn't read her thoughts. She had been like a small child who bursts into tears when disappointed, her outbursts unmediated by self-consciousness. The time she wanted to go to the rally at the Waldorf with me but not with Val, it didn't matter what she said, because what she felt was obvious. But, I pointed out to myself, we were closer then. Maybe her new friends or her roommates understood her now.

Then she said, "My roommates don't like Daniel." So I was the reliably friendly friend. And yet, wouldn't it have been simpler to leave with Daniel and avoid the roommates? All these years later, I see that everything Helen did—the long series of changes and decisions that were beginning for her—she did ambivalently. It didn't seem so at the time, but it was so, and when she felt hesitant about the life she was rushing toward, she turned toward me. I was safety; I was the past that had almost been sufficient, and maybe I could have pulled her back—or maybe I could have gone a distance with her, and that might have modified the life she led during those years, essentially alone.

I took the long ride on the rattly IRT to her apartment in Morningside Heights that Sunday afternoon, a little worried that the
apartment would be full of bugs and mice, a little afraid that it would
be so enticing—even though Helen was sleeping in the living room
and had roommates who criticized her choice in men—that I'd be
wretched with envy. Helen came to the door in an old green sweater,
with something white on her jeans and hands, and there was a scat-
tering of white on the worn parquet floor: wood strips in an intricate design, now ugly with ancient stains. Later I realized the floor
had once been covered with carpet, because occasional bits of gray
string were held down by tacks. The floor was a hint of what I was
walking into: not just young people figuring out adult life. Everything spoke of other times and places, ideas that had been argued
through decades.

I hadn't seen Helen in a while, and she looked thinner. Her brown
curls too were dusted with white. "What's wrong?" I said, before I
completely took in that all this white was flour.

"Oh, Angie's mad," she said. So something *was* wrong. "Come
on." She led me into the kitchen, where ingredients for baking were
on a small green wooden table with flaking paint.

"What are you making?"

"Banana bread," she said. "The bananas got brown."

I stood there in my coat. Helen mashed bananas with a fork. Then
an untidy woman—a girl, we said "girl" until about 1970, when the
women's movement told us we were women—came into the kitchen.
She wore glasses with black-and-white frames and overalls. I was afraid
of her.

She glanced at me and said nothing. Helen was scraping mashed bananas into a bowl, which seemed to give her the excuse to ignore both of us, like a scientist at a delicate stage of an experiment.

"I'm Olive," I said.

"Olivia," Helen said. The correction pleased me: she was protecting her investment in me. "This is Angie."

Angie and I nodded.

"The point," Angie said to Helen, "never had anything to do with showing up or not. We were always going to show up. This was a given."

"I know," Helen said.

"Whether *they* did or not."

"I get it." Helen turned and crouched, trying to light the oven. It was a gas stove, and the oven had to be lit with a match.

"Pull your hair back," Angie said.

I offered to light the oven. "My hair is shorter," I said. Nervously, I leaned over and struck the match. Angie's was shorter yet, but she stayed where she was. There was a pop when the gas caught, and I jumped. I've never liked that kind of oven.

"Thanks," Helen said. "I hate it."

As if she'd been waiting to make sure we all survived the lighting of the oven, Angie left the room, and Helen offered me tea. She put a kettle on the stove and then scraped the batter into the loaf pan.

"What was she talking about?" I said.

She didn't answer for a moment, then said, "Half a million troops," maybe indicating the reason for whatever people did or didn't go to. When the banana bread was in the oven, she took out a box of tea bags. She reached for two mugs and put tea bags into them. "Can you imagine?"

I knew there were now half a million American troops in Vietnam. Helen continued, "All this marching and chanting. We've accomplished nothing."

The kettle boiled. "Did you see those pictures?"

A series of photographs that everyone was talking about had come out a week or so earlier. I didn't want to think about them. "What did Angie mean about going to something?" I asked.

"I don't remember," Helen said. "Probably the gym. She thinks I'm wasting time on that stuff. She thinks Daniel only cares about me because he wants a white face at the protest, so the cops won't shoot."

For a second I thought she meant flour on her face and was baffled. Then I said, "Daniel's Afro American?" using the term I believed was correct at the moment. Her boyfriend, it became clear, was a black Columbia student who'd become involved in a fight that Harlem people were having with Columbia over a gymnasium. It was scheduled to be built in Morningside Park, with an entrance at the bottom of the hill so the neighborhood people could use it, while the Columbia students would enter from the top.

I had heard about this. "I thought having an entrance at the bottom was a good thing," I said. "So it's not just for students."

"Yeah, separate entrance for the ghetto, so they can lock it when they get tired of black faces. Tearing up the park for the benefit of outsiders."

I felt a moment of embarrassment for Helen—did she have a right to use the word "outsiders"?—but put my feelings aside, watching her methodically adding milk and honey to our tea. I pulled a chair out from the table, arranged my coat around its back, and sat down.

Before, when we weren't out in the wind, Helen and I were in school, in public places, or in our parents' apartments. "I *love* this," I said too loudly, waving an arm. The tea was hot, strong, and sweet, and I wanted to move in. Maybe throw Angie out. But I didn't want to think about those photographs and what we had to do to stop the war or about a gym that would be bad for Negroes or blacks or Afro Americans or whoever they were. I wanted us to be happy people drinking tea in a warm apartment. We were finally adults.

The doorbell rang before the banana bread was done, and Helen admitted Daniel. He was a boyish, light-skinned black man with a big Afro that was brown, paler at its edges, so he had an ethereal look. She led him into the kitchen ("This is Olivia," she said firmly), and he smiled at me while reaching from behind her to take her into his arms, then turning her shoulders so she faced him, pressing her face into his chest. It was the first time I saw Helen touched by a man, and she was a strange mix of child and wanton woman. She pushed back instead of burrowing in, but I thought it was not distaste but a need to take charge herself, and then, indeed, she turned again and drew his hands in front of her, where they might have chastely hugged but instead lay on her breasts.

Daniel, at first glance, was the perfect boyfriend for Helen—like her, someone who had never been a teenager, having moved directly from childhood to adulthood. The tea made me want to love everything, and I was moved by the way he touched her. He spoke in a hurried, intense whisper: "I am *really* glad to meet you." Or, "I most *definitely* want banana bread." It came out of the oven, and we waited just until it was cool enough that Helen could take it out of the pan.

We ate it. Angie ambled back in and nodded at Daniel. She picked the crust from the pan and ate it.

I assumed the second roommate wasn't home until she appeared, a tall girl, also with glasses, but with coiled hair. "I overslept," she said. "Now I have to get out of here." She stood next to the table, ignoring Daniel and me, breaking off pieces of banana bread and nibbling. "I have to write that thing."

"What are you writing?" I asked.

She looked at me. "You mean who the hell am I, or what am I saying about the war that I didn't say yesterday?" She wore a heavy black sweater—big enough for a large man—on which the sleeves had been rolled several times. Her arms were long and thin, with narrow hands she frequently raised to brush hair off her face. When she did that, the clumsily rolled cuffs dropped along her forearms, and without noticing, she would shift one of the sleeves a little, or unroll and reroll the cuff.

"The second," I said, though I didn't know who she was, besides being Helen's roommate. It turned out that she wrote pamphlets for the local chapter of Students for a Democratic Society. Maybe she thought I should have heard of her. I wasn't angry or hurt by her tone, just curious—admiring her air of significance, her looks. She was not rushing out, but she didn't sit down.

"Those photos will keep me busy for a while," she said, more to Helen than to me. "Reaction from Europe, all that. We're putting the worst one on a pamphlet."

She stretched out her arm toward Helen's head and mimed aiming a gun, and as if it appeared behind her thin arm with that big, lumpy woolen sleeve hanging off it, I saw again the black-and-white photograph I'd seen in the newspaper and on television the week before: the unbending arm of a South Vietnamese general stretching a pistol toward a young Vietcong prisoner with mussed, straight black hair and a checked short-sleeved shirt, his face tense but not terrified. In the previous picture, an American Marine guards the man in the checked shirt. In the following picture, the man in the checked shirt crumples, dead.

Barb—someone said her name—held her arm stretched out for a while, and Helen looked up and returned to drinking her tea. Her hands were around the mug, not on the handle. Her feet were on the seat of her chair, her knees drawn up. Helen had sliced most of the banana bread but hadn't taken a piece, which didn't surprise me.

They were all talking now. Not paying close attention, I looked at the walls, which had cracked yellow paint that looked like the topmost of ten or twelve layers. The windows looked painted shut, but a draft came past the edges of the steamy panes. There was cracked green-and-yellow linoleum on the floor. Years earlier, it had been new, and a grandmother had cooked soup for her large family in this kitchen. She spoke what—Italian? Spanish? Yiddish?

Angie said, "But we're saying something. They don't hear us, but we're saying something."

"I get that, I get that," Daniel said. Then he said something different. "We have *tried* that."

I waited to find out from this young man with his innocent look what they had tried and who had tried it. I thought Daniel was our age, but as I listened, I realized he was older, a veteran of the Civil Rights

Movement who had taken time between high school and college. What they had tried, I slowly understood, what had not worked, was nonviolent protest. Daniel was thinking about carrying a gun.

"That's stupid," Helen said, looking up sharply.

"Baby," Daniel said.

"Yeah, you've tried everything else, but you can think of new things. Or you can try everything else again." Helen leaned forward, her voice raised. "That's *just* what they want. Carry a gun, someone shoots, you all get killed. *We* all get killed. End of protest."

"Oh, don't give me that," Angie said. The argument was more complicated than I had thought, and I figured it out only later. Angie didn't like Daniel and thought he was simpleminded about guns, but she too was tired of nonviolence. She was interested in protesters in California, who smashed windows and committed other acts of vandalism but didn't carry guns.

"Are the cops around here violent?" I said. "They've been peaceful when I've marched."

Nobody answered and I felt like an idiot. Helen was crying. Her nose ran and her eyes streamed, but she didn't dig in her pocket for something to blow her nose with. She didn't even wipe her face with her arm. Then, as she cried and snuffled, she reached for a piece of banana bread. It broke as she took it, and she ate what was in her hand quickly, put the fragments that had fallen onto the table into her mouth, and then reached for another piece.

I stood. "Don't go!" Helen said.

I didn't want to be there. "Where's the bathroom?" I said, an excuse for standing up. I did need a bathroom. Barb said, "I'm

leaving. I'll show you," and I followed her from the kitchen and saw
where she pointed down a hall. In the living room, Helen's things
were crammed behind a sofa: a single mattress, a bookcase made of
bricks and boards. The bathroom was like the rest of the apartment:
thirty years earlier, someone had been proud of it. The floor was tiled
in chipped black-and-white trapezoids in concentric circles.

I washed my hands and tried to decide which towel was Helen's.
It seemed unpleasant to use the towels of her combative roommates.
If I stayed, I'd have to let myself think freely about the war. I had
dealt with my horror by trying not to think about it much or about
how little I'd done. We all felt a responsibility then, though in retrospect it seems foolish that we ascribed so much power to ourselves. I'd
never thought about the questions these people were debating, never
thought to question the tactics that were announced by the leaders of
organizations I joined, never wondered who started a group or why.
When I marched, I thought we were spontaneously expressing rage.
Now I saw the obvious: someone had decided that rage might best be
expressed by marching, and not some other activity. Helen's towel, I
decided, was the fluffy green one, the one that looked as if it might
have come from her parents' apartment.

When I returned to the kitchen, I intended to pick up my coat and
put it on. But Barb—she had not left—was sitting in my chair, opposite
Helen. She'd turned the chair at a right angle to the table, and her
long legs stuck out into the room. When she did leave, her legs seemed
to announce, she would go fast. My coat was squashed behind her, and
it was too hard to claim it. Angie was in another chair, and Daniel sat
on a high wooden seat with steps that swung out, a contraption I'd

seen in my grandparents' apartments. It was painted in scratched and marred yellow paint. The four of them, it seemed, had been left by ancestors—somebody's ancestors, anybody's ancestors—as the unlikely responsible parties, the people who now had to make things right. For a moment, before my skepticism and irony returned, I was awestruck by their willingness.

The banana bread was almost gone.

"*This* is our ally!" Angie said.

"Yup." Barb's voice became louder and more sarcastic. "The general is the guy we're fighting for. All those dead soldiers—this was the worst week of the war for us, did you know that?" She meant the South Vietnamese general in the photographs, the man who shot the Vietcong soldier. I was startled that she said "us."

"So who *cares* about a fucking *gymnasium*?" Angie said. It was the first time I'd ever heard a woman say "fucking." "With this war going on—who the fuck cares?"

Helen leaned forward so her head was on the table. Then she sat up. "Oppression is oppression," she said, but she sounded tentative.

"Look, sweetie," Angie said, "we're not going *back* in *time*. We don't have *slavery* in this country. We have stuff to worry about, sure—and prejudice? well, sure—but it's not *slavery*. Get that? Fighting the gym is not the *Civil War*, get that?" She stood, leaning forward with her hands on the table, then walked heavily from the room.

"Let's get something to eat," Daniel said. He looked at me. "Come with us."

Barb, at last, left when we did, but she went in the other direction at the street. It was dark. Helen, Daniel, and I ate eggs at a nearby greasy spoon. Daniel said, "Helen told me a lot about you"—what my mother might have said. I asked Daniel about his family, and he said he was from Baltimore, the youngest of three. He had grown up in a household of cherishing adults. I saw that he'd always feel sure of himself, certain that he belonged wherever he was. How many black men would spend an afternoon with four white women and never look as if he'd rather be elsewhere? I asked myself the question and then I said it out loud in those words, because it was a day for taking chances.

Daniel laughed. "I always think people want to be with me," he said.

Helen looked up from her eggs—she was eating heartily in my presence for the second time that day—and I almost heard her considering that maybe he didn't like *her*; maybe he simply liked everybody. He stretched an arm around her and transferred his fork to his other hand.

"Where do you two go for privacy?" I said, because I suddenly felt in the way.

"My roommates and I have a signal," Daniel said. He smiled like a child. After we paid the check, I got up to leave and nobody stopped me.

four

Jean Argos

The outgoing president of my board is a white guy who used to run a shelter, and another board member, Lorna—a black woman, so shrewd and decent you can easily not notice that she is sometimes wrong—used to work with him. They make a little voting bloc. They worry that we'll be sued, so they try to set standards that would limit us too much. They got us to pass a rule banning anyone found with a weapon. I don't want guns at Barker, but we can't frisk people or put them through a metal detector—which we can't afford, even if I didn't hate the things—so how will we know? Some sweet lost soul carrying a knife because he's scared of the shelters is going to drop it on the floor and be thrown out.

Joshua Griffin is the board member least likely to have a beer or a phone conversation with the rest between meetings. I've mentioned Ingrid. The remaining three members are businesspeople. They believe in what we do, but they don't know the panhandlers by name. The rest of us get distracted from the agenda, bringing one another up to date on whether someone we all know is in the hospital or in jail, has gotten sober, or has died. The businesspeople watch with surprise. For them, the clients are a category. A board needs some members like that.

When we nervously meet to elect a president, I still don't know whether I did the right thing when I hired Paulette Strong. But I don't want any more advice from that lot, so I don't talk about her. Aside from the president, the agenda is all money. I've applied for a grant that would let me rent the soon-to-be-vacant third floor. I don't know yet whether I'm getting it, and the board had doubts about this project, so I don't bring it up. There are other money issues.

Eight members show up, and Jason and I make ten. We're in the larger first-floor room, around one of the tables. I smell cold cuts from lunch. The president finally says he's really quitting. Everyone assumes I want Ingrid for president, because we're friends and sometimes go out to dinner together. And, on the whole, I do. But she doesn't always agree with me about the departing president, and she may be too close to Lorna—whom I love, but still. Years ago, Ingrid's kids went to school with Lorna's grandkids. They tell PTA stories.

Joshua Griffin and Ingrid make short statements saying why each of them wants to be president. I expect Ingrid to win, just because she's been on the board longer, and we just finished with a man, so a woman might seem timely. But Joshua Griffin is elected by secret ballot. I shake hands with him and say I look forward to working together. For a moment I wanted this outcome, and now I'll find out if I was right to think life would be more interesting.

As the meeting breaks up, Ingrid puts a hand on my arm. "Drink?" she says quietly.

"Drink." I figure she needs consoling. I look at my watch. I need to write three emails. "An hour?" I say. "Meet you—where?"

"My house," she says. "I've got a bottle of red."

I've been there often. I squeeze her shoulder, call my goodbyes to the others, and climb the stairs to my office.

But as soon as I'm alone, I close my office door and drop onto the couch, and for several long minutes I can't move. I've been faking nonchalance. I don't want to work with Joshua Griffin. Eventually

I move my left hand, and it falls on the book—that book by Valerie Benevento. I open it and find the page where I was reading before.

The Vietnam protester with the boyfriend has emotions so intense she can barely get through her days. She's a college student and lives with a friend from high school, also against the war. They are in love with the same man. The friend, a dazzling woman—mysterious but lovable—goes to bed with the boyfriend. The narrator suffers. The book holds me. The narrator's need soothes my own battered feelings. Now and then I see brief comments in the margins, mostly illegible, some in ink and some in pencil. This book held someone else as well.

The boyfriend teaches the alluring, scary friend how to make a Molotov cocktail. He has firm, muscled arms, and people can't help touching him. She touches his shoulder. He tells her he's decided to be faithful to the narrator, but then he explains some political idea. I put down the book for a moment to mourn my own lack of a man, then pick it up again. I read thirty pages. Now and then I look up to imagine inner conversations with the poet who I still think has left it for me. Off to the side of my mind are the emails I should be writing, and Ingrid. I don't look at my watch because I don't want to know what it says.

Then someone pushes open my office door, and Joshua Griffin's ordinarily well-behaved fingers, with carefully trimmed nails, appear at the edge of my door and open it. I recognize the fingers and the crisp white cuff before the face appears, but I'm alarmed before I recognize them, so I am simultaneously scared that a stranger is sneaking up on me when I thought the building was empty and the front door locked, and furious with Joshua Griffin for scaring me. I'm also furious with him for coming in without knocking.

"You're here!" he says in his lively voice—it goes up and down—not apologizing for walking in without leave but maybe laughing at himself for getting caught. I know then that he will never knock and never apologize. "I was making some calls downstairs, but my phone died," he says. "I came to use your phone." He looks abashed and says, "If I may."

But then, as I stand up, my finger keeping my place, and move the book closer to my body, he says, his voice intense, with a tone I never heard before, *"Where did you get that?"*

"Get what?"

"Let me see it."

I look down to see what I have stolen and there is only the book.

"Where did you get it?" he says again, sharply.

"It was here," I say, feeling in the wrong and angry that my other reasons for being angry are now apparently beside the point. "It was on my couch."

"Oh my," Joshua says, and then he bends his head—turns his face down fast to hide it—as if he may cry, which changes everything, as if stage managers grabbing furniture have turned an operating room into a nursery school. It's suddenly hard not to hug him. I don't, but I put the book down on my desk—losing my place—and he picks it up.

"May I sit?" he asks. We both forget the phone calls, and he never does make them. He sits on the chair opposite my desk, and I sit down on the desk chair, so we become the executive director conferring with her board president. But he holds the book close, then riffles through it and puts it on his lap, his hand on it. "I did this once before," he says. "I came into your office when you weren't here."

"I was here this time."

"Yes, yes, of course."

"The note," I say, beginning to understand. "It's *your* book?"

"Olive's book. My wife's. I lost it."

"You left it here when you wrote that note."

"Apparently I did," he says. "Don't tell me how it ends!"

"I'm only at the beginning." I don't want to let him take it, and I find myself mentally trying out lies: I bought this copy years ago! Your wife gave it to me last week!

"I was reading it," he says. He puts the book on the corner of my desk and rests his hands on his thighs. His face is not tearful, but he's smiling with disarming frankness. He's older than I. His wrinkles are concentric circles, deep clefts in his forehead and cheeks. He was a smoker once. And he's a worrier.

"What an idiot I am," he says.

I am happier having an acknowledged idiot as the president of my board than someone who thinks terribly well of himself in all circumstances, like the old president or like my idea of Joshua Griffin. But I still don't want him to carry the book off, whether it's good or not. It seems unfair. It *is* unfair.

I smile in my turn. "You can't have it. It's interesting."

"I will overnight you a copy," he says.

"Don't be silly!" I say, standing. I have remembered Ingrid.

"I must get it back to Ollie. She's writing about it."

"She's a writer?" I say. Joshua's wife must have written the comments in the book.

"Yes. She'll want to know what you think. She knew the author."

"She knew the author?" I say.

In the end, he extracts my street address, because he insists on sending me the book—which I'll now have to read whether I like it or not, I note, so as to report not to the poetry teacher but to this Olive of his, and to the president of my board.

"I have your email address," he says. "We'll invite you over. We should know each other. Now that I—"

"Have the legal right to fire me?" I say, and immediately regret that. It is not the sort of mistake I ordinarily make.

"Hardly!" says Joshua Griffin, but he does. I still shouldn't have said it. When I stay too late at the office, my judgment goes.

The meeting ended more than an hour ago. I see that I'll have to answer those emails at home. Living alone, without people to distract me with what's on their minds, I have to work to keep my house from becoming an extension of the office. Writing emails in the evening makes me wake in the night, imagining the answers and checking my phone. But Ingrid needs me. I hustle Joshua Griffin out. He turns and shakes my hand, then holds up the book like our secret.

Ingrid lives near Wooster Square, and when we meet for a drink at her place, we mostly end up eating pizza or pasta on Wooster Street, which is all Italian restaurants. As I climb the wooden steps of her porch, I decide that I won't go to dinner this time. I'm tired. And there are those emails.

Ingrid has a mass of brown curls, with gray hairs here and there, that she brushes back and keeps neat with metal clips at work, but when she's relaxed, she runs her fingers through her hair, and one by one the clips fall out. They hold her thoughts in place, and now she can think whatever she wants. She sprinkles hair clips over her car and her house, and other people's houses, if she's comfortable. I save them and return them after she visits me. They look old—silvery things with curlicues. When she opens the door this evening, her hair is about half free.

"I'm sorry!" I say, and step forward to hug her. "I wanted you to win!"

"Less work," she says. "It's okay."

"No, it's not."

"That's true, it's not. Griff—well, he'll be fine."

"*Griff?*" I say.

"That's what he's called."

"You and I would have had long spaghetti dinners, figuring things out."

"No," Ingrid says, running her hand through her hair. A clip falls, and she stoops to pick it up and puts it into her pocket. "*Now* we can have long dinners. If I were president, I'd distance myself." She'd have had to keep her barrettes in place, she seems to be saying.

I sit on a soft chair, and she hands me a glass of cabernet. My back relaxes into the upholstery, and I notice again how tired I am. "How do you know Joshua Griffin?" I ask.

"He's controlling," she says, answering the question I haven't asked. "I love him—but. Did you ever hear his father preach?"

"Hellfire?"

"Oh, no. Not that kind of church—don't you know that? Congregational," Ingrid says. "Mainline Protestant. But the man was in *charge*. And this is his son—who somehow didn't go to divinity school." She pauses. "I hear he's a damned good principal—but, what can I say, he's a guy. He knows that he knows the answer."

Ingrid, like me, was married early, but she had two kids before she got divorced. Now she's come out as a lesbian.

"He just walked into my office without knocking," I say.

"There you go." She kicks off her shoes. "Want something to eat? But what I was going to talk about," she goes on, interrupting herself, "is security. I didn't want to say it in the meeting—they'd get worked up."

"Security?"

"Doors and windows. I heard something."

"Someone's sleeping in the building?" Some homeless people avoid the shelters. We lock up, but anyone who figures out how to sneak in gets heat, water, toilets, even food, if he's careful. Now and then, it happens.

Ingrid says, "'He sleep at Barker, you know?' That's what I heard. I thought you should know."

"Thanks." I drink wine.

"An excuse to get together," she says.

We end up at Pepe's for pizza and beer. It's late and cold, and for once there's no line. We talk about family, then relationships. Ingrid's had a couple of girlfriends but has been alone for years. I tell her about the Eight-Year Disease, and she says she has it, too. "It's the worst," she says. "Love that goes on so long you stop worrying about the future—and then it ends."

"It's fun to feel sorry for ourselves," I say, but it isn't.

She pushes her hair off her forehead as we gather our things to leave Pepe's. "Any news on that grant?" she asks. She's taming her hair—returning to the subject of work. She means the grant that would let me take over the third floor.

"No."

"Does that mean you didn't get it? It might be just as well," she says.

I'm surprised. "Just as well? But you were one of the few who *didn't* scream at me."

"That's true," she says, "but Griff is so strongly against it."

"He is?"

"You don't remember?"

"No." I remember strong opposition from others at that meeting, but not from Joshua Griffin. "Was he even on the board yet?"

"He tried to talk you out of it," she says.

As I remember it, the businesspeople led the fight. "I guess I thought Joshua was just trying to get involved," I say.

"I don't think so," she says.

"Well, I don't know if I got it. I wouldn't expect to hear yet."

I'm a little annoyed. It will be—if we get it—a substantial grant from a foundation. I'm not confident because the value of the program I've planned is difficult to describe—subtle. Subtle doesn't get grants. I want to set up small private rooms on the third floor, where, during the day, homeless people can have a few hours alone. I'm not sure how the rooms will be used—for naps, I guess, maybe for reading, crying, thinking. People with stomachaches or colds might rest on our third floor instead of going to the emergency room—and that would be a tangible benefit, but I can't prove it will happen. Jason could finally get his raise.

The plan wouldn't give homeless people places to live, and the board argued that that made it irrelevant. Someone said it would increase homelessness because it would make homeless people slightly less unhappy, so they'd resist change. I think homeless people with slightly easier lives will be *likelier* to change: that a taste of civilized living—for which privacy is essential—would give them the strength to ask for more. Of course, I can't prove that either.

The board doesn't like to do what it hasn't done before. I remember several negative comments—though not Joshua Griffin's—about what might go on if we allowed clients to be alone in private rooms. Drug use was the obvious crime, but it's impossible to prevent drug use anywhere.

"I think it's a *good* idea," Ingrid is saying. "But I don't think you'll get the money."

The next day, I repeat to Jason what Ingrid told me about people sleeping in our building, and he says, "I'll look around," which I know means "So what?" If these intruders are so unobtrusive that we don't know they're there, they don't matter. He's said this before. It's cold in our building at night—the heat is on, but just enough so the pipes don't freeze. It's not luxurious.

Still, unobtrusive break-ins can lead to bad break-ins: thefts, vandalism. I say some of this aloud, and Jason interrupts me: "Okay, Jean, I get it. I just don't like barring people if they need to be in."

The next day, he says, "It was true."

"What was?"

"Somebody was sleeping here. The lock to the door into the laundry room was taped in a tricky way."

"You fixed it."

"I fixed it, and I think I know who it was—it was that Arturo." It takes me a minute. Paulette's volunteer—the stranger. "He was mopping," Jason is saying. "He watched me when I took the tape off."

"That doesn't mean he was the one . . . ," I say, but I think it probably does mean that.

A few days later, as I eat salad downtown between meetings, checking messages on my phone because I'm not sure where I'm supposed to go next, I get the email I'm not thinking about at that moment, from the foundation—the big grant. They're giving us 80 percent of what we asked for. I read the message three times, making sure I haven't overlooked a "not."

The afternoon meeting is at an agency across town, and by the time I arrive, I have several ideas I hadn't thought of when I wrote the proposal, some because I have to make changes now that I know exactly how much money we'll get, some that come with a rush of excitement. The receptionist tells me where the meeting is, but the room is empty, so I sit there making lists about this great luxury: additional space for an agency that people think has too much space already. I think of a woman with menstrual cramps lying down until a pill kicks in, which seems like the essence of civilization. The one time I mentioned this idea to Jason, he said, "Those ladies have dealt with *that* problem," as if homeless women weren't women. It will be better not to start with that.

Simply put, I want a place where people can be alone when they can't manage whatever they can't manage. Homeless people are often alone, but rarely when they're comfortable or when they're getting help. They line up for handouts, eat at communal tables, get flu shots in church basements, sit in clinic waiting rooms, reveal their pain in groups. We who have houses can go inside and close a door. I can't argue that homeless people should be let into the respite rooms so nobody can talk to them if they want to read, though I know some of them want that, too.

I don't want to offer people privacy in which to drink, sell drugs (and take them), plan crimes, or participate in unsafe sex. But I have some ideas about how a space can be private for naps, crying, or daydreaming yet open enough that it wouldn't feel welcoming to crime or even sex. I think of the privacy in an office—at least when the board president isn't barging in. I can read or cry in my office, but I wouldn't take off my clothes or do something illegal. When I look up, the paper I'd found in my purse is full of writing and a half hour has passed. The meeting must be elsewhere. I find someone who knows and go to the right room.

In the next days, four of us—Darlene, Paulette, Jason, and I, occasionally joined by the outreach workers—begin figuring out how to make the project work. I get to know Paulette Strong in these meetings about what we call "upstairs," with a glance at the ceiling, as if to invoke the Lord. She listens intently, back stiff, never leaning into her chair. She knows she will object but doesn't yet know about what. We're usually in my office, with extra chairs if Tommy or Mel, the other two outreach workers, are there. Tommy's an Iraq war vet who's been homeless himself. He's good with clients but can't help changing the subject in meetings. When I sit near him, I'm tempted to pinch him when he does it.

"What I think Jean is saying . . . ," Jason says, just about every time I open my mouth, turning his large, shaved head to look slowly around the room. At first I think, *Wait a minute, didn't Jean just speak English?* Then I realize he's slowing the pace, holding Tommy to the topic, postponing Paulette's objection. "We tried that where I was before, and it didn't work," she loves to say. If her contribution is postponed, she's likelier to say something worth hearing.

Jason used to argue for whatever he believed and considered it dishonest to do anything else. But if there was one thing I learned when I worked in business, it was to choose when to argue—to figure out what I might actually get and how I might get more if I waited. Once, I said to Jason, "You argue so hard because you think we can't do *anything*!" He thought all anyone could do was shout the right answer, hoping to be remembered for it when everything came apart. Now he pretends not to understand me to give Paulette time to puzzle it out—a trick I didn't think of.

It's a happy time. Paulette has a snarky way of saying something helpful just when I've given up on her. "I don't suppose you think it makes sense to give a woman with cramps a place to lie down for a couple of hours?" she says one afternoon. I almost kiss her. She continues, "When I was homeless, my periods—the worst. You know what I'm sayin'?"

"You were homeless?" I say, caught off guard.

"Nothing I'm ashamed of," Paulette says.

"Of course not," I say, hoping I haven't lost her confidence just when I've decided she's indispensable.

The hardest problem is access: who'll get in, how we'll decide. It won't be hard to throw them out when their time is up—if they're trouble, Jason can walk in on them *after a knock* (I keep thinking of Joshua Griffin) and escort them out, firmly. But the method of choosing is difficult. I figure we can put twelve small rooms with cots up there and two bathrooms. We'll assign rooms first-come, first-served—or possibly allow people to reserve a space in advance.

By the end of March, the snow is diminishing, the upstairs tenants have moved out, and we have figured out what we want. An architect Mel knows comes to a board meeting.

I don't talk to the board about the project for as long as I can hold off, but when I do, Lorna says immediately, "Girlfriend, all you want is to give Jason more money!" But she's impressed, not angry. The others look nervous, and somebody laughs when nothing is funny, as if I'm hilariously naïve. They're worried, skeptical, and afraid of crime, danger, and lawsuits. But Joshua's eyes sometimes brighten. The discussion goes well—until access comes up. Then they agree that what I propose will certainly not work.

"You may be wrong," Joshua says, looking around the table at them.

"Sex?" Lorna says. "We're going to send them up there—"

He ignores her. "Even a lottery would be better than nothing," he says. "People understand luck." Then he says, "The doors won't lock, Lorna, and sounds will carry. Are we agreed that the walls won't go quite to the ceiling? Sounds will carry over the tops of the partitions." I acknowledge that partitions instead of walls will solve potential problems.

Joshua follows me to my office after the meeting. "It's good, it's good," he says, as we mount the stairs. He takes the extra chair without being invited. "Did you read the book?"

"Oh. I forgot," I say. *Bright Morning of Pain*, as he promised, arrived at my house the day after he carried off his copy. It's a used paperback with a different cover—a picture of a woman who looks distraught or deranged—and it doesn't appeal to me the way the old hardcover did.

Joshua now invites me to a dinner party—something that hasn't happened to me in years—and I remember that he said something before about having me over. The party, he explains, is because someone won a dinner with him at an auction to raise money for his school. His wife has offered to cook.

"I don't know why I agreed to have it in the first place," he says. Two strangers have won, and he has decided that the only way to endure the evening is to include other people as well.

It doesn't sound wonderful, but I've already said yes.

"So I'm supposed to protect you from the strangers?" I say, unable to not tease him.

"Of course not," he says seriously, drawing himself back, offering a little less than he seemed to offer. "It's a chance to know you better."

■

The renovations will take time. We four keep meeting, and what we plan to do becomes clearer. One thought I haven't said out loud: someday, maybe we'll use the respite space overnight. How much of a respite can you get if you're thrown out at 6:00 p.m.? The question of overnights had come up when I talked to the board about applying for the money in the first place, and I assured them it was not what I had in mind. What we *did* plan required quite enough work and money as it was.

Several times I've noticed the man named Dunbar this spring, the man who joked about eating my sandwich. I hear his deep, humorous voice as I pass through the lunchroom one day: "And we have no *proof*—no *proof* that the sandwich is made of human flesh." I don't wait to find out if the sandwich is the one he has just eaten or whether others disagree. I don't eat our cheap lunch meat, even though it's elitist to carry salads of mixed baby greens to my desk.

I also see the volunteer Paulette allowed into the kitchen, Arturo. Twice, he's mopping the floor when I pass.

I'm still working hard on not quarreling with Paulette, even though she's been terrific at times. One day, she's talking to a bag lady who comes often but never sits down or eats. The woman stands in the empty space between the tables and the door, her bags around her, like a 1950s Irish grandmother, waiting for her bus with the week's marketing at her side. I've heard her speak only once, just answering someone's greeting with a clipped "Good, thanks."

It's Mel's or Tommy's or Jason's job to make friends with her, and they've found out that she's more willing to talk to men. If Tommy's around, he stops to chat, standing next to her as if he too is waiting for the bus. Once, I saw her pick up her bags one at a time, then make her way out the door. I trust that if she's hungry and afraid to eat, Tommy will persuade her. The day I see her leave, he comes over to where I'm surveying the room and stands companionably next to me, silently, for a few minutes. I know he's upset. Then he says, "She sleeps in a dumpster."

"How do you know?"

"I followed her."

"She's so clean. How does she stay clean?"

"A Chinese takeout downtown—they let her wash up. She's not that clean close up."

One day when I glance into the dining room, Paulette is talking to the old woman. I tell myself to keep going, but I walk in. The woman begins to step away from Paulette, and then she shouts, "So? So?" She crouches and gathers her bags together on the floor. She seems to be looking at the floor—her brown coat spread around her—so Paulette can't see her face. Then she stands with her arms around her assorted canvas tote bags and white plastic garbage bags with red drawstrings. Usually she hangs the tote bags by their handles on her arms, then picks up the others in one big bundle. But Paulette has startled her. The woman shuffles toward the door and out, her bags in disarray. I am afraid she may never come back.

Paulette is on her way back to the kitchen. I call to her, and she turns. Several people eating lunch look up, and I walk over to her, since she hasn't come to me. "Do you know her name?" I ask, tilting my head in the direction of the door.

"That's Craig."

"Craig? She looks like a Mary."

"Craig. Maybe Mary Craig, I couldn't tell you. You want to know what I said, right?"

"Yes, if you don't mind telling me."

"You think I have no sense, but you don't know me," she says. "I mentioned to her that I know her. She used to come into the clinic where I worked. Diabetes. She'd come in for her feet."

Paulette had been the assistant director of the social services department of a health clinic—that was the credential that impressed our board. I put aside the thought that she has violated confidentiality, telling me Ms. Craig's problem. "I'm afraid you upset her," I say. "What if she doesn't come back? I was hoping she'd calm down enough to eat."

"She doesn't like our food," Paulette says.

"Neither do I," I say.

"But she'll come back," Paulette says. "Don't worry."

"How do you know? You should have left her to Tommy."

"Tommy's not here. This way, she knows two of us—Tommy, Paulette." She counts the names on two outstretched fingers, as if I might not be able to do the arithmetic. "It's like you and me," she continues. "You don't trust me, am I right? But I can get you to do something. How? I ask in just the right way, at just the right time, and I get you when you aren't grabbing all the bags so hard. That's what I have to learn: *when*. All a question of when."

She walks away into the kitchen without saying more, hastening as if I've rudely disrupted her routine. As so often with Paulette, I try not to think about this incident. The next two times I look into the dining room, I don't see the old woman. The third time, there she is, standing, her bags at her feet again.

■

So now I have to read *Bright Morning of Pain*. I remember the beginning only vaguely, so I decide to start over, but that will be boring. Also, I'm working so hard on the third-floor project that it's hard to settle down and read when I get home. I fix a quick supper and pace, holding the plate, listening to the radio or glancing at the TV. Or I sit down at the computer, going from website to website, never reading all of anything, and eat late at night.

A few days before Joshua Griffin's dinner, I make up my mind to behave like the kind of person who might read a book. It's a warm, almost hot, day in April. I come home at a reasonable time, picking up ingredients for a salad, including smoked turkey and cheese. I carry my aunt's lamp table out to the back porch, where I put it in front of a wide, slanting wooden seat she used in summer. I make a salad and bring it—with a wineglass, an open bottle of cabernet, and *Bright Morning of Pain*—to the back porch. I pull the little table up to the wooden seat and begin to read, drink, and eat.

I drip salad dressing on the paperback. The sun goes down, and the air turns cold. I keep reading by a dim overhead light, drawn up sideways on the wooden seat. I drink wine.

Finally, I can't stand the cold—and my need to pee—any longer. I forget the lamp table and that night rain pocks the finish forever. I carry in my plate and the empty glass, with the bottle, nearly empty, wedged under one arm and the book under the other. I put down the plate and glass and bottle. I carry the book to the bathroom, where I gratefully empty my bladder. Then I go upstairs, still freezing, and get under the blankets as the fastest way to warm up. I continue reading.

The woman and her best friend, the one who loves the same man, remain friends while arguing. The narrator is studious; her friend neglects her college classes. The narrator is cautious; the friend takes risks and is arrested at protests. Then someone called Harry—who believes in violent protests—appears. The last fifty pages move quickly. The women still compete over men. Harry persuades the scary friend to carry a gun, and the man they both love joins in the crime. Then comes the violent ending.

I can't stop thinking not about the narrator or the dangerous friend—who is really the main character—but about this Harry, who is from a family of black clergymen from Hartford. I fall asleep late at night in my clothes, not looking at the clock because I know I have to get up for work in the morning, no matter what it says.

five

Olive Grossman

In 1968, Patrick and I handed out leaflets on street corners for the peace candidate, Eugene McCarthy. And we marched. A group would meet on a subway platform; for a demonstration outside the city, we crammed into somebody's car. Someone brought a bag of bagels, and we passed around a thermos of coffee. Having my thighs scalded through denim seemed like part of ending war.

I liked walking down the middle of streets at first, and then it got boring. People screamed at us—well, a few. Hungry, cold, and dirty, we became unself-conscious, falling against one another's bodies when we had a reason to laugh or cry, without caring whose body it was—male or female, friend or stranger. There was frequent sex in odd places. Brooklyn College is a commuter school, and most of us went home to our parents after these events, if we didn't crash on someone's living room floor—or someone's parents' living room floor. Home in the middle of the night, abruptly parted from the group, we didn't recognize our families' safe, upholstered lives. Home was a place to watch the news—screaming at its inaccuracies and calmly reported horrors—to shower and get ready for the next march or rally.

Sometimes, as we shouted and waved banners, I thought of Helen's friends saying, "We tried that." I was sure it was important to keep protesting; if the antiwar movement vanished, nothing would stop our government from unlimited ferocity, maybe nuclear war. And electing a peace candidate was surely a good idea. At times, I accused myself of doing what I did only to make myself feel better—and to be part of a group of friends. I felt more justified when cops showed up, cops with visible nightsticks, and when some of us began getting arrested. Helen was constantly being arrested. For a while, I couldn't quite bring myself to let that happen to me.

Patrick and I still slept together, though not often. Later I learned he was gay. The rare times we were alone, he preferred to work on our singing, and though I hoped there would be sex as well, I too took singing seriously. Our friends were tickled when we were introduced at a rally. It was a kind of fame. Often, we'd listen to the speeches from behind the platform, where you couldn't hear the miked voices clearly—but there might be coffee. I'd be so cold I wouldn't know how I could sing, but the crowd's cheers made it easier. The protest songs we'd practiced—songs by Bob Dylan, Joan Baez, the Weavers, Malvina Reynolds—seemed profound.

I saw Helen about a month after the day we spent with Daniel. We talked about President Johnson, who had not yet announced that he wasn't running for reelection. He pulled out on March 31, after McCarthy did well in the New Hampshire primary and Robert Kennedy announced he was running, so it was probably early in March that I phoned her and we met. I wanted to tell her about our most exciting invitation, from a stranger who asked Patrick and me to sing at a big rally north of the city. I was excited to be chosen for our skill, not because we knew the organizers. And I wanted to hear about Daniel and the roommates. In retrospect, the day we'd spent together seemed like one to replicate, though it hadn't been easy. I told myself I should be more involved in what I thought of as the grown-up antiwar effort, and seeing Helen would lead to that, would make me smarter and clearer. She'd had a birthday, and I had a present for her, a long string of bright blue wooden beads I'd found at a shop in the Village.

When I phoned, she said I could come along on an errand on Saturday. She had borrowed a book from someone downtown, and he wanted it back. I obediently agreed to meet her on a subway platform near her apartment, all the way up at the top end of Manhattan, and express our friendship by accompanying her on a noisy subway ride through geography I had just traversed. But maybe there would be a walk through the downtown neighborhood at least, before a meeting with yet another stranger.

Helen cried out with pleasure when she saw the beads as we waited for the train. She opened her jean jacket to put them on over her flannel shirt. Maybe she hadn't even told her new friends about her birthday. Maybe birthdays were too frivolous for her present life. She leaned over to kiss my cheek. We got on the train, Helen clutching the book.

The friend, Eli, didn't answer the door when we eventually reached his apartment on Bleecker Street. I didn't know whether he had told Helen he would be home, and it felt intrusive to ask; she wouldn't want me to know she was being treated badly.

"We shouldn't leave it on his doorstep," Helen said. I reached to see what it was: *The Power Elite* by C. Wright Mills, a book I'd never heard of.

"Did you read it?" I asked.

"It blew my mind."

"How did you find time?" With everything else, I had time only for assigned books, except that sometimes I shoved the whole pile to the end of my bed and got under the blanket with *Cheaper by the Dozen* or some other book I'd read many times as a child.

Helen shrugged. "Homework isn't the essence of life, Olivia," she said. We'd both been scrupulous about it in high school, and I still was.

We had to do something while we waited for Eli. "Let's take the Staten Island ferry," I said. It was a short subway ride downtown, but I was a little worried. Would Helen regard taking the ferry as somehow bourgeois or establishment? We had done it often in high school: it cost a nickel and felt like travel. I loved the smell of the harbor, the sound of the gulls, the bumping and sloshing of the boats. The day was cold and windy. Helen would have scorned the ferry if the weather had been perfect, but if we suffered a little, she might consider it fun. I quickly talked her into it.

"How's Daniel?" I said, as we started back toward the subway.

"He has moved on," she said, with a lofty indifference that tried unsuccessfully to make it a joke. She lowered her face and stuffed her hands into her pockets. Her jacket seemed light for the weather.

I put my hand on her arm. "Moved on?" I trudged beside her in my heavy winter coat with its coffee stains. It had that late-winter dullness.

"He's going with someone else," she said in her ordinary voice.

I was astonished. "Are you upset?"

Helen was silent. We made our way along the crowded street. Then she stopped and faced me. "I loved him." She became, again, the girl I went to high school with—something about the shoulders, or the ungloved hands, which she took from her pockets and raised, palms open.

"Oh dear," I said. "Oh dear."

"I wouldn't have slept with him if I weren't in love with him. I thought he loved me."

"So did I," I said. "When did this happen?"

"Two weeks ago."

"Why didn't you call me?"

"Oh, I was busy." Once more, she was above heartbreak.

"You mean politics?"

"Of course."

I'd have skipped all that and stayed home to nurse my broken heart. *I'd* have called *Helen*, I told myself.

The ferry wasn't crowded, and the passengers were mostly inside. We sat silently on wooden benches on the deck, Helen with the book on her lap, and I listened to the bumping and crashing as the boat scraped itself away from the dock. I watched the choppy gray water. I was freezing, even in my winter coat. I told her about the invitation Patrick and I had. We would open the rally before a line of speakers— the only singers.

She didn't answer, but when I persisted, she said, "Olivia, come on."

"What?"

"Isn't that a little childish?"

"What do you mean?" I'd allowed myself to think she'd be pleased.

"You think singing is going to accomplish anything?"

"Well, no," I said, my voice breaking a little. Despite the long argument in Helen's apartment, I continued to assume that no antiwar act was much different from any other—assumptions reassert themselves—and that Helen would approve of mine. I'd imagined her inviting Patrick and me to sing at Columbia. Now I saw I'd been foolish.

I said, "Singing won't end the war. But getting people to rallies might. The demonstrations are getting bigger. They have to pay attention sometime."

"What signs have you seen that they're paying attention?"

"What are we doing this for, if we don't believe in it?"

Helen was silent for so long I thought she'd change the subject. Then she said, "Precisely."

I was furious, not at the political analysis, which I was used to, but at the slight to my singing. I stood and felt the wind in my face. I was wearing a green woolen hat, and I pulled it off so it wouldn't blow away. Now the wind blew through my hair and made my ears ache. I stuffed the hat into a pocket and put my hands over my ears; I must have looked like someone saying she would not listen. When the ferry docked, we didn't linger in Staten Island, just took the next one back, and this time we rode in the stuffy indoor compartment all the way.

Helen seemed to have forgotten our quarrel when we got off the boat. "I like sex," she said, and laughed.

"Me too," I said. She put her arm around my shoulders for a moment. "Are you sleeping with anybody now?" I asked, hoping she wasn't, not out of concern for her but because I wasn't—or was, but so rarely that it didn't count.

"Eli," she said. "He makes the rounds—I know that. It's fine." She held up the book—Eli's representative.

I was startled. "Who *is* he?"

"He's older," she said as we walked back to the subway. She said he was a screenwriter who'd been blacklisted during the McCarthy years and now edited a magazine for a union. When we rang his bell again, he came to the door, a loose-limbed man in a sweater with a gray curly beard. Putting his hands on both our shoulders, he drew us into his apartment—lamplit, littered with newspapers and mail, with a record player on which an opera recording played. I stepped out from under his hand.

There was something stealthy about the way Eli walked, maybe because he was in socks. Two black shoes, laces flung wide, were in widely separated spots in his dim living room, with its cones of warm light under lamps. A cat rubbed our legs, and tufts of her orange hair floated to the carpet, which was already full of it.

Eli led us to the kitchen and offered us a drink, nodding without interest at hearing my name—Olivia, of course—and Helen accepted for both of us. She opened her jacket, and the blue beads looked odd and sweet over her brown plaid flannel shirt—a combination that a little girl might choose. As we drank Scotch at Eli's kitchen table out of chipped teacups (I added extra water to mine), he left the room and returned with a plastic bag of marijuana and ciga-rette papers. He was good at rolling joints. I'd mostly smoked lumpy joints Patrick rolled, with crumbs dropping. This was better grass, and more deftly handled. Eli talked about an article he was writing, something about the economics of the war, its effect on business. He moved his arms wide and leaned back in his chair. At first he seemed like a show-off, but then I saw why Helen might want to sleep with him. His earnestness was attractive.

He began to talk about someone called Rhoda, who, I realized, was a woman he'd slept with, probably in this very apartment, earlier that day, and not a student. So he hadn't been out when we'd come by earlier. He wanted to engage Helen in a discussion of Rhoda's political naïveté, and Helen complied.

Helen had spoken casually of Eli's women, but I was sure she was hurt when she too pieced together the story of his afternoon. It was so soon after Daniel had hurt her; I was angry with Eli on Helen's behalf and even Rhoda's, whoever she was. Soon, we stood to leave, C. Wright Mills on the table, the drinks partly drunk.

"She can't think an independent thought," he was saying, padding behind us toward the door. He opened it, the heavy New York door with its peephole and two locks. This was a year or two before everyone suddenly had four or five locks. "Whatever I say, she agrees with me— when she's not just quoting the Black Panthers or Tom Hayden."

"I know what you mean," Helen said. I wished we were back with Daniel, even though he was not what I had thought. "That's how she thinks—or refuses to think."

"Thank you for the drink," I said. He didn't answer.

When we got outside, I asked Helen, "Was that fair?" I'd forgotten to feel bad about the insult to her and was thinking now of Rhoda.

"Fair to whom?"

"Rhoda, whoever she is. I hated that."

"Oh, you don't know her," she said.

"So you know so much? You think so well?"

After a long pause, she said, "I'm trying. She's just repeating what she hears at rallies, singing folk songs. Nothing personal."

She turned in the direction she had to go, as if sure I'd follow, but I told her my mother was expecting me for supper. We had to use separate subway entrances to reach opposite platforms in the same station. We hugged, and she touched the beads under her open jacket. Then she said, "I told Daniel I wouldn't sleep with him if he carried a gun." Before I could answer, she hurried down the stairs.

If I'd followed her, would anything that came later have been different? I crossed the street and walked down the downtown stairs and put in my token. The uptown train was just pulling out when I reached the platform, and when it was gone, the platform on the other side of the tracks was empty.

■

A week or so after Griff showed up for oatmeal in the middle of my breakfast, I was working late at home, alone, on a difficult chapter from the book about weaving. I have fairly good eyes and a fairly good eye, as they say, but I'm no designer. I prod my authors—many of them visually gifted but not comfortable with words—to write explanations so clear and diagrams so elegantly simple that the reader could start with either, grasp the idea, and confirm it with the other. I'm not the designer, and I'm not the copyeditor—we have a sharp copyeditor—but this was one of the long evenings I spend at my dining room table with a good lamp, looking. I tell my authors that their first job is to teach *me* the subject. "Confused!" I may write.

The chapter was about doubleweave—weaving two patterns at the same time, so the top and reverse of the cloth look different. Griff was out, and I was determined to finish a section and its diagrams before getting up and preparing something to eat. Otherwise, I'd forget what I'd just read. I was happy: not quite getting the point but about to, making intellectual progress about a subject that held neither personal meaning nor threat. I wouldn't even have to thread a loom or weave something to prove myself—just catch on.

Then Barnaby barked once, and I heard Griff's car, his steps on the walk. Sometimes the predictable entering bustle of a body that has come home daily for decades proclaims that what's ordinary saves us; sometimes it's spam in the inbox. This time it was spam—and then, as his footsteps mounted the porch steps, I grasped what the paragraph I'd read three times meant, glanced at a diagram that had stumped me, and knew that I had it. With my pencil, I made a suggestion that would clarify the ambiguous phrase that had slowed me, and only then came Griff's call. I turned and saw his face, which looked interestingly odd.

"What?" I said. The dog was pressing against his legs, and Griff reached absently to touch him.

Whatever had happened was good but complicated. I looked from the angles in the diagram—the illustrative pattern from which a weaver might work—to the lines in his aging face.

"Look," he said, his smile deepening. He put his briefcase on the corner of what I think of as my table and drew out my copy of *Bright Morning of Pain.*

I seized it, brought it to my face. The dust jacket, the little rips in the paper. I'd have to write about it after all. A rush of irrational thoughts, then anger again—if he could find it, why hadn't he found it sooner? "Where?"

"Jean had it. Jean Argos." He started to tell me how he discovered that the book was in, of all places, the office of the director of Barker Street Social Services. I said, "Why didn't she return it?"

"She was reading it."

"She was *reading* it?"

"Why not?" he said. Then he added, "She didn't know how it got there," and interrupted himself to tell me about a different occasion, which he'd forgotten until then, when he stepped into her office in her absence to use the phone—he rarely remembers to charge up his phone—and apparently left the book.

The mention of Barker Street had made me remember what had occupied him that night: a board meeting. I interrupted. "Wait, were you elected?"

He took a step back and looked guilty but unable to keep from smiling. I told myself that I didn't want to stop him from doing what he actually *wanted* to do, just to stop him from doing what he'd persuaded himself he ought to do. Except that that wasn't true. I wanted him home and noticing me—not on the phone, not maneuvering through the inevitable crises entailed in the management of a non-profit. I didn't say anything.

"I'm sorry this doesn't suit you," he said, all but formally. The excitement had gone; the friendliness had gone.

I had hurt his feelings. What was there to say? It didn't suit me. I wanted to be the sort of person who'd congratulate him and ask for details, but I wasn't. I said, "Have you eaten?" Hunger made me impatient. I'd eat, with him or without. "Are you going out again?"

"I'm interrupting you," he said.

"Are . . . you . . . *hungry*?"

He smiled. It made me want to touch him, but though I lifted my arm, I didn't.

"Yes," he said. "Hungry. You?"

I turned off my desk lamp. "Very. I'll cook something quickly." I stretched. My back hurt. His phone rang.

"But why, Ollie?" he said ten minutes later, coming into the kitchen behind me. I'd fed the dog and was boiling water for spaghetti, cracking eggs for carbonara.

"Why what?"

"Why are you still mad?"

I rummaged in the fridge for something green and found a package of baby spinach, not disgustingly old, that I could stir into the pasta with the egg. Not for the first time, I wished Griff and I could drink wine together. At least he didn't mind when I did. He'd never liked wine. I poured him some iced tea and found an open bottle of cabernet.

"For the same reason I was always mad."

"You're not being fair," he said. "Of course I should have remembered where I'd been that Thursday. . . ."

"Oh." I stood up. "That's not why I'm mad. I'm mad that you got yourself elected president of that board."

"So you forgive me for losing the book?" Which is exactly the way he thinks. I laughed. Then I understood that, indeed, I was no longer angry about the book.

"So what's she like?" I said. "Does she *want* you to be president of her board?"

"No."

I was more interested in the details than in preserving my antagonism. I sipped wine; I whisked eggs. "Tell me," I said. The wine helped.

I heard a long account of the many issues about which Jean Argos was correct or wrong. "She's smart," he said. "I couldn't work with someone dumb."

"But?"

"She has too many good ideas," he said. "Remember the science teacher?"

I remembered the young, idealistic science teacher at his school, whose good ideas had included a predawn trip up a forested hill to hear birdcalls, during which a boy broke a leg and had to be rescued by EMTs. Griff had given permission—that was the problem. He felt responsible, all these years later, for the leg.

"I promised to send her a copy of Val's book," he said. "I'll overnight it."

"Why?"

"I snatched it out of her hands."

"But it wasn't hers!"

"But I promised." He arranged our plates and silverware on the table. I put spaghetti into the boiling water. "I think I should invite her to that dinner," he said then.

"What dinner?"

"Oh, you don't have to worry about it—you can hide upstairs," he said. "I'm sure you'll want to. If not leave altogether."

"What are you talking about? You're planning to invite a woman to dinner and I'm supposed to leave? Are you going to seduce her?"

"No," he said soberly, looking particularly elderly and distinguished. "Others will be present. Six or seven."

He thought he'd told me. He insisted we'd had at least two conversations about this dinner—which was the result of a silent auction, a fundraiser for his school. Someone from the PTA had persuaded him to cook a dinner for the highest bidder. He'd been studying cookbooks. I now remembered the cookbook lying around upstairs.

"You didn't sound interested," he said, "so I've been assuming you'd stay upstairs or leave. You can walk through, if you want—or whatever else you want. You can eat." He paused. "I don't know how to cook for so many people."

I tried to make sense of this. Griff, my husband, had agreed to host a dinner at our house (in the speech I was making in my mind, I said "*our home*," a locution I detest), which he assumed I would not attend. As if I'm always leaving—I, whose trip to Boston was my first time away from him in months, who works only three days a week and is home by 6:00 p.m. on the in-office days, who is otherwise home every minute.

"But who *goes out* in this marriage? Who is always *out* somewhere?"

He looked at me, surprised.

"Right this minute," I continued. "Who spent the evening here in this house"—it was almost nine—"and who was *out*?" I drained the spaghetti. Facing the sink, with my back to him, I said, "Who was *out* getting elected *president* so as to spend even *more* time out? *You* accuse *me* of not wanting to stay home for your fucking *dinner*?" While I mixed up the spaghetti in the hot pan with the eggs, I began on all the breakfasts he missed.

"Grated cheese," I said, interrupting my tirade.

"I know," he said. I looked over my shoulder, and he was sitting there at the table, grating a big block of parmesan. "I know how you fix this."

"You do?" Something about this kind of attention stopped me. "You watched what I was doing?"

I put the food on the table. We ate. I drank wine.

He said eventually, "That's not fair. You don't *want* me here when you're working."

Which was often true. He'll never get over the fact that all those years ago I'd insisted on a separation—first sending him to live in the apartment that had emptied out upstairs, then sending him elsewhere. And indeed, that evening, I had not been glad to hear his footsteps.

There was a pause. Then I asked him about the dinner party. It was fairly soon, it turned out, and he had no plans.

"I'll cook," I said. I wanted to meet this formidable Jean, who had tried to steal my book. Or I wanted to take back what I'd said. I was not an adept giver of dinner parties, but I was better than Griff.

"Thank you. I didn't expect this."

"Obviously not, if you didn't even tell me about it."

"I did tell you."

"Well."

"Thank you," he said again, with a look I hadn't seen since the day he borrowed *Bright Morning of Pain*.

When I stood at the end of the meal, I touched the back of his neck with one finger, and he stood as well.

"Let's leave the dishes," he said. "I'll put them in to soak." I knew what he meant. It wasn't the most thrilling coupling that ever took place, but when we were done, Griff rested his warm hand on my belly.

■

Still, auctioning off a dinner with the principal didn't seem like a great idea to me, and I said so often in the next few days. When I volunteered to cook it, I thought I was doing Griff a favor, but it was a favor to the school, or the auction committee, or the guests who had bid on it, and I had little interest in them. I insisted that Griff find out how much the winners had paid and how many people had bid.

"It's a small school. Most of the kids are poor," he said, as if I didn't know. I also knew there was a volunteer fundraising committee—outsiders, people who were not poor.

There had been eight bids on the dinner, he reported, and the winner had paid one hundred eighty-four dollars.

"Eight bids? How many people bid?"

"I don't know."

"So the same two people bid back and forth?"

"I don't know."

He was eating oatmeal—again—standing up.

"One hundred eighty-four? How do you get to one hundred eighty-four in eight bids?"

"I can't imagine." He ran water into his dish, put it into the sink, and turned to leave.

"Sit down," I said. "Drink coffee."

He sat down.

I kissed the bald top of his head as I walked past him, and he touched his pate as if to learn whether the kiss was still there. I couldn't have said why I kissed him. Possibly because when he came closer, I noticed him—spotted him as one might spot a walking figure in a painting of a storm, after first observing the swirl of weather. I was not seriously unhappy with Griff those weeks, not having fantasies of throwing him out, but it was rare to like him, much less love him.

■

Martin Luther King Jr. was assassinated on April 4, 1968, and Helen showed up at my house in tears. When we talked, eventually, I told her about a paper I was working on, and she mentioned one she'd written. "I didn't know you did homework," I said.

"Oh, Olivia," Helen said.

Shortly after that evening came the student rebellion at Columbia. Black students—and Helen—marched against the gymnasium. The mostly white antiwar group, to which Helen also belonged, had learned that Columbia was working with the government on developing weapons, and the protest against the gym turned into an antiwar protest. Students occupied university offices, even the office of the president. Helen didn't camp in one of the offices, but she relayed messages and food. At first she was engaged, happy, phoning me to report as the occupation went unchallenged. Changing the world was easy. Then the police beat up the antiwar students. I was shocked; Helen said I was naïve.

I associate my meetings with Helen in the spring of 1968 with the topics we discussed. There was an argument—I recall that we were hungry, but there was nothing in the refrigerator—about Eugene McCarthy or Robert Kennedy's chances of being the presidential candidate instead of Hubert Humphrey. We exhausted ourselves, waiting for someone—a roommate or a boyfriend—so we couldn't leave, in those days before cell phones. Eventually we gave up and ate at the neighborhood place, irritable with hunger.

Back at her place, we kept talking—about men, I think. I changed the subject to talk about Patrick—I was making more of that connection than there would ever be—and because talking about the war scared me. I would suddenly realize I could lose her, and back off. I couldn't get her interested in the question of whether I should be faithful to Patrick, who didn't care whether I was or not. I accused her of finding my boring sex life boring. She said, "Maybe it is boring. There are more important things."

I said, "You are so goddamn pure; I can't stand you," and then she cried.

It was too late to go home, but eventually we were friends again, and Helen said I should sleep over on the sofa. I phoned my parents. Helen got into pajamas and offered me a pair, but I knew they wouldn't fit. She found me a blanket, and we turned off the light. Sometime later we got up, hungry again, and cooked spaghetti, throwing frozen peas into the pot at the end, and crumbling dry American cheese on top. We ate in the dark, drinking Chianti, listening to angry music coming from one of her roommates' bedrooms. I heard Helen eating rapidly and could just see her on her mattress, hunched over her plate as I was, trying to keep the peas from rolling off.

I said, "You never used to eat."

"I ate."

"Yes, of course you *ate*," I said. "You didn't die. I meant I never saw you eat."

"In high school, we were rarely together at mealtimes," Helen said, with precise emphasis. "And that cafeteria took my appetite away."

She sounded offended again, but I persisted. "That's not what I meant. You were different."

She seemed to let it go. I saw in the dim light from a streetlamp outside that she put the plate and fork on the floor next to her bed and lay down. "If I fall asleep," she said, "put the plates in the sink when you're done. We try to keep the bugs in one room."

I continued eating. Then she said, out of the dark, "I'm different in lots of ways."

"You've had these boyfriends."

"Not that. I used to be a liberal. Now I'm a radical."

I considered this. Was that so different from what I was? "We're all pretty radical these days," I said. "What other choice is there?"

All I really wanted was to change the subject, but she wouldn't, reminding me yet again how many people had already died in this war, which was badly planned and badly waged and couldn't be won. All that. "No," she concluded. "You're a liberal. You're trying to decide between McCarthy and Kennedy, for God's sake."

"One of those men will be president," I said. "Humphrey, McCarthy, Kennedy. If we're lucky. We have to nominate the best one."

"Maybe not," said Helen.

"Maybe *not*?"

"If we make enough trouble, maybe not," she said. "They'll be too busy putting down our rebellion to hold an election. Maybe they'll be too busy to send more troops over there."

"Oh, don't be silly. And my God, Helen, don't we *want* an election? We give up elections, who knows what could happen?" I *was* a liberal.

"No," she said. "We don't want an election." She sat up again. "It will either confirm what we already have or make it worse. Have a little faith, Olivia. The American people . . . Look, the way you see it, we're helpless. But the American people can put together something better than this!"

I didn't answer. She sounded idealistic—like a patriot—but what kind of anarchy was she talking about? Finally, I said, "Can you agree that there is a twenty-percent chance that the war will end if we work to elect a peace candidate?" Even twenty percent—if there was that kind of chance, I thought we should stay with what we had: campaigns and elections. Helen laughed.

My food was gone, and I reached for Helen's plate and went into the kitchen, keeping my eyes closed for a minute after I turned on the light, hoping the cockroaches would disperse. There were other dishes in the sink, and I washed them all, piling them next to the sink, because Helen and her roommates didn't have a dish drainer. Maybe Helen was a radical and I was not. I knew—I was not proud of this—that when I had my own place to live, one of my first purchases would be a dish drainer.

I wanted to be a radical. I wanted to believe the American people would somehow come together and create a new, just government. Did it prove I wasn't a radical if I wanted a dish drainer?

I stayed in the kitchen until it was clean, not just to discourage the bugs but in the hope that Helen would fall asleep. But when I came back I could see the outline of her thin body sitting up once more. In the dark she looked like a little girl, and the words of a Bob Dylan song pounded in my mind. She was leaning forward, waiting for me, I saw, so she could speak.

"You didn't answer."

"Didn't answer what?" I said.

"What I said. You don't agree. You're still trying to change things by writing letters to the editor."

"I never write letters to the editor!" I said. What I did—marching, shouting, singing—wasn't that more than writing a letter to the editor of a newspaper? I lay down on the sofa and pulled the blanket up. The kitchen had been cold, and I relaxed into the scratchy warmth of the wool blanket.

"I'm going to Chicago," Helen said.

"What?"

"The convention. In August. I'm going to disrupt the Democratic convention."

"Disrupt it?" I hadn't yet heard of plans like this.

"The convention is tainted. Humphrey's going to win, and he's as bloody as Johnson. More of the same if he wins, more of the same if Nixon wins. Or some other Republican who's even worse."

"I think McCarthy has a chance," I said, weary to be starting up all over again. "Or Kennedy."

"Don't be a fool," she said. "This is boring, anyway. Wouldn't you rather do something that makes a difference?"

"Like, what, shooting people?"

"I didn't say that."

"I thought you were for nonviolence."

"I didn't say shooting."

"So what kind of disruption are we talking about?"

"Just whatever we can do," came the voice out of the dark, sounding almost wistful. "Breaking things, smashing things. Getting our heads bashed in so people will know what's what."

"Can we sleep, Helen? Please?" I was frantic with exhaustion.

She ignored me. "What else is going to work?" she said. "Don't tell me *singing*."

I knew as I lay there that singing was good for me, good for me and Patrick—but that it would not work. The antiwar movement would change the government, I thought, but so slowly that it was beside the point.

I need to make clear now, all these decades later, how bad it was, how the war in Vietnam was different, worse than every other military operation of my life. We knew so little—but enough to see that something had gone sickeningly wrong. The My Lai massacre had happened in March. An American company that had been scrambling through the jungle for months, taking casualties at times from snipers but seeing no combat, walked into a tiny village supposedly cleared of civilians—so anyone they found, it seemed, would be Vietcong—and found 504 old people, women, and small children. They drove them into three ditches and systematically bayoneted them. This wasn't public knowledge for a year and a half, but at the time, we knew something like that was likely to happen.

"You're right," I said to Helen, and turned onto my stomach to cry, like a child who has just learned she can't have what she wants most. I didn't know if Helen would ever swing a baseball bat or break a window, like radicals I'd read about, and I didn't think I could— maybe I should?—but something had to change. Helen could not compromise with truth, no matter where truth took her, and people who have that incapacity are finally convincing.

She said something else then, and it meant neither of us would sleep that night: "I've dropped out of school."

six

Jean Argos

Dinner at Joshua Griffin's house is on a rainy night at the end of April. Driving over, I'm not nervous, just pleased to be invited out, and by someone from Barker. The old president would not have let me through his front door. I've brought a bottle of wine. I'm wearing jeans but with a white shirt and a blazer. Only thing is, I'm in too good a mood. I look at myself in the rearview mirror and say, "You behave yourself!"

"Rain!" I say too cheerfully to the young, light-skinned black woman who answers the door. I hold up my closed but dripping umbrella. I say, "I'm Jean!"

"I'm Martha," she says.

Joshua comes toward us, saying by way of introduction, "You are good to come! My daughter."

He takes the umbrella and my wine bottle, and Martha and I both say what we should. A black dog approaches too, a thick, short-haired boy with a glossy coat. He wants to lick my face and I lean over to let him, since he is too polite to jump. At the near end of a long room, a table with eight chairs is set for dinner.

Guests are gathered at the other end, on a dark oval rug that covers part of the wooden floor, making a living room. There's Ingrid, with her barrettes still in place but her hair trying to work free. She's standing, holding a wineglass. Laughing. She has a rusty laugh. The substantial white woman listening to her must be Olive.

"I'm Jean," I say, while Ingrid says, "This is Jean," and Olive says, "Olive Grossman," and we shake hands. Olive has gray hair cut short and glasses with big frames.

"You know Lorna?" Olive says, and I turn and see Lorna from the board with what looks like a glass of water, wearing a red dress and sitting on a red sofa. The dog lies down on Lorna's feet. "Red?" Olive asks, and I manage to say yes to red wine without commenting on the red sofa and Lorna's red dress.

Lorna and Ingrid, they tell me, came together in Lorna's car. We agree that it's raining. Martha Griffin brings me wine. "I didn't know you were in town," Ingrid says to her.

I remember that Ingrid knows Joshua a little, and apparently also his family. Martha says she lives in New York. She's getting a doctorate in history, teaching part-time at two different colleges. She's sturdy, like her mother, but doesn't wear glasses. Maybe she wears contact lenses.

The three of us—Ingrid, Martha, and I, all drinking red wine—stand around Lorna. She beams at us, stroking the dog. Martha says, "I needed a weekend away from the city, and it turned out they were doing this." She says when she was a child her parents had people in often, but it hasn't happened lately. She claims to be glad she's here for her parents' party. Nice daughter.

"In the seventies, I knew how to cook," Olive says, joining our group. "But that kind of food doesn't count these days, and I never learned anything else. You're getting a seventies dinner."

We all say we're grateful to have any sort of meal cooked for us.

"This is happening only because Dad can't say no," Martha says. "No offense—you guys are the reward."

"Oh, I bet he knows how to say no," I say.

"Maybe to some people," Martha says.

I wonder whether the mysterious guests who won the dinner will mind Olive's presumably plain cooking. "Imagine if nobody bid. . . . ," I say.

"I am told the item did well," Martha says airily. "I am told by my dad, who may have reason to lie but never does."

"So who's coming?" Lorna asks.

"Yvonne Something and Guest," Martha says. I'm more at ease with her than with either of her parents. Olive brings in a plate, which she places on a table in front of the sofa I think of as Lorna's. "Dad doesn't think he knows her," Martha says.

"Maybe she won't come," Olive says. It's a plate of huge bright-green olives, cubes of cheese, and crackers. We fall on it.

Suddenly, I remember *Bright Morning of Pain*. "Oh, did you want me to bring the book?" I say. "Are we going to talk about it?"

"What book?" someone asks.

"Yes, you had my book!" Olive says, a little tartly, as if I did the whole thing on purpose—which was Joshua's attitude as well, I recall. "I don't suppose you read it."

"Of course I read it," I say. "Wasn't it an assignment?"

"Hardly."

"He said it's your favorite book."

"Something like that," Olive says. She sits down next to Lorna, and though she's making me feel somehow in the wrong, I like a hostess who doesn't fuss at her own party. Like me, she has on a blazer and jeans, but I like her tan blazer better than my black one. The doorbell rings, and Joshua, who has not been in the room, shows up and answers it.

"I'm sorry we're late," a breathy voice says. "I'm Yvonne. . . ." But the rest of what she says is obscured, because Joshua and the man who has come with Yvonne are both exclaiming.

"No, no," Joshua says, "Come in," but they are already walking toward us, still in wet coats. They don't have umbrellas. They are maybe forty, both white. The woman has long blond hair and a rain hat, and close up she's older than forty, but the man is the one I notice: he has laughing eyes. He's happy, not apologetic, though he apologized. "I recognized the *street*," he's saying, "but I didn't think it was the same *house* . . . and I didn't know you guys still live here."

"Why wouldn't we?" Joshua—following them—says sharply. Olive, a cracker in her hand, is scrambling awkwardly to her feet, resting a hand on Lorna's shoulder to push herself up. We all stand up, even Lorna.

"Forgive me," the man says, reaching two hands, which must be wet, to take Olive's.

"Zak," Olive says. She looks more flustered than I knew people that confident can look. "What are you doing here? What in the *world* are you doing here?" She sounds—well, maybe happy.

"I live in New Haven now," he says. "I'm a physician."

"I heard you went to medical school," Martha says, coming toward him. She shakes hands with the woman. "I'm Martha Griffin."

"Zak Lilienthal," Martha says to all of us, and then says our names—all but mine. "I'm sorry. . . . ," she says gracefully.

I step forward. "Jean Argos." Martha is less flustered than her mother.

"Zak Lilienthal," he says, unnecessarily. I feel attractive when he looks at me—my short blond hair, my white shirt. I'm reasonably good-looking, though not as attractive as Martha, who impresses the hell out of me—her calm, her charm, her good looks, and her comfort with her parents and herself, despite her ragged life running from classroom to classroom in New York, and whatever surprise this arrival entails. Zak seems to add more than one person's presence to the room. Do people like that move their arms more than the rest of us? They are not always tall—Zak is tall—but if not, they seem tall.

When asked, Zak says he's a pediatrician. "I just moved to New Haven," he says, "and I'm working in my old pediatrician's practice! I have to remind myself not to take off my clothes!"

He has nothing to do with Aspirations High—the embarrassing name of Joshua's school, which Zak pronounces with joy—or the auction. He knew "the Grossman-Griffins" when he grew up in New Haven, he says, but he didn't know where "Griff" works these days. "Yvonne just said 'dinner at the principal's house.'" He widens his eyes theatrically and waves a hand at Joshua. "The principal!"

Yvonne is the foster mother of two kids at the school. She stands there silently, not quite up to the phenomenon of the man she's brought. She's definitely older than Zak, maybe my age.

"We've met," she says to Joshua. Another foster child was in the school some years earlier. Joshua smiles and nods with fake but polite agreement.

The conversation turns to foster children. Lorna has opinions on this subject, and when she speaks from her sofa, we turn toward her, but Olive calls, "Let's eat." She and Martha have been carrying food in.

I sit next to Ingrid at dinner. The dog inserts himself under the table and lies down near me, and now and then I slip my foot out of my shoe and stroke him. He lays his head on my knee. There's spinach lasagna, salad, roasted vegetables, and bread. More wine.

"Are you a vegetarian?" Yvonne asks Olive.

"I figured somebody would be," she says. I take a big piece when the lasagna comes my way. The spinach has a little bite, still, and the noodles aren't leathery except at the edges. The tomato sauce smells wonderful.

I hear about Joshua's school and Yvonne's kids. She's funny. She likes being a foster mother, and I wonder if she's always been single. I feel a thrill of admiration, thinking I may try to make friends with her. If we got together, maybe I'd see Zak again.

Then Zak asks me what I do, and I talk about Barker, explaining my connection to Joshua and Lorna and Ingrid. Zak looks interested, so I don't stop talking, as I surely should, and I tell everybody about the third-floor project. By now our committee has worked out a clear plan for permission to use the new rooms, and maybe I describe it in more detail than is necessary.

"There's a freight elevator we're fixing up, too," I say, in case anyone is wondering about accessibility for the disabled. I say—still unable to stop—that we'll put disposable sheets on the cots and throw them away after each use. The community service people will clean the rooms. A staff member will always be up there in the corridor. The rooms will not lock, and the cots will be narrow, to discourage sneaking in sexual partners. Maximum allowed use will be four hours.

"Not overnight?" Yvonne says.

"No, not overnight," I say. Then something makes me say, "At least not yet."

"*Never* overnight," I hear Joshua say in a low, clear voice. Then he says it a second time, with even more emphasis. He's at the end of the table away from me, sawing grimly with his table knife at a crisp brown curl of noodle.

I look up and laugh—because he makes me nervous—and try to make it sound as if what he's said is charming but not relevant. He doesn't look up from his plate, and Zak asks me who comes to Barker Street. I describe the bag lady who doesn't eat.

"That's sad," Martha says.

"It *is* sad," I say. We don't usually think of that woman as sad, just atypical. I drop out of the conversation for a moment, trying to decide whether I should have handled my conversation with Paulette differently.

Maybe that's not why I drop out. Maybe I need a moment to come to terms with the fact that I have talked too much and the president of my board has said something hostile and bossy at a dinner party at his house, at which I am a guest. I try to believe he's just nervous: it's an odd party—first, because it's happening only on account of that auction, and second, because of the mix of guests, and third, because of Zak, whatever his history is with Joshua and Olive. Still, it's a friendly gathering, and that makes the anger in Joshua's voice more upsetting.

When the subject of *Bright Morning of Pain* finally comes up—Olive tells how Joshua lost the book and found it on my lap—Ingrid says *she* read it. "Of course I read it. Everyone did. The Vietnam War . . . feminism . . ."

"Feminism?" I say.

"It was regarded as feminist," Olive says drily, "because a woman shoots someone to protect her man, instead of a man shooting someone to protect his woman."

The ending. I hadn't thought of it that way.

"Did you ever read it?" Zak asks Martha, who's near him. "Your mother talked about it plenty."

"I did," Martha says. "The way kids in high school read the books their parents make them curious about. I may have skipped some parts, but I found the sex."

"It sounds good," Lorna says.

Joshua looks up. He has cleaned his plate and laid his knife and fork straight across it. "That was delicious, Ollie," he says, and the rest of us join in, though we have praised the food before. Olive ignores us.

Joshua rises to clear the table. He's wearing his napkin tucked into the neck of his shirt. Olive takes the lasagna dish into the kitchen. "Can I help?" Lorna says. She carries in plates. I stand.

"Sit, sit," Joshua says.

"I think only Yvonne and Zak should sit," I say, "since they bid on the dinner. They have to get their money's worth." I see that I am dealing with my regret for talking too much by continuing to talk too much. I've had plenty of wine, too. I carry the salt and pepper into the kitchen so I can say nothing else for at least a few moments.

Lorna and Olive are talking about Lorna's family, and I realize that she belongs to the church where Joshua's father was the pastor and knows the family from way back. In some ways, New Haven is a small town. The people in the living room are talking again about

Bright Morning of Pain. Olive and Lorna take their time with coffee and dessert—maybe they need a break—so I go back to my seat.

Joshua is saying, "I don't care if the characters were real people or not—that's not my objection. What difference does it make? It's a story."

"I loved that book," Ingrid says. "I kept on loving it even when there was that trouble—remember, about what Valerie Benevento said in interviews?"

"I remember," Joshua says quickly, and before I can ask what they mean, he says, "I still haven't read the ending, unfortunately." Which is surprising, since he wrested it from my grasp for that very purpose. "But what I'm saying is that I don't care if it makes things up about the people it's supposedly about—it's a story. But I object to historical errors. The Tet Offensive was not in 1970! How could she not know that?"

"Are there a lot of mistakes?" I ask. I didn't notice. "I didn't remember when the Tet Offensive was." I am dying to know whether any of the book is about real people—such as Joshua? The black guy at the end? I am determined not to ask.

"It *couldn't* have been 1970," he says testily. "Surely you know that much. Johnson wasn't even president in 1970!" Joshua never speaks in a loud voice, but I have learned that when he cares about something, he enunciates more clearly, landing hard on the consonants, and he does that now ("Tet" has at least four *t*s), looking at me. I wonder if I'm still in trouble for saying that keeping people overnight on our third floor isn't out of the question. I don't like the snide remark about how much I might know.

"But if it's *fiction*," Ingrid says. "Why does it matter whether the facts are true? I don't *expect* it to be true. In fiction, you can have a talking elephant, or what might have happened if the South won the Civil War. Isn't that the *idea*?"

"You don't expect the Tet Offensive to be in the right year?" Joshua persists. "Didn't she think people would remember it?"

"You told me it's a great book!" Olive calls from the kitchen. "You loved it. You *wept*!"

"I didn't weep," Joshua says, taking his napkin from the neck of his shirt and folding it carefully. "I don't believe I *wept*."

"You loved it," Olive calls again.

"Well, it not *David Copperfield*," Joshua says, in a voice loud enough to reach the kitchen.

"Not everybody thinks *David Copperfield* is a great novel," Olive says, still shouting. All this is funny because of the shouting, and because they're having a fake argument (I know they're teasing each other) between two rooms in front of a group. But something isn't funny about it. I'm afraid of both of them.

"But I loved it, despite myself, yes," Joshua says. "As far as I got."

"And why haven't you finished it?" Olive calls.

He doesn't answer.

"Because he doesn't want to read the ending?" I say. "That guy Harry and everything?" Everyone looks at me, but someone had to say something.

"Can we *please* change the subject!" Joshua says.

I have done precisely what I determined I would not do. I have twice antagonized the president of my board. And I still don't know if the character of Harry—the man who persuades the main character to carry a gun—is based on Joshua.

Olive and Lorna now bring in a coffeepot, a tray of dessert plates and unmatched mugs, and a chocolate cake. "It's from a bakery," Olive says, placing the cake in the middle of the table, then leaning over to cut wedges. We are suddenly a group of friends, eating cake and drinking what we are assured is decaf (Zak asks if he can have real coffee, and to my surprise, Olive says no). Those of us on the side of the table away from the wall pull our chairs back, so we're arranged in a loose circle.

My mug is ridged and handmade, and the cake is good, not too sweet, with thick dark chocolate icing. I want to keep knowing all these people as I sit there sipping decaf, and I consider sending around a piece of paper on which we can write email addresses. But I don't. Lorna is telling a long story about one of her grandchildren, whom Ingrid knew. It has to do with high school sports, on which everyone has an opinion. Yvonne, I notice, disagrees politely with the majority, whatever the subject. It grows late, and the table becomes pleasantly untidy, with crumpled napkins where people have finished eating. Some of us make our cake last. Zak helps himself to a second piece.

At last Olive begins gathering empty plates. A couple of people stand, but she says, "Don't stand up; I'm just being compulsive."

The dinner has been a success, and I am impressed. Olive and Joshua can do this kind of thing even when they can't, I think fuzzily. As Olive carries the stack of plates into the kitchen, I am looking the other way, at Zak, who is talking about his own experience of high school sports (long-distance running), and at Martha, who is looking at him. But out of the corner of my eye, I see Olive's sleek gray head abruptly tilt toward the table, and, with a cry, she grabs for something. And falls. A bad fall. She hits her head on the table; the dishes crash; she lands heavily. The chair she's been sitting in, which must be what she grabbed, clatters to the floor. I run to her—I am kneeling before I notice that I've left my seat. The usual outcry—"Are you okay? Are you all right?"—and then people step back, except for Zak and me, because everyone remembers not to rush her. Olive says, tight-lipped, "Leave me alone."

"Careful," Zak says. "I think you hit your head."

Obviously she hit her head.

Olive turns on her side, pulls her knees up, and turns her face away from all of us, like someone alone in bed.

"Zak, do something!" Martha says. She's shoving the dog away from her mother.

Ingrid picks up the chair.

Zak is holding Olive's wrist. Surely she has a pulse! "Ice, Martha," he says, and she scurries into the kitchen. Zak says, "I think you'll be fine pretty soon, Olive."

"Zak, do we need an ambulance?" Joshua asks sternly.

"I don't think so," Zak says.

"I'm getting up," Olive says.

"Are you dizzy?" someone asks. Zak—not Joshua—kneels in front of Olive, and she leans on him, then says, "No, I can't. My ankle."

Lorna puts a cushion from the couch under Olive's head. Martha brings ice wrapped in a dish towel and kneels to put it against her mother's forehead. Ingrid leans down to pick up whole and broken plates. Then she says, "Oh, my God!"

"What?" Olive says. "What's wrong?"

"It's my fault," Ingrid says. "I think you tripped on this." She holds up something, and I see that it's one of her barrettes. Ingrid was at ease with these people who began to feel like friends—and of course she ran her hands through her hair, as she does when she's comfortable.

And that has caused Olive's accident, and maybe everything that will follow. (It's the last time I will see barrettes fall off Ingrid's head. She will cut her hair short the next day. But I'm getting ahead of myself.)

Nobody but me pays attention to Ingrid. I stand up, uncomfortable so close to someone I barely know who is as dignified as Olive and now in need. I sit on a chair, watching, but then I turn to Ingrid and put my arm on her shoulder. "Maybe not," I say, but I think she's probably right, that Olive's foot skated across the wooden floor on the little metal clip and pulled her off balance.

"No," Olive says. "The floor was wet." I'm grateful for that, though it won't convince Ingrid.

Olive lies there—now with ice on her ankle—making tense wisecracks about taking it easy at her own party, where the guests will do the work and she'll supervise from the floor. Indeed, the table is now cleared and the sound of dishwashing comes from the kitchen, where Lorna and Yvonne have gone. But Olive makes a sharp sound when she tries to move, and Zak says, "We need to get you to the ER."

"No," she says. "I just want to go to bed. Sorry, everybody—go home. I'm going to bed."

"That's what you should do, throw us out!" I say, crouching at her side again, though Olive isn't the sort of person who needs encouragement to do as she likes. She ignores me. I look around for my purse, then decide to take my time leaving. I have been present at emergencies, and I know Olive needs to be examined, but it's impossible to insist on that with both her husband and a doctor present. I think they both agree with me. Maybe because Zak knows Olive better than I, he knows he has to take it slowly.

While I dawdle, Ingrid and Lorna are sent on their way. "You, too," Olive says to Joshua. "Go upstairs. You're too worried. I can't stand it. Get out of here. These people will get me up."

"No," Joshua says. He's been hovering, silent, distraught.

"Yes," Olive says. I consider quickly and selfishly that Joshua is being dismissed and will not forgive anyone who witnesses it.

Yvonne comes in from the kitchen. "I've been on the point of going for the last hour," she says. "I'm sorry—I'm worried about my kids."

Zak, who's been leaning over Olive, stretches and stands, saying, "I can't leave yet—but someone will drive me later."

"I will," I say quickly—which gives me the right to stay. Joshua has disappeared, and finally everyone else is gone except Martha, Zak, and me. "Maybe the ER?" Zak says quietly.

"But no ambulance," Olive says, so I know he's won. She can roll onto her stomach, crawl to the sofa, and stand with help, then lean on Martha and Zak.

The rain has stopped. I run the block to my car and drive it to the house, and the two of them manage to get Olive into it, then climb into the back seat. I drive to Yale New Haven Hospital, feeling odd—I didn't know these people three hours ago—where Olive is taken in quickly and Martha goes with her.

Zak seems hesitant to make himself known as a doctor. He and I sit in those hard chairs for a long time. He tells me that he and Martha were sweethearts in high school—his word, "sweethearts." It's clear that whatever they were, it didn't end well. Also, he has to be forty, or younger. I'm disappointed. I want him to be closer to my age. He has a comfortable smell, and sitting next to him makes me a little giddy. I'm also wary of him, a little surprised that any doctor hasn't identified himself to the ER staff and offered an opinion. It's like he might be overstepping if he says he's connected to Olive, even though they're such old acquaintances. By now, I'm headachy, worn out, but Zak is buoyant. He asks more questions about Barker Street.

Olive has a mild concussion, we learn, and has torn a ligament in her ankle. I expect that they may admit her, but eventually she's put into a long, rigid cast and sent out with crutches she can't manage, leaning on Martha. It's 2:00 a.m. I bring my car around, and we get her into it somehow. I drive everyone back to the house and watch Zak help Martha get her inside.

Then Zak comes back to my car and gives me directions to his apartment, not far away. "Come in and have coffee," he says when we get there.

I say, "Coffee sounds good."

"Not decaf," he says.

"Definitely not."

"We did well, Jean," he says, pulling out his keys and ushering me in. "We got her there." I'm trying to figure out the age difference. I stand next to him in my coat in the cold apartment, while he makes coffee. Later I won't remember anything about the layout except a long hall to the bathroom and bedroom, but I haven't seen those yet.

He turns and faces me as the coffee drips through the machine. "Would you be offended if I kissed you?" he says.

"No," I say, and his mouth is suddenly biting and thrusting at mine, and then we are all over each other, grasping and clutching as if we've waited for months. I know this is a discharge of anxiety, but so what? I've been trying to keep myself from knowing that I'm attracted to him. It's a relief to let myself feel it. We delay going to bed only long enough to have a few swallows of coffee each, between struggling to press our bodies together, standing up. We do need coffee.

The corridor is narrow, and we laugh, stumbling down it moments later, leaving the coffee in the kitchen. The bed is made—I am grateful for that—and smells clean, and Zak helps me out of my clothes and into it. Then he climbs joyfully on top of me, but soon he thrusts me around to be on top of him, which I prefer. It doesn't occur to me to be self-conscious about anything, including the age difference. I get that he's one of those younger men who likes older women. I guide him into me and thrust my tongue into his mouth, while he seizes my buttocks with both hands and, thrusting and bucking, brings us both to climax.

Later—I sleep briefly—I get up, freezing, and reach for my clothes. Zak is asleep, wrapped in blankets, the back of his dark head visible; he looks like a boy. Half-dressed, I remember Yvonne. I forgot that the man I was in bed with apparently has a girlfriend. Might they only be friends? No. I am not in the habit of competing for men with other women—especially with a woman who, like me, is old enough to be delighted and a little surprised to have a boyfriend at all, let alone a young one. I feel a little bewitched and a little guilty.

I find the bathroom, find my raincoat. Our cups of cold coffee are on the kitchen table, and I put mine into the microwave for a bit, then drink a few more swallows. I begin talking to myself as if I were a troubled client. "Go home and warm up," I say. But I write my phone number in large numbers on a piece of paper I see on the counter, then anchor it with my cup.

I let myself out and try to remember where my car is. Down the street, three or four cars to the right. I have left my umbrella at Olive and Joshua's house, and it's raining again. On the way home, I feel the elation of new love, managing to separate it from the fear and remorse I also feel. A woman who sleeps with a man someone else loves knows that he may do to her what he just did to the other woman. Women of fifty-two side with other women. And Yvonne is so *good*— all those foster kids. I get home—it's 5:00 a.m.—and put on flannel pajamas, which I already put away for the season. I take some ibu-profen. Everything hurts, but I'm happy. I sleep.

seven

Olive Grossman

When Griff found *Bright Morning of Pain,* I put it on a corner of the large table in the living room, under some papers. I didn't need to start work on it yet, and keeping it out of Griff's sight seemed wise. But I had to finish another essay soon, so as to be free for this one. On a warm Thursday in April, I made up my mind to reread a novel I planned to write about over that weekend and start a draft of the essay.

Griff hadn't asked to borrow *Bright Morning of Pain* again. Finding it seemed to have done away with his wish to read it. I ate early Thursday evening and settled down at the big table. I'd answer some emails then, to give myself even more time over the weekend. Griff was at an obligatory fundraising dinner for I forget which worthy organization. He had asked me to go with him, but I'd refused. I hadn't been able to think of a good reason. I didn't want to go—but he didn't want to go either. "No," I'd said; that was all. He looked upset.

Griff came in about nine. He'd chat in his coat—there was something about coat-chatting that kept the conversation light—and take it off only when he was on his way upstairs to watch basketball or baseball on the TV in Annie's old bedroom. It interested me that I knew so precisely how he'd behave, from the moment I heard his tired footsteps. I stood to open the door instead of waiting for him to fumble for his key.

That all happened, just as I expected. But ten minutes after going upstairs, Griff came down again, in his socks. I could hear the sports announcer in the background. Basketball. Griff's step irked me—there was something not quite straightforward about it. I turned around from the email I was writing. "What?"

"I should have mentioned this," he said. "I mean, I know I did mention it—but I should have reminded you. I think you've forgotten." I looked at him. His worry lines were deeper. He was embarrassed. "And you'll need to take everything off that table, of course."

The fundraising dinner on Saturday. I had agreed to cook but never put it on my calendar, thus never planned or shopped. And once I'd agreed, he hadn't talked about it. He must have forgotten, too.

If I hadn't been looking forward to a weekend without obligations, I might have forgiven him. We could laugh at ourselves for forgetting and then rapidly figure out how to hold a dinner party anyway. But after a moment of reverse nostalgia—a longing for what hadn't happened: the friendly and consoling conspiracy we wouldn't enjoy—anger won out. If only cooking hadn't been involved. I had a store of feminist rage always ready: over toilets I'd scrubbed, meals I'd cooked, diapers I'd changed, because women did these things. Our household had been formed and our children born just as the women's movement called into question any old assumptions we'd been carrying around about what women did and what men did. As marriages go, ours wasn't sexist. But Griff didn't clean toilets, and he knew how to cook only two or three meals, all basic weeknight stuff. I was no hostess, but I'd gotten used to cooking for company when the children were little.

"I should have remembered," I said, "but you should have reminded me."

"I know," he said.

"How many people? Did you ever invite Jean Argos?"

"Yes, she's coming."

For some reason, that was the detail that sent me into a rage. Though while I was raging, I knew it made no sense. Maybe the anger had to do with Griff's abstractedness, his being elsewhere—and Jean Argos was connected with the reason for that. In another marriage, I might have been accusing him of sexual infidelity. Griff would never be unfaithful—he was too moral; he was *irritatingly* moral. But it was more than that. We had a reasonably satisfying sex life, but it didn't dominate our dreams, our fantasies, our insecurities. That was true for me, and I was fairly sure it was true for him. What interested, threatened, and consoled both of us was work, and the rest of the serious business of life—politics, ethics, civic obligation. Infidelity, in our lives, didn't have to do with bodies. Griff was unfaithful because he had stopped being curious about me.

When I said something about that, he said, not for the first time, that I was always pushing him out. "You refuse again and again to have anything to do with me," he said. "I asked you to come with me tonight, and you said no. When I come home, your feet are on my chair."

"And why not?" I said, though my feet were nowhere near his chair at that moment. "Your butt is never on it."

"You insist on working in the living room. You make me uncomfortable in my own home."

Eventually, I stopped shouting and began to plan and cook. Martha, it seemed, had told Griff she might come. Good. Someone would talk to the strangers. He had invited Annie, too, but he said she texted that she didn't like faking friendship with people she didn't know. As if I did. I knew Griff would not quite join the party. When I had offered to cook, I was accepting the entire emotional load.

The dinner I then figured out would have been fine for family or old friends but wasn't much for strangers—strangers who had paid enough to buy the fanciest meal in the city. I prepared spinach lasagna, salad, and roasted vegetables. The single task I gave Griff—buying wine—defeated him. Even in his drinking days, he didn't drink wine.

On Saturday, once the food was ready, I cleaned. I drove to Marjolaine for a cake. I piled my books and papers in my study—where I rarely work—so we could eat at the long table. But then I couldn't work, so I cleaned some more. Martha, who is an adjunct professor, arrived with papers to grade and spent the afternoon working in her sister's old bedroom.

Griff had invited one guest I knew: Lorna Anderson, from the board of which he was now president. I'd met her at innumerable Griffin family events; she'd been at our wedding. She would report to Griff's family what I cooked and how well, and they'd wonder why they hadn't been asked. Still, I liked her. A serious churchgoer, she had room in her cosmology for me, the offhand Jew, and even for Griff, who had felt required, in his twenties, to inform his father that he was an atheist. Back then, Lorna had defended Griff to his mother.

After I changed my clothes and was surveying the living room, I got mad all over again about Jean Argos, the woman in whose office Griff had mislaid *Bright Morning of Pain*. Presumably she already considered us fools.

"I don't see why you had to include that woman," I said, passing him on my way to the living room with napkins.

"What woman?"

"The woman who had the book. Jean Argos."

"Why not?"

"It's one more thing, Griff," I said. "It's as if you tried to make this as hard as possible—adding in more and more people." This wasn't fair, and I knew it. I'd been glad to add Martha. It wasn't the numbers and the food that mattered as much as the time it was taking from my work. Now that it was going to happen, I should have put aside these issues and made the best of things. Maybe Jean would be pleasant, or at least interestingly peculiar. But once I began to complain about the numbers, I kept at it.

"You shouldn't have offered," he said. "What kind of a meal is spinach lasagna?"

"Now you say it."

"I'll leave. How about that? You don't want me here."

It was true; he was one of the difficulties: his imperious emotions interpreted all events as potential tragedies, requiring desperate acts that, carried out, made minor occasions worse. But I said, "Don't be stupid."

"You want me out of here." He turned away and then turned back. "Maybe we should turn the house back into two apartments. Maybe I should move upstairs again. That's what you want, isn't it?" His voice shook.

I turned and looked at him. "Yes," I said. "Yes. You get harder all the time. Maybe you should."

The doorbell rang.

And in they came. Lorna—in uncharacteristic red—was unexpectedly bashful. She came with another board member, also silent. Into this dullness walked Jean, a robust woman of fifty with flying yellow hair, a determined smile—for which I was grateful—and gray eyes too close together. She never stopped talking. I thought she and Griff would talk shop, but he hid in the kitchen. Martha emerged, smiling and in a pretty dress, and drew a group together. The mystery guests were late. If both were women, Griff would be the only man, and he'd flee to the bedroom and get under the covers.

I hated the mystery guest, partly because she was late and partly because, when she did arrive, she looked apologetic. The only way to carry off having bid all that money on a dinner supposedly cooked by the principal—and then coming late—would be to take command. She should have exclaimed over the room, house, and dinner with either joy or dismay, preferably the latter. Wasn't it her task to be rude, so we'd unite in opposition?

But I hated her primarily because she brought Zachary Lilienthal— Dr. Zachary Lilienthal—who had broken my child's heart twenty years earlier, who had broken, for heaven's sake, *my* stupid heart, and who would never have done what he did if he had it in him to experience remorse. I saw quickly that he had not told his companion that he knew us. When Griff saw Zak, I was afraid he'd walk out, since he was incapable of throwing anyone out of his house, any more than he'd throw a student, however nefarious, out of his school.

I didn't want to walk out. At last, I had an interesting reason to stay. Evil doesn't bother me quite the way it bothers some people, and Zachary Lilienthal's crimes didn't make him less fascinating. Griff withdrew even more. When somebody began talking about *Bright Morning of Pain* at dinner, he started an argument with me, just as I was struggling to serve dessert with no help except from Lorna, who had finally turned human. I was excited to see Zak—and terrifically upset.

And then I tore a ligament in my ankle, falling over a chair leg or my own feet or somebody's hair ornament. The dinner ended, and Jean and Zak and Martha drove me to the hospital.

Joshua Griffin

Zak Lilienthal humiliated my daughter twenty years ago and didn't understand why what he did was wrong. I hadn't seen him since, until the dinner tonight, when I now note that he apparently doesn't know that it's wrong to take advantage of an unforeseeable coincidence and walk uninvited into my house. If he doesn't know that, he can't possibly be a competent doctor, so he would not know if Olive needed immediate help or not. Olive could have been dying.

Yet I turned to Zak. I asked his advice. I scurried upstairs when Olive dismissed me. I am pacing in the dark in Annie's old bedroom, then lying down on the bed, standing up again, thinking about the reckless plans of the irresponsible director of Barker Street—an agency for which I am now responsible—and the pain in Martha's eyes when she saw that even her parents' home was not safe from the man who hurt her all those years ago.

I don't want to finish reading that book, because I know what's coming. I know what book Val wrote. I know what happened. I didn't read this book for years and never should have. I knew what to do about this book for the rest of my life, and I didn't do it.

I am not turning on the light because as long as I pace in the dark, I can talk to myself about the failure that was my dinner party and not have to consider the ultimate failure: that the woman I love—the woman I have always loved, will always love—sent me away when she was in trouble and in pain. Sent me away while Jean smirked; I know she smirked. Sent me away—and had made clear, before the party, that she doesn't want me in her life.

The children are grown. Maybe there's no reason to stay with her, if my presence is painful, if she doesn't love me. She took me at my word when, in a moment of hyperbole, I proposed dividing the house again. It's what she wants. It could be done—there's a bathroom on each floor. I could cook up here with a microwave. A door with a lock could keep me out of her domain. Those years I lived in that apartment in West Haven, near the water—where I was always afraid the children would drown, afraid every hour, but it was the only clean place I could find in a hurry—she taught herself to be separate from me, and she is separate from me, whatever my address, whatever she cooks.

I am twelve years old. I am twelve years old! And I am the principal, which means that I don't even have the comfort of being known as a fool when I am a fool. I am known as the principal.

I heard them bring her outside. They must have taken her to the hospital. They didn't come up and tell me what they decided. They forgot I was here. Even Martha. I am lying on the bed in the dark. I won't turn on the television while Olive lies in the emergency room without me.

I won't forgive her for wanting to be apart from me, all those years ago. No, wrong terminology—I won't forget. I won't stop arguing inwardly with her choice, even though she took me back four years later. I knew that, ultimately, she wanted me out because I could not forgive myself for what I had done. I still haven't forgiven myself, and so I cannot read a version of it in Val's book. Cannot endure to learn Olive's idea, what Olive knew or remembered—as told to Val—of what I did. It's between us every day.

■

The first time I saw Olive, she was walking ahead of me, looking down, in a dull blue dress. That heavy hair was loose, but it was a hot day, so she swept it off her neck, let it go, swept it off again, as if she didn't notice what she was doing, as if, notwithstanding all the talk and shouting, Olive had nothing to say. She walked forward, and maybe the war would end if she didn't stop.

I was student teaching at a high school in Staten Island. Those kids didn't know there was a war, except that they might be drafted and have to fight, which might be good and would definitely be exciting. They didn't know what to make of their black teacher.

The friend I marched with had told me about Olive. He had called her, and they picked a place to meet. We met, we shook hands, shook hands with other people, waited in hot weather, walked. We'd all done it many times, knew how we managed. Someone brought a canteen; someone brought cookies.

I talked to her. I thought about taking her to bed.

But for a while, I'd been pretty sure that marching was over, that violence had to happen, that nothing else would work. It was tragic, but it was also exciting. Some boys want to go to war, and this was something like that. I was never good at sports, never in trouble. In part, I wanted some trouble. Or I was open to some trouble. I wanted it, and I thought I could justify it.

When I bought a gun from a friend who wanted the money so he could buy a bigger one, I was pleased with myself in the way I'd have been pleased if I'd ridden a horse or climbed rocks. It was something like the way I felt the first time I got drunk—and even the tenth time, but by then I was disgusted with that, which should have told me something. Owning a gun was a way of being strong and powerful that was not my father's way. We had to do it. There were scary and tragic reasons to do it, and we also liked it. My friends, black and white, felt the same way. There was target practice, shooting followed by the drinking of beer, though around that time I switched to Coke. My first two shreds of self-knowledge: not going to divinity school, not drinking beer.

The protest in upstate New York was not going to be a big deal. The big deal had been the previous weekend, a confrontation at a draft board. I'd lost sleep wondering if I'd shoot—and if I didn't shoot, would it be because I was a coward? Then it hadn't come up. The cops had made some kind of decision to let that protest go, and it never became confrontational—and never got the attention we hoped for. But the protest in upstate New York was different: simpler, like what we'd done all the time a couple of years earlier. College students waving signs, chanting, and singing. Someone asked my group to show up in support. So we did—or a few of us did. Half a dozen on a Greyhound bus, expecting to be back in the city early.

But the students were unusually innocent and disorganized, and the cops had somehow misunderstood. And one cop was stupid or bloodthirsty. When he started bashing heads, another rushed, shouting, to his side, as if he'd been attacked. The kids were suddenly at risk. Nightsticks hit heads, there were screams, blood, a girl was down and trampled, another, another. I looked at the cop's hand with the stick as if it were a tin can I'd set on a milk crate when I practiced. I took my time. I squeezed the trigger. It wasn't manly, wasn't exciting. I thought it was regrettably necessary, and I did it as I might kill a rabid, snarling, matted animal that had been fluffy and sweet before it was infected. The cop lost his hand. I never wanted to touch a gun again—but Helen knew all about it and paid attention.

■

Looking at my watch in the light from a streetlight outside, I see it's midnight. Olive and Martha aren't back. Martha's phone goes right to voicemail. It probably doesn't work in the hospital. I turn on the light next to Annie's old bed and walk across the hall into Olive's study, where she's piled everything that was spread on the long table this morning. It doesn't take me long to find *Bright Morning of Pain*. Maybe I can't save my marriage. Maybe that old trouble—what I did, what Helen did, what Olive thought, and what she said to Val and what Val wrote—can't be fixed now. But at least I can finish the book. I keep the lamp on and lie down on the bed. But then I stand up again and put the book back where I found it.

■

Martha didn't like the sweater I put on. She picked out a shirt without a sweater, and I was uncomfortable. I thought that shirt should be worn with a necktie, but I wore it anyway, without.

All right, I said, just before the party. The spinach lasagna was in the oven. I don't like spinach lasagna, but that is most definitely neither here nor there. All right, then, just let me go. I can't go now, because I promised the auction committee. But after that, just let me out of here. I said that.

But I never wanted to leave.

You understand *that well* what you do?

I understand, yes, what I habitually do.

Olive Grossman

I've never been celebrated for my looks, but I was never prettier than in the summer of 1968, when I was nineteen. I let my hair grow, and it was thick and dark. When my neck was hot, I took out a rubber band and bundled my hair into a loose knot that looks messy in one photograph, sexy in another, distracting the observer, maybe, from my stubborn nose—as Eli called it—and shiny forehead. Ordinarily, as a young woman, I looked like somebody's babysitter, somebody's reliable assistant—a secondary character.

It was the only time in my life I ever thought more about public concerns than private ones. My predominant emotion was rage at our government—rage about the war and grief over my helplessness. You might imagine the war in Vietnam robbed me of my sexual coming of age, but it intensified my sex life: the personal freedom of the late sixties came in the context of political events. I doubt that the "sexual revolution" would have affected me had there been no war to protest, but the sexual revolution itself would not have happened without the war. Caught up in events larger than the personal, we lost shyness and caution. I slept with a half dozen men that year.

The summer of '68, I worked as a counselor in a day camp run by a reform synagogue on Manhattan's Upper West Side—at last, not in Brooklyn looking after my brother and sister. Responsible for twelve nine-year-old girls—along with my co-counselor, a barefoot Israeli named Tova with fetching black curls—I was distracted, during the day, from national politics and the war, though Martin Luther King and now Robert Kennedy were dead, the nominating conventions were imminent, and the headlines were full of downed planes and bombing raids in Vietnam. Every day, the newspaper named those from the New York area who had died the day before—a short but heartbreaking list.

I led my campers—chubby, timid kids, thrilled by what they considered an adventure—through Central Park, then hurried them back for swimming. While the swimming counselor kept them busy and Tova swam laps, I lazed in the deep end of the pool, floating and daydreaming. Emerging into the city at 3:30, I still smelled of chlorine, despite a shower. Tova was picked up in a car and driven off to Westchester. Free and alone, itchy-eyed, I was like someone rising from a day in bed, thinking like a child and moving slowly into the hot city.

Gradually I would remember who I was and what I thought. It wasn't all political: I was hurt when Patrick told me he wanted to date someone else—only later did I understand that this vague person was a man. Other men disappointed me or hurt my feelings. But it was mostly political. Robert Kennedy had been shot to death in June. The social order might soon vanish. The city was dirty and humid, a troubled place—but mine.

Helen had a job in a dark grocery store with intense smells, a grotesque version of her parents' wholesome and predictable establishment. The groceries looked like dusty props, and strange transactions took place. Her parents hadn't questioned Helen's choices when they had to do with Barnard, but they were stunned when she dropped out of school. Her father stopped giving her rent money, but she told me that her mother, apparently with his unacknowledged awareness, handed her folded bills when they met for lunch. They must have hoped the money would help them keep her: even Helen couldn't live without money. But the store paid her a little, and gradually she stopped seeing her mother.

When I couldn't think of anything to do after day camp that summer, before going home to Brooklyn, I would visit Helen in the store, waiting around while she straightened pathetic merchandise and took money from rare customers. In her free time, she was busy with meetings—the job itself had come through movement connections—and sometimes I went along.

Eli, Helen's friend and sometime lover, was a presence at these meetings. I had not liked Eli when I'd met him—or maybe I was afraid of him—but now his combination of bluntness and shyness, as if he wasn't certain he pronounced words correctly, attracted me. It turned out he was an autodidact who had spent only a few months in college. At meetings, he urged reading lists on us, setting up study sessions about political philosophy, and I began attending a Thursday subgroup that Helen didn't belong to, near his apartment in the Village. The readings were difficult, but I was proud to participate. We couldn't be accused of superficiality, of arguing for peace because we liked torn jeans and free love. The discussions were earnest and unpretentious—everyone was just trying to get it. Eli would make a point, then look quickly down and up again, his eyes bright, as if he was a little surprised to have spoken. When he suggested, one night, that he and I have "a glass of wine and a bite" after the meeting, I agreed, knowing what was coming, so aroused that brushing against his blue shirt sleeve as we passed through a narrow doorway was erotic.

He didn't wear jeans like the rest of us, but loose khaki pants and a shirt with buttons. He guided me into an Italian restaurant with an arm around my shoulder. Candle wax dripped onto Chianti bottles, and the waiters had accents. "You'll come back with me?" he said as we ate the bread, waiting for our spaghetti and meatballs. That bright-eyed look again.

"Yes," I said.

As we ate, he said, "You're smart," which pleased me more than if he'd said I was beautiful. "You made two good points tonight." Then he repeated and enlarged upon them. By the time we left, I was leaning against him, letting myself put my hand on his back. We kissed hard in his apartment. Eli had vacuumed the rug, and I wondered if he'd planned in advance to bring me—or somebody—home.

I wasn't being stupid when I slept with Eli. I knew what I was doing, and I knew Helen would be hurt or angry—possibly both. I hadn't changed my mind about Eli's carelessness with women, but I wanted to touch his penis, to put it into my mouth, to be pressed into the mattress by his wide shoulders and big arms. It was refreshing to do something reckless for once. I phoned my mother and said I was staying with Helen, then phoned Helen to say I was staying with *someone*, worried that my mother would think of something to tell me and call me there. Life was different before cell phones, before caller ID.

"Okay, I'll say you're asleep," Helen said, not too interested. "But you know, Olivia, you'd better move in here."

I said okay, as pleased by the invitation as I was about Eli.

She said, "Can you pay me something? You can sleep on the couch."

"Okay," I said again, and returned to Eli, afraid he'd lose interest while I talked on the phone.

My parents were accustomed to the truth from me and didn't guess I was with a man—or perhaps they thought I was so sheltered that if I went to bed with a man, I'd blurt out my inevitable shock and regret. In that case, they'd reassure me. They'd agree it would have been wiser not to engage in sex before marriage.

But when I said I was going to stay with Helen for a few weeks, my parents were troubled. They were uneasy about my participation in meetings and discussion groups having to do with the war, and they saw living with Helen—correctly—as a change that would lead to more of what made them uneasy. They were old Roosevelt Democrats. If they had ever been politically engaged, they'd lost that excitement,

and they regarded patriotism—emotional attachment to country—as
something one outgrew when one no longer had to stand in the aisles
of Public School Something-or-other and recite the Pledge of Alle-
giance. They didn't feel obliged to approve of the war in Vietnam just
because their government waged it, and they didn't approve. It was
clear early that the war was a waste of time, money, and lives, and my
parents thought our government should pull out. Loyalty and pride—
emotions that motivated pro-war Americans—were patently silly to
the Grossmans.

But they felt the same way about antiwar activism. Our government's insistence on fighting a losing war had become criminal, but
the Grossmans weren't the police. They remembered Hubert Humphrey's opposition to racial discrimination in 1948 and hoped he'd
be elected. When I came home from marches and rallies—spent, dirty,
and discouraged, once my initial elation dissipated—my parents were
embarrassed. What had made me think this was my business? Was I
neglecting my college courses? (Yes, but not too much.)

Now, as I packed my bag to move to Helen's, my mother said, "You
could find other friends." I might get arrested and spoil my life, she
said. I might be hurt. She shook her head. "Time after time, 'Oh,
Mrs. Grossman, I'm not hungry.'" She imitated Helen's breathy,
childlike voice, which made me realize how much it had matured.
Now she had a low-pitched speaking voice, uninflected but emphatic.

"Of course she was hungry!" my mother said, watching me pack
underwear and blue jeans. "Did she think I was stupid?"

A week or two after I moved in, Helen went to Chicago. There was
no television in the apartment, and I followed the events taking place

at the Democratic National Convention—the protests, the arrival of the National Guard, and the violence of the Chicago police, who kicked and clubbed demonstrators and arrested hundreds—as best I could. Humphrey criticized the police but criticized the demonstrators far more vigorously. He was nominated while thousands protested outside.

I was lonely while Helen was gone—and I'd been lonely before she went. I don't know what I expected. Though Helen took any money I could give her, she was no more interested in me when we were roommates than she had been before. Barb was mostly gone now, living with a lover, and Angie was generally out or shut in her room. Camp ended, and I was free most of the time. Eli had found me a job waitressing a few evenings a week in a shabby restaurant.

Helen returned from Chicago sick from gas and exhausted from a long, hot drive in a crowded backseat. She had a sprained ankle and a painful bruise where a policeman had smashed his baton into her arm. She wouldn't talk much. Apparently she hadn't been arrested—she'd been too sick and hurt to keep protesting. The night she came home, she slept in Barb's bed. I woke up when it was not quite light and made my way to the bathroom. I was going back to my sofa to try to sleep some more, but Helen called me.

"What's wrong?" I said. Barb's room was dark and stuffy.

"My foot hurts," she said, sounding like a child again. "I'm so hot."

I opened the window as wide as it would go. "Let me see."

She sat up and showed me her swollen, purple ankle. Her hair looked dirty, and of course she hadn't eaten properly for days. I wanted to take care of her. If I could no longer be close to her through talk and shared thought, I wanted to help her to the toilet, to wash her hair, to wash her belly and breasts. You will say it was a sexual wish, and of course that's so, but it was more a wish for the physical. I wanted anything that was Helen's, and her body was part of anything.

I was not to get it for long, but the next week—the end of August and the beginning of September—was the happiest time for me since those walks after school when we had just met. Now, leaving her lying there, I extracted the last four ice cubes in our tray, put them into a sock of mine, and tied it around her ankle, which I raised on a pillow. I brought sofa cushions and propped her up in bed, her back against the wall. She looked straight ahead at her foot, her face child-like and weepy. We had nothing to eat but stale bread and instant coffee. I hacked off bread and found strawberry preserves. I brought her breakfast and put it on a chair I had drawn up to the bed, then dressed and went out to buy food. The ankle was bad. I know now that she needed a doctor, but I was living in a fantasy—only I could help her.

She didn't object. Later that day, I helped her into the tub and didn't wash her breasts—I was embarrassed—but scrubbed her back and shampooed her hair. We were all but silent. I got her into bed again, gathered her clothes, took them to the laundromat. Then I scrubbed the kitchen and bathroom and dusted the walls and ceilings in the other rooms, making myself sweaty and hot and happy. Angie woke late and left, and Helen and I had the place to ourselves.

After a few days, Helen could walk gingerly with her ankle bandaged, leaning on me. I got her down the stairs and outside, where we sat on the steps of the building. In the apartment, we read at opposite sides of the room or ate. The weather was hot enough to make laziness acceptable, but then the temperature dropped, and in the fresh autumn air, she began to fret about doing nothing.

One afternoon we made our way downstairs and sat on the cracked red stone steps in front of the building, squinting into the sun, our feet stretched out onto the sidewalk. I wore huaraches, but Helen was in bedroom slippers—her shoe wouldn't fit on her swollen foot. For several minutes, she ran her finger over the flaws and broken corners of the step we sat on. Then, in a small, almost apologetic voice, she said, "Could you let up?"

"Let up?"

"You're not leaving me alone for a second."

"I'm sorry." I was abashed. "I was trying to help," I said, unable to explain what these days had given me.

Her finger made taut whorls between us. "No," she said. "You want to make me soft. You want me to stop struggling."

I hadn't thought about it, but I'd have been relieved if Helen relaxed a bit, if she could become a part-time activist like me. "No!" I said anyway. "That's not what I want. You have to do what you think you must."

I meant it as I said it. I felt guilty. I was glad when something distracted me from the war, from my frustrated rage and the grief that overcame me when I saw something about dead civilians or our local dead soldiers, with their ordinary, New York names—Italian, Irish, occasionally Jewish names, or names that sounded as if the holders might be black—but I too had the inchoate idea that it would be preferable not to be distracted.

She was quiet. Her hair caught the sun, and she shaded her eyes with her hand. "Okay," she said. Then, "What about Eli?"

"Eli? What about him?" This was early in my affair. Eli and I saw each other a couple of times a week. He acted thrilled and nervous—dazzled. He somehow knew I'd respond to vulnerability, and maybe I even knew he was faking, in part, but didn't care.

"You shouldn't have done that," she said solemnly, after a long pause.

"Slept with him?" I hadn't been sure she knew. "But I didn't think you—"

"Not because of me," she said. "I don't get hung up."

I turned. "Oh, come on, Helen, of course you do!"

"No, I don't."

"But?"

"But *you* do. If you're so into health and safety, you should have protected yourself, Olivia. You should have stayed away from him. You know what he's like." The finger made more whorls. "We don't have the luxury to make ourselves as unhappy as you're going to be when he drops you."

"What?" I laughed at her. "Since when is it a luxury to be unhappy?"

"You know what I mean."

I examined my feelings. How much would I mind when the affair was over? Two images came, one after the other. First, I pictured myself shaking the hand of a shadowy woman, putting my hand on her shoulder and squeezing, then releasing her so she could hurry into a bedroom. But then I pictured something else: myself screaming, leaning out a high window and screaming, my arms spread wide.

"You're jealous," I said, to distract myself from these unsettling thoughts.

"You don't understand me," Helen said. "I don't know if you've ever understood me."

I didn't think she was jealous, but I would have preferred it. What she had said was true: I wanted her less angry, less political, more vulnerable about men.

"I don't know if you're capable of sacrifice for a cause," Helen said. "You don't know what it means."

I had been a fool. So I moved—briefly—back to my parents' place, saying I needed to be closer to the college. Classes started. For a couple of weeks, I kept to myself, studying, though I belonged to Students for a Democratic Society. I was a junior, thinking about graduate school, taking advanced literature courses. English majors were less involved in protest than people in some departments. I didn't talk to Helen, just lived at home, spent time in the library, and worked.

But even at home, there was plenty of discussion of political subjects. My parents were trying to persuade their friends to vote not for the protest candidate, Dick Gregory, but for Humphrey, despite the violence in Chicago. My father shouted and pounded the dining room table. Humphrey had been a progressive all his life, while Nixon had been a reactionary. Whatever else happened, he repeated, Humphrey was the better choice. It was the argument I'd made to Helen in the spring: we were going to have one of these people, so we might as well pick the best.

My friends and I thought voting for any candidate in this election (in which most of us were too young to vote) would be a mistake:

nobody with sense should participate. That fall, Helen had persuaded me, and I could not believe that the vote, when I got it, would be worth much.

The night of my worst fight with my father, I came to the table reluctantly, knowing the conversation would turn to the election and the war, maybe knowing that I'd take it there if my parents and brother and sister—who were now developing opinions as well—did not. Humphrey had said that if he were elected, he'd end the bombing of North Vietnam, but the speech in which he had said it had been so full of attempts to please everyone, so defensive, that it infuriated me—while impressing my father.

Sure enough, while the food got cold and my mother fretted, my father and I screamed at each other. My brother cried. He wanted me to keep living at home, to get along with our parents. The pull was intense—I too wanted to be at home, to forget, to allow myself to believe what part of me knew was the sensible position. For hours at a time, away from home, I thought the protest movement would succeed, that the American system might be radically altered. At home, that seemed as impossible as what I *knew* was impossible—that my mother would stop bringing platters of chicken to the table, that my father would stop calling my sister "my fine feathered friend." He'd said it all her life, and nobody knew why.

My throat was sore from shouting, and my mother kept saying, "Stop it, Olivia, stop it!" though she usually called me Olive, as requested. As I shouted, I understood what Helen had meant, why taking care of her—all that silly cooking and cleaning—was wrong. I'd seduced both of us away from the war. Nothing should have let us forget it.

"Some kind of *genius*, you're supposed to be!" my father shouted. "You with your fancy brain!"

I stood, went into my room, and paused. I could sit down and start studying, but I'd be shirking my duty to help clear the table and wash the dishes. If I wasn't home, I wouldn't be shirking. The logic seemed fine at the time.

Again, I stuffed a bag with books and a few clothes. I carried it and my portable typewriter into the dining room, where my sister and brother were finally carrying dishes into the kitchen. I kissed my mother. "I'm going to Helen's," I said. "I need to write a paper. I need to think." I didn't want to be dramatic. I said something friendly to my brother and sister, said, "See you, Dad!" and left. It was close to ten when I got to the apartment.

After that, I lived with Helen most of the time for more than a year—when the restaurant gave me enough hours and I had money to contribute, when avoiding home was worth the long subway ride, when my parents' fretfulness and my sister's and brother's questions made me too uncomfortable to continue there. I was living beyond my means, not just financially but emotionally too, and when I was home, I was always in danger of seeing that. The surest sign that I was living on bravado was that the cockroaches in the apartment no longer bothered me.

In general, I was too busy to care where I lived. I was in class, or on the subway—where I read or wrote papers in notebooks, typing them later—at the restaurant, at a meeting or rally, or in the apartment just trying to sleep, sometimes on the sofa, sometimes in a room nobody else was sleeping in. Barb still lived there now and then, and I noted with some surprise that I didn't mind her dirty sheets. When the lack of decent food was too much, I'd go back home for a few days, restlessly bypassing family life, using my parents' apartment primarily as a place to sleep.

My classes remained real. I was someone else at school, and my professors would have been surprised to learn that I didn't lead a regular life. I remember no books I read that fall except nineteenth-century British novels—*Middlemarch*, for one—but I must have taken other subjects as well. At the apartment, I read those long books as a way of being alone, because what went on in the apartment disturbed me, too. When I couldn't bear the war one more moment, I sat on the floor with my typewriter, typing up the long papers I'd scrawled in pen.

One Sunday, I came back to the apartment after a demonstration —dirty, starving, exhausted—to shower and eat quickly, then write a paper, due the next day, on a story by Henry James, "The Private Life." It's about a writer whose alternate self goes out among people while the real man can be glimpsed working alone in his room. I was that writer, as I read. The story was about me, except that I didn't know how to perform the supernatural feat James had allowed his character, and so I never got enough of the private life, the inner life. I felt in the wrong when I wasn't out there shouting or when I retreated to my parents' apartment.

Helen was usually at meetings I didn't have time for. She had boyfriends who sometimes scared me. Eli still wanted to sleep with me, and I thought I might lose interest before he did—when the cat hair and the knowledge that there were other women got to me. But I turned up at his apartment once or twice a week, partly because it

was cleaner than ours (except for the cat hair) and because he introduced me to people. Sometimes I wrote papers there, where I could
sit at a table and not have to deal with my mother. Once, Eli made
love to another woman in the bedroom—a stranger to me, young and
blond—while I wrote in the kitchen. That's what I mean when I say I
lived beyond my means. *I didn't mind.* I was so certain I shouldn't mind
(exclusive sexual ties were bourgeois, boring, fussy, unimaginative)
that, at least consciously, I didn't.

When Barb definitely moved out, Helen got her room, and now I
had the space behind the living room couch that Helen had occupied
before. Angie was in and out. I sprayed bugs and cooked, comforting
Helen—who regularly got arrested and spent all-night sessions on
strategy I didn't want to hear about (but was intensely curious about)—
with whatever food I could buy cheaply.

Gradually, I met Helen's other friends. Somewhat to my surprise, most were smart people who made clever arguments and didn't
become self-congratulatory and sentimental. I'd been assuming that
anybody more involved in antiwar work than I was probably a hot-
head, and hotheads didn't make sense. If these shrewd, well-read
people thought protest could change the system, it might be so. There
was a group at Columbia, where Helen still had connections, and she
had friends at City College as well.

Two who didn't have a connection to any college were a woman
named Mallon, who came to the apartment several times and whom we
saw at some meetings, and a man they spoke of as Raz, whom I didn't
meet for a long time. Mallon had a long, reddish braid down her back
and a wide face with freckles. The first time I saw her, I thought she

looked atypically easy to approach, but when I tried to make friends, she didn't look at me or speak. She and Helen were smoking weed and drinking tea, and I—coming into the apartment late in the afternoon, a bag of books over my shoulder—was an intruder. Mallon's and Raz's names confused me, and I asked Helen the next day if they were first or last names, if they were made-up names.

"What difference does it make?" she said, though we'd always been fascinated by names.

"I can't get them straight," I continued, almost *trying* to make her mad. "This famous Raz is a man? Have you actually laid eyes on him? Why does he matter?"

"He matters because he really knows," Helen said. "And yes, I've met him. He was in the Marines—he saw it all himself. Last month his group broke into a draft board and poured blood on the records. Some kid won't get killed in 'Nam because there's blood on his name. Or that's the theory."

"Mallon wants you to join that group?"

We were in the part of the living room where I slept. I had been putting on my socks and shoes when Helen came in and asked me for money, and I gave her five dollars. I sat on the mattress I slept on, my foot extended, looking up as we spoke about her friends. She stood above me, the window behind her, with its broken venetian blind. From below, her face looked puffy.

"They're trying something a bit harder next," she said. Then, "They think I'm not ready."

I saw Mallon again, in the street with Helen, a week or two later, as I walked from the subway station, again with my student's sack of books.

"I'll be late," Helen said, waving, and I went to the apartment alone and read Thomas Hardy.

On Election Day, I cut classes, or maybe school was closed. There were protests all over the city, and Eli told Helen and me to come to Union Square for a rally urging people not to vote. It interested me to realize that Eli's presence at the rally wasn't my primary reason for going, that I wouldn't spend my time looking for him. I had at last succeeded—I thought—in attaining some of Helen's detachment about men. Being preoccupied by the war was something like having such a bad cold that you didn't care what happened in your life. Intense rage about the war and the government wasn't enough to make me indifferent to whether the man I was sleeping with dumped me, it had turned out more than once. But too little sleep and food, and too much coffee and marijuana, could do it. I had no wish except to do what came next: to storm the police without having my head bashed in, to bring more people, louder people, to the next protest and the next, until the roar of our voices would be so loud that what we wanted would occur.

We never found Eli at the rally on Election Day, where someone in a pig mask teased and amused the crowd, waving a Vietcong flag. Miming horror, the pig man clasped a Nazi flag to himself, while people around him screamed, "Oink! Oink!"

Of all my parents' objections to the movement, calling the police "pigs" bothered them most. "They're ruining their own cause," my mother would have wailed. "Those cops are just doing their jobs."

By then, I'd seen policemen who were not just doing their jobs. But that wasn't what made me yell along with the others: the *idea* of police was our enemy, whether particular cops deserved my hatred or not. That day, the place was massed with them.

Before the rally broke up, Helen seized my arm: "Let's go." We made our way to the edge of the crowd. "This is stupid," she said. "And my ankle hurts."

The protesters were supposed to go on to Rockefeller Center for a demonstration there, and even then, hundreds were heading for the subway stations. We walked slowly up Broadway and rested on a bench in Madison Square. I knew by then that I should have made Helen see a doctor in August and felt this had been my failed responsibility, as if she were my child. Now I wanted only to take her someplace quiet. The subway would be crowded, with too many steps, and I didn't have money for a cab. People who'd left the rally were walking up Fifth Avenue toward Rockefeller Center, so I led her the other way, onto Madison Avenue. We walked slowly for many blocks. I offered to let Helen lean on me, but she said she was fine.

At Thirty-Sixth Street, we came to the Pierpont Morgan Library, a building I knew. I'd gone to one or two exhibits there, taking as much pleasure in being allowed to wander around a nineteenth-century mansion as in the art. "Let's go in," I said.

"Pierpont Morgan? Not without a bomb!" She looked up at the grand old building. There was still something childlike about Helen, an unself-consciousness in the way she stood, not arranging her body like a young woman of twenty.

"It's a library," I said. "We don't have anything against libraries." It was small in those days. You could almost imagine living in it.

"It's all one system, Olivia," she said, but I knew she wanted to see the inside of the place.

"We must inform ourselves about the moneyed classes," I said. "Come on. We'll wear out the floor with our shoes and contribute to the fall of the military industrial complex."

"Are you making fun of me?" Helen said.

Her tone was teasing, warm. "Never, my darling," I said, and led her inside.

In the abrupt quiet, we stood before a row of drawings in a long glass case—drawings of people, created centuries earlier in Europe, some by artists we knew, like Rembrandt and Dürer. I was too tired to note who had made each one, but looking at them slowed my metabolism. Tears came. I thought of the man with his Nazi flag and his pig mask, while looking at these pictures in which a few strokes seemed to have created life and mood: a woman with a child, or a man who looked up, awestruck.

"Does your ankle hurt?" I said, after we'd looked silently at five or six drawings.

"Yes," she said, but she moved on down the row. On one page, studies were grouped: three sketches of a man's head and torso in a hat, one above the next. Two sketches, to the side, of the hat alone. Above them, a woman's face, suggesting compassion, grief, sorrow.

Helen kept looking longer than I did, standing motionless before each drawing, her head sometimes tilted to the side. At last, we sat down on a bench. No one else was there. Helen searched in the denim bag she carried over her shoulder and removed a small spiral notebook with a dark reddish cover, bent and wrinkled from the months or years she'd been carrying it. The pencil she had stuck through the metal coils was too large, so it had loosened the spiral. She poked the pencil free and began drawing on an unused page near the back of the notebook.

After a while, she said—casually, as if what she said was obvious—"When something *happens*. That's it. That's everything."

"I don't understand," I said. She was copying, I saw, a depiction of a woman in a billowing dress with a bucket at her side and a small child, also in a billowing dress.

"It makes my heart hurt," she said.

"The drawing?"

"Not this one particularly—the idea that they might not have . . ." She put the notebook away. "They were made quickly."

"Yes." I had thought about that too—a few sure, swift strokes.

"His wife calls him to lunch ten minutes earlier—no woman at all."

I thought. "You mean the drawing might not have been made."

"I mean," she said. She tapped the elegant hardwood bench on which we sat. "This building. Everybody building it could have dropped dead, but Mr. Pierpont Morgan would have said, 'Oh, too bad, haul away those stinky bodies—but here are the plans, get someone else.'"

"But a drawing . . . ," I said.

"Right."

"Right, what?" I said. I thought we agreed, but I didn't quite know what it was we agreed.

"The woman. She's there, or not. If she's there, that's enough. I know how the artist felt when he drew her. I know what she's feeling. If he doesn't draw her, nothing can change that."

We stood and looked at some more drawings, speculating on which stroke was the very first.

"Making is destroying," Helen said then. "Making is everything—but making is destroying, so it doesn't count."

"Destroying? How?"

"The drawing destroys the blank surface," she said. "If you value the drawing, drawing is making. If I drew on the wall over there, the guard would call it destroying."

"So what?"

"If making is destroying," she said, "sometimes destroying is making. Doing something. That's what counts."

When we left, the library was closing and it was dark. We took a bus, finding seats in the back for our long, bumpy ride uptown. Helen sat silently next to the window. Then she said, "I forgot it's Election Day."

"We went to the rally," I said. "We made our point."

"What did we *make*?" Helen asked.

The bus struggled noisily up the avenue, letting people on and off. I was glad we had seats, and I wasn't giving mine up, no matter who got on. I hoped Helen would keep looking out the window. She could be difficult on the subject of ethical behavior, sore ankle or no.

"We didn't *make* anything," she continued. "Those drawings are something somebody made. We just *talked*. We just *said*. There's no value in that." She shook her head vigorously. Her hair was very curly that day.

"Wait a second," I said. "How can you claim that saying something isn't worth anything? What about poems? What about novels?"

She was silent, looking out the window, and I thought she wouldn't answer. The bus continued northward. Then she said, "Poems and novels don't seem to be ending the war."

"So they have no value?"

"They have value," she said. "They have value—for pleasure, for leisure. But, no, Olivia, they're not what we need. Not now."

"They teach us," I said quickly. "They tell us how to live. How to think." She was silent. "Like the drawings. They're no different from the drawings!"

"I guess you're right," she said. "No different."

I'd have thought she was trying to shock me, but Helen never said what she didn't mean. "You don't believe in literature," I said. "In art."

Helen turned and looked straight at me. "Oh, honey, I wish I did!" The bus stopped, and she was silent while the doors creaked open. People stomped off and others got on; the doors creaked again. "That was so nice, what we used to think! When we wrote poems. When we took those walks."

I pulled her into a sideways hug.

Then she said, "I love you, but you're a liberal. You want to talk. You want to convince them. That's over."

"If we can't talk, we have wars," I said. "I thought we were trying to stop a war."

"We are," Helen said. Now there were so many people around us that talking was awkward. We were silent until we reached our stop. The apartment was still a few blocks away, and our usual coffee shop was on the way.

"Let's get some eggs," I said. I was starving.

"The way to end war," Helen said in a low voice, as we waited for our food—as if she'd been waiting all this time to say this sentence—"is not commentary, but action."

"Destroying something?"

"Maybe. Sometimes. A draft board—wow," she said. "I'd like to blow one up."

Our plates of egg and toast and potatoes arrived. "Aren't they in buildings people use—in city halls, stuff like that?" I asked.

"Maybe."

I was too hungry to let the food get cold while we argued. I ate half a slice of toast, slathered with salty butter. It tasted wonderful. I was the only antiwar activist who hadn't gotten thin—maybe that was how you could tell I was a liberal. "Helen," I said then, with my mouth full, "you'd do that? You'd blow up a building? What if somebody got hurt? Or killed?"

Helen was eating, but now she put down her fork. "We're careful," she said, and I noted the "we." "I don't want anyone to be killed. I don't want to be killed. But you know, Olivia," she said, "this is not a new idea. Sometimes people have to die to bring about something that matters. You know that."

"No, I don't know that!" I said. "I thought we were fighting to save kids in Vietnam from napalm, not to kill somebody else."

"We have to do what it takes to save those kids," she said, "and if Americans die—well, they're probably helping to bring about the war. We're all helping, even I'm helping. There I am"—she smiled sadly and shook her curly head—"adding to the luster of Pierpont Morgan."

I put down my fork again. I had not yet eaten any potatoes and was looking forward to them. "How can you love the drawing of a human being, and not the human being herself?"

"The drawing is nothing," Helen said. "When this civilization is gone and someone finds one scrap, it won't be one of those drawings. It will be this napkin or a cigarette ad." She pointed to the cash register near us, with a display of cigarettes next to it.

"So?"

"So—everything disappears. No one person matters that much."

But the drawings spoke to me, indeed, of the value of one person, at one moment. Nearly all the figures were busy being ordinary. "No," I said. "No, no, no."

Helen said, "Think of the woman with the big wide dress that I copied. If she died fifteen minutes after this drawing was made, it wouldn't change the drawing."

"That has nothing to do with it!" I stopped eating. Our conversation made no sense. I couldn't even follow it. "So, you'd kill?" I said.

There was a long pause. "No," Helen said. "Well. I hope I don't have to. But if it is the only way, and I have to—then yes. To say the government has to change."

"But you said 'say,'" I said. "That's talking—how is that not just talking? Like literature? Like poems? Like those drawings, damn it! The death of one person wouldn't stop the war—it would just make a point, badly. Isn't it better to make it in words?"

"Action brings more action," Helen said. "Action against me, maybe. What brings action is action, not just commentary."

She arranged her knife and fork at the side of the plate. "As long as action follows action, there's a chance for change. That's what we have to do, start chains of action."

There was nothing more to say. I knew Helen had no money. I paid the check and we walked slowly back to the apartment to hear that Nixon would be president.

eight

Jean Argos

By the end of the long evening of the dinner party, I'm thinking—nervously—that Olive and I may become friends. She makes everyone do what she wants when she gets hurt. I admire that—except for what she does to Joshua. But who knows anything about somebody else's marriage? Later, though, I decide she would disapprove of me for sleeping with Zak. He calls me right away. We're both busy, but we see each other a few times a week. I wonder how Olive is doing with a bad ankle and a shaken brain, but I don't call. I also keep making up my mind to talk to Zak about Yvonne, but somehow I never think of it when I'm with him.

He tells me that he and Martha were together for most of high school. "She had the best parents," he says, leaning back to look out a window in my kitchen. "They were my friends. I lost them in the breakup. I was a dope."

"Kids are dopes," I say.

"Not always," Zak says. He says Olive will be laid up for weeks. Casts like that are hot and uncomfortable.

"Have you called her?" I ask.

"I don't think she wants me to," he says. "But you should."

So I call. Olive sounds glad to be talking to someone. "All I can do is work," she says. "I can read, I can write—I just can't *live*." She needs crutches to walk, so she can't carry anything or use her hands while standing.

But she says she'd like a visit, and I go over after work, bringing a cold bottle of pinot grigio with some sheep's cheese and good crackers. Olive calls, "It's open," when I ring the bell. The dog, who I have learned is called Barnaby, pushes his nose through the door, and I'm wary for a moment, but he licks my bare leg and leads me to where Olive is stretched out on the red sofa. The crutches are propped nearby. She reaches to squeeze my hand and motions me to a chair. The room is bare without a party. On the low table near Olive's sofa is a laptop. The long table we ate at is covered with books and papers, a radio, a television, old mail.

"How are you managing?" I say. "Are you alone?"

"Mostly. Griff works most of the summer. Martha's in New York, my other daughter's in Philadelphia. She came for a week right after I got hurt."

"Joshua isn't taking time off?"

"Thank God. He drives me crazy."

This has quickly become none of my business. I show her what I've brought, and she waves me into the kitchen for glasses and a knife to cut the cheese. I look into cupboards and find a plate and paper napkins.

"How civilized!" Olive says sarcastically, but I think she's pleased. She sips. She has a slightly rigid way of moving, made worse by the awkward cast, which seems to make any gesture harder, even if it doesn't involve the leg. But she isn't prim. Her gray hair is messy, and her glasses are smudged.

I offer to clean them and she accepts. "Anything else, while I'm up?" I ask, but she shakes her head. She's like a big wooden mario-nette. I wonder how much older she is—five or ten years.

On second thought, she asks for a box of tissues and a glass of water and sends me upstairs to her bedroom for a sweatshirt. "I don't need it now," she says, "but it will get cool before Griff turns up."

When my errands are done, I pick up my glass and sit opposite her. I ask about her work. "Are you a professor?"

She says she writes books and articles about women novelists, mostly early twentieth century. She has a job as an editor and can work temporarily from home. She remembers something else she needs that's on the table, and I go for that, too. Obviously Griff is neglecting her.

"You're writing a book about Benevento?" I ask. The book is on the table—the copy I found in my office.

"An essay."

"Joshua said you knew her?"

She begins to talk about the party and her fall. In a sense, we're already intimate—we've gone through her accident, the ER, and now my pawing around in her things. She's a reserved person, and I have a feeling she talks more easily than she would if we'd met in a more ordinary way. I'm dying to know about Valerie Benevento, and finally I ask again. Olive says, "Oh, Val. Yes, we were friends."

"Were you close?"

"At times," she says.

I persist. "Was she fun to know?"

"Fun. Yes," Olive says. "She'd do stuff. Once we went to a play in New York, and when we left the theater, one of the actors was coming out. He had a small part, but Val said 'That's so-and-so—he played the uncle.' Before I knew it, she went up to him and got his auto-graph, and we ended up having coffee with him."

"A lot of men in her life?"

"A lot of men. That one lasted a few weeks—he was middle-aged. She got bored with him, actor or no."

"It must have been exciting when she published the book," I say.

"Oh yes," Olive says. Something about it makes her uncomfortable, and she changes the subject. She asks about Barker Street, so I talk about the third-floor project.

Eventually, much of the cheese and crackers are gone and we're on our second glasses of wine. "We should eat," Olive says, and begins heaving herself to a standing position.

"I'll get takeout," I say. "But isn't Joshua coming home?"

"Not for hours," she says. "Would you mind eggs and toast? And would you mind cooking it? I'll tell you where everything is."

"Sure. You stay there." But she reaches for the crutches and thumps into the bathroom. Then she perches on a stool in the kitchen with the cast extended, and I follow her directions. There's a basket of peaches and plums, but most are soft and wrinkled. "I'll bring you better fruit," I say. I cut up what's still good for fruit salad.

We eat at a little table with two chairs. It's an old house, but the kitchen is small. On the wall across from me, next to a window that looks out on a tangled backyard, is a framed print, black lines and a red polygon. I've been looking at it for a while without seeing it. "I've seen that somewhere else," I say.

"Seen what?"

"The picture . . . oh. Zak has it." I am so at ease that I've forgotten Zak may be a tricky subject. Or maybe I'm heading straight for the tricky subject.

"Zak?" she says. "Where does he live?" I tell her, and she says, "They bought me that print—he and Martha. They saw the painting at MoMA. I guess he bought one for himself at the same time."

"And framed it and kept it," I say. "He's crazy about all of you. I mean— I don't know what happened. . . ."

Olive is silent for a long time. "You and Zak are lovers?" she says.

I hesitate. "Yes." I wait for her disapproval.

"You seemed like his type," she says. "He likes older women—sorry, I don't know how old you are. . . ."

"Older than Zak!" I say. I have a thought, and suddenly all this feels scary. "Olive, was he your lover too?"

"No," she says firmly. "My daughter was in love with him, and he was a child. More or less. And I was married. More or less." She looks out the window and back at me. "I'd have done it in a minute, otherwise."

We eat. The window is open. There's a breeze, and I hear birds and insects. I stand. "I should wash the dishes and go," I say.

"You don't have to. . . ."

"Of course I do." I put them into the dishwasher. I clean the pan. "Shall I help you back? I'm nervous leaving you this way." I want her solidly on her crutches or, better, on the sofa. "Do you climb the stairs to go to bed?"

"I bump up on my backside," she says. "Griff will be here."

I position the crutches, and she grasps them, stands, and makes her way into the living room, pausing at the table to look over the piles there, her straight back toward me. She's in a dark top and a loose, calf-length skirt. Her feet are bare. I pick up my purse, which has been on the floor all this time. "I'd better tell you what happened," she says then, still facing away.

"If you want to . . ."

"He didn't tell you, did he?"

"He just said he was a dope." I don't particularly want to know what happened between Zak and Martha, so I don't sit down again. I stand in the empty space between her table and the sofa on its dark rug, holding my dilapidated, zipped tote bag. She makes her way back to the sofa, lowers herself onto it, and sits, her back propped against its side, facing me.

"He was her boyfriend for maybe two years," she says. "She'd be in the bedroom doing homework and he'd wander into the kitchen and lean over the counter, talking, while I cooked supper. He stole pieces of raw vegetables. Once he gradually ate an entire raw cauliflower. He was the first boy vegetarian. Is he still a vegetarian?"

"No."

"Well, anyway," Olive says. She's going to make a long story short, I can tell, maybe because I don't sit down or even put down my purse. She tells me that Zak took a filmmaking class and enlisted his younger brother to film him and Martha making love. He'd deceived her into thinking nobody else was in his parents' house, so they did it on the living room floor, where his brother had a good view from an adjoining room. There was music to muffle any sounds from the boy or the camera. The film told a story—Zak played a boy who cheated on his girlfriend with a black girl who appeared only in that scene. Martha—without her consent or knowledge—was the black girl.

"That was almost as bad," Olive says. "The invasion of privacy was the worst—but also, the black girl was just a sex object. We'd never thought Zak was thinking, 'I've got a black girlfriend—look at me with my black girlfriend.' My kids identify as black—they have no choice—but this was different."

Martha and her family found out about the film after Zak showed it in the film class. Martha's face wasn't visible, but students who knew him knew who it was, and one of his classmates told Olive's other daughter. The teacher confiscated the film and destroyed it. Zak was suspended. He had already gotten into college—they were seniors—and the school let the college know. The college questioned him but didn't revoke his admission. "I guess they thought he was worth it," Olive said.

He and Martha were going to different colleges, but they hadn't planned to break up. Now, they did. Olive said, "She went from loving him to hating him while still loving him. It was a hard time for my girl."

I listen. I drop my purse to the floor and sit down. I have a date with Zak later in the week. I lower my head and close my eyes.

"Did I just spoil your life?" Olive says.

"No."

It isn't completely different from what I've thought about him from the first. I still don't know if he's told Yvonne he's sleeping with me or if he's still sleeping with her. Bodies aren't private for Zak. He'll never understand some taboos and restrictions that other people feel. But this is not what I expected. I expected—foolishly, I see now—that what happened back then was that he and Olive slept together.

"He went to medical school," I say. "He's a doctor."

"I don't suppose he's filming his naked patients," Olive says. "He was very, very sorry. He said he understood—belatedly—and if not, it wasn't for lack of explanations. The teacher, the principal, his parents, Griff. I couldn't talk to him—I never spoke to him again until the other night."

"So do we forgive him now?"

"I don't think he expects Griff and me to forgive him. You—you have nothing to forgive him for."

"I love Martha," I say. "First sight."

Olive smiles. "She's fine."

"I wish you hadn't told me," I say.

"I'm sorry. It was selfish."

"Oh, you had to. But I wish you'd forgotten for a few more weeks."

"It's been nice for you."

"Gorgeous." I step forward to kiss Olive and hold her close. "I'll be back in a few days," I say. "With fruit."

I leave, intending to break up with Zak, but I don't. I keep Olive too and drop in often during the summer. I never do ask about Yvonne, and after a while I understand that it's because I am afraid Zak would lie to me. That's an upsetting thought, and I don't think it for long. I tell myself I am a good, hardworking woman and I deserve a boyfriend. That it makes sense to enjoy him while I can. Before he takes up with a third woman. I point out to myself that I didn't cast my eye on Zak in the first place because he was so particularly moral, and maybe I'd better put up with whatever that says about me.

A few days after that first visit, Zak and I meet in a Mexican restaurant, then go to his place and make love. We finish and roll apart, spent. After a silence, he asks, "Did Olive tell you the whole story?"

"Yes."

"I thought she would," Zak says.

I am silent for a while. Then, "Zak," I say.

"Yes?"

"When you came to that dinner, you knew where you were going. You knew it was Joshua and Olive's house."

"Of course I knew," he says. "I saw a flyer about the auction at Yvonne's house. I made her bid. I paid."

■

One morning early in summer, I go running before breakfast. At home, while I eat, I scroll through the *New Haven Independent* on my phone. A headline reads TIME OFF FROM BEING HOMELESS, so I stop, and the startling subhead is BARKER STREET'S NEW PROGRAM. This is impossible—how does the paper know? For a moment, I'm afraid without knowing what I'm afraid of. Darlene and I have talked about seeking press coverage—but not yet.

Then I understand that one of our group phoned a reporter, and the reporter happened to be looking for a story. Doing this without my approval or knowledge is outrageous, but interesting: Who on my staff is *this* gutsy? Anger is delayed for a few seconds, and by the time I do get angry (it must be Paulette, and when I have a face in mind, I'm furious with it), I am also impressed—but mostly scared that the story will harm us. The public is irrational when it comes to the homeless. I read it quickly.

As I read, I'm less troubled, because the story seems fine. It's short, and I'm frustrated that I've missed the chance for a longer one later. I wonder if we can stage a ribbon-cutting and get the reporter to come back. But I see no mistakes. Yes, sure enough, there are quotes from "Paulette Strong, assistant director." Then I come to the last paragraph, which says our agency plans to expand the third-floor program to include overnight stays within the next year. Now I'm seriously furious. Jason, Paulette, and I had precisely one conversation about this topic—one vague conversation.

Probably Joshua doesn't read the *Independent*, which doesn't have a print edition. Surely he reads the *New Haven Register* on paper, with his morning coffee, as his father and grandfather did. There will be no story there. Maybe I have a little time. I put my hand on my phone, and then decide an email will be easier and clearer—a couple of respectful paragraphs. I stand up, taking my coffee with me, to go upstairs and type an email to Joshua Griffin on my computer. I'll apologize for the premature story in the *Independent*, in case he's seen it, especially for the last paragraph. I'll make clear that Paulette ("The board's favorite, remember, Griff?" I say out loud, though I don't dare call him Griff to his face) did this. It's another instance of her poor judgment. Maybe the newspaper will run a correction.

When I turn on my computer in the bedroom, I see that a message has just come in from Paulette. The subject line reads "Look!" and the message is a link to the article. She doesn't know she's done anything wrong—or she'll claim she doesn't know.

Then one comes in from Zak. His messages are brief, about scheduling. This one cancels a date, but before I can reply, another arrives that reinstates it but moves it half an hour. I reply and start telling him about the story. By now he knows all about my job. I explain what I plan to say to Joshua, telling myself I'll write a better email if I sort out my ideas first with a friend. But before I can send it, my phone rings. Joshua's number. I say out loud to myself, sternly, "Don't answer." But I do.

As I say hello I start walking out of the room and down the stairs. My heels pound the floor. "I saw the *Independent*," he begins. No "Hello," no "How are you?" As he talks, I walk all the way into the kitchen, take another mug from the cupboard, and pour more coffee into it. I swallow, then put it down and walk some more.

He goes on: "I have to say that you might have discussed—"

"Hold it," I say. I intended to begin with an apology, but now I'm mad. People who call on my cell instead of my work phone, or at least my aunt's old landline, get unadulterated me. I'm in the sweatclothes I ran in. I haven't had a shower. "Can this wait?" I say.

I intend to blame Paulette, to say we have no intention of adding an overnight program.

"I should have explained why letting people stay overnight would be disastrous," Joshua is saying.

"Look, Griff," I am amazed to hear myself say, "I didn't see that story until ten minutes ago. I didn't know it was going to be in there. I don't know every single thing in Paulette's head." I'm talking fast. "I don't have full control over her or Jason, because that's not the kind of program I want to run, with everything checked three times in advance and no mistakes ever. If you want to fire me for not having control, do so—because I never will. Maybe she made a mistake, going to the press, and maybe she didn't, but—"

I am halfway up the stairs again, but now I turn, go down more slowly, return to the table, and sit down with my second mug of coffee in front of me. "I never want to run a program where I've got such tight control that something like this can't happen," I conclude. "*That* would be the disaster."

"It's not just the expense," he continues. "We can't afford round-the-clock staff. And if we could, it wouldn't be a good use of the money. But it's not just that. It's not safe."

"This isn't the time to discuss this, Joshua," I say.

"In theory," he says, "there's no reason why keeping people over-night is a bad idea, but institutions that do it all the time—large-scale, like shelters, hospitals—*think* differently. You can't have now-and-then overnights, especially with this population."

"Joshua, I have a meeting in forty minutes, and I need a shower. I'll talk to you later."

There's a startled pause. "Oh. Well. Well, of course."

I say goodbye, hang up, swallow the last of the downstairs coffee, and walk upstairs yet again. By the time I step out of the shower I'm embarrassed and sorry that I was rude to Joshua Griffin, even if he started it. Yet though I'm sure I've gone about it the wrong way, I give myself credit for supporting Paulette. I'm angry with her, but I didn't say that to Joshua.

I don't speak to Joshua again until I've gone to meetings at two other agencies—where nobody mentions the story. I have no emails about it. I don't know whether to be relieved or disappointed.

It's hot when I get to Barker Street, and I stop for a moment as I step inside. The rooms with their high ceilings are naturally cool, though we don't have AC, besides a few window units on the second floor. Paulette stands in the middle of the main room, talking to one of the community service workers, her narrow body shifting. She's a restless lady. She waves when she catches sight of me, and I nod and point upstairs. She puts up five fingers, meaning "when I get around to it."

When she comes, I sit her down and say, "Don't say anything until I'm done."

"Okay." She shrugs.

"First," I say, "you seriously screwed up." I tell her that Darlene and I decided not to talk to the press until after we talked to the board. I tell her I got an angry phone call from the president of the board that morning. I don't tell her what I said. And I point out that we have no plan to open overnight—we've scarcely talked about it.

"I figured it was likelier to happen if I said it was definite," Paulette says, with a little smile. Her long arms are twined around one knee, which she's raised, and the long heel of her white sandal is hooked on the edge of the chair. Her hair is cut close so I see the good bones of her head and face.

"I told you not to talk until I'm done," I say. I know I have to keep criticizing her until she listens. If I say at the start that I have mixed feelings, she'll hear only praise.

Finally, she asks, "Am I fired?" Even now, she looks defiant and slightly amused. If I fire her, she seems to say, it will only be because I'm dumb.

"Paulette," I say, "I am not sure." I tell her she has serious problems with judgment.

My phone has rung twice while we talked. I tell her when to return, then send her back to work. There are two messages from Joshua, both apologetic. I call him back and he picks up right away, though he's at school.

"I'm sorry!" I say. "I shouldn't have talked that way."

"I interrupted your morning," he says. "It was my fault." Then he says, "You didn't know about the story?"

"That's right."

"You'll have to fire Paulette," he says. "She should never have done such a thing."

"I know she shouldn't have," I say. "I told her. I'll tell her again. But I'm not firing her."

"Maybe one of the other two is still available," he says.

"I'm keeping Paulette," I say.

That afternoon, I tell Paulette she's not fired, but every day she has to tell me what she's done and what she's going to do next. I should have made her do that in the first place. We follow this plan for a few weeks, until we both forget about it.

nine

Olive Grossman

Active, take-charge people are enraged—not merely upset—by confine-
ment. If I hadn't been hurt the night of the dinner party, I might have
been pleasanter to Griff in the following weeks. The party had been
a success up to then. I liked Jean, liked watching the guests admire
Martha, and it's always good to see Lorna Anderson. Zak's arrival was
disturbing, but I was more interested than shocked. If I hadn't been
injured that night, I might have admitted the next day that I'd over-
done rage and hurt feelings in advance of the party. But the cast kept
my mood as well as my leg immobilized. Before the party, Griff and I
had all but agreed to separate—or pretend to be separate in the same
house—and when I was lying on the floor in pain, I sent him upstairs.
He wouldn't forgive that without an apology, but I had no impulse
to apologize to someone whose movements were unimpaired, while I
hobbled and crawled and needed to be waited on instead of managing
others. Griff asked about my needs and comfort as if he were a polite
neighbor. And he continued being elsewhere—to the point at which I
no longer expected to see much of him in the evenings. We slept in the
same bed most nights. A few times, I just didn't bother and remained
on the sofa where I spent my days.

Jean Argos visited me often that spring and summer, sometimes
just dropping in after work, sometimes bringing wine or cheese or
both, settling in for a visit. I was grateful, but didn't like feeling
grateful. I preferred doing things for others. When she brought wine,
I'd send her for a plate and glasses, then follow, thumping along on
my crutches.

"Talk to me about people doing things," I said, on one of those occasions, when we were back in the living room. "Not just sitting around getting fat." My clothes were tight.

She sipped her wine and began to talk about Barker Street. A volunteer, a street guy, had begun working for the program a few hours a week, and Jean had just come from a conversation about him with the assistant director. "Either I should fire her, or she's the best person there," she said. "Joshua wants me to fire her."

"Don't let him push you around," I said.

She looked at me with an odd smile. "He's probably right," she said, "but she makes me think."

"Griff preaches caution, but he takes chances at school."

Jean began walking around, as if *somebody* had to. She looked out the windows. "You need to leave?" I asked.

She turned red and sat down on the arm of a chair. "It's hard to keep still."

"You're telling *me*," I said. Then I heard Griff's key in the front door. I hadn't expected him until late and preferred to keep Jean to myself. He came in carrying two green cloth grocery bags. He had decided to surprise me with a decent meal, walking out of a meeting to do it. That's how we were: not getting along, but with friendly exceptions.

"Hi, Jean," he said.

"Hi, Joshua."

Not that I appreciated the exception. I wanted to be alone—to eat inadequately, nurse grudges, feel sorry for myself, watch an old French movie that Griff would hate. My leg itched under the cast.

After bringing his groceries into the kitchen, Griff slid into a chair. Jean had moved from the arm of her chair to the seat. Propriety increases around my husband.

"Wine?" Jean said, rising, prepared to go for an additional glass.

He shook his head, raised his hand, disappeared into the kitchen yet again.

"Why does she make you think?" I asked Jean. I wanted something to happen in this dead room, where I had accomplished nothing for many days—I wanted *anything* to happen.

"Paulette?" Jean said. "She's certainly not perfect."

"So she—"

"Okay. For example—she held a prayer meeting. Didn't tell me. Man gets up at the prayer meeting, says Jesus ruined his life." She gestured dramatically.

"You were there?"

"I didn't even know about it until the next day. Jesus ruined his life, and he gets into a screaming argument, and there's a fistfight, but nobody is hauled off to the hospital, and they decide to have a meeting to talk about religion once a week."

"Which is good," I said.

"Of course."

"What's good?" Griff asked, coming with his usual ice water. She told him.

"But she didn't tell you in advance? It's the same thing, Jean—"

"She's worth it."

"People like that are not fixable," Griff said. "What if it had been a knife? Or a gun?"

"Same as what?" I asked. It turned out that the woman, Paulette, had talked prematurely to a reporter about something they were doing, something Griff opposed. He sat straight up in his chair, and his skin took on a certain dull color it gets when he's upset. Jean was smiling, relaxed.

"We'll discuss this," Griff said.

Jean poured herself another half glass and held out the bottle to me. I shook my head. Now I didn't want another half glass's worth of conversation. She drew her feet out of her shoes and tucked them under her.

"So, Joshua," she said, "did you finish *Bright Morning of Pain*?"

"Not yet," he said.

I wondered if he even had a copy. I had mine, and Jean had hers—had he bought *two* used ones? I wasn't planning to lend him mine again.

"The end is exciting," she said. She tapped her knees, which were thick, in snug leggings. She wore leggings and a loose gray shirt. "I won't give it away. But—the character of Harry . . ." She sat forward. "Did you get to that part? I'm not sure we're supposed to like Harry, but I did."

I was silent. It's never smart to want something to happen without deciding what kind of something. Asking about the character of Harry in *Bright Morning of Pain* was not a good idea.

"I mean—is this just coincidence?" she said. "I know Olive knew the author, but—"

Griff and I didn't help her. He brought his glass to his lips and took it away without drinking. He stood.

"I bought chicken," he said. "I'll go cook it."

"I don't feel like chicken," I said.

Jean looked at me. "Don't be cranky," she said. "It's not our fault you're hurt."

Secretly, I liked this. "'Our'?" I said, as if I were accusing them of sexual malfeasance, which I was not.

"I mean, the way Harry advocates violence—and then what happens. In a way it's all his doing, and yet—"

Griff set down his glass on the table. He looked at Jean. "I have not finished reading the book," he said. There was tension in his cheeks. "But I am aware of the passages you refer to." It was thirty years now that Joshua Griffin had been aware of those passages without reading the book. Maybe we'd never have separated for those long years if he hadn't been aware of those passages.

"Yes," he said, "Olive knew the author. The character of Harry, I believe, is an African American man from Hartford, Connecticut, who, from what I understand, turns up late in the book. He influences the main character. He is the son and grandson of clergymen, but he has refused to go to divinity school and has become a peace activist, going so far as to . . ." He picked up his glass again, brought it once more to his lips, and again set it down without—as far as I could see—swallowing. "He participates in a violent episode and is found not guilty on a technicality, but it is his act that leads to the final events of the book." This time he picked up his glass and drank. "Because he influences the main character, who becomes violent in imitation of him."

He drank again. "I have never lived in Hartford," he said. "The rest is true, Jean. Make of it what you will."

"But I *liked* him," she said. "I respected him. The times they lived in . . ."

"No," I said, and sounded not just cranky to my own ears but angry. "No, it's not true. Griff, you've never actually read those scenes and you don't know if they're true or not—maybe the summaries you've heard sound true, but *it isn't true!*" I gasped like a crying child.

"Perhaps," Griff said. He stood, turned toward the door, as if Jean had announced her imminent departure. Indeed, she stood—I was furious with her for complying, though I wanted her to go—and she came forward to hug me where I sat. Her bare arms and hands, touching my arm as she crouched, felt cool and regretful, as if her arms were wiser than the rest of her, and I stretched to embrace her.

"I'll see you soon," she said, and left.

I lay back, watching Griff—visible from where I lay—close the front door. His back—clean white shirt, dark brown neck, gray hair— disappeared into the kitchen. I thought we were going to fight.

And it began as I expected. "What's her game?" he said. "Likes the character of Harry! I'm supposed to admire that? Or be grateful?"

"She doesn't know us," I said, now exhausted. "She doesn't even know how far back we go."

"Of course she does. She met Martha. She knows we didn't meet last week."

"People don't understand about fictional characters," I said.

"Ollie," he said.

"I know," I said. "All these years, you didn't read it. That was prob- ably better."

"But I knew. I knew what you told Val." He sat down opposite me, his hands on his knees, his face wide-open. "I never expected to like the book," he said.

"Why don't you finish it?"

"Because I know what happens," he said, and the wild, open expression I'd seen disappeared. "I know what I did."

"It's fiction, Griff."

"Don't give me that."

"But it is," I said. "It's a work of imagination."

"You told Val—" He leaned back, and his fingers played with the upholstered surface of the arm of the chair.

"And she *imagined*. . . ."

"It's probably worse than I think." His face held so much pain, I couldn't have been angry with him, no matter what was going on.

"Yes, it's worse," I said at length. "But it isn't you."

"But it is."

I stood, laboriously, with the crutches. "It's not. Harry tells Hannah Cohen that violence is the only way, and no one else says it so clearly to her. Black critics protested when the book came out—Harry is one of only two violent people in the book, and he's never sorry. You know that's not what happened in reality."

"Why are you getting up?"

"I need to pee," I said. Then something gave me the grace to say, "In fact, I do feel like chicken."

"I'll go cook," he said. What would people do if it weren't for food? Food and dogs. Barnaby followed Griff into the kitchen. Without food and dogs, we would live in the past and the future. I thumped my way into the bathroom. We ate. But before the meal was over, we were quarreling yet again, this time about Annie, who had a boyfriend Griff considered worrisome. Then he interrupted himself to say, "The night you got hurt—the night of that damned dinner party—"

"It was a good dinner party," I said. "Until I fell."

"It was not," he said. "Before it, you said you wanted me to move upstairs."

"You said that," I said.

"But you said it was what you wanted." We were in the kitchen, still. The food had been only adequate, and we remained sitting at the table when it was done, maybe each hoping the other would imagine into being a dessert, an elegant cheese tray, something. "It wouldn't be too expensive," he said. "There was that door at the foot of the stairs. It's still in the basement. I don't need a whole kitchen upstairs. A micro-wave and a coffeepot will do."

"Is that what you want?" I asked.

"I think it's what you want," he said.

"Maybe you're right," I said. "Maybe we should just take a break. At least bring the TV up. I don't like television much. I don't like sports." After I was injured Griff had brought it down, and on a few evenings we'd watched together. Now I wanted it back in Annie's old room, where it had been for years. It was half true that I didn't like sports. In some moods, I looked forward to watching with him.

■

Helen's mysterious Raz turned out to be a man in his late twenties with a thin, light brown beard, patches of skin showing through it, and a bald spot starting on the top of his head. In the spring of 1969 he could often be found in the apartment. He couldn't learn my name, neither Olive nor Olivia. Helen was respectful in his company—maybe awestruck—and when I heard him argue politics, I saw why. He kept the history of the war in his head and could be specific and persuasive when even Helen could not. "The French did that," he'd say. He remembered Vietnamese place names and knew how to pronounce them. If he'd looked at me, I'd have become his disciple too—maybe. Maybe he could tell I was not worth his time.

Helen was bitter and defeated as the war continued and protests became less common. I knew she missed school. At rallies, radical groups interrupted the speeches, screaming destruction. Helen grew bonier, moving about the apartment with books or papers in her hands—never, in those days, with food or kitchen utensils or even sheets or clothes. Daily life had become pointless, along with reasoned discussion. Angie moved out, and Mallon moved in. Eli had found a lively young woman who took up much of his time, and I gradually stopped hearing from him.

I kept to myself that summer, working at the camp during the day and at the restaurant in the evenings—a little place in Murray Hill where the owners cheated me but spoke to me kindly, as if I was a stupid but loved relative. Some old men came in every night, alone with a book or newspaper; ate a chop, meatloaf, or Friday fish; and left tips calculated to the penny. The place was never crowded but never quite empty.

At the start of my senior year, I rented a small apartment in Brooklyn. Finally all my clothes were in one place: all at once, I moved out of both Helen's apartment and my parents'. I decided to go to graduate school for English literature, irrelevant as that sounded, and felt almost as if I'd decided to enlist in the army: submitting to a second university's rules and practices, getting an advanced degree, was acceptance of the prevailing system. But I wanted to read more books, and with a fellowship, I could do that. I took the GREs, applied to programs.

I kept the job at the restaurant. I had a roommate, an art major I'd found through a notice on a bulletin board, but she worked two jobs and often slept in her studio. Patrick and I had stopped singing together, I'd left the chorus, and I had little to do with other students at Brooklyn—except that I suddenly saw more of Val Benevento.

The interactions of people on a campus change when a new term starts and they walk different paths at different hours. Val and I had two classes together in the fall of our senior year—one a lively course in which we read most or all of James Joyce—and I found myself seeking her out for more conversation as we left the classroom; or she might propose coffee or a meal during a gap in both our schedules right after class. Val was taking a course that required going to plays around the city, and she talked me into attending a couple of obscure off-Broadway plays with her. She slipped into the role vacated by my mother when I moved out: she told me what was wrong with me, such as how long to wear my hair so it had the romantic sweep I wanted without looking uncivilized.

"But I spend my time protesting the war. I *should* look uncivilized," I said.

"Nobody needs to look uncivilized," Val said firmly. I laughed and felt looked after. I had my hair trimmed. In fact, we hardly ever discussed the war—which made me guilty but happy.

Val also had opinions on my love life, though hers, I pointed out, was more of a mess than mine. She didn't approve of Eli when she heard about him, but she too fell for older men, and they too weren't serious about her. One afternoon over coffee, she put her hands on the table and said, "Do you think we could get together some time with Helen?"

"Helen?" I didn't think she ever gave Helen a thought.

"Well, you know Helen and I were friends when we were little kids— best friends. I know she's terribly, terribly pure and busy"—Val shook her curls, and they fluffed out and resettled—"but maybe we could— oh, I don't know, have lunch? Go for a walk? Give me her phone number."

I most certainly didn't know Helen and Val had ever been friends. I seriously doubted that it was true. But I gave Val Helen's number.

And I asked Helen about it, when I stopped at the apartment on my way to a meeting that weekend. She was asleep when I got there. She awoke and washed her face; she gulped coffee.

"Friends?" she said. "Her sister was my babysitter."

I remembered then that she'd said that before. She was silent while she pulled on some clothes and took another swallow of coffee. "We were in kindergarten, maybe first grade. Her sister was in charge of us after school." She disappeared into her bedroom for something, but when she came out, she stood still, as if reliving something she liked thinking about. Her voice softened. "Val was bigger than me, so

I thought she was older. She was bossy. She didn't get what I meant. I'd say something, and she'd look at me. But sometimes we played in the park. Her sister would talk to her teenage friends and we'd pretend to be lost, running into criminals, getting our lives saved. We were always getting killed by bears."

I don't know if Val ever called Helen, if they got together. But I'd detected in Helen's voice something I felt too: you couldn't quite dismiss Val; you couldn't quite do without her. I wanted her approval. I wanted her ideas—I wanted to hear the next surprising thing she'd say, about me or something else.

And then the term ended, and in the spring term of senior year, I didn't see her often; plenty was going on elsewhere. We continued to have a meal together now and then, but time with her made me restless, as if I were in the wrong place, as if there was something I should have been doing elsewhere.

My roommate and I didn't have a television set, and I didn't subscribe to a newspaper. In November, the news had broken of the American massacre, more than a year earlier, of hundreds of defenseless Vietnamese civilians—including children—in the hamlet of My Lai. But it broke slowly. Seymour Hersh, an independent journalist, discovered that the Pentagon was investigating a case involving a Lieutenant William Calley, and he gradually learned what Calley and his soldiers had done. Calley eventually served three years for ordering and participating in the massacre of more than five hundred people. When Hersh broke the story, newspapers resisted it. It was published obscurely in mid-November, but a week or so later it became well-known, and Mike Wallace of CBS interviewed a soldier who talked about being ordered to kill men, women, and children, and who did so. "And babies?" Wallace asked—again and again—and the soldier, each time, said, "And babies."

I heard about My Lai from my parents, who saw the interview. "Babies!" my mother all but screamed when she phoned me, close to tears. After that, if she continued to think my participation in antiwar protests was foolish, she didn't say so.

That weekend, I once again rode the IRT uptown and found Mallon, Raz, and some people I didn't know in the living room. Helen—they pointed when they saw me—was in the bedroom. I knocked, heard nothing, and went inside. She was in bed and sat up. She wore a loose T-shirt—blurry printing of a date, a raised black fist. "What is it?"

"I'm sorry—did I wake you?"

She shrugged in the direction of the living room. "What are they doing?"

"Smoking pot, planning something—I don't know."

"Olivia, I want to die," she said.

"Because of—"

"I knew, we all knew," she said. "It's not that. It's not, Olivia. This is just the My Lai that somebody found out about. There are hundreds. Every town in Vietnam is My Lai. We killed those babies, Olivia. And the army's protecting the guy. This happened months and months ago. Do you understand that?"

"I understand."

My parents had blamed the soldiers. Helen didn't. "The soldiers didn't do this—the people ordering them to go there did this. The system that brutalized them. You and I did this."

The window shade was pulled low, and the room was smelly. "When did you eat?" I asked.

"You're always talking about food," Helen said, but she smiled a little. "Did you come to save me again?"

"Maybe I did," I said. I had come to find out what I should be thinking, to catch up, but also to save her—maybe even to save her by joining her. For once, I didn't think that if I could only forget about the war and lead my life, I'd be better off. Now—like Helen—I knew it would be reprehensible to forget, and of all my acquaintances, Helen was the one I trusted to know what we should do about it, even though she scared me. I didn't think she meant what she said about violence. Helen was kind. What My Lai proved was simple: the system—the organization of people and power and money; the military industrial complex, if you will—was not fixable.

Again, I began spending time in the apartment, not living there but making myself heard at meetings, visiting when I could. Helen didn't encourage me, but she didn't stop me either. She was sleeping with Raz, and often as not they'd disappear into the bedroom. I'd watch her walk through a room, mostly wearing clothes you couldn't go outside in, looking bereft, even confused. It was hard not to seize her by the shoulders and wrestle her out of there.

One night, I saw no one but Raz. He was leaving but said, "Stay. Helen knows you're here." I sat there reading. There was silence when I knocked at her door, so I returned to my book. The evening passed. In more than one way, it was too late—too late for me to be where I didn't belong, too late to become whatever Helen was or to persuade her to change.

As I was finally packing up, Helen came out of the bedroom, pulling something around herself to keep warm. When she saw me, she leaned on a chair back. "You're still here. I fell asleep."

"I'm just going."

"I'm weak," she said. I thought she meant weak from hunger, but when I said, "Oh, for heaven's sake, let's find you some food," she said, "Not weak like that."

"Then what?"

"It's hard to be tough," she said. "We weren't raised that way. It's not—natural. Raz thinks I'm not making progress."

"What kind of progress?"

"Something's coming up. He wants me to be part of it, and I'm trying. It's harder than I thought, Olivia."

"You mean—"

She stood. "Never mind. Wait a minute—I'll be right back." She went back to the bedroom. I waited ten minutes, then left. I was not mugged on the subway. The night was cold, and I got home late. In the morning, it was a relief—a guilty relief, despite my resolution—to turn my attention to a paper I was writing about Jane Austen, who knew about friendship and loyalty. I knew Helen eventually came out of that room, expecting to see me.

Griff used to say he saw me for the first time at a march, but I don't remember that. I noticed him at a peaceful sit-in at a draft board. I noticed him watching Helen. We were all arrested. By then, this was routine. Helen was out in front, screaming. Griff talked to her and then to both of us: a black guy, not very tall but tough-looking, with lots of hair and a brisk, purposeful way of moving. We were released late that evening. He was with a woman, and the four of us ate hamburgers in the middle of the night. The food was pretty good, and I watched Helen eat—greedily, that time. I also watched Griff eat: his neat, precise fingers on the hamburger bun, his lips taking civilized sips of coffee. I didn't think the woman was his girlfriend because of the way he looked at Helen. As if I were her mother, I wished I'd washed and combed her.

The woman with Griff had a beautiful, big Afro—even bigger than his, which was big—and glasses. She looked sleepy. I thought she disapproved of Griff for eyeing a white woman. Griff—it was how he introduced himself; I didn't know his actual name for weeks—told us about the school where they were both student teachers, a high school in Staten Island. "All the kids are white," he said.

"Do you hate them?" Helen said. I was startled.

"Hate them? God, no."

"The Black Panthers—"

"Do not all hate white people, no," he said. He told us he had friends in the Panthers but had not joined. He was thinking about it, he said. His parents would be distressed. "Maybe I've already distressed them enough," he said, "but maybe I have to do it."

"But the kids in your school," Helen said. "Do you like them *too much*?"

He looked puzzled. I was sitting next to Helen.

"I love people too much," Helen said. "This is a problem I have. I start with love. I have to learn to start with caution—to be cautious, to leave room for hatred."

It was very late, and I knew Helen would say anything if it were late enough, but this seemed remarkable. I didn't change the subject but tried to shift it slightly. "You don't love everyone," I said. I remembered how she used to see things from every viewpoint, when we took those windy walks through Brooklyn.

"I'm not mushy, no," she said.

"But eventually, you forgive everyone," I suggested.

"It's not good," she said.

"Why not?" I said. Then I said, "Not Adeline. Remember?"

"No," Helen said, "not Adeline."

"Who's Adeline?" the other woman asked. She probably thought Adeline was a rival for love, but Helen would have forgiven a rival. Adeline was the woman who had wanted a color TV and stopped letting Helen tutor her child. When I explained this, Griff smiled and said, "Oh. You can't forgive ideological impurity."

Helen stared at him. "But that's what Raz says is wrong with me—I do forgive."

"Apparently not," he said.

"That's why I asked you about hating white people," she said. "I think if we're going to make any progress, we have to do some hating. Black people have so much reason—I thought it might be easier."

"I was raised to look forward to Brotherhood Week," Griff said. He'd grown up in New Haven.

"Church?" Helen said.

"Indeed." He wiped his long fingers, one by one, on the paper napkin. "I do not hate children, no," he said. "But I don't find it hard to hate General Westmoreland. Or whoever is in charge."

"Could you kill him?" Helen asked quickly. She pushed her food aside and crossed her arms on the sticky table. How many times had I seen that gesture, on a table similarly sticky? I wanted to go home—somewhere—and sleep. Griff had a car and had offered to drive us to Morningside Heights once we'd retrieved it from wherever he'd left it that morning.

"I'm not sure that killing a general makes tactical sense," he said. "But I could kill, of course. I could kill some of these soldiers who rape and kill civilians."

"Really?" Helen said. His friend got up and went to the ladies'. I didn't know if she was disgusted or just bored and sleepy.

"Really. No question."

"How?"

"I think if I had the chance," he said seriously, "and I was sure who they were, I could do it any way you like."

It didn't make me think ill of him. It's hard, decades later, to remember how things felt at that time: how weary and angry we were and yet how excited about the possibility of big change—of revolution. I too thought revolution was the only way to change, and I kept returning to protests, or just to Helen's apartment, because I didn't want to be one of those who failed to see the revolution coming. It was an exhilarating thought, and there was little else to be exhilarated about. The people who opposed us—who approved of the war—hated us and were excited about nothing. We hated them and also were excited. We were sure that they too—that everybody—would benefit from change.

Things would become chaotic, we thought, and committees of ordinary people would start to organize life—without killing, without racial prejudice, with help for those who were poor. What we envisioned—what I think I remember—wasn't like the Russian Revolution. It was a coming together of people of goodwill, of sense. Unique to this period in my life was the feeling that soon things might actually be new. Schools would change; what we read and thought and how we worked would change. It sounds naïve, but it wasn't, not entirely, and some of what changed in my life then has never reverted.

When Griff's friend came back, she put on her coat, and I stood, too. I took our check, went to the counter, and paid it. When I came back, Griff stuffed some money into my hand. He sat down again—Helen had not moved—and continued talking earnestly to her, while his friend and I leaned on a wall in the harsh light.

"This does have to do with being a black man," he said.

"Yes?" Helen leaned toward him.

"I can't participate in powerlessness," he said, "even if I'm squeamish. I must exert power if I have to."

"Would you shoot a gun?" Helen said.

"I have shot a gun," Griff said quietly.

"At somebody?"

"No. Practice." He didn't gesture much, I noticed. When he wasn't talking, he was motionless. There was silence, and then he spoke again. "It would be different if the war didn't involve our country—if we weren't directly involved. We could make nuanced observations. But we don't have that luxury. We oppose it—or we don't oppose it."

Helen stood up then and leaned against me. I put my arms around her. "I oppose it," she said.

I thought Griff might try to walk next to Helen as we left, but he stepped back and put his arm around his fellow teacher, and she leaned her head on his shoulder. His car was a long walk away.

As we drove, Griff tossed a small notebook into the back seat. "Olive, your phone number, okay?" he said. "I need to talk to you." He'd heard me say that my name was Olive, though Helen still called me Olivia.

"Sure," I said, and scribbled it.

Griff had a good lottery number—that topic came up the night we met—so this was after December 1969, when student deferments ended and a lottery determined the order in which young men would be drafted in the new year. Numbers from one to three hundred sixty-five were pulled at random from a box—I believe it was a shoe box—and the following year, men were drafted in the order in which their birthdays came out of the box. The day after the lottery, some men were absent from class—on their way to Canada or home in bed, sick with dread. Some enlisted, to get it over with.

The morning of the lottery, I talked to a quiet young man named Greg in my Victorian literature class, and he told me his birthday: October 18. He was one of those absent the following day. He was right near the top, was quickly drafted, and died in Vietnam. I didn't know him well, but well enough that I could imagine the life he might have led—one of the lives we'd been trying to save, with our marches and protests. And indeed, those activities seemed more and more foolish. How could we have imagined they'd prevent what happened to Greg or to anyone?

When the Weathermen—later called the Weather Underground—mistakenly blew up a building in Greenwich Village with bombs intended for protests, Helen said on the phone, "I envy their certainty."

"Oh, for God's *sake!*" I said. "Two people died!" These were activists we'd heard of; Helen had met one. I hadn't quite believed until then that educated young people like us were constructing bombs.

Helen said, "They should have been more careful."

"Fooling around with that stuff?" I said. "You can't be sure."

"You can be sure." She was quiet. "You can do it right."

■

Griff called me a week after I gave him my number and invited me for coffee. He had questions about the movement in Brooklyn, he said. Later, he would say he liked me from the beginning—he claimed we'd met before—and had found Helen fascinating, but not that way.

When we met on a street corner, he raised a hand to brush hair off my face. It scarcely touched my skin, but in response, I raised my own hand. I meant to touch his sleeve, but he moved his right arm and I touched his hip, the rough canvas of his pants. I felt a sexual charge and reached for his hand, as a child might, to acknowledge something we'd both experienced. Then I saw what I was doing and pretended to be shaking hands. He laughed and hugged me. We went for coffee, and he did have questions, though not about the movement but about my friendship with Helen—how we'd met, what she was like. We didn't sleep together, though sleeping together in those days was almost automatic. I was confused, stunned by desire. I decided he worked for the FBI, investigating potentially violent activists, and that he'd befriended me to find out about Helen.

That spring, in 1970, there were protests at campuses all over the country, especially after the announcement at the end of April that we had secretly been bombing Cambodia. Thousands protested in New Haven when nine Black Panthers were tried for murder. I wondered if Griff had gone home for that and fantasized about going there myself, maybe coming across him. Then he called me again. He had been to New Haven, where violent protests had been expected, though the Yale administration and the Panthers had kept things relatively calm. He said, "I want to know you—but I can't now."

"What are you doing?"

He paused. "I'll call you," he said, and hung up. I was irked, unimpressed. He seemed more self-important than dangerous. But I stopped thinking he was working for the FBI. He couldn't lie, I sensed. That turned out to be true. Nonetheless, he was full of himself, and I didn't bother to think about him.

One rainy night several weeks later, Mallon walked into Helen's kitchen, where the two of us were drinking tea. "Isn't Joshua Griffin a friend of yours?" Mallon asked.

"I don't think so," I said.

"That's his name," Helen said. "That's his real name—*you* know."

"Griff?" I said.

"Yes. From the draft board protest. What happened to him?"

"Shot a pig," Mallon said.

I stood up, startled, and inadvertently knocked over my tea, then was down on the floor with napkins, mopping, as she told Helen what she'd heard. I was excited—I'm afraid it made me feel more legitimate to know someone who'd done this. Some of Mallon's group had joined a protest at a college in upstate New York. A policeman had brought his club down on the head of a young girl, and Joshua Griffin, now in custody, had drawn a gun and shot the policeman in the arm.

"Crazy," Mallon said. "What if he hit the girl?"

"He's not crazy," I said, scrambling to my feet with my sodden napkins. "It will turn out he had a clear shot."

In the next days, I could think of nothing else. Mallon knew only the bare fact, told to her by a friend: a policeman had been shot, not killed; Joshua Griffin had been arrested. I found nothing in the New York papers, and it seemed important to Helen not to make a fuss, positive or negative, about what Griff had done. "Yes," she said, nodding vigorously. "This is what it's going to be like now."

I had imaginary conversations with Griff, in which he regretted without regretting. "I'm sorry this was necessary." I'd seen him only twice but knew what he looked like: the compact way his body moved; the worry lines on his face, made deeper by smoking.

After a week, he phoned me. "I thought you were in jail," I said.

"You've heard something," he said. He wanted to meet for coffee again. We met on a street corner, and for a second I didn't recognize him. He'd shaved and cut his hair. He saw my momentary confusion, touched his head, and said, "Court." We had coffee and doughnuts at a Chock full o'Nuts, sitting way at the end of the counter. He mumbled something I didn't hear. "What?"

"I shot—someone."

"A cop," I said. "I know." Then I said, "How did you get out of jail?"

"I'm out on bail. My father came to that town and prayed with everyone," he said. "The cop's parents . . ."

"I have limited sympathy for the cop," I said.

"No. No," he said. He stirred his coffee. "Look, I need to ask you something. Can I see you again?"

I said, "You asked me out for coffee to ask me if it's okay to ask me out for coffee?" He had an innocent smell—he smelled of schools and libraries and churches, I decided later.

"See you more privately. May I visit you in your house?"

"Sure," I said. I was amused by this formality but liked it. He looked in both directions to make sure our conversation was private, then didn't talk about the shooting but expressed a fear that I would be offended by what he called "my interest in you" because of what he'd done.

I was startled, not so much that he was expressing sexual interest—I knew when he touched me that he found me attractive—as that his interest required this kind of acknowledgment. In our circle, sex was so easy and un-momentous that nobody was surprised when someone suggested it.

"I want to make love to you," Griff said.

I hesitated—but it was what I wanted, too. My roommate was home that night, but he came the next evening. When I opened the door, he stepped into my apartment and pressed me into a long, trembling hug. He kissed me as if he'd been wanting to do it for a long time, not aggressively but with a series of questioning, exploratory, tasting nibbles and thrusts of his tongue. I led him to my bed. I wanted each moment to last, because what if we never did it again? Surely Griff would go to prison.

He was a vigorous lover. I felt beautiful. When we lay sated, he began to talk. "Your friend Mallon. Did you know her real name is Beverly?"

"She's not my friend," I said, but I wanted to hear everything, so after that, I didn't speak. He too was sure he'd go to prison.

"I'm on a bus," he said, "Little town out in the country, no black people except at the university. A demonstration—and when we got there, four of us, it was mostly girls. This sweet little girl I talked to, Kimmy. I had a stomachache, and she smuggled me into her dorm so I could go to the bathroom. We're going to keep it peaceful, for their sakes—and really, there was no reason not to have a peaceful demonstration. We've done some complicated stuff, but this was nothing. Nothing that would make those girls do what they promised their mothers they would not do."

I nodded. I wondered if Kimmy was black or white.

"But I had a gun. I had one." He paused. I was startled but didn't say anything. He said, "I don't know why I brought it—I guess because I usually carry it, and I was so sure we wouldn't be arrested that I didn't bother not to." He paused again. "The fact is, I always had it. I owned it that night we ate those hamburgers, but I'd left it home because I figured we'd be arrested."

I was still silent.

"I am sorry, my darling," he said then. "I must use your restroom." I told him where the toilet was. I lay still. "My darling" was a surprise.

When he came back, he drew a blanket over us, tucked it in around me, and I drew up my knees to lean into him. His skin was warm. We faced each other in the bed, and I thought we might begin touching again, but he kept talking.

"The cops started. They were swinging batons, so we threw what we could pick up—broke some windows. Then six or eight cops started bashing heads. They put twelve kids in the hospital. This one cop— well, I found out later his name was Lambeth, Carlin Lambeth. So when Carlin Lambeth aims for Kimmy, I—"

He stopped. Then he said, "They knocked the gun out of my hand. They beat me up—I was in the hospital. They could have shot me, but they didn't."

"Did you aim carefully, so as not to hurt Kimmy?"

"When he hit her, she rolled away. There were steps, and she rolled down the steps. I thought she was dead. So sweet—and not too bright, so I felt responsible. She was in the hospital. One of the girls—she's brain damaged. Honor student. I thought it would be in the paper, but nothing."

He paused. "He was alone up there," he continued, "looking for the next girl to hit. So I shot his arm. It was easy. I destroyed his hand."

He held me close, and I realized he was crying.

"What is it?" I said, but he shook his head with its shortened curly hair and was silent, holding me as a child might.

Then he said, "Do you have anything to eat?"

I fed him, and we kept talking. A volunteer lawyer was oddly optimistic even then about what would happen to Griff, and in the end —months later—the charges against him were dropped, apparently because the cops feared a trial on account of the injured students. That night, he so regretted what he had done that he almost wanted to go to prison.

I had kept away from discussions at Helen's apartment involving bombs and guns, but not because I was certain—as I am now—that nonviolent protest is the only reasonable option. At that time, the willingness to risk getting hurt and hurting others had come to seem essential ("putting your body on the line"), and an undeviating pacifism seemed naïve. I wasn't violent, but I wasn't proud of that.

I understood what Griff was telling me: maiming a boy's hand for life—Carlin Lambeth, we learned, was twenty-one—was too harsh, and not the province of one citizen but of the society; the proper outcome might have been the loss of his job, prison. But if instead of shooting, Griff had rushed to the nearest police station and filed a complaint about an officer bashing in students' heads, nothing would have happened—and even if something *had* happened, the bashing would have continued. When he shot Lambeth, the other cops turned from the girls to him. So I assumed that Griff's regret—which he asserted again and again—was temporary: nerves. I thought he'd performed a heroic act. Carlin Lambeth might have killed the next young girl.

■

I received my BA soon after that evening. I was going to graduate school, even though part of me believed that artificial arrangements like degrees and universities were about to disappear. I had gotten into Columbia with a fellowship.

Helen, when I told her what Griff had done and how he felt about it, said, "We can't let ourselves think that way." She was suspicious of him because of his regret, and thought I shouldn't sleep with him.

One evening that summer, while waiting for her, I noticed that some papers on the kitchen table were instructions for making pipe bombs. Not that this was unusual. Several years earlier, *The New York Review of Books* had included an exact diagram for making a Molotov cocktail on its cover. I knew Helen and Mallon had handguns, though I hadn't seen them. Raz had bought them on the street.

Others besides Raz and Mallon began turning up at the apartment or living there. When I visited, I was met with unpleasant stares from strangers. Helen would come out of the bedroom, put her hand gently on the arm of the person rigidly holding open the door, and step past him or her to embrace me. She would silently lead me back to her bedroom, or quickly get what she needed, and come with me.

Her hair in those days was bedraggled, and she wore loose men's clothes that made her thin wrists and ankles more noticeable. I knew she and her friends were planning something, but she shrugged. "We're just doing what we always do." She didn't want to take walks and would eat only occasionally. We'd stand talking somewhere, then separate. She and her roommates had had the phone removed because they were certain it was being tapped. I couldn't call her, so I turned up often—stupidly, pointlessly. I still had fantasies of getting her out of there permanently, but I couldn't get her out even for an hour.

Whenever I didn't hear from Griff for a few days, I began to be afraid he'd been called back to court, maybe sent to prison. He was brave and cautious at the same time; I admired the caution and envied the courage. I wondered whether he'd continue to regret what he'd done. Maybe not. Maybe he'd take up violent protest as a way of life. I considered whether I might live that life with him, shoot a gun beside him. It would be unbearable to be given the choice—do this with me, or forget me.

When he appeared on my doorstep or met me in the city—more and more often—I had to adjust my expectations to what he actually was. He never changed his mind about what he'd done. He insisted he shouldn't have done it. Each time, I reassured him: he had done the right thing. He had no choice. He'd shake his head sternly. I'd go back to worrying about prison, worrying that I'd lose him that way. He was sexy and a little scary—which made me fall in love fast—but he was also something else. He had a studio apartment near Columbia, where I was touched to see a neat row of clean socks drying on the shower rod. He had a coffee percolator and made me a cup of coffee: not instant. Once he had a tin of cookies his mother had baked. His parents were upset about his arrest and what might come of that, of course. "They are beside themselves, to put it plainly," he said. He was finishing up a master's degree and hoping that the arrest would not keep him from teaching.

I moved in with him. My lease was up, and I had been on the point of looking for something in Morningside Heights, now that I was going to Columbia in the fall. Griff and I couldn't be apart anyway— the move seemed like the obvious choice. The apartment was too small for both of us, but we managed somehow. I worried even more about the threat of prison now that we lived together. He had become a three-dimensional person who could suffer, not just someone to daydream about.

One evening we ate at a little Italian restaurant on Broadway, and when we stepped outside, I heard a laugh that I recognized. Val

Benevento was walking past, talking intently, head bent, to a man who looked older than we were, in a jacket and tie. We dressed to express our politics in those days: my hair was loose, and I was in jeans and an embroidered peasant blouse I'd bought at a store that also sold drug paraphernalia. Dress codes were loosening; Griff wore a tie to teach in but managed to look like a revolutionary anyway, and he too was in jeans that evening. Val, in heels, spotted me. She hugged me, and we laughed as if meeting this way was miraculous. We introduced the men. She and her date had been to a foreign film—Val made sure to let us know—and were on their way to dinner. "Come with us!" she said, and named their destination, an expensive place. I knew she didn't expect us to say yes; she'd probably even seen us coming out of the restaurant. I wanted her to behave differently, to behave like someone I'd be friends with. Moments of ease and comfort with Val were touched with anxiety (Did she really like me? Was she someone I wanted to like?), and moments of anxiety were touched with love. I could almost discern the friend I cared about. I could see she was nervous, and I liked her more because she cared what we thought of her. Maybe she thought that having a black friend—being friendly to her friend's black boyfriend—would make her a worthier person. But I felt Griff dislike her; he was putting polite pressure on my arm, moving me away. Val wasn't serious. It was what Helen thought: Val was not worthwhile. For once I could see the whole woman, see through the show, and I wanted my lover to like my friend, to discern what I liked about her. Later I could remember nothing about the man except his tie and a thicket of neatly cut straw-colored hair over pale eyebrows. Hair too neatly cut for the era we were living through.

■

From Griff's I could get to Helen's easily, and twice she came to our place. The first time, she walked in while we were eating, late at night. She accepted a glass of water, then a chair and a little spaghetti before she fled. The second time, it was also night, but I was alone. Griff had gone to New Haven to see his parents. I recognized her knock— tentative and defiant at the same time, as if to say she didn't care whether I let her in or not. It was a pleasant, late-summer night after a hot stretch, and the windows were open to the fresh air. I had been reading. Griff had a television set, but I avoided the news.

"Olivia," she said, "I need to tell you something."

"Okay . . ."

"I may have to leave New York. Don't worry about me if you can't find me, okay? And—don't go to the apartment anymore." Helen's hair was longer now, and she looked older, pushing it off her face with a weary, harried gesture. "That's all."

"Your roommates don't want me?"

"Some things are delicate at the moment," she said.

"Tell me what's going on!" I said.

She looked at me, silent—embarrassed for me.

Griff's place—our place, now—had kitchen equipment in an alcove, and after a long silence I went over to the refrigerator for a glass of ice water to give her. Even back then, Griff kept a bottle of water in the fridge. "I have cookies," I said, and put the package on the table between us—chocolate chip cookies. She took one, and then another.

I watched her. "You don't like this life," I said. "Why don't you quit?"

"Oh, stop it."

"You could."

"What would I do? Move in with my parents?"

She was sitting at the edge of the bed, and she shifted to lean on the wall, drawing up her legs, kicking off her shoes. She wore ballet slippers.

"That's not impossible," I said. "But no. Come here. We'll help you figure out what to do next." Even then, I knew Griff was too high-minded to object to this offer, whether he wanted to or not, whether it was even possible or not.

"It's not simple, Olivia," Helen said. "No, I don't like this life. I'd rather have a pretty life."

I knew she was tempted because she'd begun not with the ideological argument but the practical question—where would she go? So I persisted.

"You could go back to school. It doesn't have to be Barnard. The city colleges are all right."

"I'm not a snob about the city colleges," she said.

"You could get a job. We could do this. Stay here. Don't go back."

She stood up. "I'm disappointed in you," she said. "I didn't know how confused you were."

"Never mind, never mind," I said, panicky. I started talking about something else, but she left quickly. At the door, she turned back, took me in her arms, and pressed her face into my shoulder. I clutched her thin back, stroked her hair.

A week later, Griff came into the apartment, where I was putting a meal together, and snapped on the TV without speaking.

I turned. "What?"

"There's something. . . ." He waved his hand impatiently while the newscaster went through stories that were obviously not the one he was interested in. "It was probably the lead story," he said. At the end of the news broadcast, the lead headline was repeated. Armed radicals had held up a bank in Westchester. A security guard was dead, and a policeman was injured. One of the criminals had been identified in photographs as Beverly Mallon. Another woman and two men had fled with her.

In the next days, I wandered the apartment, reading newspapers and exhausting myself with TV and radio reports. Helen's name appeared in the *New York Times* two days after the holdup. There had been at least two guns. Apparently, Helen carried one but did not shoot. Raz, who was arrested the next day, had killed the bank employee. The fugitives were sighted here and there—or people claimed to have sighted them. It sounded as if they were upstate.

Weeks passed. I would walk into a store and think I heard people say, "Helen Weinstein," and maybe I had. I had constant fantasies: seeing Helen in the street; going to her apartment and finding her in bed, hungry; hearing her knock at my door. I didn't go to the apartment. I did little of anything. Griff became withdrawn, maybe jealous. We were too new a couple for something like this. He had just gotten a teaching job, a miracle with all his arrests.

I went to see my parents and Helen's. If my parents were anxious about my black, non-Jewish boyfriend, they didn't say so, and even

Helen's apolitical parents looked nervous but wished me luck. They wept and hugged me, longing for news. Riding back to Manhattan on the subway, I noticed I no longer had trouble believing in nonviolence and regretted my impatience with Griff on that topic. A moment later, I decided I should have been at Helen's side in that bank, shooting along with her, destroying the system that killed and oppressed.

Those weeks, I was angry with Helen, and also with anyone who attempted to comment on or even mention her. Has a piece of your private life ever become public? Suddenly, you are no longer the expert on your own friend, your own family member. Everyone has an opinion, and yours is irrelevant. Nobody got Helen right, and at first I said so everywhere and was pulled into pointless arguments. Nobody deserved to judge her. But I judged her.

■

My torn ligament, the summer after Griff's dinner party, had nothing to do with old age, but because I was past sixty, I thought of it as a sample of what was to come, and that made my mood even worse. Everyone irked me. Jean, my new friend, was easiest to take. Others tried to help— my colleagues at work, writer friends, neighborhood friends—but each had irritated or disappointed or bored me at least once in the past, and I punished them now in my helplessness. My sister phoned often. She's a clinical psychologist; she lives in San Francisco. My brother, a New York lawyer, emailed. But I didn't feel like talking to them.

Jean was present when I got hurt and thus seemed to understand. And she'd just read the book I had to write about—an assignment that became more urgent as the weeks passed. At first I wasn't pleased that she'd read a book that was almost my private property (now that it had mostly been forgotten), but one Saturday, when I was finally walking around outdoors again and we met for coffee, she said, "In *Bright Morning of Pain*, the characters itch."

I laughed.

"They're always scratching mosquito bites or noticing a rash. Nothing else is like all that scratching. Did Valerie Benevento have skin trouble?"

I didn't know, but I knew what Jean meant. Itching had nothing to do with love or politics. *Bright Morning of Pain* is one of those books that's about a slightly tidier and more dramatic existence than any we know. All events are life-changing. I hadn't noticed Val's lapse on the topic of itching, but I too relished certain unstudied gestures that seemed to have slipped in by mistake, messing up the literary smoothing.

I always tried to make Jean talk about Barker Street. She resolved not to, I knew, worried that I'd tell Griff—I didn't—but then she did talk. That summer, they were getting ready to open rooms where clients could go for privacy. They were also just doing what they did, coaxing people into entering the building, eating a sandwich, accepting a ride to the health center.

Jean thought her fellow workers were hilarious and repeated to me the jokes they told her, which I rarely found funny. When I could go, she brought me there—big spaces, tall windows. The agency accepted the logic of its users, and I saw that running it, Jean had become both less and more sensible. She knew that feeling is rarely logical, and that it's undeniable.

All this, I knew, would suit Zak. Jean suggested that the four of us go out to dinner at a new Indian restaurant, and I wanted to do it. I was sure Griff would say no, but you could never guess where Griff's conscience would take him. The evening after Jean made the suggestion, he and I watched a Red Sox game, with the TV still on the big table in the living room, even though I'd said I wanted it upstairs. I was on the sofa, with the dog on the carpet near me.

I told him Jean's proposal.

He quickly said, "Zak?"

"Yes."

"She's going with Zak?" I had spoken during a commercial, but the game began again. The other team was batting, and he paused until each pitch had been resolved.

"Yes."

"Jean Argos and Zak Lilienthal," he said. "This is my fault. They wouldn't know each other if I hadn't been persuaded to have that cursed dinner."

"Jean's happy. I suppose Zak is." There was a pause until, again, the ball was no longer in the air. He watched from a straight chair at the big table; during commercials, he was reading a long, official report. I had reread *Bright Morning of Pain* that week, and my activity was making a list of pages I had marked, using a code.

"Does she know—?" he said.

"About Martha? I told her," I said. "Jean can keep her mouth shut. Should I have asked Martha's permission?"

"No. What did Jean think?"

"She's still seeing him."

He said, "She's casual about trouble."

I considered. "It's why I like her."

"Me, too. Up to a point," he said. "Let's go to dinner. He'll behave if he knows we're keeping an eye on him. We owe it to her."

His face became abstracted. Griff was so familiar to me that I knew not just what he was thinking but what he was doing about his thoughts: directing himself not to draw conclusions about Zak, no matter what took place, as a judge might admonish a jury to dismiss from its collective mind what the law didn't consider pertinent.

Now I wanted to prolong the conversation. We sounded like Griff and Ollie, for once, even though I still hadn't figured out how to write that essay.

Then Griff said, "Maybe it's okay to keep the TV down here."

"No, I need to work at night," I said quickly.

"You could work in your study."

"I can't. You know that."

He was silent. Then he said, "And you know—it's about time we had that wall broken down, enlarge the kitchen."

"What made you think of *that*?" I said. "That's all I need, car-penters! Griff, I really meant it about taking a break. We're just not together right now."

Before the dinner with Jean and Zak, I went away for a week—to the Cape with Martha and Annie. Griff was too busy to come; school was starting soon. "If you'd gone earlier . . ."

"But my ankle. Which I wrecked at your ridiculous party."

"I'm not blaming you," he said.

"You don't like vacations anyway," I said.

"That's true."

"I mean," I said, "I'm going without you not because we're separated but because of scheduling conflicts."

"We aren't separated," Griff said. Once a couple has tried separation, it's too easy to think of it again.

"Well," I said, "we are separated."

"We're eating meals together. We're even going out with friends. Friends of a sort."

"We're people who live apart but get together to eat," I said.

He didn't answer. He might have pointed out that we slept in the same bed, but that happened only sometimes. I knew he was too upset to speak, and I had let it happen. How could I? I didn't know. I looked at him, his worry lines, his expressive eyebrows. I thought that I was being ridiculous, but I didn't say so. For the first time all summer—an exaggeration—I cherished Griff, the consistency with which the man was who he was. But it was no help.

When I came home from the Cape, the television was back upstairs. Now, again, I heard the faint sound of the crowd at a game—the ups and downs of the announcers' patient or resigned or excited descriptions, but not the words—and Griff's occasional cries of dismay or pleasure.

Joshua Griffin

We are not separated. When Olive is away, I feel her absence whenever I am home. We spend most of our time in the house apart—she downstairs, I upstairs—but I feel her through the floorboards, hear her indignant mind, seething and justifying and reconsidering and seething some more. There are thoughts she comes to in a moment that would take me a week, but then she thinks something else a moment later.

When she comes home from the Cape—loud, sandy, sunburned, tired—she likes me better. That comes from being with Martha and Annie, who like me just fine. Neither has ever allowed either parent to criticize the other—they took that position early and have never changed it. I know Olive didn't spend the week complaining about me. She comes home with both girls on a Sunday, in the late morning, and after lunch, she drives them both—thoughtful Martha and impetuous Annie, both gleaming with youth and loveliness—to the train station. They kissed me with joy, and I joyfully held them close.

When Olive comes in again, alone, I'm washing the lunch dishes. I turn from the sink, wiping my hands on a kitchen towel. She still looks more like a traveler than a woman in her own house, dangling her car keys, her graying hair windblown.

"I'm glad you're home, Ollie," I say.

"Me, too."

"But it was good?"

She leans on the wall. I say, "Let's talk in the living room." I pour two glasses of water, and she follows me. We sit, I on the sofa, she on a chair.

"Olive," I say. "Please. What is wrong?"

She is quiet for a long time. "I want you somewhere else," she says, but she sounds tentative, as if she's reading a note someone has passed her that she doesn't understand.

"Why? I want to be with you."

"I don't think so," she says. "You love the idea of me. I think when you're somewhere else and something makes you think of me, you have great admiration for the idea of me. But when you're home, it's the same. You have an idea of me. You're not having to do with the actual person."

I consider whether this might be true. "Isn't that true of any two people? We can't read each other's thoughts."

"I can read yours," she says.

"I don't think so."

"Sometimes."

"Maybe." I put my glass down on the table next to me. There is no coaster, so I put it on top of a folded newspaper. "I don't want to put up the old door at the foot of the staircase."

"Neither do I," she says. "It was a stupid idea. We'll go on as we are."

"So we're not separated?"

"It's easier for me," she says, "to think we are. I expect less of you. Be my housemate."

"What would be different," I say, "if you felt that I'm your husband?"

She doesn't answer.

ten

Jean Argos

I like a guy who speaks. Too much history with the other kind. You know what I mean.

Jean: Blahblahblahblahblahblahblahblah.

Man: Blah.

Jean: Blahblahblahblahblahblahblahblah.

Man: Blah.

Right away, talking is one of Zak's good points. Possibly he talks too much. Zak has an opinion about everything in my life. He wants to hear about my job, especially Joshua Griffin, and these are conversations he goes back to. "No," he says one morning—I've stayed over at his place—and it takes me a while to realize he is disagreeing with himself. With what he said the night before about my life. "Griff argues, but he's really on your side."

"He thinks I'm a nut," I say.

"I don't think so."

It's a weekday morning, and we're hurrying to shower and dress, but he starts talking about Joshua and himself. I know this is a hard subject. Joshua was Zak's imaginary father—the one who took an interest and could be a bit stern for Zak's own good. His actual father, he says, was shy, out of his depth with such a loud and noticeable son. Joshua was a history teacher then, and he helped Zak with assignments.

"More than he helped the girls," Zak says. "He was crazy about me."

"Then why did you—?"

"I know. I must have known he wouldn't like it. I was looking forward to the scolding, I think, and then the understanding."

"You thought he'd *understand* why you secretly filmed his daughter having *sex*?"

"He's a humanist," he says. "A mensch." He leaves the room and returns with his shoes. "I thought Martha would be mad-slash-not-mad. She'd think my film was brilliant. But I should've written a story on paper, not made a film with actors. It had to do with race too, which I thought they'd love, but, oh boy."

As we're heading out to our cars, he suggests that we try to arrange a dinner with Joshua and Olive. I see that he wants more than anything to get their friendship back. Part of my appeal is my connection with them. I'm not offended—I know he likes me for myself, as well. Why not use what's there to be used? I too think making friends with Joshua and Olive would have benefits. More than that. Zak, who is at ease with bodies of all sorts in all situations, is entirely open but not particularly intimate, and I've rarely had close friends. The dinner party at Joshua Griffin's gave me a massive dose of intimacy of more than one kind, and much that I do in the months after it is an attempt to get some more—to make friends with Olive. I broach the question of a dinner with her, and she says she'll get back to me, which sounds like no—but she says yes. We make a date to meet at an Indian restaurant.

Our dinner is almost at the end of summer. Zak bikes over to my house when he gets off work. I live near Edgewood Park, so I take my own bike from the garage and we ride in the park for a half hour. Then we go to bed. The sex isn't right. Zak is too exuberant, all but manic. Nervous. Then we're late. We shower fast and dress fast, and I feel alone. I'm with someone who's not particularly aware of me, just contemplating his evening with powerful people. We take my car, since he came on his bike, and it's like I'm the taxi driver.

Joshua and Olive are seated side by side, staring at the door of the Indian restaurant, looking tense amid red-and-tan cloth hangings, glints of gold. Zak holds the door open and I walk in first, beneath his arm. I'm in a turquoise sleeveless dress and sandals—no jewelry; no jacket, though the air conditioning will make me cold. I'm carrying a little black pouch instead of my usual big stained tote bag. Very Saturday night, though it's Thursday. Zak is also in summer clothes— an open shirt with his chest hair showing—and sandals. Olive is in a neat white T-shirt and tan cargo pants; Joshua is the most formally dressed: no jacket, at least, but—of all things—a red necktie.

"You look as if you spent the day on the beach," Olive says.

"Biking," I say. "After work. Sorry we're late—we had to shower."

Which is stupid of me, the first of several stupid remarks that evening. I know she sees "bed" on my face. But Zak talks easily about the food. Papadums and sauces appear, we order beer for us, wine for Olive, a Coke for Joshua. Zak—waving the cracker—points out that it's crisp and peppery. We order. We decide to share. We pick out dishes, but then the waiter wants to know how hot we'd like them. Zak and I say, "Hot," just as Olive says, "Medium," and Joshua looks anxious. He mumbles, "Medium," too, but I realize an Indian restaurant may have been a mistake. Olive says maybe we shouldn't share, but "Medium," Zak says firmly to the smiling waiter. Eating assorted appetizers, we talk about the weather, Olive's recovering ankle, and the geography of Zak's new life—where his practice is, where he lives; we don't mention my house.

The main dishes arrive, with naan and basmati rice. The waiter snatches the lid off each dish as he names it. It's like somebody snatches the lids off us too, and we talk more easily. I order another beer, aware that it's too early to order a second beer. "So," I say then, "is risk necessary? If you're going to accomplish anything, I mean."

"Risk?" Zak says.

I'm thinking of Paulette. Zak and I talked about her this afternoon, just as we were taking off on our bikes, but what am I doing? I know how Joshua feels about Paulette. I'm doing it because I want Zak to be right about Joshua: I want to see Joshua, after a little argument, turn open and warm. But surely he won't. For a second, I wonder if I'm getting myself into trouble just to prove that Zak's fantasy about Joshua makes no sense. But I don't have time to think this through. I have to explain about risk, and now I can't think of an example *except* Paulette. "I was telling Zak. A woman who works for me—well, you know—"

"Risk is a romantic fantasy," Joshua says. "Take risks! Teach kids to take risks! It's what everybody says. I teach kids *not* to take risks. I teach them to figure out what will *work*, and do *that*." I see that he's taking some rice and putting on top of it a tiny mound of aloo gobi, like he's illustrating the rule.

Zak laughs. "Maybe risk is good for timid people but not for the brave."

"Not good for anyone," Joshua says. He eats some of his rice. He has the intent look of an old man for a few seconds, as I glance across the table. His napkin is tucked into his collar. His attention is on the process his hands carry out—while Zak scoops food and tears bread and eats and argues all at once.

"That woman who works with you?" Olive says.

"Everything she does makes *some* kind of sense, though yes, everything is at least a little dangerous. But she *tries* things!" I'm excited about Paulette's newest scheme, and for a moment I am sure Joshua will be excited, too.

He makes a noise, and I interrupt myself. "Joshua wants me to dump her, but he's wrong," I say to Olive. Coyly. I can't believe I'm doing this.

"The woman who put that nonsense in the paper?" Joshua says. "What now?"

I am still hopeful. "She's paying clients to do little jobs. I said we don't have a budget for that, even though it's so little—so she said she'd earn it. Today I find out that twice, she's taken teams of homeless people and gotten them to clean people's property for money. The clients get some, and she keeps some, which pays for other clients—or the same clients—to work at Barker."

"Is she with them when they do the work?" Griff says, putting down his fork. "What is she telling the homeowners? We can't guarantee these people—we don't know them. They could be rapists, murderers. What if they get hurt? We don't have insurance."

"If they're murderers," Zak says, "maybe they deserve to get hurt."

With a gesture that shows me what things were like between them twenty years ago, Olive reaches across the table and slaps Zak's hand, and he pats hers. He begins to talk about another doctor in his practice who's difficult but good. He's trying to help—broadening the topic to "screwy but worthwhile people."

Then Olive says, "What about political risk?"

"What about it?" I say.

"Never mind," Olive says.

Then I know what she means. I say, "Like in *Bright Morning of Pain*," but she is speaking again and doesn't notice. She's asking Zak what it's like to be a pediatrician.

"I'm a kid and an adult at the same time," he says, happy with the subject change, not noticing that Olive is working hard to keep us friendly. "We talk shoes. When a baby knows six words, he'll talk about his shoes. '*My shoes.*' I try to wear cool shoes."

"Like running shoes?"

"I want the kind with flashing lights." He scoops up food with a scrap of naan. He gestures with it—talk about risk!—and a hot splat of chickpeas and sauce falls sideways onto my bare arm. I jump, flick the food onto the table with a finger, touch my napkin to my arm. Zak doesn't notice any of this, though I see that Olive does. I shift my chair away from my date. It makes a sound when it moves, and now he glances at me and goes on talking. He's saying cute things, as always.

I wish I had said, "Hey, you dummy!" when the food fell on my arm, but it's too late now. I want Zak to stop sounding young and perfect. So I change the subject again, but I'm not going back to the topic of Paulette. And I think Olive wants to talk about the book. So I ask Joshua—again—if he's finished it. Olive looks at me as if she thinks I'm crazy, and I remember that this book is a complicated topic for the two of them, even though Joshua says he loves it, even though Olive knew the author.

There is a long silence. Then Joshua says, "I did."

"And what do you think?" I say, while Olive is saying, "Where did you get it? You didn't read *my* copy. I keep it under lock and key."

"I borrowed it from the New Haven Free Public Library," Joshua says, slowly enunciating the library's formal name. Then he looks at me and says, "That's not how it happened."

"How what happened?"

"What's in the book. It's not true."

"You mean about you?" I say.

"I don't count," Joshua says. "No. About someone else."

"I thought it was a novel," Zak says.

"It *is* a novel," Olive says. "Of course it's a novel."

"Yes and no," Joshua says. "It's a novel if you didn't live through certain events. If you did, it's not quite a novel."

"You mean," Zak says, "it should be accurate about verifiable events?"

"Of course, and despite its charm, it's not," Joshua says. "But that's not what I mean." He's stirring his food with his fork. I'm eating away.

"Charm?" Olive says.

"I want it to be accurate about the people it's based on."

"Is that fair?" I say, looking up from my plate.

"Yes, it's fair," Joshua says. "I love this book. But it takes off from the life of someone who became well-known. It shouldn't lie about her."

"It doesn't use her name," I say. "I don't even *know* her name."

There was silence. "Her name," Joshua says now, "was Helen Weinstein."

I've vaguely heard the name. "But the character of Harry?" I say, immediately regretting it.

"This is more important. But that's troubling, yes. The book glorifies violence."

"My entire life," Olive says, "has consisted of you caring about the character of Harry, and that's not much of an exaggeration."

"But I'd never *read* it," he says. "The other is much more important. It lies about what Helen did."

Now I want to know more—about Helen Weinstein, about Griff and the character of Harry—but Olive pushes her plate away, folds her arms on the table, and says, "Fiction establishes its own truth."

"What?" I say. "What does that mean?"

"It's a work of the imagination," Olive says. "You can't argue with it—not about accuracy, at least."

"Wait a minute," I say. I expected her to say what she said before—that the book is inaccurate about the character of Harry. "You're not happy with this book. You're *mad* at this book!"

Olive ignores me. "In one novel, history is accurate, in another, it's distorted but recognizable, in a third, space aliens assassinate the president. Each thing is true within each book."

"But how do you know which kind you're reading?" Zak says. "If a book says Abraham Lincoln was president in 1980, how do I know if the author is doing something tricky or he just doesn't know?"

I laugh at that, and Zak, belatedly listening to himself, adds, "Could Lincoln have beat Ronald Reagan for the Republican nomination?" but Olive is serious. "The book tells you," she says. "It tells you how to read it. Like a Hollywood movie with a secretary living in a fancy house—you *know* whether you're supposed to wonder where she got the money. The fancy house could be part of the plot—or it could just be real estate porn."

"She stole it," Zak whispers.

"I'm serious, Zak," Olive says.

I don't know why Olive cares so much—or why she's defending the book—but Zak ought to know enough to shut up.

"Yes, Mrs. Griffin," he says. He's almost sarcastic.

"I've never been 'Mrs. Griffin.'"

"Sorry, I forgot. Ms. Grossman."

"My cousins wanted her to hyphenate," Joshua says mildly. "They didn't mind if she kept Grossman, but they wanted Griffin, too."

"Grossman-Griffin is a mouthful," I say. Is it possible that we can get away from all these topics?

"That wouldn't stop my cousins," Joshua says.

The waiter asks if we want anything else, and Griff orders tea, which nobody else wants. We are silent as the man clears the plates and dishes. We watch Joshua drink tea. I think we're okay. Then Zak says, "Why does the author owe Helen Weinstein anything? It would be different if she claimed it was true, but I gather she never did."

Now I sort of understand. "I do *like* novels to be true," I say. Maybe we can turn this into a conversation about how everybody's taste is different. Nobody glares at me, so I keep going. "I figure a novel *might* be true—I do! I shouldn't admit this, but I don't even *want* to know what's not true in this book. Which I loved. To me, it's all true." Then I remember our previous conversation and add lamely, "Not the character of Harry—that never seemed true."

"So, once you know who it's about, you think it's true about her?" Zak says. "Maybe the problem is that the author said who she was writing about."

"You want her to keep it a secret?" Olive says. "That's not a bad idea. But Val talked all the time about Helen, as if all she'd changed were the names. At the time, people would have guessed she meant Helen, anyway."

"Aren't you contradicting yourself, Olive?" I say. "Whose side are you on?"

Olive sighs and picks up her wineglass, which is empty, and glances around for the waiter, then seems to think better of it. "My personal preference," she says, "has nothing to do with the ethics of writing a novel. Helen was my friend."

This is the first I know of that.

"I thought Valerie Benevento was your friend," I say.

"Not really."

"Not really?"

"No," says Olive. "Helen." She continues. "But novelists don't owe anybody anything. That's what it means to write a novel. That's art. Nobody can complain that a novel lies."

"Are you kidding?" I say.

"Well, of course people *do* complain," Olive says, "but no, I am not kidding."

And then something at the table changes. Joshua, who does not raise his voice, says, "The end of the book—" He pauses. For the second time in our acquaintanceship, I think he may cry—and it interests me that the first time was when he found this very book. "The end of the book glorifies violence," he says again. "It romanticizes violence. I love this book. It's not always accurate, but I love it. Until the end. It doesn't have to tell the truth about everything, maybe, but that's one truth it should tell."

"What truth?" I ask.

"What's wrong," he says, his voice shaking, "is *wrong*. What is destructive—" He pauses. "Destroys." His tea is still in front of him, and he clutches the cup but does not drink. "Blowing people up. Shooting people. It's wrong when it's terrorists now, and it was wrong when we did it. There's no difference." He picks up the cup this time but still doesn't drink. "It's not like a play—you don't wash off the red makeup. It's blood. Helen knew that and did it anyway. Give her *that*!"

Olive now turns to him, and when she speaks, she sounds as if she too may cry. "You say what bothers you most about Val's book is the way she wrote about Helen? The fake Helen? That's not what bothered *you*. That's what bothered *me*." She pauses. "I'm the one who cared about Helen. I suffered over Helen. *You can't have Helen.*" She sniffs, and her voice wobbles. "Helen was an idea to you. You didn't love her. You didn't love her and lose her."

"You think I didn't suffer over Helen?" he says. "You still think that?"

I consider the end of *Bright Morning of Pain*. The two women—who loved the same man in college—again love the same man, a different man. Harry has urged the narrator's friend, Hannah, to follow her convictions and carry a weapon. The narrator and her boyfriend cook up a plot: the boyfriend will pretend he loves not the narrator but Hannah, so he can then persuade Hannah not to use a gun. He will feign love to get her away from Harry's influence. But the plan fails. Hannah talks the boyfriend into agreeing that violence may be necessary. The two of them participate in a raid on a draft board. When the police come, a policeman aims his gun at the boyfriend. Hannah, who loves him, shoots and injures the cop. Another policeman shoots her. The novel ends without telling us whether she or the cop lives, whether she goes to prison, but it's clear that the narrator and her boyfriend will be together.

Joshua's intensity—and Olive's—scares me. Maybe the novel does glorify violence—I'm not sure. At the end, I was sad for Hannah. I didn't think she was a villain. I gather my thoughts. I have to disagree with Joshua—though of course I should keep quiet. I search for the right words.

"That sounds . . . *unforgiving*," I say. "A lot of what we do at Barker is based on the idea that if you think hard enough, nobody's unforgivable—no matter what he did. Otherwise we'd throw all our guys out. Plenty of them have been violent." I stop to see how he's taking it. It's central to everything I think. "This matters," I finish.

"Well, that goes without saying," Olive says, but Zak interrupts her. "Oh, for heaven's sake," he says, much too loudly; I see a couple of heads at other tables turn in our direction. "Would you let that go, please, that *forgiveness* shit? Forgiveness doesn't help anybody. Would you like to be"—his voice becomes loud, even nasty—"*forgiven*? I don't want anybody's forgiveness for anything I've ever done." He glances at Joshua.

"But why not?" Olive says. She has calmed down. "If Helen were alive today—and I wish she were—well, I don't know about *forgiving*, but I think we could all work out a way of understanding. . . ."

"You *understand* what Helen did?" Joshua says, suddenly turning his head to look straight at Olive. "You *understand*?"

"Maybe not quite forgive, maybe not quite understand," she says, "but . . ."

"Okay, Zak," I say, because Olive seems to have fallen silent. "How about *understanding*? If you don't want forgiveness, don't you want understanding for—for whatever you've done?" Of course, I'm thinking about what he did to Olive and Joshua's daughter, and I know he is, too. And so are they. Why *doesn't* Zak want them to forgive him? Can it be true that he doesn't?

"I don't want forgiveness or understanding," Zak says. "I lead a fine life. Nobody needs to judge it." Then he says, "I bet Helen Weinstein didn't want *forgiveness* either."

I'm mystified, stung by the sarcastic way he repeated "forgiveness." Is he dismissing what I do for a living—which I believe in as I believe in nothing else? "Wait a minute," I say. "Wait one minute."

Zak turns in his chair to look at me. We're too close, physically, for ordinary talk: that close, people murmur or shout. He pulls back a little, but the table is small. "I mean it," he says. "About me. I don't know much about Helen Weinstein."

I say, "Look, I don't go to your medical office and tell you how to be a doctor."

"What does *that* have to do with it?" he says.

"I put it wrong," I say. "What we do at Barker makes sense. Paulette makes sense."

"Of course, of course," Zak says. "You're a great woman, Jeanie— but forgiveness is sentimental crap. Let's all hang onto our crimes."

Joshua looks supremely uncomfortable. The waiter hovers with the check. But Zak's body relaxes, and he turns to face the table and shrugs. The waiter puts the little folder on the table, Joshua picks it up and looks inside, and Zak hands him a credit card. Joshua takes out his own and puts both of them into the folder. I retrieve my purse from the floor and reach into it—Zak doesn't usually pay for me—but both men wave it away.

When they've paid, Olive and I mumble in what I think we both hope is a friendly way. I am pleased to learn that their car is in the opposite direction from mine.

"What was *that* about?" I say, after a block of silence. "Of course you want them to forgive you!" We get into the car, and Zak says nothing for half a mile. I say, "I'm dropping you off at your place."

"My bike," he says.

"You can get it another time."

He is silent for another half mile. Then he says, "I want them to say I don't need forgiving." He sounds like a boy.

eleven

Olive Grossman

After the first days, Helen's crime—even Raz's killing of the security guard—was no longer a front-page story. I bought the paper every day. Before the internet, you had to turn all the pages. Sometimes I'd find a relevant item, a short column near the bottom of a page, and I'd read it again and again. A gun that had been used in the holdup turned up. The injured policeman was released from the hospital. A ceremony honored him. After that, I saw nothing for weeks, months— well into 1971.

I was embarrassed on Helen's behalf—had she made so little difference?—and angry at her for having an unrealistic idea of what kind of difference even a violent crime could make. I was fundamentally at a loss. Alone in our tiny New York apartment, I sobbed uncontrollably more than once for the dead security guard, his kids, his wife. I'd stop where I was, unpredictably, sit on the floor, cross my arms over my head, and sob. I sobbed for Helen too, and for me. I'd start crying for the guard and end up crying for myself. Whatever happened, I would never have Helen back. I was too scared to imagine in detail what might happen next.

But first and daily and in every part of me, I was stymied. Helen had not been insane or even mistaken when she couldn't eat the hot dog because Norman Morrison had immolated himself, and she had been right to seek ethical choices on those windblown walks, deciding what to do next, and next, and next. She had wept when Daniel, her first boyfriend, spoke of violence, and only after intense inward scrutiny and the passage of years had she concluded that he was right. I never put much credence in what Mallon or Raz said, but Helen—though I didn't agree all the time, and I *still* thought Adeline had the right to wish for a color TV—was subtle, thoughtful, scrupulous. What should she have done—what should I have done—to end the war? What should we have done *instead*? To say "nothing" would condemn us to complicity.

Yet the logic that had led Helen from step to step—the exercise of conscience—had killed a man who had not caused the war nor fought in it nor, for all we knew, approved of it. I didn't know how Helen had come to think that the bank holdup made sense, but I knew that because she was Helen, she had concluded it was regrettable but necessary.

I pretended interest in my graduate courses as a courtesy to the professors, but I felt no conviction, not because I had stopped loving the nineteenth-century novels that had seemed to offer a legitimate life's work, not because I was bored or even—as before—unable to think about anything but the war, but because I was distracted by my sense that something incomplete could not be completed. I lived in a parenthesis that did not close. Griff—the person whose arms and legs, whose noises and silences, were the climate I now lived in—was, again and again, a startling presence. I never forgot Helen, but I sometimes forgot that I lived with Griff, and would wonder at the sound of a key in the door. I was surprised when I woke in the night and heard him breathe in his sleep. Surprised but thrilled, as if he were a present I had forgotten I'd received. How had I come to be paired with this other person now of all times? Did I even know him? Helen's crime made me, by turns, shyer with Griff, needier, warier. He

was a good man who didn't deserve to be dragged into my life; he was
a man from a persecuted race who deserved more than I could give; he
was an intruder in the bed. Sometimes he was just an ear, and that was
useful. Often I couldn't stop talking—speculating, justifying, working
out possibilities and trying to find one that ended well, arguing out
loud all sides of all questions. Griff often didn't answer. Sometimes
he'd pick up a magazine or a newspaper, and I'd say, "No, listen, this
matters, *listen!*"

"I'm listening," he would say. "You just said, 'But she won't.'" I
often imagined out loud that Helen might suddenly appear in our
studio apartment, where we'd have to hide and shelter her—which
presumably could land us in jail. And how would it be possible? But
indeed, I'd always end such speculations with "But she won't."

This was a few weeks after the crime, around the time when Griff
was having frequent phone conversations and a few meetings with
the volunteer lawyer about the charges against him. I became more
and more anxious in the days before he learned that the charges
would be dropped. One afternoon I came back from the library and
heard the phone ringing from the hallway outside. It took too long
to dig out my key, and whoever it was hung up. I always expected
Helen to call. Maybe the lawyer had called—maybe with good news,
maybe with bad news. I sank into a chair we had bought. When I
moved in, it had soon become clear that we needed another place
to sit and read, or to face the bed and talk to someone sitting on it,
and with a sense of great consequence we chipped in on a chair in
a junk shop. It was soft and gray, and I loved it. I sat back in it and
could not move even a finger. Griff came in quite a while after that

and found me still in my coat, still with my bag at my feet and my key in my hand.

"What?" he said.

"The phone rang."

"Who was it?"

"I didn't get it in time."

"It will be all right."

"Maybe not." I'd never changed my mind about Griff's crime. He had been defending people who were being attacked; he was as justified as he could be, and the law should let him go. It was too bad he had to do it—but he had to do it. And also, I didn't want this man—this young teacher, this idealist, my lover—to experience anything bad, anything that would take him away from me. He had a way of crossing the room diagonally in my direction, a certain way his arms and shoulders looked—vulnerable and not, at the same time— that made me want to seize him and hold him close. Sometimes I did, knocking him a little off his feet. He'd laugh and stroke my head and hold me in his turn.

Now I didn't stand up and seize him. I had never been so tired in my life. He looked at me, then turned away. He went into the bath- room, and I heard the toilet flush. He opened the refrigerator. Griff, unlike most people I knew, shopped once a week as his mother did and kept food ready to turn into meals: frozen vegetables, hamburger meat. With his back to me, he was taking things out. Minute Rice. He said, "She wouldn't have done it if it weren't for me."

"What?" I said.

"Helen."

"I know who you mean."

"I gave her permission. I taught her. I shouldn't be allowed to teach."

"That's not how it happened," I said. "That was one conversation." I was too tired to remind him of the years of arguments and discussions, of Raz and Mallon, of all that made up the Helen who had done whatever it was she had done.

"You don't know how it happened," he said.

"I don't know? Who would know if I didn't know?" Helen was mine.

"No," he said. "Baby, no. I did it."

I didn't have the energy to argue—didn't know how to prove what I knew. And he was my boyfriend, my fairly new boyfriend, so instead of making me angry, his ignorance of the topic touched me. It gave me the energy to put my key back into my bag, take off my coat. Griff began patting chopped meat into hamburgers.

■

That fall, a classmate asked me to join a women's consciousness-raising group. All my life, women had been joking and griping about the ordinary insults we lived through, from nasty remarks about "women drivers" to the assumption that women would do little except clean and care for children. Even politically active women were relegated to typing and sex. We didn't need to raise our consciousness: as soon as it became customary to talk about sexism, our consciousness swelled like rising bread. In our group were students and teachers, as well as wives of students and teachers. Four women in the group left their husbands that year.

At the first few meetings I said little, partly because I hadn't felt much discrimination personally. I was grateful to have time off from thinking about Helen and the war—to have a political topic that wasn't cause for despair—and I listened with interest to stories in which men had failed to respect women or women had failed to respect themselves.

I was silent too, because I couldn't talk about my own, unrelated trouble. At one meeting, I caught myself silently glorying in my connection to Helen. I was horrified. I hadn't had the courage—or the passion, or whatever the hell it was—to risk my life as she had. But now I was preening on my connection to someone who took action—while I continued to disapprove of her. I missed part of the discussion, sitting there scolding myself. When I returned, I was humbled, which made it possible to speak: for once, I didn't need to be sure that what I said was relevant, accurate, and fascinating all at once.

"I live with a black man," I began, not sure how this fit, and two black women—sitting next to each other—looked up at me sharply. A few sentences later, a white woman interrupted me. "You're not black," she said, "so you can't speak to the double discrimination black women feel."

I hadn't been about to complain. Nor did I want to talk about Helen—and lately Griff and I talked little about her. If I mentioned her, his face clenched. I wasn't sure how the topic I wanted to talk about related to feminism—or to Griff's race—but I had a feeling it did, I told my friends.

One morning, I said, Griff had emerged from an intense silence and asked, "Do you believe in God, Ollie?"

I was looking for my lipstick. "God?" I said. "I guess so."

"You don't *know*?"

I explained. Jewish prayer repeats, again and again, the information that God is God, that there is only one God, that God is good, and that it is good that God has commanded us to do whatever we are about to do or has given us whatever we have. I had been brought up hearing those prayers—not often, but enough. Jewish observance, in my mind, was for periodically reflecting that it was good to be alive. If you wanted to call the giver of life God—this is what I said to Griff, and now to the women's group—then I did believe in God and was grateful. If you thought of life as a result of certain physical and biological processes, what I felt was more like awe.

"I am not sure I still believe in God," Griff had said solemnly, when I finally shut up. I thought Helen's crime had something to do with his problem—or the war, as it had led to Helen's crime and his own. I had not taken God seriously enough before to disbelieve now, but in Griff's mind, God was so irreconcilably attached to justice and goodness that if things got bad enough, it was impossible to imagine God.

"But then nobody would *ever* believe in God," I said. "The Black Death, slavery, Hitler . . . If people believed despite all that, why can't you believe now?"

"I am not them," he said—a rare grammatical lapse. He went off to teach.

After that, he and I asked, as a household, frequently, whether Griff believed. I've met others in interfaith marriages who have had similar experiences: they and their spouses may not be religious, but religion is often what they are thinking about. The women's movement, diverting as it was, was background. Maybe the women's movement gave me permission to keep whatever belief or disbelief I had, instead of adopting Griff's position.

I ended what I said to the women's group with the comment that sometimes I pictured God—the God of Griff's childhood, whom I saw as a wrinkled black man—leaning on an elbow in suspense, listening to find out if his servant Joshua still believed in him. Then I stopped talking, and there was coffee and cake and departure. Nobody answered me, but I was glad I had spoken. I'd told a coherent story to myself and apparently to them—leaving out Helen—of what my life was like. It even related to feminism.

My life, come to think of it, centered in many ways on what Griff thought. Every day he came home talking about his pupils—the troublemaker, the slow one, the sad one. I talked little about my classes. So we were one of those households in which the man's job matters more than the woman's activities, and I was as responsible as he for the disparity. What Griff did was more useful than what I did. Reading novels meant ignoring the big stuff, even if the great books I read were *about* the big stuff. Griff loved to teach, and teaching was not ignoring the big stuff— yet it was also not protesting the war. Protesting the war had become unbearable, and teaching was a kind of solution. I didn't want to teach kids. At the time, I thought I was preparing for a career teaching college students, though I was never excited about that prospect either, and except for a short stint as a teaching fellow, I never did it.

I asked myself, in those months, whether I loved Griff for the wrong reason, because he was a bit exotic. My parents worried about

me, as his did about him, but the two sets of parents worried differently. My mother worried that I wouldn't find a teaching job after
graduate school or I'd find one in a distant place. Neither she nor
my father thought Griff was the right boyfriend for me, but not—
they earnestly repeated—because he was black. My mother said she
feared that the racial difference might finally keep us from getting
married, and by then I'd be too old to marry someone else. My
father worried that my reputation would be ruined because I was
living with a man I wasn't married to.

I didn't meet Griff's parents for months. He phoned them often
and would lie stretched on our bed, his shoes removed, the phone to
his ear. In an hour I'd hear only murmurs, and after he hung up, the
silence persisted. He did tell me that he talked mostly with his father—
if his mother answered, she passed his father the receiver. She was a
kindergarten teacher, but they didn't talk about teaching.

I began to ask to meet his family. He'd met mine: we'd eaten polite
dinners, carefully planned and cooked by my mother. "Soon," he'd
say. "You'll like them." Like Helen when we first met, Griff was always
making sure I was fair to people, and maybe he thought I didn't expect
to like them. I did assume they were scolding him for having a white
girlfriend, but when I finally asked, he said, "Of course not!"

Once, during yet another argument about whether the Vietnam
War ought to make the idea of God untenable, Griff sighed and stood
up. This conversation had started as I was straightening clutter on a
Saturday morning, and now he was sorting a pile of mail and newspapers, so when he stood, he clutched papers. He sat down again. Then
he spoke: "I've told my father about my doubts."

"You told your *father* you don't know whether you believe in God?" I would never have a conversation about God with either of my parents.

"I had to."

"How long ago?"

"Month, couple of months." I slowly grasped that all these phone conversations had been about God.

"What does your father think?" I said.

"He has doubted," Griff said. "My father has doubted, too." That a father and son had talked for months about uncertainty was hard to imagine. I envied it. My parents had only certainties. I couldn't imagine these conversations, which apparently were both more and less personal than any talk my parents and I ever had.

Christmas was coming. With only a little guile, I began saying that I'd enjoy meeting his family when everyone came together for the holidays, that I could bring his mother something—maybe a calendar with photographs of children from around the world. He liked that. After one or two more phone calls, we were invited to his parents' home in New Haven for a few days, beginning on Christmas Eve. They wouldn't have room for us along with his brothers—two, both married, one with a baby—so we'd stay, in separate beds, with Griff's aunt. I'd have the spare bedroom, Griff told me, and he'd sleep on the sofa. He was embarrassed that we couldn't be together, but I wasn't surprised. All my single friends were engaging in plenty of sex, but nobody's parents felt at ease about it, except a few old Communists who'd never believed in marriage in the first place. My parents might have let me sleep with a man in their house, but their embarrassment would have ruined the occasion. I preferred the Griffins' confident prohibition.

On Christmas Eve, we drove to New Haven in Griff's VW Bug. Everyone I saw as we got out of the car in the late-afternoon sun, not far from downtown New Haven, was black. I was ashamed to notice that and, when we got inside his parents' house, to notice that both of his sisters-in-law were light-skinned. For a moment, I thought they were white.

His father met us at the door—as distinguished as I'd imagined but shorter. "This is my father, Reverend Griffin," Griff said.

The reverend shook hands. Griff's mother came forward, saying, "I'm Sally." She kissed me, and starting then I loved her until she died—a good thing, because she often drove me crazy. She was barely shorter than her husband and had straightened gray hair and a face that often looked as if she didn't know what would happen next but thought she'd like it.

Within moments of surrendering my coat, meeting the brothers and their wives, and admiring the first grandchild, a little boy crawling around on the rug, we talked about Hanukkah. I had done nothing about it, but Sally and her kindergartners had constructed paper menorahs. That was the last year I didn't light candles at Hanukkah, and since Hanukkah is actually a minor holiday, logic required me to observe, in some fashion, Rosh Hashanah, Yom Kippur, and Passover. The Sabbath matters too, Sally often pointed out, but I couldn't change my behavior for something that frequent.

After a few minutes, Reverend Griffin offered to show me New Haven, as if Griff might have been inadequate to the task. He led us to his large car and drove slowly through the streets. Later, Griff told me his father didn't see well anymore and probably ought to quit driving but would not consider it.

Passing the Green, I said, "New Haven's beautiful!"

"Parts," said both father and son at the same moment.

I liked the Christmas Eve church service. In the morning, there were modest presents, for me a pair of pink woolen gloves. Sally liked her calendar. She was a terrible cook. The oldest brother and his wife weren't unfriendly, but they were shy, which amounted to the same thing. I exchanged glances and smiles with Henry and DeeDee, the next oldest brother and his wife, whom I liked. I also liked Griff's aunt, with whom we stayed. The Griffins' house had solid, dark, old-fashioned furniture; at his aunt's, everything was plaid. She worked as a bookkeeper at a hospital.

Griff's sense of humor had temporarily dried up. His father was similarly serious, and Sally's anxiety squelched her sense of humor—I learned only later that she had one. The day after Christmas, I proposed leaving. My period was due; I had a paper to write—I wanted to be home. But Griff didn't want to go.

In the late afternoon on the twenty-sixth, I persuaded Sally to let me make a pot of coffee and serve it with Christmas cookies; they'd received several tins, some homemade, from parishioners. What was different, I understood now, as we sipped coffee in the living room, was that the brothers had left. I suspected the middle brother, Henry, agreed with us about the war, but the oldest brother had been in the army and was a hawk, so nobody had brought up the topic. Now I thought maybe we'd talk about politics. I was pretty sure Sally and the reverend were antiwar, but I knew they had been horrified by Griff's violent crime. Would they scold, or argue, or continue to avoid that topic entirely?

Griff took a last sip of coffee, placed the cup and saucer on a coaster, and told his father that he was finally sure he no longer believed in God. He apologized.

"Oh, for heaven's sake!" I burst out, and quickly saw how wrong that was. I looked at my shoes, hoping I'd be ignored, and I was.

"I'm sorry to hear this, son," the reverend said. "I don't know if I've ever told you, but I too have doubted."

I glanced up, saw that Sally seemed to be suppressing a smile, and quickly glanced down again, feeling slightly better. But the next time I looked, I saw that Sally, in her corner of the sofa opposite Griff, was crying, and I understood why she'd been anxious—why everything had been tense through these days. The trouble had nothing to do with me. Reverend Griffin went on, "But I'm not sure you've truly . . . ," and Griff said, "I have, I truly have . . . ," and they began to discuss— yet again—the question. No one else spoke; no one left.

"God has tried us before, he has tested us before," Reverend Griffin said.

At last, Griff stood and said he wanted to take me to Blessings, a Chinese restaurant he thought I'd like (at the time, the name seemed hilarious). His parents looked relieved.

On the way, he was talkative. "He'll keep at me," he said, "but I feel so much better!" He then asked, "How are you?" as if he'd just noticed I was there.

I said I had to get back to New York. He thought he'd better spend another day or two at home.

"Just to make sure everybody feels as bad as possible?" I said.

"We both need it," he said, and I recognized that he was probably right about anything he claimed about his father, whom he resembled. His brothers were different, and I guess that was why Griff was the one they had expected to go into the ministry. It hadn't seemed to be a question for the oldest, Isaac, who was learning how to repair televisions, or for Henry, who worked in a law office and studied law at night. As we approached the restaurant, Griff reached for me, and we stopped just outside the door to put our arms around each other. We'd barely touched for days. He kissed my ear before we stepped into the lighted room.

The next morning, I took the train to Grand Central, glorying in solitude. When I finally walked into our apartment, I sat down on the nearest chair in my coat, my bag at my feet, and didn't move for an hour. Finally, I felt my period start and stood to go to the bathroom.

When I came out, I saw a piece of looseleaf paper near the front door, a little to the side. I had walked on it without noticing it; there was a footprint on it. Sometimes flyers were pushed under the door, or notices from the landlord. I picked it up and brushed it off, turned it over. In blue ink it read, *I miss you so—love forever—HW.*

I sat down where I was, on the floor. Had Helen come on Christmas Day? Did Helen even know about Christmas? Regardless, I had missed her. I might never see her again. I struggled to my feet, took some pills for cramps, and went to bed in my clothes. I slept for hours, and when I woke, it was dark. I cooked some spaghetti, ate it plain with butter—all I wanted—unpacked my bag, and went back to sleep.

■

I never wrote a doctoral thesis, but I spent a second year in graduate school: teaching, taking seminars, and compiling notes that eventually—two babies and two editing jobs later—became the book about Edith Wharton. Living was cheap, and Griff and I managed on the modest sums we were paid. As a year passed, it became harder for me to imagine a life without Griff, or Griff's life—and his family's life—without me.

Helen did not reappear, not in my life and not in the news. Everyone but me seemed to have forgotten her.

And there must have been a pinhole in my diaphragm, because in late winter, a little more than a year after that Christmas visit, I found myself pregnant. I said to Griff, "I went to the doctor," and he looked up from the newspaper, his dark skin deepening, and dropped the paper on the floor. "Yes," I said, crying, and he rushed at me, seizing me and placing himself around me as if to keep me still. "The next Griffin," I said. The baby was the next Grossman as well, but my family didn't think in those terms, exactly.

Griff and I hadn't said much about marriage, but we both knew it would happen. Once, he had said, "I suppose we'll be married for ten years before we replace this chair." (It was the shabby gray one we'd bought together.) When he said that, I had looked hard at him. He'd said, "What? You don't marry schoolteachers? You don't marry atheists?"

"Under certain circumstances, I marry them," I had said.

These, apparently, were the circumstances, because we started talking about a wedding the day of the doctor's visit. For Griff, of course, a wedding involved God, whether he believed in Him or not. God was a kind of absentee landlord who'd abandoned the building.

At times I found all this fuss about religion irritating, but mostly it moved me. It was a sign of Griff's scrupulous moral sense. My boyfriend—unlike the men many of my friends were involved with—regarded a coming baby as a gift, if not quite from God, and a pregnant girlfriend as a wife, a wife for all time. Griff doesn't believe in divorce either—it's inconceivable to him—and I know he will never quite forgive and forget the years we lived apart. I'll get to that.

I listened patiently while he considered and reconsidered out loud all our options. The clerk in the Municipal Building—my suggestion —was unthinkable. "I can't ask my parents to witness something like that!" he said. I didn't like the rabbi of the synagogue my parents paid dues to and attended on the High Holy Days. He wouldn't ask whether Griff or I believed in God, but I was pretty sure he wouldn't marry me to someone who wasn't Jewish.

"My father knows rabbis," Griff said, and that turned out to be the solution. Active in the antiwar movement, Reverend Griffin knew an array of liberal clergymen. This was before clergywomen.

My parents considered themselves enlightened; they'd have been fine with the clerk in the Municipal Building. Abortion was still illegal—*Roe v. Wade* came a year later—but in New York, it wouldn't have been difficult to end a pregnancy, and my mother delicately asked. I clutched my stomach, burst into tears, and declared that Griff was the man I loved, the man I'd always love, and I loved my baby, too.

"Okay, okay! Now I know!" she said. She and my father became bubbly—all but drooly—about the coming grandchild. And, in fact, about their son-in-law. Maybe it was true that they had worried primarily about my chance to become anybody's wife.

We were married in New Haven, by a rabbi assisted by Reverend Griffin, in an ugly room lit by fluorescent lights at a community center, in the presence of about forty people, most reveling in the interfaith aspect. Our families turned out to resemble each other—well-behaved, cordial people who shunned ostentation. The gathering wasn't jolly, but it was friendly. Sally and my mother hugged. My sister was my maid of honor. I missed Helen. My parents had offered to pay for a wedding trip, but Griff and I were too busy. We drove back to New York and resumed our lives.

While we ate supper one night that spring—I was getting big; we had been thinking about neighborhoods where we could afford a bigger apartment—Griff sat up straight in the way he did when he had something important to say, some moral requirement he had recently detected: a need to invite my crabby professor to dinner, for example. This one was larger.

"Can you write your dissertation away from campus?" he asked.

I was fairly sure I wasn't going to write a dissertation. I was trying to think of what I might do if I didn't become a professor, but I hadn't talked about it. "I guess so. . . ."

"I must teach in New Haven," he said.

I felt a swirl of unreasoning panic. I was angry—and had no idea why. As he talked about the poor black community in New Haven and his obligation to make a difference there, I grasped at the only argument against moving that came to mind—that New York was my home, the only place a reasonable person might live. New York is comprised of people who dream of getting out—replacing subway commutes with driving, walkups with sprawling lawns, snow and slush with warmth—and those who can't imagine living anywhere else. Even when I expected to become a professor, it didn't occur to me that academics find jobs where they can.

It was our first bad fight. I screamed. He accused me of not wanting to be part of his family. It was true that I was doubtful about living near Griff's complicated family, but I was also tempted. It was like being offered a job, maybe a job I wouldn't always like but in which I'd have a certain usefulness. I was already the Jewish Daughter-in-Law, supposedly an expert on certain topics. I was also the woman who'd kindly married their beloved and impossible youngest son. I was the expert on Griff.

Finally, a few days later, as I walked through the aisles of our neighborhood grocery with a basket on my arm that kept bumping into my belly, I realized why I didn't want to leave New York—why I'd even been wondering if the baby might fit into our tiny apartment if I just shifted this, got rid of that. If I lived elsewhere, Helen could not find me. I began to sob in the grocery store, put down the basket on the floor, and fled. I went home and crawled into bed, then returned to the store, where I found the shabby canvas basket just where I'd left it, still containing the rice and soup I'd chosen. Someone had added cornstarch.

It's hard to remember now how difficult it used to be to find people one had lost touch with. Or to be found. Before Facebook, the internet, and email addresses (which don't change just because someone moves), the only way was a phone book or calling Information in a distant city. You had to know which city, know your friend's married name, maybe. In the seventies, it was new for married women who weren't actresses to keep their birth names. Helen could find me through my parents if we moved, but I knew she wouldn't. I had kept my name, but our phone number in New Haven would be in Griff's name.

Meeting a high school or college friend in the street was thrilling, and these reunions, just because they were so chancy, meant more than they should have. After Helen's crime and disappearance, I kept expecting to run into Val, but I didn't. Then she phoned me, sometime in my second year of grad school, though she had to call my parents first to get my new number. As always, I felt a mixture of relief, curiosity, and annoyance talking to her. How could I have kept Val and lost Helen?

"All right," I said to Griff that night. "Let's move to New Haven." I'd had a vision of Griff and me—stooped, gray, wrinkled—stuffed into this one-room apartment with several aging children. Helen hadn't earned this hysterical loyalty, and she didn't want it. Immediately I felt better: in that apartment, I was always poised for a knock. Somehow, I didn't think Helen would ring the doorbell.

Griff quickly found a job in a New Haven high school. I would work on my dissertation—I had decided to try writing one. A professor had hired me to help research a book, but I could work at the Yale library and meet him in the city occasionally.

We began spending weekends in New Haven, looking for an apartment, sometimes going to church, then eating Sally's Sunday dinners. Griff's sister-in-law DeeDee was pregnant too, and we joked about little Griffins taking over the world. I pretended to feel more comfortable than I did with this family—I guess all brides do that—but now and then I felt at ease with Sally, who was straightforward and who wanted to like me. I was lucky in my mother-in-law.

Griff relaxed a bit too; being an official atheist was easier than becoming one. Sometimes the reverend—I had learned that his first name was Isaac, like his oldest son's, but I called him Reverend, like everyone else—looked at Griff sadly. But he gave me generous, somewhat distant smiles, and he told me each time he saw me that he was excited about our baby—also that he understood that I probably wouldn't want him baptized, which made me feel guilty. Their neighbors told me the baby would be a boy—something about the way my stomach tilted. It was a few years before ultrasounds made it possible to know.

I listened for Helen's knock during the weeks before we moved. The war was a steady, depressing fact that suddenly, now and then, became unbearable once more. One day in June, we all saw for the first time the famous photograph of the naked, burned, screaming Vietnamese girl running with others from napalm. President Nixon had been reducing the presence of American troops on the ground, and there were peace proposals, but air strikes increased. It was an election year again, and we were for George McGovern, the peace candidate.

We moved in July, with help from friends. We filled Griff's VW, and somebody had a pickup truck. I looked for Helen on the block as we drove away. Then I got interested in living in New Haven and fixing up the apartment we'd found. The Helen part of my life was over, I decided—and so was the Val part, apparently. I didn't let her know where I'd gone. But one day that fall, when I took the train to New York to see the professor for whom I worked, I thought I recognized Mallon from the window of a bus and jumped off. I ran back a block on Broadway, searching for the tense shoulders and reddish hair that I had seen, peering into stores, not wanting to go inside lest I miss her.

"Olivia," a low voice said behind me, as I hesitated. Mallon had come out of a grocery store with a pack of cigarettes. She paused to light one, offered it to me, then said, "I see you're—," nodding at my stomach.

I told her I was married to Joshua Griffin. "I thought you were in hiding," I said.

"I'm mostly not in New York," she said.

"Is Helen all right?" I asked.

"I'm not with them," she said.

"You know where she is?"

"I know where she is."

"Can you—can you tell her I'm living in New Haven? Can you give her my address?"

"I can't promise," Mallon said.

"I understand," I said.

"I don't think you'll hear from her," she said.

"Okay," I said weakly. I just wanted to see the piece of paper I handed her disappear into a pocket. She turned away, and I was sorry I'd chased her. Now I had reason to be anxious again, to wait again. I heard nothing.

The fall continued. Nixon won reelection in a landslide—which was depressing until Watergate, just a few months later. Griff and I got ready for the baby. One day, alone in our second-floor apartment, staring out a window at a bare, wintry backyard, I felt certain that I'd never see Helen again, never know what had become of her, and I felt a certain calm—what people nowadays call "closure."

Martha, a big girl who looked like the reverend—he was light-skinned, paler than Griff, and she was the same, and also had his placid dignity— was three months old and spring was coming when I saw a short, blond woman cross the street toward me as I bumped the carriage down the porch steps of our three-family house. I knew the woman mattered. Her elbow bent slightly as she mounted the curb on my side of the street; I saw that she was Helen, Helen in makeup and black pants she'd never wear, false breasts and a tight black sweater with sequins, and that wig. She had dressed up as a parody of what she most passionately opposed. But it was Helen. I couldn't speak.

"Olivia," she said.

"Mallon gave you the address?"

She was carrying a map of New Haven. She had come on a bus from downtown—I don't know what, before that. "What do you think?" she said. "She's not a bad person, Olivia. You could have trusted her."

I embraced her and started to cry. She shook off my hug and said, "I have to see my nephew."

"Niece," I said. "Martha."

The baby was asleep. Helen crouched at the side of the carriage and put her hand on Martha's back through the blanket. In those days, they told us to put babies to sleep on their stomachs, not their backs.

Martha's face was sweetly turned to the right, and her thumb was in her mouth. Helen slowly traced Martha's shoulders, her head, her face, her thumb, with her own forefinger (she wore dark red nail polish), grazing my daughter's edge so lightly that Martha stayed asleep, just worked her thumb a little harder.

Then Helen stood and we walked, as we always had. "Don't call me by my old name," Helen said. "I'm Mary."

"That doesn't sound Jewish," I said.

"I'm not Jewish. I'm Mary Walsh. I'm risking my life to tell you this."

"Not your life," I said. "Maybe your freedom. But I won't tell."

"My life," Helen said. I suppose she meant that if the police came for her, there would be shooting. Maybe she carried a gun. "And you have to promise not to tell my family you saw me."

"I promise." I felt a pang of guilt.

"I had to see the baby."

Mostly we were silent. I couldn't ask the obvious questions. I still don't know where she was living, who with, what her plans were. At last, I said, "Helen, I wish it hadn't all happened. I wish I could have you back."

She shook her head and was silent. Then she said. "We have to do hard stuff, Olivia."

"Oh, Helen!" I said, forgetting to even consider saying "Mary," but when I looked, she wasn't Helen at all—or so I thought for a moment of excruciating embarrassment. She was quite well disguised, and the disguise made me as sad as if she really had become someone else.

She wouldn't come upstairs with me, wouldn't tell me how she'd come or how she'd get wherever she was going. She said, "I wish I could tell you to tell my parents I'm okay, but I can't," and I wondered as she hurried down the block whether she meant I was supposed to tell them after all. I decided I couldn't risk it. Maybe someday she and her companions would decide they could come out of hiding, that nobody cared anymore. I would hope for that. I yanked the carriage up the steps.

■

After our Indian dinner with Jean and Zak, I didn't see Jean for a few weeks; I supposed she had broken up with him and wanted nothing to do with people she'd think of as his old friends. I was angry with Zak for driving Jean away from me. He wasn't an old friend, more like an old enemy.

I was trying to write my essay on *Bright Morning* that fall. I wrote openings that were far too personal, stopped in mid-sentence, opened a new document, and started again. Griff was busy at school and spent his evenings upstairs.

One late afternoon, I took Barnaby to the park and met Zak, running in baggy shorts, on a trail near the river. He stopped and stood wiping sweat off his face. His hair flopped on his forehead. "Olive!"

"Hi."

"Wait," he said, though I had stopped, too. He bent to pet the dog. "I was a prick that night," he said. "At the restaurant."

"Did Jean break up with you?" I allowed myself to ask.

"No," he said. "Break up with me? Did she say that?"

I should have known Zak would get what he wanted. "I haven't seen her. You were such a pest, I figured she might have."

"We did have a fight," he said. "I didn't even register that Griff kept looking at me like I should be taken out with the garbage. The next day, all I could see was that look. I hadn't seen that look since . . . since you know when."

It was funny that he said that about the garbage, because at the moment he smelled of sweat—but fresh, vigorous sweat, and I was not repelled but attracted.

Zak said, "Olive, I've missed you!" It was the first time we'd been alone together since he'd returned to New Haven.

I had liked him so much back then that I couldn't feel as angry with him as I knew I should, as Griff felt. Griff had loved him but had withdrawn all his affection when we learned what Zak had done. I stared at him, there in the woods, but didn't say I'd missed him, too. I began to walk, and he fell into step beside me. Our feet crunched leaves. The leaves still on the trees were sparse, but some were yellow, and the sun shone through them. The river glinted. The dog sniffed bushes and tree roots.

"It wasn't that I was in love with you," Zak said finally.

"*What?*"

He was silent again. Then he said, "Of course, you have to know that I've spent the last twenty years of my life trying to figure out why I did it. Why I filmed Martha like that."

I didn't know what to make of that—I had *not* thought this. I thought he'd spent the time justifying it to himself. "But you said you don't want to be forgiven," I said.

"Hmm. No, I don't."

"But why not? If you think you did the wrong thing, why not be forgiven? If possible."

"Oh, forgiveness." He was hugging himself. "I meant that. It takes away who we are. I'd rather be me."

"Are you cold?" I said. "Do you want to run?"

"I'm cold, but it's okay." He sounded like a boy. "I shouldn't have been so disgusting, but it's not forgiveness I want."

"Then what do you want?" I asked.

We came to a narrow footbridge, and though the wind had come up, he paused and looked upstream, leaning over the railing. Barnaby watched ducks. I patted his skull, pressing it into my leg. Clouds were gathering, and now the river looked dark.

"I thought you'd be interested, back then," Zak said. "I did it to get your attention."

"You thought I'd be *interested*? In pornographic photographs of my daughter taken without her knowledge?"

"I think I knew Griff would be angry," he said, "but I thought you'd be different. What I imagined—I know this is incredible, but what can I say? I was a kid. I imagined Martha complaining to you, and you reassuring her, telling her it was like the sixties, like the way you all lived back then, that it was *advanced* to do things like that, like John Lennon and Yoko Ono, like . . ." He paused, then said again, "Like the sixties."

There's nothing quite like discovering what someone has been thinking when it's unlike anything you ever imagined. "The sixties weren't—" I didn't know how to put it. "We were serious."

"I know. I've read *Bright Morning of Pain*—after our dinner, I got hold of it."

Now I had no idea what to say or do. *That book* was his idea of the sixties? Of seriousness? Wasn't that the problem? Wasn't it many people's idea of the sixties? I wanted him to read the book I might have written.

"My dog needs his supper," I said.

"I'm sorry," Zak said.

He didn't start running again; we continued walking together. I had a mad idea that I could make him understand everything—what I'd done in the sixties, what I felt about *Bright Morning of Pain*, what effect his act had had on Martha. But I said nothing.

When we stepped out of the woods a few minutes later, he said, "Not telling Martha seemed incidental. If I asked her, she'd say no, but if I just did it and then told her about it, she might love it—and if she didn't love it, you'd help her love it. I do see that was crazy. I saw that quickly. Griff and my film teacher made me see that."

We were in College Woods then—the only part of the park that is *not* woods—and in this more public place, with wide paths and benches and playgrounds, our conversation became general. Zak was still appealing—a thought that felt disloyal to Martha. I said goodbye, and, dismissed, he began to run again. I went home and fed Barnaby. Griff came home; he went upstairs. I could hear bits of the *PBS NewsHour*, so I went up and watched with him. I didn't tell him the whole story, just that I'd met Zak, that Zak and Jean hadn't broken up.

"He won't do," Griff said.

"He's not the kid he was," I said. He didn't answer.

■

In November 1976, Martha was almost four and Annie was a year old. We'd moved to a larger apartment, not far from where we live now. I was working at a press in northwestern Connecticut that specialized in books about American history. I had my driver's license, and we bought a second used car so I could go back and forth two days a week to the office, leaving a bottle of breast milk behind, returning with piles of manuscripts. On the other days, I worked at home. The kids went to a lefty day care center in a church basement. I'd forgotten my rage about the war—I was sometimes ashamed to realize that. People who had opposed the war, back at the start of the movement, were often those who cared about social justice: legal aid lawyers, social workers, teachers. When nonviolent protest began to seem pointless, those who resisted the turn to violence by the Weather Underground and lesser-known groups like Helen's returned—maybe hardly noticing the shift—to social justice. I had been atypical, with my love of moral subtlety and ambivalence in old novels. The women's move- ment had made even childcare political, so I could tell myself I was still in the struggle just because we'd joined a cooperative day care center, in which fathers were required to work a few hours a week along with mothers. Griff and I both put in hours taking care of the children, he after school.

Meanwhile, the United States had signed the Paris Peace Accords in 1973 and Saigon fell to North Vietnam in 1975. The war was over. As all this happened, I wondered where Helen was and what she and her friends thought. Now I know from books that their opposition to the American government was so general that it didn't matter what the government did.

One Wednesday, Griff went to work as I was sleepily nursing Annie in bed. He liked to be in his classroom well before the children. Annie was an even bigger baby than Martha had been, and she crawled and walked later, content to rock her hefty middle back and forth from her perch on her hands and knees. After I nursed her that morning, I showered and dressed, hauling her around, putting her into her crib when I needed both hands. Griff had fed Martha breakfast, and when he left, she was playing on the floor of our bedroom in her pajamas, singing about a giraffe who couldn't fly. I got her dressed and then gave her a second breakfast—this was her routine most days—while Annie sat in the high chair with toast cut in squares. I sat down with my mug of coffee and my own toast. The weather was still warm, and I enjoyed the children, as well as the knowledge that I wouldn't have to look after them all day, nor drive to work: I'd walk them to day care in our big stroller and come home to the manuscript I was editing. It was about women in the Revolutionary War.

I remember it all so many years later not because anything particular happened that morning but because when something did happen—later that day—it was the thought of the peaceful morning, the solid, rumpled bodies of my children (somebody nonchalantly leaking pee, shit, snot, or drool) that I went back to: this was the story I told myself, trying to sleep that night.

Working at home, I kept a leisurely schedule, and at day care, nobody cared if children were dropped off late; that day I was slow.

Eventually I got everybody going and pushed the stroller to the day care center. It was a windless, warm day. A few leaves were left on the trees. Martha was still singing about a giraffe. I left the stroller and my daughters after kisses and squeezes, a little conversation with the people on the turn, then walked home unencumbered, poured another cup of coffee, and settled down to work.

I didn't talk to anyone all day, as often happened. I spent those hours in the solitude of engrossing but not terribly difficult intellectual work, stopping only for food or more coffee.

When I was approaching the day care center at five that afternoon, I saw one of the other mothers, a woman with a loud voice and emphatic opinions that she told you before you knew what the topic was, so you found out which side she—and presumably you—were on (anti, generally) before learning what you were against. She had no sense of humor. She wasn't a bad person, only irritating.

I caught up to her, and we walked along together. I wanted to tell her something funny her son had said to me that morning, to see if she might laugh, but before I could speak, she said, "So how *exactly* are they bringing down the military industrial complex by robbing a suburban bank and shooting three cops? Tell me that. It's a tragedy, a stupid, stupid tragedy. That girl!"

"What girl?" I stopped where I was. "What girl?"

"The one who got killed. It was on the radio just now."

"I don't know about it. What happened? Who got killed?" I was shouting.

"Not around here, nobody you know—someplace in Pennsylvania." I fought down panic. Nobody I knew lived in Pennsylvania. She went on, "The same radical politics we all believed in—up to a point! Up to a *point*. They make me madder than the assholes in Washington."

She touched my arm lightly, as if to say, "So much for that," and started walking briskly toward the gate. Once inside, we couldn't talk about a bank robbery. I stopped, dropped my purse, and seized her forearm, squeezing so hard it must have hurt. "You have to tell me!" I said. "I don't know what happened."

"Easy, take it easy," she said. "A bank robbery. But a girl got killed—a Jewish girl from Brooklyn. One of the radicals."

I would have to go inside, take my children, behave as if everything was fine. This could not be done.

"Do you know her name?" I asked.

"Something like Weinberg."

"Please, stop," I said. I was whispering, helpless and not caring who saw or knew it. "Was it Helen Weinstein?"

"Maybe," she said, and at that moment, Griff's car came to a stop beside us and he jumped out and seized me in his arms, sobbing. Whatever happened to Griff and me later—the long separation, the strangeness between us, still, at times—we were joined indissolubly, married for real, at that moment.

He steered me to the car, and we sat and cried there for quite a while, seeing people emerge from the day care center, leading or carrying or pushing children. We were the last to pick up our kids, but the woman who'd told me must have finally worked out what was going on and told the parents on the shift. When we went inside, Martha and Annie were being quietly read to by one of the fathers. He hugged me, patted Griff on the back, hoisted his own little boy to his shoulders, and left us alone to get ourselves and our children out of there.

We had many chances to learn the whole story, and people still remember it because it was one of the few times during those years when a radical white woman died. Helen had carried a concealed gun. She had gone into the bank and quietly approached a teller with a note. When the teller gave a signal and a security guard approached Helen, she took out the gun and killed him. Cops rushed in; her companions shot at them. A cop killed Helen with one shot.

The photographs in the paper, which I stared at for hours, were bizarre. It was one of those ugly little banks where customers are greeted with insincere platitudes and halfhearted ornaments wish them whatever is appropriately wished at the season. There was a picture of Helen, an old picture of the girl I knew. And there was a picture of the place where the crime had taken place, after it was cleaned up. Above the spot where Helen died, a string of limp letters hung in an arc between two pillars, spelling out "Happy Thanksgiving."

twelve

Jean Argos

Zak doesn't make a distinction between getting along and fighting. As I'm driving him home after our disastrous dinner with Olive and Joshua, he says, "Griff still loves me."

"I'm not so sure," I say.

"Paranoia by proxy," he says. "Let's fuck." We've reached his house, and he's just about to get out of the car.

"We already did."

"Hours ago."

I'm thinking that if I had any sense, I'd break up with him. Even before Olive told me what he did, he was too good to be true, too ebullient and curious and sensitive not to be a bad guy. And, indeed, someone else's boyfriend—too good and too bad at the same time. I imagine he is still someone else's boyfriend, and sometimes I still feel a pang of guilt about that, though mostly I figure she knows whom she's dealing with. Sometimes I think I'd have preferred to have Yvonne for my friend instead of her boyfriend for my boyfriend. But now I go inside and we go to bed, though I'm feeling sleepy and angry more than sexy, and I have to work tomorrow. After a while, of course, I'm aroused, and I watch Zak's flexible arms and legs roving my body. His big, hard penis plunges into me.

The next morning, my phone rings while we're drinking coffee, he in his bathrobe and I in one of his T-shirts. The phone is in my purse in the living room, and Zak runs for it, as if the call might be for him. He hands it to me. Jason.

"I got here early," he says. "A cop just came by. Somebody was in our building last night." He pauses, and his voice takes on a slight, humorous edge. "They called your house, but you weren't there."

"My private life is private," I say, teasing back. I haven't told anyone at work about Zak. My staff doesn't run into Joshua.

Zak is staring at me, still poised for an emergency, mine if not his. I shake my head: we won't need a pediatrician in the next ten minutes.

Jason says the cop on the beat saw a light, walked around, and found an open door—but nobody was there. Whoever it was woke up and hid, in or outside the building. It wouldn't be a priority for the police, but I'd given my phone number to the cop we know best and told him I'd be grateful for a call. Apparently I gave him my landline. Jason sounds guilty, or maybe he's just uncomfortable about catching me away from home.

I hang up and say to Zak, "I'd better go home and change."

"You let them push you around," Zak says, as I hurriedly put on the dress I wore last night.

"No, I don't," I say. Zak doesn't notice that I'm annoyed. It will be days before he says to me, "I was awful that night. Griff must hate me. What should I do?"

At work, I ask Jason how the intruder got in this time.

"Same door," he says.

I try to remember what he told me the last time. "Didn't you replace the lock?"

"I did." He still seems uneasy. I assume that with our customary stinginess, he took a lock from an unused door lying around in our basement or his house instead of buying a good one, so the replacement was as easy to pick as the original. I should have checked. I should have insisted that he spend the money on a decent lock. One difficulty of running a nonprofit is that available money from the government or foundations is mostly for new programs, like our third-floor respite rooms. But if a program works, it's no longer new, and it's hard to get money to keep it going and harder still to get money to keep the lights on and the rooms painted.

I don't get another call, and then I forget the back door—and even forget about Zak's drawbacks for a week or two—because the third-floor respite center opens at the start of September. Paulette does well. She's hired a couple of the people who worked on her summer yard project to help with painting, moving, and setup. One, I'm surprised to see, is the man called Arturo.

"Wasn't it Arturo who was sleeping in the building?" I ask Jason. "The first time?"

"He has a place of his own now," Jason says.

Arturo is often around after that, a thick guy with an odd expression but a great willingness to work. He's useful, but—

"But stupid?" Zak says, when I think out loud with him about Arturo. We're together for the first time in a while, eating pizza we picked up and brought to my house.

"Not stupid. I think he's smart. He gets jokes."

"Evil?"

"Out of touch."

Arturo speaks without an accent, but he seems to not quite

understand when we speak to him. At first, I think he's rude. When we're setting things up on the third floor, I ask him to carry up a box that's blocking the staircase and he says, "No." Just that. Then I realize, from what I hear the others say, that he's carrying things up in a prescribed order. It just wasn't time for that particular box. He didn't explain—but neither did he passive-aggressively obey me when he knew I didn't understand. The next day, he smiles, and I like him. Like many people who have been homeless, he looks clean enough and wears regular clothes, but he has bad teeth. He has a big, bare forehead; sparse gray hair stands straight up starting halfway to the back of his head.

We thought the respite rooms would catch on slowly, but right away, people want a couple of hours alone in a room with a cot and don't protest when we don't let two people go in together. Maybe some ask to use the rooms only because we offer them, figuring there must be something good about them. Twice in the first week, somebody goes into a room and comes out fifteen minutes later. "It's like jail," one man says, though we painted them yellow and put up posters. After he's proved he can leave, that man comes back.

We look through people's stuff to discourage shooting up. We know we can't prevent it entirely, but finding someone unconscious at the end of his time will not be acceptable. People like being alone, being able to sit or lie down, just taking a break.

By the second week, we have a waiting list almost every day, so we have to decide whether you can reserve a room in advance. I have a meeting with Jason and Paulette to figure it out. Paulette says, "You let these people sign up in advance, you're running a hotel. What about no-shows? What if somebody reserves the whole week?" I finally make the decision: we won't let people reserve, but if you don't get in on Monday, we bump you to the top of the list on Tuesday.

"That's the same as reserve," Paulette says. As we predicted, menstrual cramps are a big motivator, and we sometimes move women to the top of the list just for that. "I won't have no cramps tomorrow," somebody points out.

Mel and Tommy take turns at the desk on the third floor, and they claim that people who have been in the rooms are more open to other changes in their lives—to referrals for medication, to job training.

When I tell Zak this, he shakes his head. Counting off on his fingers, he says, "Drink, drugs, sex, stealing."

"What?" We're at Archie Moore's, eating hamburgers just before the kitchen closes. It's raining out, and the smell of rain comes into the bar when the door opens. Zak called me when he got off work late, and I'd just gotten off work late, too.

"When you come right down to it, that's what's going on with your clientele," Zak says. "And one way or another, that's what they're doing upstairs."

The assumption that I don't know what's going on makes me angrier than the slight against my clients. I'm not naïve, and I know that drink, drugs, and sex happen up there occasionally—not stealing; there's not much to steal. But when they happen, it matters mostly because drink may lead to vomit, sex to used condoms. Our problems have to do with scheduling, housekeeping, laundry—the boring, nonlurid parts of life. We use up more disinfectant than we expected, wash more blankets. Whatever goes on in these people's lives, whatever makes them poor or likely to die young or go to jail, is not what we contend with on our third floor.

"Okay," Zak says eventually. He reaches across the table to eat my French fries, since his own are gone. "It's not all stuff from the movies."

"Correct."

I'm tired, and after we pay, we go in separate cars to our separate houses. Sometimes he talks about living together, but that's silly. Am I going to give up the house where I've lived so long? Am I going to let him in, to deal with him daily, hourly? Paulette is loud, and her voice is the soundtrack of my days; talky Zak at home every night would not do.

In my office, I have plenty of chances to see how Paulette works up close, because she's always running past me. I've never had clients above as well as below me, and the old tenants were few and mostly silent. The respite rooms upstairs are supposed to be quiet. Clients call them the Quiet Rooms, and I sometimes hear, "I need one of them quiets." But I often hear Paulette loudly ushering someone up, shouting warnings about quiet—"No radio, no girlfriend, no singing songs!"—in a voice that must be heard by anyone already in the rooms. Some people need the freight elevator—which is noisy.

There are more readers than I expected, many taking one of the donated paperbacks from a box on the first floor, often without looking to see what it is. Some people make cell phone calls or write something. I think some are writing-writing, as we put it, but most are filling out forms—applying for something, documenting something. As I hoped, giving homeless people something other people have in their houses brings out the ways in which they are the same as anyone else.

Mostly, getting people to leave isn't a problem. They get lonely—except for those who want to stay all night. Right away I see that that issue isn't going away. If you give people a warm, safe room, more likely than not they will want you to give it to them overnight—which is why most comparable agencies are shelters. The first person to make a fuss is a woman with a bad cold. She spends the afternoon on our third floor and protests when it's time to go. It's fall, getting dark by the time we close at six. "It's cold," she says. "The shelter is across town. I go there, ten people get sick. I stay here, nobody's sick but me."

Jason comes to talk to me about that one, and I tell him no. We don't have input from the board or permission from the city, we don't have insurance, we don't have someone to keep the place safe, we don't have someone to call an ambulance if she gets sicker. She'd be alone in the building.

"When you're home in your house, you're alone in the building," Jason says.

"That's different."

I go with him to talk to the woman. I give her a ten-dollar bill—my own money—so she can buy food or bribe someone to give her a place to stay, or buy booze, I suppose. Then we both escort her out. I watch her back as she walks away. The wind blows into her face, and she bends her head, or she pretends it's blowing in her face because she knows we're watching. I don't like sending someone sick out into the night, whether it's windy or not.

Jason looks at me, and I lay my arm across his shoulders. "I know," I say. "Me, too."

During the setup, members of Paulette's neighborhood improvement group worked for us—hauling, painting, arranging. Now, only Arturo still puts in a few hours a week. Then Paulette says she needs one more person, to keep the third floor staffed all the time. "Somebody smarter than Arturo but dumber than me."

"Cheaper than you," I say, "but worth more than we can pay." There's a useful category in my business: people who can do things but have trouble getting hired, so they'll take a job for less money than they'd get if they used proper grammar or had been to school or hadn't been to prison. We need someone tough but with good judgment, someone who will throw out dangerous people but know when to do nothing.

I talk to the board about hiring someone, and Joshua says, "Are you doing this so you can keep people overnight?"

"No," I say fast.

He taps the table with a pen, a gesture I've seen before and don't like. "Then why isn't your present staff sufficient?"

That makes me mad enough that I slow way down. "Well, let's see," I begin, and describe every damn thing that I do, then every damn thing that Jason does—or the first twenty damn things. They all begin saying, "Okay, okay." They know that no nonprofit that isn't stealing the grant money has staff with free time.

Paulette hires someone, and she brings him to meet me: a tall, skinny black man whose legs are too long for the rest of him. When I look at his face, I almost recognize him.

"Dunbar," he says. I remember now. He always says his name with some irony, as if he finds it hard to live up to it. He's the man I met all those months ago, outside on that windy day with the sandwich.

We shake hands, and I ask him about himself. "I used to work for the schools," he says.

"What did you do?"

"Cooked. Until I got busted. I did time."

"You're clean?"

He nods. "I'm clean," he says. He's a little more of a street person than I want, but Paulette—as usual—has gone ahead and promised him the job without consulting me. Not that I have anything against people with complicated pasts. Still, they might go back to whatever they have done before, and they might be just a little too creative. I want my employees to take risks but to worry a little about it. People who've taken big risks in the past may be a little too used to the sensation.

Still, I figure someone who cooked for the schools has skills I can use. He'll know how to follow directions. He'll know there are such things as directions.

"Years," Dunbar says.

"Years?"

"Clean for years."

"Oh, right."

Paulette turns back when they've left, waits until Dunbar is out of earshot, and comes back into the office. She spreads her long fingers and brings her open, arched hand down on my desk. I am sitting again, and I blink across the desktop at Paulette's hand. It's the gesture you might use to grab something small that was scuttling away. "Trust me," she says.

"You are a great woman," I say. "I don't totally trust you, but I am in awe of you."

She leaves laughing. Paulette is too creative. But I decide Dunbar will work out, because Paulette is tough on former volunteers who now get paid, as if they're parking meters and she has to take handfuls of quarters from her own pockets and feed them into a slot in their necks. "I'm paying you!" I hear, her voice rising with *paying*.

Dunbar works about half time, and she quickly trains him not to play favorites with the clients and not to waste time. He keeps records of who's upstairs and whether anything happens. He helps the outreach team.

Sometime in October, I run into the cop on our beat, and he tells me he's pretty sure people are sleeping in our building again. "You get a feel," he says. He shrugs.

I say, "Whoever it is, he hasn't made a mess so far."

He shrugs again, but he says, "It's not a good idea."

"Yeah," I say. I thank him and continue on my way. He's an old-fashioned cop: Irish, middle-aged, burly. Usually they're more boyish—or girlish—and skinnier, darker-skinned, less sure. I'm thinking about cops, almost receiving his permission not to think about what he's told me.

I don't even think about it when I see Jason, not until the next day. Then I find the old back door lock in my desk drawer. We never throw anything out. It's a snap lock that could be opened easily with a credit card or any thin plastic, and as I turn it over, I decide to take a look at our back hall—a small room off the laundry room, which is a small room off the kitchen. There's nothing in the back hall, just a dark old cement floor and dark walls, probably unchanged since the old factory was built.

When I get there, I realize that it has changed after all. The door from the laundry room to the back hall has a lock on it—not the modern deadbolt we have on the front door but an old snap lock like the one I just found in my desk. That doesn't matter, because it isn't the door to the building anymore, as it clearly once was. But somebody (Jason? Paulette? One of the community service workers?) is supposed to lock that door, between the laundry room and the back hall, every night.

I've been here, of course, but I've never looked closely. The back hall itself, I see now, was originally not an indoor space—probably a loading dock. At some point, it was enclosed, maybe to keep merchandise secure and out of the rain. The hall is now a windowless wooden shed built onto the brick building, and the door there leading to the outside has a good lock and a deadbolt after all: Jason's new replacement. But it's standing open. So the old snap lock is all that's keeping anyone out, at least at the moment—not just out of the laundry room but the whole building. The offices have locks, the door to the staircase up to the third floor has a lock, but everything else is open. An intruder could do laundry, eat from our cupboards and refrigerator, sleep on the ratty sofas in the computer room, even steal the decrepit computers used by our clients. Nothing has been reported missing, which means he or she is more interested in just being indoors than in walking off with a refurbished computer, but people change their minds or invite along their greedier friends.

I go looking for Jason, whom I find in Paulette's office. "I should have asked you about this sooner," I say to him. "Somebody's still sleeping downstairs." I explain about the cop and the open door to the outdoors.

Jason rubs his hand slowly over his hairless head. "I'll make sure it's all right down there," he says then. "Don't worry."

Behind me, I'm aware of Paulette in some way. Maybe her breathing changes.

"Listen," he says, "will you be in your office? There's something else I need to ask you about. Be right there."

"Okay." I go back to whatever I was doing when I found the old lock, or avoiding whatever I'd been avoiding when I started rummaging in a drawer.

Jason comes in a moment later. "I thought we should talk about this without Paulette." He sits down and says, "It's Arturo. I promised her I wouldn't tell you—so you can't say anything to her." He's laughing a little, as if he's deciding whether or not to be embarrassed at this small deception.

"You told me he found a place."

"He does have a place. He's not here all the time. Look, Paulette let this happen, but I know why she did it—I've been pretending not to know, but honestly, Jean, it's not a big deal."

"If he has a place . . ."

"Something about a girlfriend's kids. He's here when somebody else is there."

"Is Paulette the girlfriend?"

"No."

I'm angry with Jason. Angry with myself for never checking the back doors before too, but primarily angry with Jason. I talk for quite a while about what it means to have rules rather than just a bunch of case-by-case decisions. If Arturo is allowed to sleep in our building, the whole homeless community knows it, and anything can happen. Paulette has taught Dunbar not to play favorites, but he must know she's playing favorites herself—breaking rules for another part-time employee—and he may be learning from her example, not from what she said.

"You told me the cop didn't think it was a big deal," Jason says.

"But it can turn into a big deal."

"Winter's coming," he says. "Arturo is someone we know. He needs a place. Only some of the time."

All true. Even so, I tell him to tell Paulette to stop letting Arturo sleep in the building. Then I phone a locksmith and have a proper lock with a deadbolt installed on the door between the back hall and the laundry room.

Zak is delighted to hear all about this, delighted with everyone's quirks and foibles. He wants to drive over to Barker Street and look at the doors. He scolds me for not going down to look in the first place. "So it's not in your fucking job description," he says. "So what?"

"It was Jason's responsibility, and I trusted Jason to do it," I say.

He mumbles something and goes to the bathroom—we're in bed at my house—which is often when he reconsiders what I've just said. I hear him talking to himself while he pees. As he gets back into bed, he says, "Micromanage, all that."

"Right. I don't want to micromanage."

"Makes sense," he says. "But you know Jason's going to find a way to let Arturo in—because he can't stand up to Paulette."

"He's not," I say, "because now I am taking charge."

Soon everyone at Barker knows the story of the back door and the locks. I suppose the clients hear it from Arturo. And by a sequence of ideas I don't entirely follow, the improved locks on the back doors lead to the renewed demand that we keep the respite center open overnight. I guess the story somehow demonstrates how New Haven's complicated shelter system doesn't meet everyone's needs.

Paulette starts urging me to apply for money so we can open the respite center overnight, but government money is getting even scarcer, so foundation money is more in demand. I'm feeling like I'll never see substantial money again. A proposal to extend a program I was surprised to be able to run in the first place seems silly.

"Sure," I say, "and while we're at it, let's apply for ten billion dollars and buy houses for homeless people. Then we can close down."

It isn't just that I think we can't have overnights. I don't *want* overnights. Paulette—and now Jason—keep telling me they are the obvious extension of what we have, but, like Joshua, I think other organizations do the work of providing overnight shelter better and more cheaply than we can. Also, all the talk among advocates for the homeless nowadays is about finding permanent housing, not increasing shelter beds. Still, conversations with Jason, Paulette, and the outreach workers regularly circle back around to the issue of whether the third floor should be open all night. "What is the point of a bed if nobody can spend the night in it?" Tommy asks at one meeting, looking left and right as if someone might finally tell him. "We have beds!"

"They're narrow cots," I say.

"I can introduce you to several guys who are sleeping under bridges because they're afraid of the shelters—and they would be happy to sleep on our narrow cots," Tommy says.

"It's not that simple," I say, and keep saying. And because it amazes me to have a boyfriend who wants to know in detail what I'm doing, I tell Zak all about it. Half the time he argues with me about what I think or what I've done, making the same arguments I've been refuting all day, but now he can't make up his mind. Sometimes I'm right, sometimes Paulette and Jason are. He comes up with new arguments every few days. He even thinks about my stuff when we're not together.

He's much less willing to talk about *his* work. The requirement of confidentiality baffles Zak, who doesn't understand anyone's need for either privacy or secrecy, but his incomprehension makes him studiously careful about it, especially after his experience with Martha and a few mistakes he made as a medical student and a resident. His instincts don't help him follow the rules, so just in case, he's usually *too* scrupulous. He wouldn't say, "I saw a kid with the flu," any more than, "Hector Diaz has the flu."

So we talk—after bed, or before bed, or on the way to eat, or while eating—about my life, my work. We don't have many other subjects, except the state of the world and the country, restaurants, books, and bike routes—impersonal topics, that is. No kids, pets, or rooms in common. We do have Olive and Joshua, and we often talk about them. Olive and I have met for lunch a couple of times, but the four of us haven't gone out since the Indian meal at which Zak got angry—because he hadn't had enough sleep, he told me later. I didn't believe him but was glad he felt bad enough to come up with an excuse.

"Let's set up another dinner," he says more than once. "We're natural friends." I do not think this is a good idea for about ten reasons, and I'm sure they'll say no, but I like Olive and am always curious about Joshua, so after Zak brings it up for the third time, I say, "If you want to try, you do it."

He kisses my shoulder as he gets out of bed that morning, as a child might kiss the nearest part of someone rather than the customary one. "Send them an email," I say. "Both of them together. Copy me."

"I'd rather phone," Zak says. A few days later, to my surprise, he tells me that he and Joshua have had a friendly conversation, and they do want to go out to dinner. Then Olive writes to all of us, and we make a plan.

Before the date of our dinner, there's a board meeting, which I expect will be short and easy. I will report on the success of the respite program and on Paulette's improvement. And some members who work on fundraising want a go-ahead for an event. For some reason, the meeting is held in our small computer and sofa room instead of in the dining room. When I come downstairs, Joshua is already sitting in one of our shabby armchairs, which Darlene has drawn up to the table. His arms stretch along the armrests like Abraham Lincoln's on the memorial.

"How are you?" I ask.

"We have a dinner date."

"That's right."

I pull up a straight chair and arrange papers, and by the time I finish, a few more people have come. Then, looking straight at me, Joshua says, "I hear you want to stay open overnight."

"What?" I say. "It's something my staff wants—but no."

"What's that?" somebody asks cheerfully.

"*No?*" Joshua says.

"No."

More people come in, and the meeting begins. Joshua looks restless. He follows the agenda Darlene has prepared, but at the end, instead of adjourning, he turns to me and says, "I see you didn't put all that down—but don't we have a right to discuss this enormous change you seem to have in mind?"

To say, "How do you know about it?" would admit there's an "it." At some point in the tangled discussion—in which board members try to explain to other members what I mean or what Joshua means, while other board members say, "Wait, maybe that's not what she meant, but isn't that a good idea?"—I realize that Zak must have told Joshua that we've had conversations about third-floor overnights, and I am so distracted by this thought that I can't pay attention. I keep trying to prove to myself that Zak wouldn't have done it, deciding again that he has, trying to understand what this now means for him and me. I am angry—and astonished, which, in retrospect, is stupid. Meanwhile, the more we talk, the more overnights become a real question: Yes or no?

"Could that fellow you hired to work up there run such a thing?" somebody asks—meaning Dunbar—putting that issue ahead of the question of what such a thing might be.

"This is Paulette Strong's protégé, correct?" Joshua says. "I've had doubts about her for a long time."

"No, Paulette is doing fine," I say. I've said so in a perfunctory way during the meeting, and now I wish I said more. Paulette still drives me crazy, and she can be wrongheaded, but she thinks shrewdly out loud and in practical steps. I know she still doesn't quite believe I'm in charge of her and not the other way around, but I can deal with that. I try to explain some of this, admitting she isn't perfect—but of course Joshua won't let go of the imperfections. That makes me defend Paulette more energetically, and soon I find myself repeating Tommy's argument about the scared people under bridges and what it would mean to them to have a place that's simpler and less overwhelming than the shelters.

"She's not reliable," Joshua says. "I understand she's been leaving the back door open for some homeless friend of hers, in addition."

"Wait a minute," I say. Zak said that, too? I'm now so angry that nothing can stop me. "I think that shows her compassion," I say. "We're all so afraid to take chances, we risk having people freeze to death. Winter's coming. There's no good reason not to let a few people stay on the third floor overnight, and I'm going to try it before the year ends." I explain that we have a little unallocated money (which is true, but I had something else in mind) and can hire Dunbar for the extra hours. If the program works, I continue, we'll apply for money to do it long-term. Paulette, I say, has already risen to meet responsibility and will do even better with more responsibility. And there's now a strong lock on the back door; Joshua needn't worry about that.

In the end, we decide to try it: if we can get permission from the city, we'll let twelve people sign up to spend a night—no food, no frills, no laundry privileges, just a cot and a bathroom in a heated building—during the last weeks of the year, and if nothing goes wrong, maybe we can get funding to stay open through the coldest months. Joshua, who surely was always conflicted about this issue— he's more compassionate than any of us—resumes the Abraham Lincoln pose and says he never opposed overnights absolutely, just opposed deciding hastily. The rest of the board, led by Lorna, is now excited about waifs from under bridges coming in out of the snow. Probably I'm the only one who's still against the idea when we finally end the meeting, and I've just made it happen.

I'm not supposed to see Zak for a few days. The night after the meeting, I ask a friend out for a drink, and she listens while I cry about Zak's faults at a table in the back of Archie Moore's. I run out of tissues and blow my nose on scratchy toilet paper from the women's room. It's that kind of rage I'm feeling, the kind that is part shame, because I should have known—I did know—that Zak was capable of doing what he did. I know he did it innocently, because he simply didn't—*couldn't*—know that what I said was confidential. Why didn't I keep quiet, in that case, or at least explain exactly what he must not repeat to whom?

I don't expect to see him until Thursday, but on Wednesday, he leaves a message on my phone, and I listen to it at work. He wants to come over that night. I text him. It's too hard to do more than set a time.

Takeout? he texts back. *Will bring.*

He doesn't know we have a problem. If I tell him to eat before he comes, I'll have to cook something for myself, and then he will come without eating after all, because he never has time to eat, and I'll end up feeding him. If he brings takeout, at least there will be food. I don't look forward to a breakup without food. Also, this way, we'll start with eating instead of sex; it would be impossible to break up after sex. *OK*, I answer.

He comes bearing Chinese food, smiling and hurrying with his plastic bag of hot containers—shrimp, vegetables, rice, pork. Dumplings to start. It's hard to break up with Santa Claus. He leans over to kiss my lips domestically and begins arranging his boxes on the kitchen table. I go for plates and beer.

"Something happened," I say, my back to him, as I open the fridge.

He doesn't hear or doesn't pay attention. For once, he talks about his work. "Four kids in the hospital," he says. "But everybody's going to live," he adds, "except the crazed parents."

At last, I sit down at the table, my plate in front of me, and open a beer. I take one sip and start to cry, push my plate aside, and put my face down.

He sits down, still in his coat. "What? Sweetie, Jean, what?"

"I can't," I say. "I can't."

"Can't what?"

I get up and go to the sink to wash my face, then turn back. Standing there, my back pressed against the rim, I say, "You told Joshua Griffin everything I told you about work."

"I did?" He doesn't even remember.

I describe the meeting. I tell him I was against third-floor overnights and now I have to make them happen so as not to betray Paulette—I had to claim she was heroic to avoid demonizing her, or so it seemed at the time. He listens. At some point, he takes off his coat—a corduroy jacket that's too light for the weather (it's November) and too casual for a grownup doctor—and goes out of the room (I know he's putting it on the same chair where he always leaves it) and returns. Then he begins eating. So I do, too. I'm hungry.

"Are you breaking up with me?" he asks. I guess he's turned a little pale, because I'm suddenly aware of his black hair and eyebrows in contrast to his face.

I don't speak for a long time. Then I say, "Yes."

But I'm not sure. I haven't planned on his agreeing with me, but he does. "Oh, my big mouth, my big mouth!" he says more than once. He's no longer the innocent who arranged to have Martha Griffin— and himself—photographed; he has learned that he can get into trouble for failing to respect secrets and privacy. He's like a longtime member of Alcoholics Anonymous who keeps relearning that he will trick himself into drinking if given a chance. It's hard to be angry with people like that—they are on the same side as you, while the scamp who did wrong is rejected by all.

Also, I want the tasty food, and he's paid for it—somehow that figures into it. It's like I'm remembering some long-ago instructions from my mother about how to behave toward a visitor who brings a present. We eat; we go to bed. I'm not happy.

I tell him—again—that I don't really want to have overnights in the Barker Street respite rooms, and now Zak sounds a little less innocent, a little less surprised by his own badness. "I knew you didn't," he says. "I can't say I figured out what would happen—but maybe I thought Griff would talk you into it, in a backward kind of way."

He was meddling. Now we finally have a fight—a real argument, with shouting, the kind of fight that people have who are not fighting to break up but fighting to persuade the other person. When he leaves the next morning, I'm still angry.

But we're having overnights at Barker Street. Paulette hugs me. She thinks she talked me into it; in a way, she did. Jason is quietly pleased.

We set about planning and conferring with officials, and they have us make a few alterations. The first week we let in six people a night, twelve after that, with a signup sheet. I expect demand to be low because there won't be food or socializing—you have to stay in your room—but people sign up right away. Privacy may not mean much to Zak, but it means something to our clients. We carefully check everybody's pockets and bags and rarely turn someone away.

"All right, it makes sense," I say to Zak after the first full week. This is around the time I realize that I haven't seen Arturo in a while.

I ask Paulette about him, and she says, "I fired him. He's drinking again."

"Does he have a place to live?" I ask.

"Who knows? Not with me, I'll tell you that much." Which makes me realize she was his girlfriend after all.

Paulette wants to talk not about Arturo but about heat. The furnace at Barker is old and weak. The landlord does what he can, but the building is poorly insulated, and in cold weather, it's never warm enough. We now pay more to keep it warm at night, but it still isn't as warm as people want it to be. I keep my house at sixty degrees at night, and that's what we try, but we don't have blankets warm enough for rooms that cold. Paulette says it isn't quite sixty anyway, and the landlord promises to make some kind of repair.

One cold night close to Christmas, I stay overnight at Zak's apartment and my phone rings around 4:00 a.m. It's near the bed, in the pocket of my jeans, on a chair. I grope for it in the dark and find it before it goes to voicemail. Sitting up in bed with my jeans on my lap and Zak sitting up, alert as always, beside me, I glance at it—Jason—and answer.

"Trouble," he says, and he sounds awful.

Zak leans back on his elbows, looking questioning and amused, while Jason tells me quickly that Paulette has just called him, because Dunbar has just called Paulette. "He's hysterical," Jason says.

"What happened?"

"A fire."

"*Upstairs?*" I scream the word.

Zak says, "What? What?" and I slap him.

"No—he got them out," Jason says. "They're all fine; it's not that. The smoke alarm—he got them out."

"Where was the fire?"

"In the kitchen. Dunbar called nine-one-one. Arturo's in the hospital.

"Arturo? I thought Paulette fired him."

Paulette fired Arturo, and Arturo was homeless. He spent a couple of nights on our third floor—I don't learn this until later—but there was no room that night. Since the back door was securely locked—thanks to me—Dunbar simply let him in the front door. Arturo was cold, apparently, and tried to light the oven in our ancient and dilapidated stove. I guess he was drunk. I guess the stove was hard to light, and he lit match after match, too drunk to do it right, if there was a way to do it right, clumsy in his winter coat, which was probably donated and too big, even for that big, clumsy man. At last, Arturo got the gas to light—and set his hair—and then his coat—on fire.

thirteen

Olive Grossman

Grieving for Helen should have been my full-time job for a year, but there were two small children in my life, one old enough to ask questions. "Mommy's friend went away," we said. Griff didn't think we should say "died" about someone my age, but Martha screamed in nightmares anyway. I couldn't get through the days without crying, and she must have heard me.

A reporter learned that Griff and I had known Helen, but we refused to speak to her. I felt abruptly terrible that I had neglected Helen's parents all these years and tried to call them. I reached her brother, but he wouldn't talk and wouldn't put me in touch with his parents.

In the first stages—weeping and patting backs—it was a relief to have Griff, the only person I knew in New Haven who had also known Helen. But then we began talking. Responsibility comes first for Griff. "I made violence a reasonable moral choice," he said.

"Helen thought about violence long before meeting you," I said.

"But she resisted it," he said, and that *was* true. Helen had sobbed in my presence when her first boyfriend talked, over banana bread, about carrying a gun. Griff was the first person—the only person I knew—who had said out loud that he would use a gun, and then used one. Maybe he had somehow provided an option, and maybe that made his suffering greater than mine, but all I knew then was that he was turning the conversation back to himself—his misdeeds, his grief. I wanted to talk about Helen. Or me. The long, intense friendship. The enormity, not just of losing her but

of losing her in this particular way. In odd moments, I had bitter-
sweet fantasies: Helen dying from illness, accident, even suicide,
or as the victim of a crime. Dying of anything that would allow me
to approve of the woman I still loved.

I too felt responsible: my choice to live my private life instead of
devoting myself to protest had left Helen free to be influenced by
Mallon and Raz. If I'd stayed at her side . . .

But when I started to say these things—in bed at night, or when we'd
hired a sitter and gone out for pizza or Chinese food—Griff would
shake his head and keep silent. "Words won't help," he seemed to say.
Which was true—which is true of all tragedies, I guess. But I needed to
say what we both already knew, to say it and hear it until it was boring.

There had been no funeral—or none that I knew of. No inadequate
prayers. No clichéd condolence cards. I wished for what I'd ordinarily
scorn.

Griff and I also disagreed about Helen herself. I was horrified by
her crime—frantic; sick—but I still respected her determination to
figure out what she thought was right, and do it. The more I didn't
understand it, the more I respected it. When I first met Helen, her
morality stunned me, and when I didn't agree with her—long before
she was violent—I suspected she was right because she had always been
right, even if she was too stern and strict for me. The deficiency was
mine. Now that I'm almost old, I am *sure* Adeline had the right to want
a color TV if she damn well pleased, but when Adeline was an issue,
though I said something like that, at some level I assumed that Helen
must be right, just because she was Helen. Maybe there should have
been a moment when I faced our differences and proclaimed that

Helen was no longer my friend, but there hadn't been. I was always, somehow, expecting her to make clear to me why she was right. Or expecting her to discover she was wrong.

Griff—who later became so compassionate toward students, even when they did wrong—was disgusted by what I said. "Evil does not become good when one's friend becomes evil," he said again and again. He had not forgiven himself for shooting Carlin Lambeth, so he could not forgive—or understand—any criminal. He deprived me of Helen, in all her many forms, by turning her into someone we should abhor. I condemned Helen—of course I did—but I still loved her. Her crime created a mystery, a mystery I have spent my life trying to solve.

Around that time, our landlord told us he wanted the apartment we lived in for his son, and having to find a new place was a healthy distraction. When Griff and I disagreed about moving, it was about straightforward questions like whether we could manage without a washing machine (I said we could; he said no). I thought our present landlord was uncomfortable with a mixed-race couple as tenants, and Griff said that was nonsense—he wanted the apartment for his son, just as he said. I was starting to understand how the Griffins felt about racism. Institutions were almost inevitably racist; the rage of the Griffin family was too great to talk about or was expressed with a wave of the hand that reminded me of my aunts and uncles acknowledging anti-Semitism and dismissing it as not worth discussing. *People*, however—individual persons—were rarely racist, the Griffins believed. It took a great deal for them to decide that a particular man or woman was prejudiced—the word we used then—and when it happened, it was a teaching opportunity. Sometimes I felt them teaching me.

Griff and I rented the first-floor apartment in a former one-family house: the house we now own and still live in. We were tenants, then bought it, continuing to live on the first floor and renting out the upstairs apartment. Our tenants moved out shortly before we separated, so when we did, Griff moved upstairs. Later, he moved elsewhere, and I rented the apartment. It was empty again when he eventually came home; by then, the children were almost teenagers and we had a little more money, so we spread out into the whole house.

But all that came later. In the late seventies, we moved. Conversations about Helen became less frequent. The children grew. Though life continued, and though in many respects it was a lucky life—I had my health, a husband, children, casual friends, a job, and notes for a biography of Edith Wharton that I would eventually write and publish—I was unhappy and lonely. Of everyone I'd ever known, Helen was the person I seemed to understand most easily, who seemed to understand me best, but she had become the person I understood least well. I mourned the jokes we told, our quirky mutual perceptions. I mourned her conscience.

I remembered the day she sketched the drawing at the Pierpont Morgan. What had become of that battered spiral notebook? My life was so predictable that I still had a box of notebooks I'd used in college. Her possessions, somewhere, had become trash. As she had become trash.

Now and then, someone—on the news, at some meeting—would mention her. Her name was not a household word after the first few months, but news junkies and old lefties knew it. Someone I knew would say "Helen Weinstein" without knowing I knew her, and I'd feel it as a punch to my midsection, whether the person spoke with disapproval, gossipy excitement, curiosity, or even a much-qualified sympathy. But nobody thought it was all right to kill.

One evening, when the kids were maybe two and five, the phone rang as we were eating. I picked up the kitchen phone, and when a familiar voice said my name, for a second I thought crazily that I was speaking to Helen. The voice was from the past, that was what I recognized. Val Benevento. I was wary but glad to hear from her—guilty that I'd let us lose touch—and too rattled to say I'd call her back when the kids were in bed. Val said she'd called to catch up, and I stood near the phone, waving at Griff to carry on without me, though I knew he disapproved of interrupting family dinners—and so did I, for that matter. I was pleased—flattered—as always when Val paid attention to me.

She lived in SoHo, she said, and was single. "Well," she said, lowering her voice, as I reached over Annie's shoulder to take the spoon she was banging on the table and place it next to her plate, "I'm dating my boss. My married boss. You know." I tried again to catch Griff's eye, to get him to stop Annie, but he was either oblivious or angry with me for staying on the phone, and she banged the spoon some more. Val worked as a publicist in a big New York publishing house. "Can I buy you lunch?" she asked. "Do you ever come into the city?"

It was classic: I was the unhappy lady in the provinces with spaghetti sauce dripping down my pants whose life held not a shred of glamour, and my old friend—with glamour to spare—was offering me a sniff of her corsage, a sip of her champagne. I stretched the phone cord so I could step around a doorjamb and not see what the children were doing—now they were starting a quarrel. I leaned against the wall and settled into a conversation, reminding myself how Val always made more things possible. I stuttered with gratitude at the prospect of lunch in New York and agreed to the first date she mentioned. At the time, I was about to leave my job and take one at the place where I still work, because it was nearer home, and I thought that because she too worked in publishing, she might like hearing about my work as an editor or about my manuscript on Edith Wharton. I'd hear interesting gossip about the married boss she slept with and her life in Manhattan.

At the end of the conversation, her voice turned sober. "And of course we have to talk about—well, you know," she said. She paused. "I missed you so much when it happened."

I had not thought of Val when Helen died.

I don't know what, if anything, Val said to her boss to justify treating our lunch as a business expense. We met at a nice place, not fancy but not funky. She waved from a table when I arrived: she was in heels and a snug suit, and she looked the same, or almost. Blonder. I wanted spaghetti or a sandwich, but I imitated Val and ordered a salad. She ordered Perrier, which I considered extravagant and silly, when water was free. Val reminisced about times we'd been together in high school and college. She first mentioned Helen's name when recalling an argument she said Helen had with a teacher in our high school English class. I didn't remember that we three had ever been in a class together.

"I talked about it with her later," she said. "She said it was nothing. I was shocked, of course—disagreeing with the teacher! I was such a good little girl."

That wasn't how I remembered either of them, and I said so.

"Well, she was quiet," Val said, "but she was so funny—that sense of humor could be wicked. Remember those imitations?"

I didn't remember imitations. Val said that at lunch, she and Helen and a couple of boys we knew used to imitate some of the teachers. "Maybe you weren't there," she said. "Helen used to do that math teacher who would lose track of what page we were on? Remember her?"

I remembered the math teacher and remembered laughter, kids in the cafeteria fumbling with textbooks, saying, "No! Not fifty-one, sixty-one! No, seventy-one!" But I didn't associate Helen with any of that. Where would she have been? We usually ate together. It made me a little uncomfortable. Had I forgotten something important about Helen? I had imagined that Val and I might touch hands and weep at the lunch table, brought together, at last, by tragedy. But she and I had never seen anything important in just the same way, and we wouldn't start now.

"The FBI infiltrated all those groups," Val said, when we got to the subject of Helen's crime. "She'd never have done what she did— shooting someone! It was entrapment."

"No, it wasn't," I blurted out. "For one thing, when it's entrapment, don't they arrest the person *before* the crime? And it would have come out. And Helen—" All Helen *had* was that crime. It was her career, her husband, her child.

"It didn't come out," Val said calmly, "because for some mysterious reason the agent *didn't* arrest them and they *did* do it. Nobody knows why. There's speculation on the radio, late at night." She paused. "I sometimes listen. There are nights when—well, you know. . . ." She gave me a look that suggested degrees of sexual risk and pain I had never contemplated.

I still didn't guess why she'd invited me. One fantasy was that she'd ask to see the biography I was writing, then offer to show it to an editor. Though I mentioned my work, she wasn't curious; I didn't know houses like hers didn't publish that sort of book. Eventually, I decided it was true that she missed me, that she wanted my friendship, and I was pleased—I'd *always* been pleased when Val wanted my friendship, even when I didn't approve of her.

Over coffee, she sat back, pushed her chair back. "I'm writing a novel," she said. Her blue eyes sought mine, and she blushed a little. She smiled. She waited to see what I'd say.

I was awestruck. How did one even begin? "That's wonderful!" I said. "What's it about?"

"I need your help," she said. "I *really* need your help. Will you help me?"

"Of course!" I said. "Is it about children?" I was an expert on Lamaze breathing during childbirth, on breastfeeding, on bathing a toddler. . . .

"It's about—well, it's fiction. It's about a made-up person."

"Yes," I said, as if agreeing that novels are fictional.

"It's about Helen."

My first emotion, I'm ashamed to say, was jealousy: Why hadn't I thought of that? I could write a novel! Surely I could. But I quickly suppressed that reaction in favor of dismay. We had no right to write novels about Helen! "Isn't it," I said quietly, my voice shaking, "isn't it—I don't know how to put this—none of our business to write about Helen?"

"Nonsense. That's what novelists *do*," Val said. "Don't worry, it will be fair—it will come out on her side. Well, insofar as that's possible. I'll immortalize Helen Weinstein."

"You're going to use her name?"

"Of course not," she said. "In the book she's Hannah Cohen."

Val had just bought me lunch, I slowly understood, because she wanted me to talk about Helen. To refuse would have led to hard feelings—and I'd just said "of course" about a favor. Besides, I *wanted* to talk about Helen, and Griff wouldn't let me. Val would let me talk.

Before we parted, we set another date. She offered to come to New Haven, but I insisted it would be hard to talk with my family around. So we planned a dinner in SoHo, where she lived. It was followed by many more.

Griff had met Val only that one time in New York, when he and I ran into her shortly after we began living together. He decided from her clothes and manner that she wasn't a serious person, certainly not an antiwar activist—she was someone our government had tricked into complacency about the war, or relative complacency. Val was against it, I assured him, but he said she wasn't against it in a way that counted. Now he was baffled that I'd take time from the book I was writing to help her write hers—which he thought of as a foolish project that would go nowhere. I was glad to talk with Val about Helen because Griff wouldn't talk about her at all, so I wasn't surprised when he dismissed the whole plan. If he thought I was somehow choosing Val over him when I left him with extra childcare, he was correct.

I loved my trips to New York. My new editing job was not full-time: I had negotiated a day a week to work on my book about Edith Wharton. I went to New York instead. My book waited while Val wrote hers. I felt bad about that, but seeing Val was a solution to a different problem and an opportunity. Sometimes I took the commuter train to New York in the morning and went shopping or met a friend or visited an art gallery. It embarrasses me to remember how, despite everything—the Perrier, the commercialism, the false enthusiasm—I wanted Val's friendship and valued the times we spent together.

We always met for dinner at an old Italian restaurant. We hugged briefly, then ordered. She'd take out a yellow legal pad and a ballpoint pen and ask a question. It was flattering to think the story of my life—the part connected to Helen, at least—was of interest. I liked again what I had always liked about Val: her conviction that she could do what she wanted to do, her practical courage, her impersonal warmth. We sat in that restaurant or lay around in Val's apartment with wine and sweets—Val liked cookies and pastries and cakes—talking, talking, until I'd rise and stretch and hurry to the subway and a commuter train that would get me to New Haven late at night, so I'd be grouchy and sleepy the next morning.

I told Val everything, without considering. I told her about Griff's crime and his belief that he was responsible for Helen's turn to violence. It was something like talking to a therapist. I didn't really imagine a book, a book people would read. When, occasionally, I became nervous, she assured me that I wouldn't be in the book. The only time in those early months when I said anything negative was when she told me her title, *Bright Morning of Pain*. "That sounds like a trashy book," I said, and Val laughed. I don't know what I expected—maybe that I'd be a heroic figure in her book, despite her assurances. I'd be a wonderful character, Helen would be accurately depicted, and Val and I would be friends forever, even if nobody paid much attention to her book.

It was written more quickly than I would have thought possible. I assumed there would be a long period of revision, but Val knew agents through her job, and over the last of our dinners she said in an offhand voice that several were eager to see it. I figured she was exaggerating, but a month later she phoned to say she had just come from the post office, where she'd mailed copies of the manuscript to an agent she had a good feeling about, and also to me.

Again, her call had come while we ate supper. When I hung up ("Hey, good luck!" I said), I was disappointed and ashamed of being disappointed. I had imagined seeing the manuscript before anyone else did, making suggestions to which Val would listen gratefully. I'd go into greater detail about events she hadn't quite understood. The book would make Val and me friends forever—Val would grow up a little—even if it were never published. When I now turned from the phone, the children were at play in the next room, their food still on their plates. Griff was reading a magazine while finishing his dinner.

I hauled the kids back. Griff watched, expressionless. "You might have said you'd call her back," he said. "Of course, the children felt neglected."

"They didn't feel *neglected!*" I said. He was silent. "And if they needed something, where were you?" He didn't answer.

That night, I thought things through and decided the agent would surely turn down the manuscript and Val would be hurt. It would be my job to console her, maybe to help her improve the book after all, so the next agent would be more receptive. Even if she didn't know it, she still needed me. So a few days later, when the children and I came home to find a package from Val, wrapped in brown paper and tied with string, I seized it eagerly. The children were disappointed that the package wasn't for them and watched me open it, still hoping. Inside the brown wrapping paper was a box that had once held a ream of typewriter paper and was now three-quarters full of a manuscript.

Griff wouldn't be home until late that night. I cooked supper for me and the children, while they colored on the brown wrapping paper. Annie scribbled over Martha's drawings of people and flowers; Martha hit her. We ate. I bathed them and put them to bed. At last, I began to read.

■

As Val had promised, I wasn't in the book: the character who was supposedly Helen—Hannah Cohen—had only one friend in high school, and she was a version of Val, called Violet Bonning—I noted Val's initials. I read about the incident Val had mentioned: Hannah Cohen arguing with a teacher, Violet feeling shocked. But then I came to the day when Hannah wouldn't eat a hot dog because she was upset about the man who immolated himself to protest the Vietnam War. I'd told Val that story. In the book, Violet Bonning buys hot dogs—two, not one torn in half. Eventually she eats them both.

But something more important had also changed. Hannah was not upset just about the stranger who had died. She'd been told about the death by a boy she liked. Hannah had said something to the boy that she regretted. She was afraid he wouldn't like her anymore. And secretly, Violet liked the same boy. These were attitudes Helen and I would have scorned at the time, serious little virgins that we were, but reading, I thought we'd have done better to like boys, to be more normal, to be more like Val. Helen and I hadn't had the nerve to live the life Val had imagined for us—or for Helen and Val herself. Helen would be alive, I found myself thinking, if she'd been Val's friend instead of mine. Maybe she really did imitations of the math teacher. Why had she stopped? Could Val have helped her continue if I hadn't been in the way?

When I began to dislike Val's book, as I read that night, I didn't let myself know it, partly because I couldn't admit to Griff what was wrong with it. When he found me in bed reading the manuscript, I said it was "pretty good." I moved to the living room, wrapped in an afghan Griff's mother had knitted, and read compulsively into the night.

Some incidents were just as I'd described them. Some were invented or invented except for one detail, which I'd suddenly recognize. The blue beads. But the tone was consistent, the message. Hannah—the woman who supposedly was Helen—was well-meaning but confused, distracted by sex, love, and jealousy, and thus forgivably mistaken, like the heroine of many books about girls growing into women, books in which the girl gets things straight, finally, at the end—and gets the guy. This book was new in one way: it ended just before Hannah came to see how wrong she'd been. But there were hints. And, of course, Hannah didn't get the guy. Violet Bonning would get the guy—a different guy, by then. Right after the last page.

First, I was angry with Val. Then I understood what an idiot I'd been. She had told me she was writing a novel. I told her the story of Helen and me, knowing she was writing a novel, knowing she wanted help with her novel. But Val wasn't a ghostwriter, hired to write the novel I'd have written myself, if only I'd thought of it first and been brave enough. What I knew mattered to Val, but she didn't care about my viewpoint. Why should she? The viewpoint, inevitably, was Val's, and I had disappeared into a character who was a version of Val, living our story as she would have if she'd had a best friend something like Helen. Violet had Val's personality but, at least in the first part of the book, lived my life.

The invented action mostly had to do with men. I had told Val that Helen and I both slept with Eli, and rivalry over a man became the most prominent theme. The second half was much more fictionalized. Hannah has committed a crime and disappeared, but in the novel, Violet Bonning participates in the first crime, though neither she nor Hannah does anything violent. She disappears with the rest of them. Living together in a safe house, they again love the same man. When Val imagined herself as me, she imagined a braver, sexier, and more reckless me. This character was something of a reproach to me—the book seemed to ask me why I *wasn't* always at Helen's side. Except in Val's book, all the political action feels safer, more glamorous, less morally suspect than it was: a fantasy.

Then, Harry arrives—the character based on Griff. Val transposed him from the period in which he really turned up in our lives—before

Helen's first crime—to the period when the group are fugitives from justice. Some of the less attractive men in the group have shot and wounded people, but the women have done nothing more than dump blood at draft boards. It is Harry, the black man from Hartford, son and grandson of clergymen, who commits a violent crime and persuades Hannah to do the same.

Meanwhile, Violet Bonning and her boyfriend agree that the boyfriend will pretend he loves Hannah, so as to draw her away from the part of their group that is planning to use guns. It will turn out that they've been infiltrated by someone from the FBI (as in the rumors Val reported), who is urging them to become more violent. This man has fooled the FBI and is an actual revolutionary—which is why he lets the crime take place instead of arresting those planning it. Violet Bonning's boyfriend tries to keep Hannah out of it but then is conned as well. Even Violet has a gun in a drawer, though she doesn't use it. It's a sexist plot in which women do nothing unless urged and taught by men, but—as people remembered at our dinner party—at the end, when a cop aims at Violet's boyfriend, Hannah shoots him. Val left it ambiguous whether Hannah (or the policeman) lives or dies.

After I finished reading the manuscript, I told Griff a little about it, but not that Val used what I said about him—and not that I said it. I was too ashamed, ashamed of my entire participation in this project. My only hope was that Val wouldn't be able to publish the novel, which had flaws unrelated to my participation. Scenes were confusing. Description was overly luscious. But despite everything, I couldn't put down the book, especially once I reached the second, imagined part. The book was large and intense and wilder than anything I would ever write in my life. Val had written about sex and violence when we were kids, and she could still do that—though there was something showy about the violence. Sometimes my words—my side comments, my exclamations—had made it into the book. I was subtly thrilled, and I was sick.

That first agent grabbed the manuscript and quickly found a publisher. Val got a big advance, for the time. A year or so later, *Bright Morning of Pain* was published. There was an advertising campaign and a tour. Val was on the *Today* show. Limousines drew up outside bookstores and auditoriums, and Val climbed out. She quit her job to write her next book.

Throughout, I pretended I was happy—pleased at my friend's success, as any nice person would be. I tried to convince myself that I *was* happy. The book, I pointed out to myself, really had nothing to do with Helen. It was simply an achievement by someone I knew, brought about with my help.

"So how much of it is autobiographical?" an interviewer asked Val, shortly after the book came out.

"Well, it's fiction," Val said. "*You* know."

"Did you ever have a gun in a drawer?"

"Let's not talk about *that*. As I said, the book is fiction."

"Were you close to Helen Weinstein?"

"We were friends as children, and in high school. We went to a protest together. I remember her crying on the way home."

I went to see Val when she read in New York, and listened to what by then were familiar paragraphs. In the question period she said again, "It's *fiction*." And smiled.

"What did you do during the war?" someone asked.

"I was involved," Val said. "Those were hard times." She sighed, and then she said, "Helen Weinstein wrote me a letter when she was in hiding. I've never told anyone this. She said she regretted her choices and wished she could get away, but she was afraid they'd kill her. She knew too much."

Someone asked, "Do you have this letter?"

"She told me to destroy it," Val said. "So—no."

When Val began signing books after the question period, I squeezed past the line, touched her shoulder, mouthed, "Congratulations!" and left. I took the next train to New Haven and got home before I expected to.

A week later, I saw the same claim in a printed interview. I phoned Val. "I'm happy for you," I said. "But of course that's not true about the letter."

Val hesitated. "You can't prove it isn't," she said, "and if you try, you'll just seem jealous." Then she said, "Let me pretend she was my friend, Olive, please. I know damned well she wasn't. And maybe if she'd let me be close to her, she'd be alive today."

I'd had the same thought myself. But I said, "Why would she be alive?" My voice was shaking.

"I'd have known how to talk her out of it." Val said she had to run. She hung up.

I didn't tell Griff about the conversation or the supposed letter. I didn't tell anyone. I was as stunned and impressed by Val's cool willingness to lie as I'd been in high school by Val's bold, embarrassing fiction.

By the time the book came out, Griff knew I was upset about it, but he thought that was ungenerous of me: that I was jealous of my dopey friend for doing something that I—with what he regarded as my better capacities—had not done. He didn't read the book. It didn't *matter*, he said. There was no reason to read it. What mattered was real life—my memories of Helen, our friendship—which no novel could change. There was always some truth to his arguments, but he never got it just right, and I couldn't tell him exactly what I'd said to Val or what I felt now, so we were less and less able to understand each other. I couldn't say—I couldn't have put into words then—that the book had created a version of Helen devoid of convictions, which were all she had. And that that was my fault.

Then someone asked Griff for the first time about "that guy Harry in that book," and he came home barely able to speak. At last, I told him the whole story of what I'd said. "You didn't do wrong," he said tensely, when I wept and apologized and wept again. "It's true. It *was* my fault. People may as well know it."

He was silent for an hour. "It will kill my father," he said. It didn't. I'm not sure Reverend Griffin or Sally ever heard of the book. He was a reader, but, like his youngest son, not of novels. Sally read novels— but not that kind of novel.

■

Bright Morning of Pain was shortlisted for a couple of prizes. It was attacked both for glorifying antiwar violence and for failing to glorify it enough. Some critics thought the writing was bad; some were entranced. It was called a feminist book—it was called sexist. As all this happened, I wasn't entirely miserable. My feelings about Val had always been full of contradictions. At some moments, I was thrilled that she'd actually gone and done this big bold thing. And I liked some things about the book. The second half trivialized Helen, if you thought of Hannah as Helen, and trivialized women, even if you didn't. But it was exciting to read. As for the other issues, I continued to believe in freedom of the imagination, in Val's right to use the material I gave her as she wanted to use it. I didn't think she had a right to lie about the letter she claimed Helen had written her, but I was so prone to self-doubt at that time, that sometimes I wondered if I had misunderstood Helen all along, if she'd really wanted to quit. I wanted to be happy about everything to do with Val's book, as a friend should be.

And it's a thrill to have anything to do with success. Like Val herself, her success made new enterprises seem more possible. I told my friends about it without disclosing everything, chuckling ruefully at Val's wide-eyed soul, the omission of the politics, but dropping her name, regardless. It was fun—but I've never been good at fun. I agreed—only sometimes cringing inwardly—with the friends who told me how special the book was for me, in particular, for someone who was close to both Helen and Val. I was asked to reminisce in a women's magazine about high school with Val and wrote a short, pleasant piece about *Sidewalks* and how the principal did whatever Valerie Benevento wanted.

Meanwhile, Martha started school while Annie continued at the co-op daycare. Griff's father had a heart attack—it was a frightening time, during which I at last began to feel close to the Griffin family. My mother had a heart attack—again, we worried, and we both became closer to *my* family. The last thing our parents needed was children with troubled marriages, and without consulting each other, Griff and I decided so definitely that we would *not* have trouble, that we stopped arguing for a while. In retrospect I see that we began then to establish the habit of having little to do with each other. I was startled to realize one day that I'd told two friends I'd finished my book about Wharton and—on the advice of the professor I had worked for—had mailed it to a publisher, but I hadn't told Griff.

I didn't tell Val either. She and I were out of touch again. I didn't seek her out, and she was always more interested in men than in any woman friend and maybe a little nervous about remarks she'd made in interviews, hints about Helen, not to mention her claim about a letter. "My sister babysat her," she said in print once. "I wouldn't say I was at her side every moment during the war years, of course." Being close to a criminal was apparently good for book sales, good for Val's reputation.

■

A couple of years after *Bright Morning of Pain* came out, I was asked to write an essay of some length about it by a friend from graduate school who edited a small literary journal, *The Rocky Hill Review*, which was connected to a university. I was delighted. The journal is long gone now—one of those earnest, slightly stodgy but witty and well-written magazines that one suspects is read only by the contributors and their best friends. This was long before the internet, so I could say what I liked without being afraid it would go viral. No one would take me to task no matter what I said, not even Val.

By then I'd published the Edith Wharton book. It sold modestly; I got a few respectful reviews in academic journals. I was asked to speak about Wharton at libraries and some small colleges, and when I paused for questions, people who'd discovered that I'd gone to school with Valerie Benevento sometimes asked about her. Nobody asked me about Helen Weinstein, who was regarded as Val's friend, not mine. Asked about Val, I again and again described the literary club and how we put out a magazine and published her stories. I admitted to some conversations with Val when she was writing, and I was praised for helping her.

So when my old friend asked for an essay, I was ready to tell the truth. I had something to say about *Bright Morning of Pain* itself, but I didn't yet know what it was. In my essay for *The Rocky Hill Review*, I told the story of my friendship with Helen—our closeness, her transformation, my grief—and my relationship, early and later, with Val: how Val, as a young woman working in publishing, reconnected with me, how I told her the story of my friendship with Helen, and how she used our friendship in the book, putting a character who resembled herself in my place. I saw my piece as comparable to essays I found in dusty bound volumes of literary journals about long-dead novelists: an eyewitness account of how an author went about writing what she wrote, a modest, secondary account that someone might find useful. I didn't say Val claimed to be Helen's friend, nor that she wasn't Helen's friend, only that I was.

As I wrote and revised my essay, I asked myself only two questions: Was it well-written? And was it true? I worked on it carefully and mailed it to the editor of the *Review*. I didn't show it to Griff before I sent it. I rarely showed him anything I wrote, because his intensity about anything that touched on him, even remotely, kept him from judging my arguments on their own terms. But when the magazine arrived, I was excited. I left it in our living room. That night, while I was putting Martha and Annie to bed, Griff found and read my essay. I was singing to the children when he came into their bedroom, probably some sixties song by Joni Mitchell or Bob Dylan. Griff came in with his arms held stiffly at his sides, one hand grasping the journal, a finger acting as a bookmark. He thrust it in my direction, interrupting me. "You shouldn't have done this, Olive."

"I'll be out in a minute," I said—furious—and he withdrew.

When I came into the living room, before I could speak, he said, sounding like the principal he hadn't yet become, "I know why you were tempted to write this, and I don't blame you for being tempted, but you shouldn't have done it."

"What do you know about writing essays?" I said.

He was sitting and I was standing, always a bad arrangement. "Nothing," he said. "But I know that I shouldn't embarrass a friend."

"She'll never see it."

"How do you know?"

"Nobody will see it," I stupidly insisted. I pointed out that I hadn't condemned Val in the essay, only said what happened. It was about me—about knowing Helen and helping with a book. Writers and readers might find it interesting.

"It was selfish," he insisted. Like Helen, he was good at blaming himself—and like Helen, he held friends and family to the standards to which he held himself. He expected more of his daughters than they could manage, and now he was expecting more of me. I suppose he was hurt that I hadn't told him.

We spoke in harsh whispers, with the girls still awake in the next room. "How do you know it won't be read?" he said.

■

I was wrong about *Rocky Hill Review*, which was not read only by the contributors and their best friends. Or maybe somebody's best friend had connections. *Harper's* ran a piece on little magazines. It mentioned a poem here, a story there, and then it quoted my essay.

The next thing I knew, I was on the phone with a *New York Times* reporter. "Yes," I said. "It's true." My biography of Edith Wharton, published by a respectable press, made me reliable. Val, when told about my essay, said it lied both about my friendship with Helen and my conversations with Val—but I must have seemed more believable than she did. I'm sure that my editor, if asked, would have said I didn't have enough imagination to invent such a story. I imagined her saying, "Grossman's as honest as dust under the bed."

The media enjoy discovering that successful people are not what they have claimed to be. Suddenly, widely read articles pointed out what I'd always known: that Valerie Benevento invented Hannah Cohen, that Helen Weinstein had a political agenda, not just sexual desire, that Valerie Benevento had let the public think she was a former revolutionary when she was nothing of the kind. By then, it seemed, it was not reprehensible to be a former revolutionary, it was exciting; it was reprehensible to have *pretended* to be a revolutionary. For a couple of weeks in the eighties, Val Benevento was everyone's favorite scoundrel.

After I got over being astonished, I was furious with myself—again—for not realizing what I had been doing. I have never allowed myself to be quite that self-deceived since. I didn't regret writing the essay, but I regretted doing it without having the courage to know I was doing it.

Val called me up and told me I was evil, that her book was a work of the imagination and she had never said it wasn't, that I was an envious bitch and she would have nothing further to do with me. She never did.

Griff blamed me again, just when I most needed reassurance. "Anything in print may be *read*," he pointed out with impeccable logic—though only a writer knows the extent to which what is in print, or even on the Web, nowadays—may be *unread*. Now I became, in Griff's mind, not only unkind but reckless. I had risked Val's happiness. I remembered Val's plea, back when the book came out, to let her pretend Helen was her friend. I didn't think I'd prevented Val from pretending—but maybe I had. The more I worried that Griff might be right, the angrier I was with him. It crossed my mind to wonder if it was Griff who'd sent the journal to the writer of the *Harper's* essay, just to prove his point—and the fact that such an idea came to me shows how far we'd gone.

I felt terrible about what I'd done, though baffled—didn't I have *some* kind of right to describe my own life? How long could Val exploit Helen and me—endlessly? Val said I had humiliated her in public because I was self-righteous. When I had written the essay, I'd felt not morally superior, only misunderstood. I was someone too, and the wave of fame that had washed over Val had touched me negatively. I was officially nonexistent—there was no character in the book who resembled me, and the one who was closest was being taken as Val herself.

Worse, my intensely principled friendship with Helen had become, in the book, a gossipy connection between two women who loved a man and thought of little else but him, while the political, moral, and philosophical issues Helen and her friends had struggled with were colorful background. The book offered the familiar, easy view of the sixties as a time of free love, patched jeans, music, and peace symbols stenciled on T-shirts. The war itself was missing from the book.

Soon my essay and I were forgotten, but Val became publicly interesting again a year later, because—of all things—she died. She had been trying unsuccessfully to write a second novel, interrupted by a tempestuous life. There were men, some who were minor celebrities, some who hurt her. One or two were mildly unsavory; she was photographed, for example, with a politician who was accused of taking bribes. Then she got involved with a charity in Africa that rescued young girls from sex slavery. Val had made money from her book. She had a kind, sentimental heart. Since she couldn't write, she had spare time, and she craved adventure. She agreed to go to Africa and serve as a spokesperson for this charity. Somewhere in central Africa, on a rutted road in the rain, she was killed in a bus accident.

Again, Val and her book made headlines, and this time she was exonerated from her crimes. The public decided that creative people, however erratic, mean well. Valerie Benevento's behavior in dying had been both noble and risky, and she was retroactively understood as someone who'd *always* been noble, if unthinking: writing her novel, she had wanted to have befriended a troubled young revolutionary so badly that she'd imagined that she had done so. Nobody blamed me, exactly. Insofar as anyone remembered my essay, I was too dull and methodical to understand the Vals of the world—which isn't far from the truth.

I had regretted that Val was angry and unhappy, and, of course, I felt worse when she died. And confused, because I was also glad she was dead. And grief-stricken. I would never figure out how to be friends with either Helen or Val. Griff made it all worse. These were the years when Griff became first a coordinator of programs for gifted children and then a principal, though he didn't yet have the small and highly effective school for troubled kids that he eventually founded, a place where he could be creative, not just hardworking and rigorous. He had done well in his profession, and his reward, during the years of our bad time, was more paperwork, more long meetings down-town—often with cynics and time-servers, whom he loathed. At home, he was suspicious of me—uncomfortable with my literary concerns, uncomfortable with my friends. His parents would never value his teaching as much as they'd have valued the ministry—or so he thought. He still didn't read *Bright Morning of Pain*, and in his imagination, the character of Harry was someone violent without cause who had indirectly killed a promising young woman.

So once Val was dead, Griff and I, according to him, were all but murderers together: he'd killed Helen, and I'd killed Val. Though he didn't quite say it, he made clear that he thought that if it hadn't been for the controversy, Val would have been quietly at home writing a novel instead of riding on that bus. I thought it was unlikely that Val would ever have written a second novel.

I'd always loved Griff for his courage and his moral sense as much as anything, but when that seriousness was turned against me, it looked like pride and a wish to control. I almost hated him. He was the same Griff, but not in a way I could use. He often worked evenings, leaving me alone with the children. He was stern with them and spoke to me, I told a friend, as if I were an incompetent employee. "What do you want?" she said, and I said, "I want him to *go away*."

He didn't want to separate. "I love you," he said solemnly.

"It doesn't feel like it."

"I do, though. I do."

Maybe he did love me, but I couldn't trust or love him after he made me ashamed of that essay, which was not shameful. That I might write what I had soberly decided I should write was part of what was holy to me. It makes me angry all over again to think of him telling me I should not have told that truth. It may seem like a strange fault to cause a long marital rift. Griff was sexually faithful, except when we'd both decided not to be, when he lived elsewhere. He was honest and hardworking, and he didn't drink or hit me. But he made me feel ashamed of that essay, and I told myself that was why we separated. The real reason was related but different. Helen killed someone and died; Val told the world that what Helen had done was trivial. I blamed Griff so I wouldn't notice how bad I felt about Helen and how Val had made it worse.

After months of argument about whether he loved me, I insisted on a separation. He said he couldn't do this to his parents, and that was one reason that when he at last went, he moved upstairs, where the apartment happened to be vacant. His family didn't have to know.

The girls told their grandparents immediately, of course, and the Griffins weren't surprised. Griff's actual parents were more observant than the ones he thought he had.

I made him buy a bed and a table and helped him move. I gave him dishes and pots. He kept following me back down, and I changed the locks. At last he saw that this was real, and he bought beds for Martha and Annie, who were ten and seven in 1983, the year Val died. A few months later, Griff moved out. The children liked climbing the stairs to Daddy's house, which they did on their own, with a parent watching at each end. They stayed with him Friday and Saturday nights and spent Saturdays with him. I'd hear them coming down the stairs, the back and forth of intent conversation, sometimes laughter. Alone with them, his sense of responsibility took over, and he was apparently kinder and more fun than I'd dared to hope. I expected to be lonely when the kids were upstairs and tried to be out of the house in the evenings, but there came a day when staying home was the most tempting option, and I discovered that I loved hearing the girls' footsteps above my head. I knew they were fine, but I was free.

I didn't miss Griff or the children. Like many parents, I had a solitude deficit: loneliness wouldn't be an issue for a long while. I remembered the years when I thought I should be in Helen's apartment and also wanted to leave, to forget the war and read nineteenth-century novels. I recognized that same wish for solitude and the delicious feeling when I finally got it.

Griff had never wanted to be apart and still didn't. He had too much pride to ask me, each time I saw him, whether he could move back. It wasn't a topic to discuss with the children around, anyway, and the children were nearly always around. He didn't mind giving me money. He earned far more than I did; I think it was a comfort that I needed him financially. The house remained his as well as mine, and we each contributed to the mortgage payments, but he put in more.

One day, when we'd been apart for a year, Griff asked if we could have dinner alone together. I hired a sitter, and we met at a restaurant where the tables were far enough apart that we could talk. I thought he'd suggest getting back together, but I'd misjudged him. It was an Italian place, and he studied the spaghetti he twirled on his fork before saying that he was moving out of the upstairs apartment. "I would like to have the chance to ask a lady to dinner," he said.

I was eating penne. I stabbed them like fish as I thought about what he'd said. I wasn't happy that he wanted to see other women, and my discomfort was the first hint that I might come to the end of this experiment and want him back—and what if he was no longer available?

I didn't want to see other men. I was still using up that solitude deficit. I was happy to go out for dinner or drinks with friends, but though I missed sex, it seemed like too much emotional trouble. Nobody asked me out, anyway.

"If this is how things are going to be," Griff said, twirling some more spaghetti, "there's no point in pretending otherwise."

I didn't say that yes, this was the way things would be. I wanted to say, "Don't take somebody else out to dinner!"

Instead, I said, "You are free to decide whom you spend your time with."

Too upset to talk about all the possibilities, I pretended I was fine with all the possibilities, but that was a bad week. I thought I'd made a mistake, I'd lose my husband, but I was powerless to keep him, and I knew I couldn't get along with him if I had him. I didn't talk to anyone. My friends would have said, "If you feel so bad, tell him you'll take him back," but I couldn't.

Then he changed his mind—after a man I met through my work asked if I were ever free for "coffee or something." We went to see *Broadway Danny Rose*. Maybe the girls found out that while they were upstairs I went to a movie with a man. Maybe Griff saw him from the window. Suddenly, he didn't want to move away—and now, encouraged by my new popularity, I wanted him to go. I insisted that he look for an apartment elsewhere. After protests, he moved to West Haven, to an apartment near the water, and I rented the apartment upstairs to a couple of graduate students, so we could continue to afford two households. I dated the man from work for months, and someone else after that. Then Martha told me Griff had a "sort-of girlfriend" who came along on outings with him and the children.

"How do you know she's his girlfriend?" I said.

"I asked him," she said. "He said, 'Sort of.'"

The girls were spending whole weeks with him by then, alternating with weeks at my house. I guess that woman was a girlfriend, because she lasted. The girls liked her and I wondered if we'd divorce and she'd be their stepmother. In some respects, it didn't seem like a bad way of living. Griff and I could be friends. Maybe we had always been meant to be friends.

Dating other men, I was experiencing a particular kind of surprise and anticipation I had thought I was done with: the moment when I knew a man was about to make a move in my direction, the little swirl of delight when he did. I was sensible enough to pick nice people, and the sex turned out to be welcome. Nice men tend to be shy, so it wasn't passionate, but that was okay; I didn't have time or energy to have my heart broken every few months.

The men were fine, but I never lost the delight in solitude I'd felt at the beginning of our separation—I still have it. The pleasure of spending an evening with these men was often pleasure I'd have cheerfully done without, as I'd realize when someone called to say he was sick or busy and couldn't go out after all.

Griff must have been reasonably happy with the sort-of girlfriend, because he stopped making occasions to talk about our situation. We'd get together more casually to plan vacation schedules or teachers' conferences. A surprising amount of time passed. Then one day, more than three years after we'd separated—toward the end of a lunch we'd scheduled to make some household decision or other—Griff settled back in his chair, as people do when they have something important to say. I thought he might ask for a divorce. I got ready to feel bad. But he said, "I think it's time we got back together."

To my surprise, I felt a surge of joy, as if this were a romantic comedy and, despite everything, the guy I loved had just taken out a ring. He leaned forward, and I noticed that the lines on Griff's face had deepened. He smiled, but with so much sorrow, so much rueful wisdom, that I couldn't give him an unconsidered answer. But I was late for a meeting at work. I didn't know what to say, so I said, "We'll talk about it."

We had lived past Helen's death and Val's book and Val's death. Griff would always be someone who thought he knew best what other people ought to do—he still is—and he still thought I'd done wrong to write that essay. I knew he did; I didn't have to ask. But I'd lived enough to feel sure of what I believed, whether he approved or not. It's tricky to marry someone who thinks for hours a day about ethics and God and how to live. I hadn't known that I too had a moral code, but it turned out that I did, and it wasn't identical to his. I believed in freedom of the imagination. I believed in Val's freedom, however uncomfortable her book made me. I could never say it shouldn't have been written, trashy or not. But that meant I too had freedom. Freedom to write what I had written. Freedom to love my reprehensible, lost friend.

So it took a few days, but then I said yes. The guys I'd dated couldn't compete with Joshua Griffin. The upstairs apartment happened to be empty when he moved back, so for the first time, we had the whole house to ourselves. A year or two later, renovations made it more like a one-family house: we took out the upstairs kitchen appliances and removed a door at the bottom of the stairs. In some ways, it still felt more like two houses, and Griff occasionally complained. The arrangement suited me.

■

When Griff—decades later—became president of the board of Barker Street, I was angry, and I guess I was right to be, not because, as I had predicted, there were so very many meetings and other obligations but because Barker Street upset him. One morning, he blurted out something about the previous president, who seemed to think his job was to prevent anything anyone wanted to do. Griff, the board must have thought, would be an improvement, and I knew he would be. But from the start, Griff and Jean were at odds. I didn't understand why he was so negative about the employee Jean kept talking about, Paulette, and since he was, why Jean kept talking about her. Finally, Griff explained that he'd persuaded Jean to hire Paulette in the first place, and then they'd both changed their minds. Whenever the name Barker Street was mentioned in our house, he'd predict trouble.

It wouldn't have mattered to me if he'd followed me around complaining about Jean Argos or her staff member. But instead, he became tense and quiet—touchy. After dinner he climbed the stairs in his socks. I heard him go, but it felt as if he was sneaking up there, to Annie's old room and the TV. I resented his departure, though I knew that if I'd let him keep the TV downstairs, he'd be downstairs with it. Lying on the sofa in the evenings with laptop and books—trying and failing to write, yet again, about *Bright Morning of Pain*—I'd hear the muffled sound of a sports broadcast: crowd noise, the announcer's sharper tone at a tense moment. Baseball—a bad end-of-season for the Red Sox—gave way to football.

I didn't spend all my time on Val's book. That fall, I worked on three projects: an intricate book about embroidery, a subject I do not care for; an essay I'd been writing about some novels written after the

First World War; and the essay about *Bright Morning*. Which still went badly. The editor sent emails: it was nearly due, then overdue. I stayed downstairs, accomplishing little, heaving myself off the sofa to move through the downstairs rooms—kitchen, living room, and the room behind the kitchen that had been our bedroom when we lived on the first floor, now used mostly for storage and wet boots. Then I'd lie down again, without having found a sufficient reason for standing up. It seemed that, after all, I had nothing left to say about *Bright Morning of Pain*.

If I had been working well, the solitude would have been fruitful. When Griff was upstairs, it was as if he had gone out, and I could think. But in the bad mood that persisted, the arrangement felt hostile: it recalled the years before he moved away. Sometimes, again, he'd be asleep before I got into bed. Sometimes, he'd have gone to work before I woke up.

One evening shortly before Christmas, I heard his phone ring, and then his urgent voice rising. "What? What did you say? I didn't hear you." The conversation persisted. He sounded alarmed, maybe angry. He hung up, and then his phone rang again, and again I heard urgency. Concerned, I went to the staircase, then upstairs.

Annie's old room is small, and the TV is large. Griff had moved a chair out when he bought it, so he mostly sat on the bed—sprawled, almost lying down. But now he was sitting on the edge, staring at his phone.

"What's going on?" I asked.

"Barker. I knew this would happen."

"What?"

"Somebody's dying. He's probably dying."

"A client? How—"

"One of those unsupervised employees, though technically I believe they had fired him."

"What happened?"

"He set himself on fire."

"What? On purpose? On the third floor?"

"No, the stove. On purpose? Of course not. He was drunk. Of course he was drunk." I finally got him to tell me what happened. A former employee had been allowed into the building by the man in charge of the third-floor rooms. The man who got in tried to light the oven and caused a fire. He was in the ICU.

"He was lighting the stove? A gas stove?"

"I suppose it's a gas stove if he was lighting it. The oven, I guess." It reminded me of something, something to do with Helen, and then I remembered the oven in the apartment. It almost seemed as if it were the same stove, finally doing the harm we'd feared.

"It took her all day to call me. It's on the news websites already—I just checked. She finally figured it was time I heard about it!"

"You mean Jean?"

"I'm the last to know. *Why* did I say yes? Why did I let them have overnights?"

"You didn't advocate letting drunks light the stove."

"If the building weren't open, nobody would have let the man in, and this wouldn't have happened."

"Griff," I said. "This is not your fault. For God's sake."

Griff stood up. He looked at me. "Nevertheless, if I hadn't agreed, it wouldn't have happened." He put on his shoes and went to the hospital to see about the injured man.

The man died. His family turned up—he was from an Italian family in Waterbury. He had grown children who hadn't seen him in years. After the accident, Griff worked closely with Jean, and, overhearing conversations, I could tell that at heart they were similar; they should have been able to work together. They apparently spent hours on the phone or sitting across from each other, talking and then falling silent, sighing and trying to talk again. Meanwhile, the fire had damaged the agency's kitchen, and repairs were necessary. An insurance claim had to be filed. Overnights on the third floor were discontinued; the agency had to close for a few days.

I wasn't in touch with Jean. Our friendship had faltered once I no longer had need of friendly visits. I wanted to see her, but a phone call might have been an intrusion on Griff's business. Then, a week or two after the fire, I stopped at a market in our neighborhood to pick up something for supper and met Jean at the meat counter. We dropped our wire shopping baskets to put our arms around each other, holding each other as if at a funeral. The store was crowded, so it was something of an accomplishment.

I told her I was so very sorry, and she shook her head with a you-don't-know-the-half-of-it look. So I invited her to come home with me for a glass of wine. During the school year, I never expected Griff early, and I thought I remembered a late meeting that night.

Jean wanted to come—I had a feeling she needed somebody to do something for her, anything. I hurried through my shopping and met her with her smaller bag of groceries outside, and we drove our separate cars to my house, a few blocks away. I poured wine and sat her down in the living room. "Tell me about it," I said. "Griff talks in riddles. Unless you'd rather not?"

Jean took a deep breath. She talked for a long while. Then she said, "There was nothing wrong with the overnight project. There is nothing wrong with Paulette. Well, there is plenty wrong with Paulette—but she's worth it."

I said, "You're angry with Griff, but don't be angry with me."

She hesitated. "No, that's right."

"I don't invariably agree with him," I said. "Hardly ever, come to think of it."

"You two are pretty independent," Jean said.

"Too independent," I said. I usually told myself we were just independent enough.

We talked for more than an hour. What troubled Jean most was something she thought Griff had been trying to tell her all along. "Everything gets trickier when you're talking about *night*," she said. "*All* night. That's what he meant. At three a.m., people think crazy thoughts. I didn't think of it as different from day, only *extra* day."

"You don't still think the project could work?" I said.

Jean put down her glass, started to get up, adjusted her pants, sat down, smoothed her knees, picked up her glass again. "Yes," she said. "It can work. I'm not sure I ever thought it could work. I do now—but we need to do some things differently."

I thought she looked younger, oddly—then realized she'd gained some weight. Her face was rounder, more attractive. "Are you still seeing Zak?"

No. "He's impossible." They had stayed together until Arturo died. She had almost broken up with him several times. Then she did. "Nothing in particular happened, this time," she said. "But I was sad—well, he wouldn't be sad. Couldn't be."

"I'm sorry!"

"Oh, so am I!"

■

As had happened once before when Jean was visiting, Griff came home unexpectedly. I felt a slight thrill when he arrived. Maybe I had taken that chance because I wanted to be present when the two of them were together. When he saw Jean, he sat down without taking off his coat. "I'm sorry to interrupt," he said. He didn't sound friendly.

"No, no," we both said.

"Did you eat?" I asked.

"No."

"Neither did we," I said. "Should I cook?"

"I'm not staying," Griff said. "Meeting Kevin." This was a former student Griff had befriended at a time of trouble. Kevin still needed counseling occasionally, or at least friendship, and they'd meet in a coffee shop.

"What about food?"

"They have sandwiches."

"Right," I said. "The last sandwich leftover from lunch—cold and stale."

"For me, they heat it in the microwave," he said, smiling.

"Mmm," I said. "Hot lettuce and mayonnaise." Griff looked old when he smiled, like someone's grandfather.

Jean put her glass on the table. "I should go."

"Stay," I said. "Griff's going."

"I hate to ruin your evening, Joshua," she said. "I'm not who you want to see in your only ten minutes off all day."

"You're not my enemy," Griff said, looking straight at her.

"So you've come around?"

"What?"

"I'm reopening the third floor," Jean said. "We're starting respites next week and overnights two weeks later."

Griff didn't say or do anything for a few moments. Then he stood, reaching reflexively into his pants pockets to check for his wallet and keys. "We'll talk about this another time," he said.

I thought that was that, but on his way out, he turned, a hand on the doorknob. "You know I've never cared for your third-floor program," he said. "And certainly not overnights." I saw Jean sit up straight. Griff went on, "Doubtless, there are elements I fail to understand. But we're not having any more suffering while I'm the president of this board, and I plan to do what it takes to prevent it."

Jean looked up at him. "You'd can me?" she said.

He was silent again. "I've been on boards that let a director go," he said. "It's the most painful process there is. I'd rather not." He smiled a weary smile, and again he looked old—and kind.

"Joshua," Jean said, as he stood with his hand on the front door, "listen to me. If we worked in a law firm where somebody caused a fire and died, we'd be very, very sad, and we would try very, very hard to make sure it couldn't happen again—but we wouldn't close the place down. If it happened in your school, you wouldn't close the school. If it happened anywhere but in a social services program, everyone would be sad, but life would go back to normal."

"This was never normal," he said. His voice got quiet. "The third floor must go. I don't mean you have to give up the space. Maybe the respite program is all right. But while I'm responsible—no overnights. No Paulette, no Dunbar. We don't even know yet whether Arturo's family will sue."

"We have insurance if they do," Jean said. "I think maybe they should. It shouldn't have happened. No one understands that better than Dunbar. He's devastated. I don't want to lose him. I want the benefit of what happened that night, not just the pain."

"You'd put him in charge again?"

"It'll be different," Jean said.

"Paulette has to go. Dunbar has to go."

"No." Jean stood. "I'm sorry, Olive. I don't think I should stay. Joshua—I don't think you'd have the votes to get rid of me. Just saying." She left. Neither of us saw her out.

I thought Griff would wait just long enough for her to drive away before he went to meet Kevin, but he sat down again. I looked at him. "You're still wearing your coat," I said.

"I'm hungry," he said.

"I'm not saying I entirely agree with you," I said.

"Have you *ever* agreed with me?" He looked older than ever, like someone who'd been the chief justice of the Supreme Court for decades and had suffered over every ambiguous case that might do harm to anyone.

"About anything?" I said.

"About anything," Griff said.

There was a silence so long that it felt as if my life might have changed. Then I said, "Yes."

"But not recently," he said. He left.

■

Waking one night, I was alone in bed. I was angry with Griff—I still considered myself, in some way, separated from Griff—but I went downstairs to look for him, after glancing into Annie's old room. In his dark green woolen bathrobe, a substantial Christmas/Hanukkah present the girls had chipped in on, he was in the living room, turning the creased pages of the *New York Times* he'd read earlier that day. The robe was elegant. "Are you okay?" I said.

He looked up, studied me for a minute. "She has to go," he said.

"Who?" I said, though I knew. But he hadn't mentioned Barker Street for a week or two.

"Jean Argos is dangerous."

"What are you going to do about it?" I said. I couldn't prove Jean wasn't dangerous, but I needed her friendship. I shopped more often at the market where we'd met but hadn't seen her again.

"I've called a special board meeting."

"Boards can turn dangerous," I said. "Sometimes they try to get rid of somebody good." I stood, looking at him. He was still turning the pages of the newspaper but not reading it.

"That's so," he said.

I sat down. We were ten feet apart. I felt as I looked at him as if an invisible iron bar separated us. We were each fastened to an end of it—we could not go far from each other—but it was rigid: we could not go closer. We stared at each other. Both of us were starting to be old.

I wanted to stretch out my arms and say his name—Joshua, or Griff—but I couldn't. I said, "You can't fire her."

"Why can't I?"

"I mean, you mustn't. Maybe you can, but you mustn't."

"You don't know," he said. "It's the responsibility."

Now he was quiet for so long I thought the conversation was over. We'd stand, turn out lights, make our way upstairs. Maybe we'd talk some more as we got back into bed, maybe not.

But he said, "You don't know what I think. You don't know *how* I think."

"Surely," I said, "if there's one thing I know, it's what you think, Joshua Griffin!"

"No," he said. "You don't. You don't know what I felt when Helen died. You don't know what I felt about Val's book. You wouldn't have broken up with me if you did."

"Don't tell me you're bringing *that* up again!"

But he was. Maybe because I was so tired, I let him talk. "Way, way back," he said. "When I first did it."

"You mean—when you shot—?"

He told me again that he'd shot the man's hand. That he felt he had to. That I had always thought he had to—and he knew why I thought that. But that his shot, for which he had not even gone to prison, had made everything possible. Had made Helen's crime possible.

I objected yet again, as I had decades earlier. Helen—unlike Hannah in the book—was responsible for her own acts. She was not led around by anyone. She made the decision. "You have to give her that!" I said. "You have to hear me. You've never heard me!"

Griff said, "But I know she did it on her own. I know that. I mean something else."

"What do you mean?" I said.

"I mean, you have never thought about my crime the way you would if I carried it out today, or if anyone carried it out, at any time, in"—he paused—"in a different context."

Startled, I stood up, reached to the side as if something had fallen: a small cushion on the sofa was about to drop off the edge, and I straightened it.

He said, "You gave Val an idealized version of what I did. You didn't take seriously what I did or what Helen did. If it's wrong when terrorists commit violent acts against random people for what I am sure they think are very fine reasons, it was wrong back then, too."

"But you had a good reason for shooting that cop," I said. "You were protecting those girls."

"I could have rushed forward and grabbed the stick," he said. "I could have kicked him in the stomach."

I stared at him. He was still sitting, but he had dropped the creased newspaper at his feet. "What does this have to do with Jean?" I asked.

"Responsibility."

I couldn't answer. I tried to remember why I had separated from him—not this recent pretend separation but the real one, thirty years before. With what felt like the kind of effort that would have been required if there really had been an iron bar between us, I stood and walked slowly toward him, bending it. I started to cry. He stood. I put my arms around him, and he put his around me. He held me so tightly I could hardly breathe. After a long silence, I laughed, and he laughed, and we went back to bed.

■

By now, my job was a little easier, with the book on embroidery done, but that just made it clearer how hard it was to write the essay. At least Griff and I had located each other in our fractured house. I brought the TV down to the living room, remembering that I'd worked reasonably well while Griff watched baseball during the summer. I sat with my laptop and typed notes to myself, watching or half-watching or not watching basketball. He muted the sound. My notes were repetitious, incoherent, disconnected. We didn't discuss Jean, but I had the feeling that he hadn't changed his mind. He still wanted to fire her. I didn't bring it up. For all I knew, I told myself, he was right.

One morning at breakfast, he sat with his oatmeal at one edge of the table, and I sat kitty-corner to him with my coffee and toast and yogurt. As usual, the coffeepot, loaf of bread, newspapers, and everything else we needed were also crowded together on the table. My elbow knocked over the milk. It was open. The newspapers were soaked, and in the confusion, the glass carafe of the coffeepot—which

I was holding in one hand when I reached for the milk with the other—fell to the floor and broke, spilling hot coffee.

As we mopped and straightened, at last I saw that sensible people who could afford it—we could—would remove the wall between the kitchen and the empty room behind it. And buy a larger table. "All right," I said.

"All right?"

"Bring in the carpenters." I waved my arm as if in a ballroom. "We'll open up the wall."

"Renovations are hell," he said, but his face broke into its old-man wrinkles as he smiled. His skin looked worn these days. I reached out a finger to stroke his cheek.

"Do you ever think of retiring?" I asked.

"I dread it."

"Yes."

He was in pajamas and a bathrobe, and as we stood next to our wrecked breakfast, waiting for more coffee to drip into a mixing bowl I'd stuck where the carafe belonged, I reached my arm under the bathrobe and around his body, over his expensive, well-made navy blue pajamas. Griff was still slim, still muscular. I held him. "I'd be nicer to you," I said, "if I could write that essay."

Joshua Griffin

Sundays, in my mind, are still yellow—egg-yolk yellow—as they were when I was a child. The other days are light brown, a functional wooden color. On a cloudy Sunday morning in winter, I drink coffee in the living room, reading the paper at Olive's big work table. Barnaby is under the table, between my feet, having created his morning arrangement of dog's body and man's body, though we aren't in the kitchen. Carpenters have begun working, after Olive mysteriously agreed to bring the kitchen wall down. They don't work on Sunday, but we've dismantled the kitchen.

Olive comes down the stairs behind me, and I turn and look at her in her old gray quilted robe, which makes a sound when she walks. Her steps on the stair are steady and even. Since she hurt her ankle last summer, her walk has become deliberate.

"Good morning," I say, but she has gone into Martha's old room, where we've put the refrigerator for the time being. Dishes and bread are on a table. The toaster oven is on the floor. I hear her assemble her breakfast.

"You want more coffee?" she says from the other room.

"I don't know yet," I say.

She says, "Do you remember when Annie sang a solo in that concert?"

"What about it?"

Annie was in high school. I remember how she walked to the front of the stage. I was afraid she'd fall off, afraid she'd sing the wrong notes, afraid I'd cry.

"Our mothers," Olive says, "sitting together and blowing their noses."

I say, "Annie did well. She sang well." All our parents are dead now. Olive's mother, the last, died two years ago. We might do anything now—disgrace ourselves.

"Of course she sang well!" Olive says. She brings a mug of coffee and a plate of toast. Both hands are full, and she lets her elbow touch my shoulder as she passes me, a morning touch.

"That was many years ago," I say.

"I woke up thinking about it," she says.

Then she stands still, behind me, her hands still full. "Griff."

"What?" I say.

"Did you have that board meeting? Do you still think Jean is dangerous?"

"Yes," I say.

"Yes to dangerous, or yes to the meeting?"

I say, "We had to postpone the meeting. It's coming up."

She says, "I don't know—I don't know anything. But I think you may be wrong."

"I know you think that," I say.

She stands quietly for a long moment. I expect that she'll carry her breakfast upstairs or sit behind me on the sofa, across the room, but she puts her food beside mine. I stand to give her my chair, but she pats my shoulder and pulls over a chair from the corner. Our furniture is in disarray.

"I think you love me more than I give you credit for," she says, sitting down.

"That's true," I say.

"I'll never stop fighting with you."

"I know," I say.

Rumpled from sleep, she sits beside me, and the sleeve of the robe touches my arm. The dog moves over to lie with his body linking one of Olive's feet and one of mine. I have his head, and Olive has his rear. He sighs. I know he isn't sentimental. He's waiting for crumbs to fall, and I suppose they do.

Olive Grossman

I wanted to invite Jean over when Griff wasn't home, but he'd walked in unexpectedly twice, as if he could sense her wherever he was. I never worried that he'd fall in love with Jean—not Griff's style—but work connections are little affairs, with intense feelings, positive and negative. Jean and Griff were hurt lovers—people who should have performed not good sex but good work together, and almost did. Their animosity came from their similar wish to help. I wanted to talk to Jean—I wanted the friendship I had thought was imminent.

Then I was invited to talk about *Bright Morning of Pain* in public once more, not because people were thinking in particular about that book—though there had been a few mentions in the press of the coming new edition—but because someone who remembered my connection to Val organized a panel discussion at a library: "Authors Up Close." The other speakers would be the onetime Yale roommate of a well-known author and the daughter of another well-known author.

The Institute Library is a pleasantly dilapidated, nineteenth-century workers' reading room, located up a rickety staircase in downtown New Haven, kept open by one or another civic hero. Jean Argos must have seen some publicity about this event, because there she was on the appointed evening, a couple of rows back in the block of chairs set out in front of the speakers. I waved and smiled, hoping I could catch her afterward. Griff hadn't come.

The panel went better than I'd expected. The novelist's daughter was uninhibited—her mother wrote on the toilet, she said—and the roommate of the other author, a psychologist, was canny about his friend. About Val, I said what I'd always said: she was dynamic and vigorous in high school, a bold writer even then; we had little contact in college; we discussed Helen Weinstein after her death. I decided it would be all right to tell the story of how I blurted out that I didn't like the title of Val's book, and Val didn't care.

"Do you like the book itself?" the moderator asked, peering over his glasses at me. I wondered for a moment whether my old essay about my connection to the book—or the ensuing controversy—had somehow made it onto the internet and how much homework he'd done. Maybe he didn't like the novel. He sat back in his chair and folded his hands behind his head—as if he expected me to speak for quite a while in response to his question.

I said I liked the book, that like Val—I smiled—it was larger than life, not quite emotionally accurate, not my favorite sort of novel, not Jane Austen. But it was true to itself. The daughter of the famous novelist said that her mother had loved *Bright Morning of Pain*, and several older women in the audience nodded and smiled.

In the question period, I was asked about Val's politics, and I said we'd once gone to a protest against the Vietnam War together. Most of the questions were for the other speakers. None of my friends were present except Jean, and some audience members had clearly not heard of *Bright Morning of Pain*.

Jean waited for me at the end, rising up and down on her heels with ill-concealed impatience while a woman I didn't know told me what *she'd* done in the sixties. "Let's go eat," I said to Jean, when I finally got away.

"Okay," Jean said, "on one condition. Your husband is trying to get rid of me, and I don't want to talk about it. I don't care whether you agree with him or not—I just don't want to discuss it."

"Okay," I said. "Fine." I wanted to talk about it, but I understood how she might feel. "I'm grateful that—" I said. "In the circumstances—"

"Okay," Jean said. "Enough."

We walked to a Japanese restaurant. It was late winter, a windy evening with the feel of spring coming.

Jean was quiet, and now that I had found a way to spend time with her (we could do this again!), I wondered what we'd talk about if *not* Griff's attempt to fire her. But when we were seated in the restaurant, Jean said, "Why the hell didn't you say what you think?"

"What?" I looked up from the menu. I didn't answer her question but talked about the woman writer whose daughter had been on the panel. I said, "I'll never think of her again without picturing her writing on the toilet."

"On a laptop, do you think?"

"Mmm, no. I bet she never switched to a computer." I proposed an IBM Selectric on the lady's lap, then felt contrite. "She used a notebook and pen," I said firmly.

Jean laughed, but then she shoved her tangled hair off her face as if preparing for action. "But, Olive, why the bullshit? That's not what you think." We were eating miso soup.

"Oh, it's what I think," I said. "It's not the whole long story, but if I have to say what I think in a few minutes, that's what I think. Don't worry—I *always* say what I think. Any of my friends will tell you I say what I think when I would be much better off keeping my mouth shut!"

"You don't like *Bright Morning of Pain*," she said. "You think Valerie Benevento should have told the truth about your friend."

I tried to explain. As Helen's friend, I might want the book to be different—but as a reader, I knew Val had to write whatever book she needed to write.

"No, she didn't," Jean said. "I enjoyed that book—but there are limits."

"Actually, there are no limits. The imagination—"

"You don't think that," Jean said again. "You've been furious with Valerie Benevento all these years."

"You're not listening," I said, getting annoyed. I spoke slowly. "I am furious, yes. But my fury doesn't change the rules. This is god-damn freedom of speech. Did you ever hear of that?"

I told her the story—the story of how I helped Val write the book, the story of the essay, the story of the controversy and Val's death. "I do care," I concluded. "I would like people to know that Helen Weinstein was my friend, even if that makes them disapprove of me. And I'd like people to know who Helen was. That she was serious. That she had reasons, whether we can make sense of them or not. But Val was free to write whatever book she liked. I should have written about Helen myself, but Val was the one who thought to do it."

"I don't say she should have gone to jail for lying about Helen," Jean said. "I just say she shouldn't have done it."

We'd finished our soup and were starting our sushi. Jean put down her chopsticks and crossed her arms on the table the way Helen herself used to—all those late-night sticky tables. Here, at least, the table was clean.

"I need you to understand," I said. "I like you."

"I like you a lot," Jean said. "And I do understand. I'm not completely uneducated. You literary types think everyone is an idiot who doesn't have your kind of education. I have a different education."

This was getting personal. "All right," I said. "What should I have said?"

"It was a perfect opportunity, and you blew it," Jean said. I noticed that her nose was bony and had a slight tilt.

"I don't need opportunities," I said. "I don't sit around waiting for justice on this issue. That audience never even heard of Val. Or Helen."

"Some of them had heard of both. And some of them thought that Hannah was Helen and the 'I' character was Val. That it happened. You should have told the real story. You should have said that Hannah isn't Helen."

"You don't know the half of it," I said, and then paused, hearing myself.

Jean's eyes opened slightly, and her head moved back. "What don't I know?"

I told her what I'd never told anyone: that Val had claimed Helen wrote her a letter—which she'd destroyed—saying she didn't want to be a revolutionary but was afraid to run away, and that when I had challenged Val about it, Val said I couldn't prove it hadn't happened.

We were silent when I finished. "She really needed to think Helen didn't mean it, didn't she?" Jean said.

"And to think Helen was her friend."

"Was she?" Jean put down her chopsticks again. Once more she brushed back her hair. It was short, graying blond hair, always untidy.

"I was sure Helen didn't like Val when we were in high school. I don't think they were friends." I paused. "I'm not sure."

"Oh, poor Val," Jean said.

I felt a little better. "Helen would have told me not to talk to her at all."

"Why did you?"

"I was lonely. Griff—Griff is a great man but little help in a crisis," I said, and Jean smiled. I picked up my chopsticks again. "Val was never as bad in reality as in my imagination. I'd think of her as shallow, and then she'd say something that wasn't shallow. It was—" I paused to stir wasabi into my soy sauce. "It was not *deep*, you understand. Being with her was not like being with Helen—plunging in over your head and thinking you might drown, every time she spoke. Still, Val's remarks were not puddles. They were—" I paused.

"Up to your chin?" Jean said. She had eaten most of her sushi.

"Mmm, no, not *chin*. Rarely *chin*."

"Bosom?"

"Bosom. Showing cleavage. She had a lovely bosom, and Helen didn't," I said.

We were silent, appreciating that.

"I like Hannah in the book," Jean said. "Your friendly local revolutionary. She doesn't mean to kill anyone. She shoots the cop because he's aiming at the man she loves. She gives him back to her friend. She's noble."

"And you want me to talk to a nice, friendly audience like that," I said, "with what's her name's daughter saying her mother loved the book and everybody nodding—you want me to say that Helen was a terrorist and I loved her anyway, and Val should have made Hannah a terrorist? I couldn't say that."

I couldn't say it at the friendly panel discussion—but at last I knew what my essay would say. Months of indecision gave way. I smiled at Jean, who had no idea why, and was still arguing.

"You're as bad as Joshua," she was saying. "You've got some wrong-headed idea and you won't let it go."

I wondered if it was now permissible to talk about Griff—and about Jean herself. But it was pleasant to discuss my own concerns. I was planning my essay. She hadn't convinced me that I should have spoken differently at the panel, but though I remained someone who believed in the imagination above all, I knew now that Val had lied about her subject. She wasn't just imaginative; she told lies. The alternative—the truth—was not something Val could have written. Helen was lovable in life but hard to like, especially when seen from the viewpoint of the twenty-first century, when principled people whose beliefs permit them to perform acts of violence against uninvolved parties are not the semi-familiar enemies of the Vietnam era but the Boston Marathon bombers and the people who perpetrated 9/11. Helen Weinstein was my principled, lovable friend, I was thinking—and she killed a man on purpose.

So it was probably with feeling leftover from the other topic that

I said, "You're so sure you're right and Griff is wrong?" I hadn't quite made up my mind about that. I didn't like the way he talked to Jean and about her, and I didn't like his threatening to fire her, but I thought he was probably correct that she shouldn't run overnights on her third floor.

She ate her sushi. She used more wasabi in her soy sauce than I did. She used it up.

"I'm right, and Griff is wrong," she said. "I know what I'm up to, and the board doesn't get it."

"The man died," I said.

"But not because of the third-floor program," Jean said "Because of Dunbar. We didn't train him properly. We didn't supervise him properly. The program works."

"I'm sure it's good," I said quickly. "But don't you think—well, don't you think it's just not possible to do it now?"

"You don't know how this simple thing we do makes a difference," Jean said, "and there is absolutely no reason why what happened before should happen again, or why anything should happen again."

"You said yourself that everything's harder at night."

"But I learned something. Dunbar learned. Paulette learned— Paulette! She'll never be the same. Arturo was her lover. She's wrecked. If I didn't let them all figure out ways to do what we have to do—"

The next thing I knew, we were in an argument—almost as if I *were* Griff.

"But what if someone else—What if something else goes wrong?" I said.

"It won't."

"Jean, that's too hard, to be so sure."

"One accident and it's all over?"

"If it were me, yes," I said, "because two accidents and you'd all go to jail."

Her voice got quieter, as Griff's does when he's extremely angry. "Then I guess you'd put a lot of issues ahead of our clients," she said. "If you and Joshua Griffin have other priorities, maybe you'd just better stay away from us."

We were almost finished eating, and, apparently, I'd just destroyed a friendship. She looked around—she was going to signal for the check.

"I don't want to choose between you and Griff," I said.

"Well, it's clear whom you'd choose—not that I blame you for siding with your husband."

"It's almost unheard of in my marriage," I said. "Will you let me think a minute?"

"What's the point?"

The waiter put the check on our table. "Can I have another glass of wine?" I said. "Jean?"

He picked up the check, apologized, and stood there waiting for her answer.

At last, I reached across the table and touched her arm. "I'm tired," I said. "I'm not thinking well. Give me another chance."

"Tea, please," she said to the waiter.

"No problem," he said.

He walked away, and she turned to me. "What?" she said.

"I hate 'no problem,'" I said. "Of course it's not a problem! He pours wine and brings tea all evening."

"He didn't mean anything bad."

"I know that. Sorry."

"So, I have to sit here and drink tea and continue this argument for *what* reason?" she said.

I lowered my face and closed my eyes. "Swear you'll be my friend and I'll let you go home."

"I'll be your friend," Jean said. How long had Helen been dead? I had finally found a friend I couldn't do without.

"But you just said—"

The wine and tea came and made a difference. Jean, with her scraggly hair and aging forehead, was brave, I saw. What had happened was a series of accidents—it would be superstitious to stop because of that.

"I care about you more than I love your clients," I said. "I don't want anything bad to happen."

"Thank you," Jean said. "But you've got to trust me. Don't tell me I'm doing the wrong thing."

I gulped some more wine. "Okay," I said.

Then Jean sat back. "I think Griff—mind if I call him Griff?"

I smiled.

"I think Griff wants me to do it, whatever he says."

I too moved my chair back a little, as if for a wider view.

"Do you know it's his fault that we started the overnight pro-gram?" she said. She explained how at a board meeting, at which she didn't put the issue on the agenda, didn't even mention it, Griff had insisted on discussing it—having been informed by our nefarious Zak that Jean's staff wanted such a program. He got her so incensed that she defended the idea, and other board members joined in. "It's his doing," she said.

"He blamed himself when that man died," I said.

"Arturo," Jean said. "Yes. Nobody I know is blameless."

"What was he like?" I asked. "Arturo."

"Oh," Jean said, "he was odd—one of those people who seems dense and may *be* dense, but maybe not. The first time I saw him, I was afraid of him. He was sober but went back to drinking. *That's* the tragedy."

"What did he look like?"

"Big," she said. "A white man. Bulky. Moved slowly—sweet, once you knew him. In his fifties."

We both fell silent. She looked at me, and an expression I didn't recognize crossed her face. "What?" I said.

"I think I convinced you," she said. "I rarely convince anybody of anything."

"This time you did." In fact, she'd convinced me twice.

We sat there looking at each other, not speaking. Jean's tangled hair was more rumpled than usual, and now and then she brushed it out of her eyes. Her eyes looked happy. The place was quiet, and I realized that two talky groups had left, one after the other. Behind Jean, I saw the waiter wipe down their tables with care, first one, then the other, bending solicitously over them. His back was to me, and I couldn't see what he used—a sponge, a rag. Beyond him was the big front window and light from streetlamps. Jean touched my arm and nodded, and we signaled to him. It was time to go.

I drove home and had another argument with Griff, about the third floor of Barker Street and whether he should try to fire Jean.

But the renovation in our kitchen was almost done, and we needed to choose a color for the walls, so after a while we stopped arguing. Pale yellow. The next morning, Barnaby ran to greet the carpenters, getting set for their workday in the kitchen, but they all—there were four of them—could be heard making much of the dog. Over breakfast at the big table in the living room, Griff said, "I was hasty. You're right. I'll cancel that board meeting."

That day, the carpenters made a racket, so I took my laptop to the communal privacy of a coffee shop. I bought a medium house blend and a cappuccino muffin and began writing my essay.

Author's Note

Warm thanks to Sandi Shelton, Donald Hall, April Bernard, and Edward Mattison, who read drafts and offered useful suggestions; to my loyal and brilliant agents, Zoë Pagnamenta and Alison Lewis; and to my editor at Pegasus Books, Katie McGuire, who understood what I was trying to do, and seemed to see through my sentences to what I had so far omitted to put into them. My thanks too to Derek Thornton at Faceout Studio, who designed the cover.

New Haven people and organizations in this book are imaginary, except for the Institute Library and the New Haven *Independent*. The *Independent's* actual stories are checked more carefully than the one mentioned in this novel.

In the late 1960s, I briefly met an idealistic young social worker. I next saw her name a few years later in newspaper headlines, when her resistance to the Vietnam War had turned violent. I never met her again, but this novel results in part from my lifelong curiosity about how such a transformation might occur, and what its effects might be on people who knew and loved the revolutionary.

We hope that you enjoyed this book.

To share your thoughts, feel free to connect with us on social media:

Twitter.com/Pegasus_Books

Facebook.com/PegasusBooks

Instagram.com/Pegasus_Books

PegasusBooks.tumblr.com

To receive special offers and news about our latest titles, sign up for our newsletter at **www.pegasusbooks.com**.